# HUNTED

# PRAISE FOR HUNTED

"This book was seriously addictive... This is a well written novel with a wonderful, detailed world building and a well explained magic system."

*– Kat Kinney, author of The Everwood Falls series*

"Hunted by A.J. Calvin is a fantasy story that brings something new to the genre. Fantasy lovers that are looking for something different than wizards and quests, will be pleasantly surprised by the time they get to the end of chapter one."

*– Entrada Publishing*

"I thoroughly enjoyed this book... [It] kept me flipping through the pages."

*– Jami Fairleigh, author of The Elemental Artist series*

# HUNTED

A.J. CALVIN

This is a work of fiction. All of the characters and events portrayed within this book are fictitious, and any resemblance to living people or real events is purely coincidental.

HUNTED



ISBN 978-1-7379204-9-6



Absolutely no portion of this book, including its artwork, was generated using artificial intelligence.
Human authored registration # 6427349,
https://authorsguild.org/human

Cover artwork by Jamie Noble (www.thenobleartist.com)

HUMAN AUTHORED

For Lindsey and Vanessa;

One could not ask for two better friends.

# INTRODUCTION

As I sit down to write this, so many years after the events within took place, I find myself lost in reminiscences of the good times, while still feeling the poignancy of heartbreak and devastating loss I experienced during the bad.

The tale I have woven here is not false, as those who follow the ways of the hunters may lead you to believe. This is my story in its fullest, the story of how an apparently ordinary young woman took control of her destiny to become something quite extraordinary. During my journey, I experienced the greatest wonder of all—true love—but also the opposite by way of human emotions—betrayal and the devastation brought about by terrible loss.

Let me remind the reader that this is no ordinary tale. It may appear to be just that in the beginning, but as you read on you will discover that it is unlike any tale you have ever heard, unlike any book you have ever read.

Some may be reading this after hearing my sister's account, but know this: my story contains the true version of the events related within.

# PART ONE

# AWAKENING

# 1

# NOT ORDINARY

My story begins many years ago, when I was called Chandra Grey, and I lived a rather ordinary life. I grew up with my twin sister, Xandra, in the midst of a small town in northern Oregon. My parents loved one another, and they loved us as well. They provided us with everything we could wish for as children, and that extended into our teenage years. We were average human beings, bearing no skills or abilities to mark us as exceptional.

Xandra and I were not identical twins; we were fraternal. As we grew older—I suppose I first noticed it when we were in high school—there was a greater difference between us than there had been as children. Xandra was pretty, but not overly so, while I had often been considered beautiful. We were about the same height, though Xandra stood a bit taller. We had the same straight, dark hair, the same dark brown eyes, but the similarities stopped there.

Xandra was outspoken with her opinions, and had no qualms about proving exactly how smart she believed she was. She caused many high school disagreements simply because that was her way. I saw the way other girls looked at her with contempt, and vowed that I would strive to fit in with the popular crowd. I did not wish to be loathed as my sister was. During those years, we fought often, and sometimes the fights went beyond mere words.

We managed to settle our differences the summer before we were to leave for college. Because we were sisters, we had been assigned the same dormitory room, and I suppose that was enough reason by itself to make amends. After our first year, we leased an apartment together, and even grew fairly close. At that time, my life wasn't very interesting.

It was during our last year of college that things began to change for me. As was to be expected, Xandra didn't like the subtle changes in my routine, my behavior. She was stubborn and resisted the transition I seemed to be going through, as though it were a thing to be feared.

My story truly began when I became friends with a young man named Theodore Connelly—he went by Teddy. He was attractive, in an unassuming, geeky sort of way, though there was never anything between us but friendship. I think he hoped there would one day be more to it, but his role in my overall transition was quite small, and he stepped out of my life almost as soon as he had become a part of it.

Teddy was studying accounting, though I will never understand why. He was terrible with numbers, and struggled to balance his own finances. I don't know why he believed he could make a living out of it. I was a business and economics double-major, and part of my coursework included some classes in accounting. It was there that I first encountered Teddy.

He was struggling with the class, which is no surprise given what I've already said of him. He happened to join a study group I was a part of, and we struck up a fast friendship. I can remember the way he smiled, always slightly crooked, the skin around his blue eyes crinkling behind the frames of his glasses. He smiled often, and seemed to enjoy life—whatever it brought for him. I think I might have envied that about him, but I cannot be sure any more; it has been a very long time since we parted ways, and my memories from that period are vague.

Teddy had a fascination with different and strange religions. He claimed no affiliation with any of the myriad denominations that exist, but he wanted to try them all at least once. He pestered me for the better part of six weeks before I finally gave in and decided to go with him to some obscure church one Sunday. He claimed he disliked going alone, and felt better about himself if he had a friend come along.

I do not recall what the name of the church was, nor its exact location. I remembered the service was tiresome and bland, and that Teddy had not seemed pleased with his choice afterwards. What I do remember was the sign-in book, placed upon a small table just inside the front doors. Though it was not required that guests write down their information, it was strongly encouraged. I found that aspect of the church's business odd.

It was exactly two days after I went to that obscure church with Teddy that the phone calls began. The first phone call I dismissed as a prank, something a bored teenager had concocted to scare the random recipient of his careless dial.

It was a late November evening, a Tuesday, dark and cool. The wind that whirled about me hinted that air far colder would soon be coming to town, and a light drizzle was falling from the sky. I had a job at a small coffee shop three blocks from the college campus, five blocks from the apartment complex where I lived with my sister. Living so close to both work and school, I rarely drove, and this particular night had been no different.

Walking home in the dark, my cell phone had begun to ring. I was unfamiliar with the number, but I answered it anyway. It could have been a friend or classmate, borrowing someone else's phone, or perhaps they had received a new number and had forgotten to mention the change. It proved to be neither.

The voice on the other end of the line was unnaturally deep and somewhat distorted. I was reminded of the devices used in some movies to disguise the speaker's voice. This alone frightened me, but the words that were spoken struck true fear into my being.

"Chandra Grey, you are unique. You stand out amongst the crowds. You have a gift. You can become something more than human—"

The voice struck such a chord of terror in my heart that I quickly hung up and stuffed the phone back into my coat pocket. It was several minutes later, after I had overcome the initial shock, that I began to question the words. What was the caller speaking of, a gift? How had the caller known my name?

My thoughts quickly spiraled out of control, circling around the possibility of a stalker. I broke into a sprint, dashing through the dark night to the apartment complex. That night I dreamed of being chased by shadows, unknown creatures that wished me dead, or something equally horrific.

I told Xandra nothing of the phone call, dismissing it in the morning as a mere prank. With the brightness of the morning, one can easily forget the terrors of the night. Even the nightmares that had plagued my sleep faded quickly from my memory.

I went about my day as though nothing had happened the night before. I went to class, chatted with friends and classmates, and went to work at the coffee shop. Nothing out of the ordinary occurred for the rest of the week. By the time Friday night came around, I had purged the phone call from my memory.

A group of my friends from class had organized a game night for that Friday. There was alcohol involved, but since I had to drive across town to return home, I consumed very little. With as many people as there were at this game night, I did not hear my cell phone ringing. It was very late when I left—"getting early" as my friend Grace had joked—and I happened to check my phone as I walked back to my car, a cheap little two-door thing that looked like hell but ran well enough despite its morbid appearance.

I had three missed calls, but no voice messages. As I scrolled through the list of missed calls, I noted that each call had originated from the same number; a number with a 505-area code, which was odd for Washington state. Most of the people I knew from school had local phone numbers.

I dismissed the missed calls and proceeded to drive home. As I pulled into the apartment complex, the phone rang yet again. I answered with a tired, "Hello".

To my horror, it was that strangely distorted voice again. "Chandra Grey, you must meet us soon—"

Unable to suppress the shudder that ran suddenly up my spine, I quickly pressed the button to disconnect the call. Suddenly the overcast night sky seemed a terrible curse; the clouds obscured the stars and moon completely, pulling the land into almost absolute darkness. There was a streetlight casting a pale orange glow over the parking lot, and I was thankful for once that our apartment was facing the lot.

Approaching the stairwell that led up to the second-floor landing and my front door, the phone rang again, causing me to jump. It was the 505 number yet again. Hands shaking, I pressed the button to ignore the call, sending it straight to my voice mail. I knew that the caller would not leave a message, since they had not bothered to do so before.

Drawing a shaky breath, I sprinted up the dark stairwell as fast as I was able, coming into the yellow glow of our porch light a few moments later. My hands were so unsteady that I had trouble managing to get my keys into the door to unlock it.

Xandra was still awake, for which I was grateful. She was watching a zombie horror flick in the living room with the lights turned off; opening the door to the terrified screams of the actors did nothing to ease my mind. I noted that Dillon was sprawled out on the floor watching the film with her, munching on buttered popcorn from a plastic bowl. The strong smell of their snack was almost overwhelming in the small apartment.

Dillon was Xandra's latest love interest, and I wasn't fond of him. He wasn't the brightest person, but was the typical jock-type guy that she always fell for. He was an exercise science major; he had a nice body, and a fairly attractive face, but that did little to make up for his lack of intelligence.

"Hey, Chandra," Xandra called as I came in. "Wanna join us for the movie? It's *Night of Horrors 3*."

"No thanks," I managed after a moment. "I don't think I can stomach it tonight." This was the truth. I was terrified of receiving another phone call, afraid that I truly *was* being stalked. A zombie movie wouldn't do much to alleviate my tension.

"You ain't afraid of zombies, are ya?" Dillon asked without taking his eyes off the screen.

"You wouldn't understand even if I tried to explain it, Dillon," I replied, annoyed. I received an angry look from my sister for the remark. "I'll be in my room if you need me, Xan."

It was as I began to step out of the room that my cell phone rang yet again. As I looked at the display, showing the same 505 number, I froze, unable to peel my eyes away from the tiny screen.

"Aren't you going to answer that?" Xandra asked over the movie, her voice concerned.

It was as though her voice had broken the fear-induced trance I had fallen into. My hands were shaking again, but instead of answering the call, I pressed ignore.

"No, I don't want to answer that phone call," I replied, my voice lost amid the dying screams of the actors in the film. Without looking back at either my sister or her thick-headed boyfriend, I walked slowly back to my room, staring down at the phone in my hand all the while. I closed my door to block out the sounds coming from the movie.

On an impulse, I decided to call Teddy. He had been at the game night, and had left only a few minutes before I had; I hoped he would still be awake. I was grateful when he answered his phone on the third ring.

"Hi Teddy, I'm sorry for the late call," I said after he answered. "I…I just had a question for you, I guess." I was fumbling around in my mind for a reason to have called him, other than I needed to hear the sound of a human voice on the other end of the line.

"It's cool," he said. "What's up? You sound a little scared."

"Um, yeah, I am a little," I admitted. My mind spun with a million things to say, but I was having trouble focusing long enough to decipher my own thoughts. Finally, I settled on, "Have you gotten any weird phone calls since we went to that church on Sunday?"

There was a pause on his end of the line, and I could tell immediately that he was confused by the question. "No, I haven't gotten any weird calls. Why would you ask that?"

With a sigh, I explained about the calls I had been receiving, first on Tuesday, then several times this night. "This just started happening," I said, hoping I sounded convincing, but feeling lame. "They encouraged that sign-in book. I thought it might have something to do with this?"

"Hmm," he replied after a moment. "Well, I didn't give them my phone number when I signed the book. It *could* be, but it almost sounds like something worse, maybe. Like a stalker, or some kind of creep. I mean, you *are* attractive, and if I were a stalker, I'd pick you…Um, but I'm not, so yeah…If I were you, I'd call the police if they don't leave you alone." He sighed. "It wouldn't be that one guy—Greg, I think was his name?—that you went out with once a few months ago? He struck me as the weirdo-type that would have trouble letting go."

I hadn't thought of Greg in months. Our only date had been a rather bad experience, and when he had asked if he could see me again, I had told him bluntly that it was out of the question. I may have hurt his feelings, but Teddy was right—he had been weird.

"You know, you might be right," I said to Teddy. "I can call Erik in the morning and see if Greg's been up to anything lately that's stranger than usual." Erik was one of our classmates, and had the unfortunate luck of having Greg as a roommate. Erik had originally rented the house he was in with his girlfriend, but they had broken up not long ago, and desperate for someone to share the rent, he had accepted Greg's offer. Greg had been fighting with his other roommates at the time, and had been equally desperate for a new venue.

"Actually, Erik's over at my place," Teddy replied. "Him and Joe and Leanne are watching *Star Wars*. I can ask him about Greg." Joe and Leanne were Teddy's two roommates. I had forgotten that Joe and Erik were friends.

I heard Teddy muffle the phone and call over to Erik, then I heard Erik's muted reply, though I couldn't make out any details from their conversation.

Finally, Teddy spoke into the phone again. "Erik says that Greg isn't doing anything out of the ordinary...well, for Greg, I mean. He says he doesn't know about any phone calls, but it's always possible. Sorry I can't be much help, Chandra."

"Don't worry about it, Teddy. Thanks for asking him, anyway." I sighed. "I guess I'll just call the police if this doesn't stop."

"I think that's about all you can do at this point," he replied. "I wish I could help you more."

"Thanks, Teddy. Have a good night." I hung up after he said goodbye. With another sigh, I tossed the phone onto my bed before sitting down to remove my shoes.

I realized belatedly that the sounds of the zombie movie had stopped and that it was very quiet in the rest of the apartment. Not certain I wanted to learn why it had become so quiet, I opted to stay in my room, away from whatever my sister and Dillon happened to be doing in the other room. I booted up my computer, intending to check my email before I went to sleep. I had a fairly new laptop set up on an old wooden desk that had been donated by one of my cousins. The desk's surface was so scratched that I had never been sure what color it had originally been, but the desk had been free; I couldn't complain.

Just as I logged into my email account, there was a soft knock on my door. I knew it was Xandra; I called for her to enter.

"Tired of the movie already?" I asked her as she sat down on the corner of my bed. I swiveled around in the rolling chair so that I could face her.

"Not really, but...there's something bothering you tonight, and I thought it would be better if I spent my time with my sister rather than

Dillon." She sighed. "He's pissed at me now anyway, because I shut off the movie."

I couldn't help it—I laughed. "He'll get over it, Xan. If he doesn't, he isn't worth wasting your time on."

She nodded. "I'm coming to find that out. He can be such an idiot at times, and he's really very insensitive. But…" She sighed. "There's some part of me that still cares for him, even though he treats my friends like dirt half of the time, and he doesn't treat me much better." She frowned, then said, "I didn't come in here to talk about Dillon though. I wanted to know what's wrong…When your phone rang out there, you looked worried."

I looked down and nodded. "I was." I paused, trying to collect my thoughts while Xandra sat inches away, watching me intently, concern clear in her brown eyes. Finally, I said, "I've been getting weird phone calls."

Looking up, I noticed she was frowning, her dark eyebrows knitted in worry. "Weird, how?" she asked.

With a sigh, I said, "I don't know who the caller is. The area code is 505, and I don't know where that's from, *and* I don't know anybody else with that area code in their phone number. The caller is using one of those voice-changing things, you know, that makes the voice sound really deep. And whoever it is knows my name." As I had spoken, my words had come out faster and faster, and by the end I felt tears streaking their way down my cheeks. "Xan, I'm *scared*."

She nodded, her eyes betraying worry and her own brand of fear. "Have you called the police?"

I shook my head. "No, not yet. I called Teddy earlier…He asked me if maybe it was Greg. You know how obsessive he was for a while. But…Even with as weird as Greg can be, I really don't think it was him." I sighed. "I thought that it was somehow related to that stupid church Teddy dragged me to last weekend. The calls started on Tuesday."

"That's why you called him, isn't it?" Xandra asked. "To see if he had received any calls."

I nodded. "But he said he hasn't had any. Then again, he also said he didn't write down his phone number in that sign-in book they had." I shrugged helplessly.

Xandra bit her lower lip, appearing thoughtful. "I really think you should report this, Chandra. What if it's something more serious?"

Despite the fact that everyone who knew about the calls had told me to report them, I was hesitant to do so. I could not explain why I felt that way.

I did not have any other calls for the remainder of the weekend. I was beginning to hope that Friday night had been the end of my mobile torment, but I was mistaken.

I was awakened at just after two a.m. on Monday morning by the sound of my phone ringing. I knew that most of my friends were decent enough not to call at such an early hour; my mind immediately jumped to the conclusion that it must be the mystery caller again. My phone was plugged into its charger on the nightstand, and I stared at it for several seconds before I finally gathered the courage to answer it. Perhaps if I heard the caller out, this harassment would end, and my life would return to normal.

I answered the phone without pausing to turn on the light. "Hello?"

"Chandra Grey." The voice was of a man; I could discern this now that the voice was not masked behind the changing mechanism. "I must apologize for the previous calls. Someone who works for me was attempting to call you, and I think that he must have given you some cause for alarm. I should not have asked him to call, and should have taken that responsibility upon myself."

"Who…who is this?" I managed after a moment.

"I cannot give you my name at this time," he replied, though there was a hint of regret in his tone. "I would like to meet with you, today, if that is possible. There is something about yourself that I do not believe you know of…A great power that you possess. I can teach you more about this, but you must trust me enough to meet with me first."

I was becoming curious, in spite of my initial fear. This man sounded sincere, and I felt that I could indeed trust him. It did not matter that his employee had terrorized me, nor did it matter that he had the indecency to wake me at two in the morning. There was something about his tone, his manner over the phone, that drew me as a moth is drawn to a candle's flame. I wanted to know more.

"Where?" I breathed.

"There is a night club downtown, a place called Dark City Hall. Do you know it?"

I shook my head, and then felt foolish. He could not see the movement. "No," I replied. "Can you give me the address?"

I managed to find a scrap of paper on the nightstand which I could scribble the address upon. He gave me some rough directions, though I believed I could find my way easily enough. He informed me that a man named Trey would meet me outside of the night club, and would take me to his designated meeting place.

Many young women of my age would have told me that I was crazy for attempting to meet up with this strange man, that it could have been part of a twisted plot that would ultimately end up with my getting killed. There was something that pulled me, however, and I knew—somehow—that no harm would come to me. I cannot explain my feelings, but I simply *knew* that I was in no danger.

As quietly as I could manage, I dressed and left the apartment, hoping that I had not awakened Xandra in the process. I made my way downtown, which even on an early Monday morning still had its share of traffic. I nearly drove past the night club—it was closed and the building was dark. There was a single sign hanging above the black double doors that read "Dark City Hall" in Old English-style lettering, but the sign was small and inconspicuous; it would have been easy to overlook.

I found an open parking garage a block away, and left my car there. As I headed in the direction of the night club, I saw a man emerge from the shadowy recess near the doors. He was several inches above six feet tall, broad shouldered, and bald. I remember he wore a black leather jacket that night over his worn blue jeans. At first glance he was rather intimidating, and I recall thinking that he must have been one of the club's bouncers.

As he approached me, he extended his hand. "I'm Trey," he said. "You must be Ms. Grey."

I merely nodded, shaking his hand briefly.

"Follow me. The man who wishes to meet you is waiting."

Now that I know who this man was, and why he wanted so badly to meet with me, I understand why I was able to follow Trey without hesitation. I was drawn to the caller, albeit unconsciously, because of his own ability—the same ability with which I have been graced.

Trey led me past the entrance of Dark City Hall, to an alley that was perhaps a half block away on the same side of the street. We walked to an unmarked metal door that led into one of the buildings from the alley. There was a woman standing outside, dressed in a full-length blue patent-leather jacket that contrasted starkly with her fair skin. Her hair was cut short, falling to her prominent cheekbones, and was dyed a garish red-orange. The street light at the end of the alley fell upon her face in such a way that her eyes appeared almost colorless, though I assumed they must be a light blue. Trey introduced the woman as Carmine.

"So, you're the girl the boss was trying to contact," she said in a flat, somewhat smirking tone. "I wonder if you can handle it?" She broke into a harsh laugh that elicited a frown from Trey.

Muttering something under his breath, Trey pulled a ring of keys from his jacket pocket and jammed one into the doorknob. He yanked the door open in an angry manner that startled Carmine from her laughter.

"Was it something I said, Trey?" she asked in a mocking tone. "I'm sure Ms. Chandra Grey will be fine once she's accepted what he is. It's the acceptance part of it that will be difficult, as you well know."

I had the distinct feeling that Carmine had very few friends. She was clearly trying to frighten me, although her words only managed to instill an even greater curiosity within me.

"You must go inside alone," Trey said, ignoring Carmine and holding the door open for me.

I simply nodded, and did as he said. In that moment, I wanted to understand Carmine's cryptic remarks; I needed to know more about this man that I had agreed to meet, and why she had wondered if I could "handle it". Curiosity had replaced my initial fear, and as I stepped through the doorway, I felt no anxiety.

The door closed behind me, and I found myself in an office area. There was a wide metal desk, and a few filing cabinets against the wall opposite the door. To my right was a round table with a few folding metal chairs scattered around it. I noticed that two of the chairs had been pulled into the center of the room, which was otherwise bare. The room was windowless, and the only door leading into or out of the room was the one I had just stepped through.

To my left was a man. He stood slightly taller than I did, and was slender. What caught my eyes—and my breath—was his appearance. He looked to be close in age to me, perhaps a year or two older, but his hair was completely white. It was combed neatly to one side.

When I had first stepped into the room, his eyes were closed, and he kept them that way until I had time to study him. When at last he opened them, I couldn't help but gasp with surprise—they were not human eyes that looked back at my own. His eyes possessed silver irises.

"Do not be alarmed," he said in a soothing tone. "Now you understand why I must have you come to me. My appearance makes it difficult to walk about the city undetected. No amount of dye will color my hair, and I have tried upon occasion to use contacts to hide my eyes, but to no avail. I cannot draw attention to myself, so when I wish to meet someone, I must arrange it so that they come to me."

His voice, so calm, served to relax me. "Why did you wish to speak with me?" I asked, surprised that my voice remained steady. My insides felt as though they were doing backflips.

He smiled, and gestured to the two chairs in the center of the office. "Let us sit down, for this may take some time," he replied. "Are you comfortable?" he asked once we were seated facing one another.

"I think so," I said after a moment. "I'm not sure what is going on. I don't know why you called me here, or how you know who I am. And I don't know *what* you are either."

He chuckled then. "Yes, I suppose I do have some explaining to do," he replied. "I called you here because you possess a great talent, one that you undoubtedly don't know that you have. I happened to notice you a little over a week ago—you were in this area of town, with some friends, going to dinner I presume. I could feel your power then, and I knew I must take this opportunity to teach you how to use it." He shook his head slightly, wonder spreading across his face. "You can become very great, Chandra Grey…You do not need to live an average life; you can become so much more than ordinary."

I was unsure of how to respond to his statement. I don't know if I had ever considered myself completely ordinary; throughout my life I had managed to excel where my friends could not, but I had attributed this to hard work and dedication. To hear something like this from a complete stranger—one who had admitted to following me for over a week—was a bit unsettling, to say the least. When I managed a nod, he continued.

"I watched you go into the church last Sunday," he admitted. "It was an opportunity I could not pass up. I sent one of my…underlings to copy down your phone number from the guest book, and bade him contact you. That was a mistake, and I apologize for my miscalculation. I understand that he had you quite scared."

I nodded again. "Yes," I replied slowly. "If the calls did not stop, I was going to report them to the police. I thought…Well, I thought I had a stalker. You aren't really a stalker, are you?" Immediately, I regretted my words. *You don't say something like that to someone you've just met!* I screamed at myself internally, before thinking, *A stalker would never admit to it.*

I was surprised when he laughed. "I don't believe I am a stalker in the sense that you mean," he said. "I do not intend to harm you in any way, and I did not contact you because you happen to have a pretty face. You have an ability that few humans possess. I must know what your decision will be, regarding being trained as a summoner."

Summoner. This was the first time I had heard of the word, and it sounded strange to me, yet somehow grand and powerful. I was intrigued.

"What's a—?"

"Summoner?" he asked with another laugh. "I am a summoner, though not a very powerful one. You can become much more than I could ever hope to be—the amount of raw talent you possess is very rare indeed." He paused a moment, reflecting, before going on. "Are you familiar with demons, Chandra Grey?"

# 2

# POTENTIAL

"What?" I asked, before I could stop myself. The question had taken me off guard. "Demons? You mean like the creatures that are supposed to come from hell? I can't honestly say I believe in that."

He nodded knowingly, as though he had expected such a response from me. "Perhaps I can make a believer of you," he said slowly, and rose carefully from his chair. I was stunned at the grace of this simple movement. There was no menace in his tone; he had spoken with an air of resignation, as though this were not the first time he had been forced to demonstrate this fact to someone.

He spoke rapidly in a language I could not identify, and spun around once with his arms crossed before his chest. I could feel my eyes growing wide with surprise as he did this, and fear began to clutch at my breast. The words, even though I did not know their meaning, sounded terrible and threatening, while his tone had been strong and commanding. I did not know what to expect, and I was quickly becoming afraid once more.

I did not remember closing my eyes. It took me a moment to understand that the darkness obscuring my vision was self-imposed. When I finally had managed to open my eyes once more, I realized that I had every reason to be terrified. The man had called forth a monster.

That was my original thought: A monster, a creature of nightmare. I looked upon it, fear holding my gaze frozen, making it impossible for me to look away. My mind raced in a whirlwind of panicked thoughts.

The thing that had appeared while my eyes had been closed retained the basic elements of a human—two arms, two legs, a head centered between its shoulders. Its skin was a dark gray color, so dark as to be nearly black, and it appeared to be hairless. It wore metal leggings—it reminded me distantly of a medieval knight's armor, although this armor was matte black and ended at the creature's knees. Its upper body was very muscular, and was covered with slightly paler areas of severe scarring. Its fingers ended in sharp talons, and it had a pair of leathery wings upon its back. Its face was contorted into a look of hatred so profound that I struggled to look it in the eye; its eyes were a deep crimson, slit by vertical pupils.

I believe that I screamed. I know that I tried to stand up, to back away from this horrendous creature, but I only managed to fall backwards over the folding metal chair I had been sitting in.

The man I had come to meet stood at arm's distance from the creature, and I realized belatedly that he appeared quite distressed.

"I am sorry, Chandra Grey," he said after a moment, his voice strained and his eyes sad. "I should have warned you of what I was about to do. This creature will not harm you; I merely called upon it as a demonstration of my own power—the same power that you possess." He looked down, closing his eyes briefly. "It has been far too long since I had an apprentice," he said after a moment, his voice subdued. "I seem to have lost my touch, and have made for a poor host."

I managed to stand up, though not very gracefully as I stumbled over the overturned chair's legs. "I was not expecting...*this*," I managed haltingly after a time, breaking the awkward silence that had settled over the room. I pulled the chair into its proper orientation and sat down once more. "You said that I can do this? I can call monsters?" Again, my curiosity was getting the best of me.

He nodded once. "Yes. This...this is a shadow demon, as they are commonly called. A creature that is loyal to me, as the summoner. I am afraid that this is the same creature I tasked to contact you, and that was a truly regrettable act. Again, I apologize for frightening you as I have."

He seemed very sincere in his apology, and I knew he had not meant me any harm. "Not to worry," I replied lightly. "I think I'm over my fright now." I thought over his words again, then said, "So this is a demon? I didn't know they actually existed..."

He chuckled briefly, and I was glad to see him smile. "Demon is truly a misnomer. They are not evil creatures, as the stories would have you believe. They merely follow orders, although some of the more powerful demons require something from the summoner in return. The word demon is derived from the Greek word *daimónion*, which in its earliest definition meant something of 'divine nature'. I do not believe that demons themselves are evil—they are only as evil as the summoner behind them chooses to be."

I nodded thoughtfully. Demons existed, that I could not deny, but to learn they weren't the terrible creatures that popular belief made them out to be came as a bit of a shock. Then again, it made complete sense—humans are capable of immense cruelty and evil in its truest sense; given the proper tools, we can spread fear and grief like a disease upon the land and never think twice about our actions.

"But they can also act of their own volition?" I asked after a time. "You said you had 'tasked' this creature to contact me—"

He sighed. "Yes, I did, and yes they can act of their own volition if allowed to. In many instances, the demon will carry out its task without causing any harm—or fear, as in your case—but once in a while they will act out of character, as this one did."

He was silent for a moment, looking down at his pale hands as he clasped them in front of himself. I had been so intent upon watching him that it took me a moment to realize that the demon had vanished. Slowly, he sat down and brought his strange gaze up to meet mine, his jaw set with determination.

"I must ask you now, Chandra Grey—are you willing to learn the ways of the summoner? I will tell you that it is not an easy path, and it is one that few people emerge from. There have been many would-be summoners who have failed in their training, and failure of this magnitude can have extreme consequences. Some have died, and those often were the fortunate ones."

His words brought forth an involuntary shudder on my part. This path was incredible, yet there was great risk associated with it. I knew even then that this was a risk I was willing to take. Somehow, I had always known there was something different about me, something that caused me to stand apart from others, even when I strove to blend in with the crowd. I had to make a choice—continue with my rather ordinary, boring life, or trust this strange man, and learn if I was strong enough to survive his proposed training.

All of these thoughts had flitted through my mind in an instant. There was only a brief pause in the conversation before I said, "I want to learn."

It was then that I finally learned his name. “Very well, Chandra Grey. I am Il’zaks.”

I blinked. “Does your name have some sort of meaning? It’s—“

“Strange?” he asked, his silvery eyes twinkling. “It does have some meaning; let me explain. My name was not always Il’zaks, but that is the name I was given at the time I completed my training as a summoner. You will also receive a name when you finish your training; at that time, you will no longer be Chandra Grey, nor will you remember that name.

“A summoner’s name is a powerful word, and one we do not give away freely,” he explained. “The names we are given are determined by our individual strength—there are many summoners whose names are far more powerful than my own. We are organized by ranks according to our strength—the most powerful of our Order is the Master Grand Summoner, Te’chok.”

We had spoken at great length, though I had not noticed the passage of time. Il’zaks stood up then, and said, “Your training will begin tomorrow evening. I must be going—and you must as well, for it is already well into the morning and we do not want to arouse the suspicion of your sister if we can help it. We must be very careful around her.” His voice was wary, as though Xandra posed some sort of threat to this new endeavor of mine.

“Xan won’t be a problem,” I said, trying to sound reassuring, though I didn’t understand his reason for mentioning her. “She might be curious, but I can come up with a reason for what I do that she’ll accept.”

Il’zaks smiled faintly, though his eyes remained wary. When he spoke, a note of apprehension was clear in his tone. “Your sister may not be so easily convinced, regardless of how reasonable your invented business may sound. We shall speak more of her later, but for now we must part ways. Find the back entrance to the Chaos Rising arcade near your apartment tomorrow evening as the sun sets. Trey will be at the door awaiting your arrival.”

When I returned to my apartment, I fell asleep almost immediately, falling upon the couch in the living room. I was beginning to feel the effects of having been awakened at two o’clock in the morning. It was the the dreamless sleep of exhaustion, and I did not hear the door open and close as my sister and Teddy came in sometime later.

Xandra awakened me by shaking my shoulder gently. As my eyes opened, I saw her face inches in front of mine, her expression concerned, her dark eyes filled with unspoken questions. Then I noticed Teddy was present, standing some distance behind her, wearing a matching expression on his boyish face. I sat up, rubbing the sleep from my eyes, which felt as though they had been filled with sand while I slept.

"Are you alright?" Xandra asked, her voice trembling uncharacteristically.

"I'm fine," I replied, and stifled a yawn. "I'm just tired, that's all."

Xandra sighed, and I could tell she was frustrated, though she wasn't prepared to say as much. "You were gone this morning," she accused, "and you left your phone here. Where were you? Teddy and I spent the entire morning looking around for you, because you skipped out on your study session. That isn't like you."

I had forgotten about the study session I was supposed to attend with Teddy. "I'm sorry," I replied lamely. "I'm tired, and I forgot about the study group. I had a very late night."

Xandra's eyes accused me of unspoken crimes as she said, "I see." Her voice was flat and emotionless, but I knew that she was seething within. She had always excelled at hiding her anger and then unleashing it when I least expected it. I had learned over the years to read the signs of her body language so that I was no longer caught off my guard when she decided to unload her fury.

"Don't be angry, Xan," I said, feigning hurt. "I had some things to take care of. At least I can say I won't be getting any more of those phone calls."

She looked away from me, her eyes flashing as they caught the light coming in from the window. "I *knew* it had something to do with those calls!" she nearly shouted. Behind her, I saw Teddy flinch and take an involuntary step backwards.

"Xan, please," I said, tired of her game already. "It's been taken care of. Drop it."

"What…what do you mean by that?" Teddy ventured in a nervous tone.

I sighed. "So, the two of you decide to wake me up just to interrogate me? I'm *tired*. I think I got maybe an hour of sleep last night. Can't this wait until later?"

Xandra turned to face me again, crossing her arms angrily. "No, it can't wait until later, Chandra. You were gone when I woke up this morning—and I was up at six because I had *intended* to go running. I know you; you don't get up that early without a reason, and you never leave without your phone. Where were you?"

I decided it wouldn't hurt to tell a partial truth. "I met with the people who were calling me," I replied with a shrug. "They won't be calling me any more. Like I said, it's been taken care of."

Xandra remained dissatisfied, but she allowed the subject drop. Teddy, uncomfortable with conflict, practically fled the apartment at the first opportunity, while Xandra left me alone to resume my nap.

When I awoke later, it was growing dark outside. Xandra had not turned on the lights, even though she was sitting in the cushioned chair in the corner of the room beside the window. A deep frown creased her pretty face, twisting it, and her eyes were as hard as stone as they glinted in the dying light. Sitting up with a weary sigh, I reached behind me and flicked on the light switch. There was no reason to argue in the dark.

Xandra had leaned forward as I was turned away, her elbows resting on her knees. "Tell me about what happened last night," she said, her voice unnervingly flat, an indicator of her suppressed anger.

"I already told you," I said patiently, "I met with the people who were calling me, and it was taken care of. No more weird calls for me."

Xandra sighed in exasperation and rolled her eyes heavenward for an instant. "You're being really vague," she snapped. "Why did you go meet with them *alone*? They could have been planning to murder you!"

Now we were getting to the real issue at hand—Xandra had been worried. As was her way, she tried to mask her concern with unwarranted fury.

"I realize that now, yes," I replied dismissively. "At the time, I wanted to make those calls stop, so I agreed to meet with them. It was actually only one of them that had been calling, and his employer was very apologetic about it. I guess they hadn't meant to scare me." I shrugged.

Xandra's dark eyes had narrowed and the frown had returned to her face, though this time her expression was perplexed rather than angry. "What on earth did they want with you that they were calling you so often? And why did they never leave you a voice mail?"

"They offered me a job, Xan," I replied, looking at her sideways and hoping this would suffice. It was as close to the truth as I was willing to admit to her. "After talking with them for a while, I accepted their offer…That reminds me, I need to call the coffee shop and tell them I'm done."

Xandra gaped at me, as though I had suddenly sprouted an extra head and she couldn't believe what she was seeing.

I laughed at her expression; it was almost comical. "It's okay, Xan," I assured her. "This offer is a once-in-a-lifetime opportunity, and I'll be damned if I pass it up. So, what if the job is working nights? *This* is something I can't let slip past me."

Xandra had recovered enough from her initial shock to form words once more. "What will you be doing?"

"Research, mostly," I replied, thinking furiously. I had been so exhausted by the time I had returned home that I had scarcely had time to come up with any sort of explanation. "The man I met last night is the manager of the night shift. He needs another person to help him with his research—economic research—because the day crew hasn't been keeping up well enough for him."

Xandra was nodding. "I see now," she said quietly. "It's the first job you've been offered that has anything to do with what you've been going to school for. I guess I'd jump at an opportunity like that too, but I don't know if I'd be willing to work nights."

I shrugged. "I'm almost done with school anyway, so I'll manage. I decided to forgo the rest of my accounting classes and graduate early, in December." I watched her face carefully; she knew what I said was true since I would finish my economics degree at the end of the current term. She merely nodded, dropping her eyes to the floor, while I pressed on. "I need this job, Xan."

My tone must have stirred something within her, because she snapped her head up and met my eyes with a fiery gaze of her own. "You do not *need* this job, Chandra," she practically snarled.

I sighed heavily. "I don't think you quite understand," I stated in as even a tone as I could manage. Her angry words had caused my own temper to flare. "This is a once-in-a-lifetime position. This is something that I could not possibly pass up. This is what I was *made* for."

She crossed her arms, frowning. "Fine."

"You're being irrational, Xan," I chided. "Why are you so angry with me for taking this job opportunity? I don't understand."

Her face softened somewhat, and she looked away, her dark eyes clouded by her inner turmoil. "It isn't the job that bothers me, not necessarily. It's the way they attempted to recruit you...Honestly, what sort of employer *does* that?"

I went to class the next day as usual, but had a difficult time concentrating on the lectures that were presented. I spoke briefly with Teddy about a possible study session over the weekend, but I remember little else of the conversation. My mind was preoccupied, and I was anxious to meet with Il'zaks again. There was something about him, and the allure of what he had to offer me, that I simply could not resist.

I located the arcade called Chaos Rising as I walked home from the college campus. It was in a shopping center a block away from the apartment complex I lived in, and looked to be fairly busy even during the early afternoon hours. The front of the store was lined with floor-to-ceiling windows, behind which stood a vast array of different arcade games painted in bright colors. I took note of the concrete stairwell that ran along one side of the arcade, a dark brown door at its end. I assumed that it must be the back entrance Il'zaks had spoken of.

I returned home, dropping my book bag haphazardly onto the floor once inside my bedroom. Xandra was not home yet—she had been scheduled to work at the supermarket that afternoon—leaving me with little to occupy my mind as I waited for evening to fall. I could not focus on my homework, excited as I was about the upcoming meeting. I paced the apartment for what must have been several hours before I realized that the light outside was beginning to fade. It was time.

I had retained enough sense to take a jacket with me before I raced out the door, practically running down the street toward the arcade. I had decided not to drive—I did not play video games, and I did not relish the idea of explaining why my car had been parked outside an arcade, should someone I know happen to see it there.

The overhead lights were flicking on across the parking lot as I neared the concrete steps I had spied earlier in the day. A flood of relief washed through me as my eyes fell upon Trey, standing resolute as a boulder near the brown door. He nodded to me as I approached, but said nothing until I stood beside him.

"Good evening," Trey said, a faint smile cracking through his otherwise stony countenance. "Il'zaks will be pleased to see you. He waits inside."

Without waiting for my reply, he pulled the door open. It made an unpleasant screeching sound as the bottom of the door scraped against the dirty concrete.

"I cannot enter here," Trey said in a hushed tone. "What goes on between a summoner and his apprentice is something that I can't be present for."

The corridor beyond was illuminated dimly by small blue-white lights attached near the top of the wall to my right side. The lights were set with enough distance between them that there were areas of the corridor black with shadow. Despite this, I was not afraid; I was merely curious.

As I strode down the length of the darkened concrete hallway, I heard Trey close the door behind me, causing the darkness between the tiny lights to intensify as the remaining daylight was shut out. I paused for a moment beneath the nearest light to allow my eyes to adjust before continuing forward.

I was uncertain of what to expect from Il'zaks, though I had not anticipated wandering into a large, darkened room to find him faintly illuminated on the far side. A single blue-white orb floated only inches from his face in the otherwise lightless room. My footsteps echoed strangely as I entered the room, as though it were a vast space; I kept my eyes focused upon Il'zaks as I navigated through the darkness.

His silvery eyes searched my own, as though he had little difficulty discerning my form in the darkness. "Good evening, Chandra Grey," he stated, his voice taking on an air of mystery. "Come closer, and we shall begin your studies."

I obliged him, walking rather slowly across the expanse of the room since I could not see where I placed my feet. As I drew nearer, my eyes were dazzled by the light coming from the orb, and I ceased my advancement once I was within arm's distance of Il'zaks. The orb's light was strong enough that I could see his features in spite of the surrounding darkness.

He gestured toward the glowing orb. "This is a *djinn*," he said by way of introduction. "It is perhaps the simplest of demons to control, though it has many useful attributes. I thought that tonight I would acquaint you with it, and tomorrow we shall see if you have what it takes to summon one of your own."

At hearing this revelation, I was elated. Tomorrow, I would learn if what he said of my abilities were true. I nodded eagerly, ready for the lesson.

Il'zaks chuckled briefly. "I am certainly grateful that you have agreed to train in this manner, for your potential is remarkable. It also pleases me to see such enthusiasm in a student." He allowed himself a small smile before continuing. "The first thing you must understand about *djinni* is that they are creatures of fire. This means that you cannot call them near large bodies of water or rivers, for the presence of so much water in one area causes them great distress.

"A *djinn*, despite its weakness to water, is a very useful creature to have in your employ. They are excellent at gathering information simply with their proximity to humans." He paused to look at me in a most mysterious manner. "For example, this *djinn* tells me that you had an argument with your sister last night and that to you, she seems overly suspicious. It also tells me that your friend Teddy is rather worried about your recent activities, and that you suspect he feels more strongly for you than mere friendship, though you do not reciprocate that sentiment."

I was astonished. That he could have revealed so much about me from just having the *djinn* present was amazing—the tiny glowing orb hanging in the air inches from Il'zaks' face was more than it had first appeared. Il'zaks had a mischievous smile playing across his lips as he studied my reaction.

"That isn't the extent of a *djinn's* abilities, either," he added once I had recovered somewhat from my shock. "A *djinn* can also take on the form of a person from the memories of any human it is gathering information from."

Briefly he closed his eyes, and as I watched in awe, the floating orb slowly stretched and widened, assuming the shape of a human. The light it emanated faded quickly as it took on more and more of the characteristics possessed by Teddy. After a moment it had grown too dark to see, but the bright overhead lights suddenly flicked on.

Startled, I turned quickly around, noting that Il'zaks had abandoned the spot where he had been standing and was now several feet away; he was standing at the back wall of the room, near a light switch and another door. I noticed the room was empty except for a small collapsible table that had been erected near the entrance, accompanied by a pair of folding chairs.

The *djinn* had taken on the form of Teddy perfectly; it stood only two inches taller than I did, and had assumed the same outfit I had seen Teddy wearing the day before. The blue eyes sparkling behind the wire-framed glasses, the slightly crooked smile, and the disheveled, red hair were so perfect a match to the real Teddy, that I could scarcely believe what I was seeing had been nothing more than a glowing spot of light only moments before.

I gaped at the spectacle before me for several moments. Only when Il'zaks broke the silence with a brief, amused chuckle did I finally realize what a fool I must have appeared to him.

"I'm sorry," I managed, though I was yet unable to tear my eyes away from the *djinn*. "I—"

"There is no need to apologize," Il'zaks interrupted calmly. "It is only natural that you should react this way. You have just witnessed an apparently insubstantial ball of light transform itself into a perfect replica of your friend, based upon your own memories. Many apprentice summoners react rather more adversely than you have."

Finally able to shift my gaze back to Il'zaks, I noted that he was smiling in an amused sort of way. "It is sort of hard to accept," I replied. "If I hadn't seen it transform myself, I don't think I would believe that this *isn't* Teddy."

Il'zaks' smile broadened. "That is the true beauty of using the *djinni*, Chandra Grey. No one would doubt that this was your friend, if they were to walk into this room right now. The only weakness to this charade is that a *djinn* cannot speak—it can only deliver information directly into the summoner's mind. It is something that may take you some getting used to."

"Are you able to make it take on any form?" I asked, glancing briefly at the not-Teddy.

"No," Il'zaks replied, "it can only take on the form of a human. A *djinn* could not assume the shape of a rock, or a piece of furniture, or even an animal, for example. There is another demon you may encounter later in your studies that can change into a myriad of shapes, but the *djinn* is limited only to human forms."

He paused a moment, motioning for me to follow him to the table, where we sat down. The *djinn* exited the room through the door near the light switch.

"Where is it going?" I asked, merely curious, though my voice sounded nervous to my own ears.

"I sent it to fetch some glasses and a pitcher of water," Il'zaks replied. "There is a refrigerator and kitchenette in the room beyond that door. I think it was used as a staff lunch room in the past, but nobody comes down here any more."

"Are the *djinni* difficult to…manipulate?" I asked, struggling to find the right words to describe this strange new experience.

Il'zaks shook his head, his silvery eyes twinkling in amusement. "Decidedly not," he replied. "There are other demons that are quite difficult and willful, some of which I am not strong enough to control. A summoner's strength is not something that comes with time or practice; it is an innate gift that we are born with. It is why I am so delighted that you have accepted my invitation, poorly executed as it was. Your gift is quite extraordinary, Chandra Grey."

Though I could have pondered this statement for some time, my train of thought was interrupted by the *djinn* as it returned carrying a black tray bearing a clear acrylic pitcher and a pair of matching glasses. It—I struggled to think of it as *not Teddy*—walked serenely across the room and placed the tray on the table before retreating a few steps away, where it stood silently.

"There is something very important that I would like you to consider," Il'zaks said quietly as he poured water into the glasses and handed one to me. The water was very cold, but felt wonderful as I took a few sips.

"The path you have chosen is not for the faint of heart," he continued, his voice grave. "There is no turning back, no running away. Your time as a mere human will end soon, and with it all things you have grown familiar with these past twenty-two years. On the night that your training is complete, the change from Chandra Grey into Lady Summoner will occur. You must devise a way to make it seem like you have simply vanished from the human world. Do not leave any clues behind as to what truly happened, because should your sister find out it will cause many future problems for you."

His last statement triggered a memory of our previous conversation. "This isn't the first time you've mentioned something like this about my sister." It was not an accusation, merely a statement.

Il'zaks nodded gravely, no longer smiling. "While you have the ability to become a great summoner, your sister has the ability to become a great hunter. Her hunter's instinct is not yet realized, but it is there nonetheless. She will be your greatest obstacle, Chandra Grey. Always be wary of her."

Hunter. This was the first time I had heard the term used in such a fashion. "What—?"

Il'zaks smiled sadly. "The hunters have the ability to track demons—or more rarely, the summoners who call upon them. Their objective is typically singular; kill whatever they are tracking."

I nodded, thinking this over. I was determined to see my training through to its completion, and Xandra would *not* stand in my way. I would have to be very careful of what I said to her from now on about my "new job".

"How is it that you know these things?" I asked him after a moment.

Il'zaks chuckled, his smile resurfacing. "It is something you will come to recognize eventually, Chandra Grey. The more exposure you have to myself and to other summoners, the more aware you will become of the innate abilities of those around you. Given time, you also will come to recognize a human's potential for summoning. Know that a human with either potential is very rare." He paused a moment, then added, "A human with a gift as powerful as yours is even rarer still."

This wasn't the first time he had said this, but I remained skeptical.

"Do not doubt yourself, Chandra Grey," Il'zaks said softly. "You have the potential to become much greater than I could ever hope to be. We must proceed with your training carefully in order to realize this potential. I would never be able to forgive myself, should you join the unfortunate ranks of those who have failed."

He was looking down at the tabletop between us as he said this, his voice betraying fear perhaps, though I could not be certain. A thick silence descended between us as we both contemplated his words. It grew quiet enough that I could hear the frantic sounds of the arcade filtering through the thick concrete ceiling above.

"You should prepare yourself for tomorrow's lesson," Il'zaks said after a time, raising his silvery eyes once more to meet mine. His voice was roughened with emotion. "Be sure to get sufficient sleep tonight. Make sure you take your normal meals—do not skip any. Try to be relaxed when you arrive here tomorrow, for unnecessary tension can cause you difficulties. You will need to be able to concentrate to your fullest ability."

I nodded. "Thank you for the advice, Il'zaks."

A faint smile played at the corners of his mouth. "I ask a favor of you, Chandra Grey. Tell Trey to escort you home. It is late and I would feel better if he accompanied you on your walk."

"Alright," I agreed. I was touched that he would show such concern for me already.

"Good night, Chandra Grey," he said quietly as I stood up to make my way to the exit. "Take care of yourself."

# 3

# NIGHTMARE

I arrived home to find Xandra in tears, curled up on the living room couch with a box of tissues on the floor near her feet.

"Oh, Xan, what's wrong?" I asked, rushing to her side. I knelt down on the floor beside her, pushing the box of tissues out of the way.

She turned her red-rimmed eyes in my direction briefly before burying her face in her hands. "Dillon…Dillon broke up with me," she sobbed.

I drew a breath, slowly, evenly. "He was always a jerk to you anyway, Xan. You even told me that on Friday night."

"I know," she sniffled. "But I'm…I always wonder, what's wrong with me? Why can't I have a normal relationship?"

I sighed. Xandra and I had gone through this same discussion with the last three or four guys she had dated. She always blamed herself, when I always believed she could do better. I decided to try a different tactic, to tell her how I truly felt about Dillon.

"Xan, it isn't your fault. Dillon was…Okay, I'm going to speak my mind here. Dillon was an ass to everyone around him—you included—and he was a complete idiot. I don't think he cared about you at all—he was just after one thing, if you take my meaning. Honestly, I always thought you could do better than his type. You *deserve* better."

Xandra was staring at me, the tears she had been shedding suddenly gone. "You're right," she said, as though this came as some sort of surprise to her. "He *was* an ass."

"Want to know what I think?" I asked.

She nodded, and her brown eyes shone with an unspoken hope.

"I think you should try to find someone who is *not* an athlete or an exercise science major. Someone different than your norm, who will give you the kind of respect that you deserve."

Xandra smiled, and practically flung herself off the couch to give me a hug. "Thanks," she mumbled, backing away slightly. "I'll keep that in mind. Um, how was your first day at the new job?"

Internally, I cringed. *Just keep it vague,* I thought. *Vague and simple.* Outwardly, I smiled. "It was great. Tonight was just some orientation training, nothing real exciting. The people I met were great though. I think this will be a lot of fun."

Although I tried my best to follow Il'zaks' advice, I had a difficult time getting to sleep. I couldn't help but be excited about the next lesson—I was going to learn how to summon! At the same time, I was terrified. What if I was unable to summon, for one reason or another? The disappointment would crush me, and Il'zaks' allusions to the horrors of such failure haunted me.

I did finally fall asleep around three a.m., and didn't wake until my alarm went off at nine, blaring an advertisement for a local car dealership. I groaned, forcing myself upright, shutting the clock radio off as I did so. Glancing outside, I noticed that it was another overcast, gray Seattle day. At least the sidewalk appeared dry—it wasn't drizzling yet.

I went about my morning routine, noting that Xandra had changed the calendar in the kitchen before she had left. Today was December first. Final exams would be held the next week, and then I would be finished with school.

My Wednesday classes went past in a blur much as Tuesday's had. Fortunately, my last class finished at three-fifty, and it was beginning to grow dark as I left the college campus. I could drive directly from the campus to the arcade, neatly avoiding any potential arguments with my sister in the process.

Carmine was standing at the door this evening as I descended the stairwell behind Chaos Rising. She had changed her hair color—it was now a vibrant lime green—though little else about her was different compared to our first meeting. She grinned cockily at me.

"Trey had some other business to take care of tonight, so you're stuck with me," she remarked snidely. "Good thing you decided to drive that old beater P.O.S. of yours. I don't do babysitting duty."

I glowered at her. Trey, while he looked intimidating, was at least civil. Carmine was giving me a headache already. "Just open the door, Carmine. I don't really have the time to chat."

She raised her eyebrows and gave me a superior look, but did as I asked and opened the door. I brushed past her into the dim corridor without another word.

"Adios, amiga," Carmine called just before she shut the door rather forcefully.

*Why on earth did Il'zaks keep her around?* I wondered. I was agitated now, and felt hot from the anger that Carmine had inspired within me. This was no good—I was supposed to be relaxed for this lesson. I pulled off my jacket and slung it over my arm, hoping that it would help me to cool off while I walked the length of the concrete corridor.

The overhead lights were on in the big room, and Il'zaks was seated at the collapsible table as I entered.

"Have a seat, Chandra Grey," he said, gesturing to the empty chair across the table from him. "We have some things to discuss before we begin your true training."

I nodded, taking the offered chair.

"You seem to me to be a bit distressed tonight," Il'zaks began. "Perhaps if we talk first, you will be able to calm your thoughts before you begin learning to summon?"

I looked down at my hands, clasped together in my lap. "I'm sorry. I didn't want to disappoint you like this. And really, I was fine until I got here, but then everything went downhill."

"Are you nervous?" he asked, concern creeping into his tone.

I sighed. "No, it was Carmine. I don't think she likes me much."

Il'zaks frowned slightly. "She is not very friendly, and I know this. Generally, I do not have her accompany me to things like this, but Trey had something important to take care of tonight. You will see little of Carmine during your training. I promise you this."

I was relieved, yet still unable to relax. I believe Il'zaks sensed this, for he launched into some lengthy explanations.

"I think it is important that you learn some of the history behind summoners," he stated after a brief silence. "It is believed that the first of the summoners developed his ability in Egypt around the year 2200 B.C.E.

It is said that when he had discovered enough of his innate ability, the transformation from human to summoner occurred, and he became known as Ae'tama. He had learned to recognize the same ability in others after he fled his home, terrified of the consequences he would face should any person see the changes he had undergone. He met his first student in what is now called Saudi Arabia, and taught her what he knew. From then on, our numbers gradually increased.

"It was not until after the birth of Christ that the summoners had any sort of order to their ranks. Previously, there had been no need for it. However, as the man known popularly as Jesus gained influence, the summoners were forced into creating for themselves what became known as the Order for their own survival.

"Jesus was the first hunter to have realized his ability. He recruited followers, some of whom had no special abilities, but most of whom did. He helped them to cultivate their hunter's instinct, as it is known, believing—irrationally—that the summoners and the creatures they controlled were innately evil."

He paused a moment, allowing me to digest this information. Perhaps it was to my benefit that I had always tried to maintain an open mind; I could see how this revelation, if presented to many of the people I knew, would bring tension or outrage. Most people did not like to change their beliefs, and would not tolerate the contradictions present in Il'zaks' words. I, on the other hand, was captivated—I wanted to know more.

"As I have said before, demons are only as evil as the summoner who controls them," Il'zaks continued. "Yes, there have been some truly diabolical summoners throughout our history, but their number is small. The belief among most hunters is flawed, at best, and they often believe they are working towards a righteous cause by eliminating any demon they come across. Their misinformation has had some devastating consequences for our predecessors. It is why we must go about our lives in secret."

"I understand," I said quietly, thinking of Xandra's as yet unrecognized talent. "I promise to be careful."

Il'zaks smiled faintly. "Good. I tire of history lessons, so let us move on to the real business that has brought you here tonight."

My heart leapt at his statement. Finally, I would see for myself some of what I was capable of. Perhaps, I would learn that some of Il'zaks' claims were true. I would know tonight if I possessed the ability to become a summoner.

Il'zaks rose from his chair in a movement that looked as graceful as a dancer's. "We will work on this at the center of the room, where there is plenty of open space. Are you ready for this, Chandra Grey?"

I felt suddenly giddy, and yet the situation felt almost unreal, much like a dream. *What if I can't do this?* I wondered, in spite of the assurances I had received from Il'zaks so far. The next few minutes would be crucial; I *must* focus.

I stood up slowly, feeling my blood thunder through my veins, filling my head with a dull roar, while my heart began racing. In that moment, I realized that I was afraid. I did not want to fail. The effect of a failure tonight, and the resulting disappointment, would be devastating to me.

I followed Il'zaks to the bare center of the room, all the while trying to swallow my sudden apprehension. I could do this. I *had* to do this, if only to prove to myself that I could.

"Listen carefully, Chandra Grey," Il'zaks said, his silvery gaze fixed steadily upon my face. "If called correctly, a demon will recognize your power as a summoner and will appear in our plane. Each type of demon heeds a different sort of call. The most difficult part for you will be to find the correct call to use—each summoner's tends to be different from the next."

"What do you mean?" I asked, feeling panic begin to well up within me.

Il'zaks' gaze never wavered. "Each summoner uses a different method to call demons to them; the best method for you will probably be very different than my own. For example, I use motion primarily, coupled with words of the demons' native language, but my previous student, Ke'tai, prefers to summon by singing."

I blinked, beginning to feel even more bewildered now than ever before. "How will I know what to do?"

An amused smile lit up the summoner's face. "It will come to you—I cannot explain to you how this process works, but the best word I have for it is instinct. What I have done in the past is to show my students how *I* summon, and most find that something within themselves as they watch, almost immediately. I have faith that you can do this, Chandra Grey."

"I'm glad someone does," I muttered, eliciting a laugh from Il'zaks.

"You *can* do this; it was what you were born to do," he replied. "You must pay careful attention to the words as I speak them. Take them to heart, for you must use them in some way to call a *djinn* to you, as I will call one to me. The same holds true for other sorts of demons as well, but tonight we will only focus on a *djinn*. The words I speak will *only* call a *djinn*, and cannot work for other demons."

I nodded. "So, the next thing you show me will have a different set of words to summon it? I understand."

"Good," Il'zaks stated. "Now, listen carefully."

He splayed the fingers of his right hand, stretching it out before him. "*Ach bin djinni sún,*" he said in a commanding tone, closing his hand into a fist with the last word.

Something within my mind suddenly clicked into place at hearing his words. I was stunned, and stared at Il'zaks unblinking for several seconds as I processed what had just happened inside of my brain.

Most of all, I was surprised—and elated—that he had been right. I *could* do this. My brain had indeed revealed how, just as he had said it would.

Il'zaks chuckled, breaking me out of my amazed gawking. "If I can read your expression correctly," he said, "I think you know what you must do. Go ahead, and try it now."

I nodded. My method was different than his; I must *think* the words, and dance—something I had not done seriously for years. The steps seemed simple enough however, and I felt that I could manage them with this new-found knowledge to guide me.

Closing my eyes, I raised my arms overhead. I stepped first right, then left, swaying gently, then dropped my arms forward as I swayed to the right once more, thinking over the words as I did so. I drew a surprised breath as I suddenly felt the presence of a *djinn* inside my mind.

Already it was feeding me information about Il'zaks. It felt as though an internet cable had been inserted into my brain and I was being inundated with all of the information Il'zaks had to offer. It was nearly overwhelming.

I winced, wishing the flood of data would stop. Abruptly, quiet descended upon my mind once again, and I ventured to open my eyes. I could still feel the presence of the *djinn* even though it was no longer bombarding me with information. Seeing it for the first time, floating inches away from me, helped to reinforce the fact that I had actually called it. I had succeeded.

Il'zaks was grinning, and his silvery eyes seemed to glow with pride. "You've done it! Fantastic."

I managed a smile of my own. The *djinn* floated in the air between us, its glow nearly invisible in the flood of light coming from the overhead fluorescent bulbs.

"I'm sure it gave you some information about me," Il'zaks said. "Tell me something I have not yet divulged to you about myself."

I blinked, having to process some of what the *djinn* had provided for me. "You trained Ke'tai almost forty years ago...Which means that you're a lot older than you look."

Il'zaks flashed another grin. "Excellent! Now, order the *djinn* to assume the form of someone from my past. I think you will be able to figure out how without my telling you."

I sorted through the various information and images I now had and settled on one of Il'zaks' memories of his former apprentice, Ke'tai. I stared at the *djinn*, willing it to transform. As I watched, the ball of light stretched and slowly became a perfect replica of Ke'tai, a tall, fairly muscular man with Asian features who kept his white hair in an array of short, haphazard spikes. The *djinn* also incorporated the gray-brown trench coat and faded blue jeans Ke'tai had worn in the memory.

Il'zaks smiled. "You have done wonderfully, Chandra Grey."

Il'zaks requested that I practice my newfound skill whenever I was able to in secret. We scheduled our next meeting to be after I finished my last final exam on the following Thursday.

"Your education is very important," he had said. "I wish you well on your exams. I will see you here again on Thursday evening of next week, when you have finished with them."

Carmine was nowhere to be seen as I exited the building, which was just as well. I thought very little of her absence, dismissing it quickly as I made my way to my car. I had parked it on the opposite end of the parking lot from the arcade, hoping to avoid the notice of anyone I might know. The parking lot was well lit, however, and I was not concerned for my own safety.

The apartment was dark as I entered it after my brief drive home. Glancing at the digital clock on the stereo as I passed by the living room, I was surprised to see it was nearly three a.m. Xandra would be in her room, asleep.

I managed to find my way to my own room in the dark, navigating successfully enough that I did not bump into anything. Once I was inside and had the door closed, I switched on the overhead light.

There was a note taped to my computer screen, written in Xandra's handwriting.

> *Teddy called earlier. Said he knew you were at work tonight, so he just wanted to leave you a message. Doesn't sound urgent. I think he needs help w/ accounting hw.*
>
> *Xan*

I left the note where it was so it would serve as a reminder for me to call him in the morning.

I yawned, realizing belatedly how tired I truly was. I had much to think about, but it could wait for the morning. I fell to sleep rather quickly, but my dreams were unpleasant.

I stood at the center of a circular chamber that felt very vast. Bright light shone down upon me, as though I were standing in the beam of a spotlight. Beyond this area, the room was filled with shadows.

I could see the dim outlines of what I believed were people, moving slowly about in the darkened expanse beyond the circle of light in which I stood. The light shining down upon me was making my eyes hurt, and I was forced to squint in order to see anything beyond its unnatural glare.

The shadowy forms seemed to be moving; they were shuffling about in a bizarre sort of dance. I turned around slowly, and realized that I was completely surrounded by these figures. I did not feel any animosity emanating from them, but I knew somehow that it would be improper for me to step outside of the light. If I did venture into the shadows, the consequences would be dire.

"What is this place?" I asked, my voice shrill and quavering. The words rang oddly in the near-silence of the place, as though the room itself were suppressing the sound.

I was met with continued silence from the beings shuffling around me. I decided to try another approach.

"Why am I here?"

Again, I was afforded no response.

A thought drifted to me, as if through a curtain of fog. Perhaps these people were unable to speak. "Can someone show me?"

Abruptly, the shuffling dance stopped. I was uncertain of the implications, but the atmosphere in the room suddenly became hostile.

I stood as still as I could manage at the very center of the circle of light, turning this way and that in an attempt to observe the shadow beings from all directions. The air had grown oppressive, and I could sense the sheer animosity emanating from the edges of the chamber. I knew I must keep my vigil, lest I be devoured by the darkness. After what seemed an eternity spent in this pandemonium, a trio of the shadow forms broke away from the masses, and began walking slowly towards me.

My knees were beginning to tremble and knock together, and my breathing had become shallow. As my heart raced, I came to the realization that I had never before been so utterly terrified.

The three stopped just outside of the light, and still I could discern none of their defining features. They were vaguely human-shaped, but dark and cloaked in shadow, they said nothing, merely stood there. I felt as though they scrutinized me, even though I could see nothing of their eyes.

They seemed to nod slightly to one another, each in turn, before taking that final step forward into the light. They were shaped as humans, though they lacked the details needed to determine gender. They remained shadowy, as though they were silhouettes of people come to life. They possessed no definite facial features to distinguish them one from another. Together, they reached toward me, placing their hands on my shoulders, my head, my chest.

Immediately, I felt a burning sensation, as though my skin were on fire at each point their shadowy hands made contact. I tried to break away, but found that I was unable to move. My eyes widened in shock as I came to this realization. I urged my uncooperative limbs to obey, but to no avail.

The burning sensation intensified; the pain was so great that I wished I could scream. When I tried, no sound issued from my mouth. My body felt as though it were dying.

Darkness began to cloud my vision, and I knew that death must have found me, at last. I welcomed the thought of release, desperate for an end to the pain. The last image I recalled was of the featureless faces of the shadow-people before my sight gave out and I was blanketed by a profound gloom.

I jerked awake violently, breathing heavily and covered in a cold slick of sweat. My body ached, as though the pain I had experienced during the course of the nightmare had been real rather than imagined. I felt wretched.

I sat up, wincing, and glanced at the clock. It was ten-thirty. I blinked in disbelief. It did not feel as though I had been asleep nearly seven hours; I was exhausted, drained, and uncharacteristically weak.

"That must have been some nightmare," I muttered to myself as I slowly stood up on aching legs that felt as though they were made of jelly.

There was another note from Xandra taped to my laptop, in addition to the one regarding Teddy. I sat down heavily on the rolling chair to read it, no longer trusting my quivering legs to hold me upright.

*Strange,* I thought, *I never heard her come into my room.*

> *I hope I didn't wake you when I came in. Grace Allen called to remind you about a study group tomorrow night. You were making some weird noises in your sleep. I hope you are OK. Call me when you get up.*
>
> *Xan*

I sighed, closing my eyes briefly. I had never felt so tired before. What was wrong with me today?

# 4

# VULNERABLE

Xandra answered on the third ring. "Hello?"

"Hey, Xan," I said, managing to stifle a yawn. "What's up?"

"Well, not too much, really. I'm just waiting for my first class to start," she replied. "I wanted to make sure you're doing alright. Usually you don't sleep through me knocking on your door."

"I got home real late," I said. "And I was having some bad dreams. Maybe I've been doing too much the last few days."

Xandra was silent for a moment, then said, "If you want to know what I think, then yes. Are they going to give you any kind of break for finals?"

"Yeah," I said. "I'm off 'til next Thursday."

"Oh, good," she said, sounding relieved. "Did you call Teddy yet?"

"Not yet. I called you first. I thought you said Teddy's thing wasn't urgent?"

"He *said* it wasn't, but you know how he is. I need to get to class though, so take care."

After disconnecting, I sat there for some time, trying to summon the energy to stand up once more. I didn't want to speak to Teddy right away, but it seemed that he had other plans. My phone started ringing and his name flashed across the caller ID screen.

I groaned, but answered the phone anyway.

"Hey, Chandra, did you get my message? I was starting to worry that your sister forgot, and—"

"I *did* get it, Teddy," I said, cutting him off. My voice had sounded sharper than I had intended it to be. "I'm sorry. Look, I had a really late night. I've been awake for maybe ten minutes."

"Sorry," he mumbled. "Is there any chance you'd have time to help me with the last homework for accounting—the one that's due tomorrow? I know you don't usually have class on Thursdays..."

"If you can come over to my place this afternoon or evening, sure," I replied. "I don't feel very well right now."

"Yeah, sure," Teddy replied. "What about four? Will that work?"

I agreed, mostly to get him off the phone so I could get some additional sleep. Thankfully, when I lay back down on my bed, sleep came quickly, and I had no additional nightmares.

It was nearly two o'clock when I next awoke. I felt much better than I had earlier, but I knew that sleeping as long as I had this day could be a detriment to my health. I brushed this line of thought away and began to go about my afternoon.

By the time Teddy arrived just after four, I had managed to shower, dress, eat a late lunch, and clean the living room. I had just set a stack of accounting books on the floor near the couch when a light knock came on the door.

Teddy gave me a shy smile when I opened the door. "Hey, Chandra," he said, as my eyes traveled past him to the other man standing on the porch. "Uh, this is Elliot. I told him he could come. He's in one of my other classes, and he said he knows your sister."

Elliot was tall, lean, and very good looking. His skin had an olive tone and his hair was black as a raven's feather, falling over his forehead in a messy, yet incredibly attractive manner. His eyes were the color of melted chocolate, and were filled with uncertainty as he gazed steadily in my direction.

"Hi," I managed somewhat breathlessly after a moment, while thinking to myself, *Wow.* "Come in. I just collected all the books I think we'll need to study."

"Great," Teddy replied. "You know me—I need all the help I can get."

"I, uh, actually came here to talk to your sister," Elliot said as he entered the apartment and I closed the door behind him. "I'm not in any accounting classes."

My heart sank, but I forced myself to sound cheerful. "Well, make yourself at home. Xan should be home any time."

Damn, but he was good looking. I was forced to avert my eyes, so that I might focus on helping Teddy with his homework. It was mental torture.

Elliot sat quietly at the table in the kitchen, in plain sight of the door. He appeared nervous, but I tried my best to keep my eyes diverted and my mind on accounting. When Xandra walked inside twenty minutes later, it was a relief.

It was impossible not to hear what transpired between them, though I tried to focus my attention upon the accounting textbook in front of me.

"Elliot!" Xandra cried when she had closed the door and had taken notice of him. I glanced up to see that Elliot had risen from his seat and was smiling anxiously, while Xandra dropped her backpack hastily on the floor and rushed toward him, clearly surprised.

"I had a question for you," Elliot said quietly. I had scarcely been able to make out his words.

"Do you understand this part here?" Teddy asked then. I forced my eyes downward to look at the passage in the book that he was pointing to. As I was forming my answer, I heard Elliot speak again.

"I know this might be a little soon," he said slowly, and I strained my ears to hear what he had to say. "I just wanted you to know how I feel, Xan. I like you very much. I know you don't usually go for my type, but would you be willing to try something different?"

*You would have to be* insane *to turn him down*, I thought furiously at my sister.

"Chandra?" Teddy asked.

"Um, sorry," I said quickly, then launched into an explanation of what the text meant, while still trying to eavesdrop on Elliot and my sister.

"'Kay, I think I got it," Teddy replied. "I'm glad you understand this stuff, otherwise I'd be totally lost."

"I think I'd like that," I heard Xandra reply in a surprised tone.

She said more, but I didn't hear it. I was excited for her; I felt that there was something about Elliot that seemed to align with Xandra in some subtle, yet profound, way. This relationship would be good for her, though how I knew this, I could not be sure. However, there was also a part of me that was maddeningly jealous at my sister's good fortune. This was something I had learned to suppress over the years as she had gone through countless boyfriends. Besides, I wouldn't have much opportunity to date with my "new job", or so I told myself.

I would be happy for Xandra, no matter how painful it became for me.

Finals came and went without incident. I opted not to walk at the graduation ceremony, since my parents were unable to secure the necessary time off from work on such short notice so close to the Christmas holiday. This served the dual purpose of allowing me to "work" on the nights following my finals, without being forced to answer unwanted questions.

Needless to say, I was thrilled when Thursday evening arrived and I was able to see Il'zaks once more. The week preceding this meeting had felt as though it had taken an eternity to pass, even though I had successfully found several opportunities to practice summoning *djinni*.

I was smiling as I entered the virtually empty basement room below Chaos Rising, but my high spirits quickly fled as I took a good look at Il'zaks. His face was grave, and lines of worry creased his forehead. His right arm was cradled in a sling.

"We must talk, Chandra Grey," he said, and his voice sounded weary.

I knew something was wrong, or had been very recently. "What happened?" I asked, frightened by his serious demeanor. I sat down upon the vacant chair across the folding table from him.

He held up his left hand in a gesture for silence. "I will come to that," he stated evenly. "When last you were here, we both were in considerable danger, though I did not know it at the time. You may have noticed Carmine's absence when you left."

"Yes," I replied warily. "I didn't think anything of it."

"I must tell you now why I employ Carmine and Trey," Il'zaks said. "Like some hunters who have the ability to seek out summoners, there are those born with the ability to seek out hunters. Trey and Carmine both have that particular ability, and therefore are indispensable. Carmine—"

"She found someone," I gasped.

"Yes," Il'zaks replied. "After you left last week, she returned here to tell me of the threat. It was a lone hunter, one with a tracking ability, who was most likely sent here looking for me. We had no choice but to confront him and eliminate the threat. Do you understand?"

I suddenly felt very cold, and nodded slowly. Il'zaks had been forced to kill this hunter. Would I have the strength to go through with a similar act if the need arose? I did not know.

"The battle we fight has been ongoing for millennia," Il'zaks said, his voice tired. "At times, we have been able to convince some hunters of our story—that we are not evil as they would like to believe. During those brief times of peace, we are able to walk this world with a little less fear, but as always happens, something occurs that shatters the fragile alliance we shared, and the battle begins anew. It has been nearly two hundred years since the last respite, and there is little hope of another any time in the near future. I want you to be aware of this."

I nodded, but my mind felt numb. I was being drawn into this world of constant conflict and ever-present danger, but I refused to change my mind and abandon this new life I had chosen. This was what I had been born for, and to deny that now would be the worst kind of betrayal one could inflict upon one's self.

"We tracked this particular hunter for two days before we thought we had him cornered sufficiently to strike," Il'zaks explained. "He still had a bit of a surprise for us; that is how I hurt my arm. I think it would be wise for you to learn to defend yourself without the aid of demons. You will need those skills when dealing with many hunters. The inability to fight back has been the undoing of many summoners in the past."

Again, I nodded. "So, what would you suggest? Should I take up karate lessons, or something else?"

Il'zaks chuckled, breaking the tension that had grown around us as he had spoken. "Actually, I did have something planned. I hope you do not mind my having already contacted someone for this aspect of your training."

I blinked, surprised, but not upset by his words. "No, of course not."

Il'zaks smiled. "Summoner Ke'tai should be arriving tomorrow night, and will help you train in that manner. Eventually, he will also take over the rest of your training. As I have said before, I am unable to teach you all that you are capable of." He paused a moment, reflecting. "We decided that some nights will be dedicated to your summoning, while others will be for combat training, for lack of a better description. Ke'tai is very skilled in both karate and jiu jitsu, and is without question the best teacher you could ever hope to have. Few humans can say they have actively practiced martial arts for sixty years."

The way he said the word humans gave me pause to reflect. Il'zaks certainly seemed to be something *more* than human, but I was uncertain of the specifics.

"Why do you say 'humans' like that?" I ventured after a moment.

Il'zaks smiled in amusement, his silver eyes twinkling. "You caught on to that, it seems," he replied. "You may recall that I have mentioned a transformation will occur on the night you receive your summoner's name. It is not quite as simple as that statement makes it sound."

I waited while Il'zaks ordered his thoughts to better elaborate on his statement. I began to grow worried as the smile fled from his face and was replaced with a solemn and concerned expression.

"What will happen is much more than just the color of your hair and eyes changing. You will stop aging, and your perception of the world around you will be enhanced. Your reflexes will be much faster. As a summoner, you are no longer merely human, but something more." Il'zaks dropped his eyes. "I know that this must sound incredibly fantastic to you, Chandra Grey. We summoners *are* at a great advantage when compared to humans, yet we all were human once. The transformation is not easy. It will be more painful than anything you have ever experienced, or anything you can possibly imagine. I have been told that it takes much longer for the transformation to complete for those who are very powerful, as you are."

He fixed his gaze upon me once more, and the sadness and pain I saw in his eyes took my breath away. I stared at him, transfixed.

"I am sorry, Chandra Grey," Il'zaks said softly. "This is a reality that a would-be summoner must face. It is not something that is easy for me to speak of, but because I have brought you this far..." He sighed. "I will understand if you are angry with me, but someone like you is very rare to find, and I could not risk losing you. I could not pass up the opportunity to bring you into this life once it had presented itself."

He did not raise his eyes, and it was apparent that he was distressed. I continued to study him, attempting to discern my emotions. Surprise, certainly, and fear concerning the future, but I was decidedly not angry.

"Il'zaks?" I asked in a quavering tone, and finally he lifted his tortured face to look me in the eye. "I…I'm not angry with you. I think I'm…scared."

As soon as the words were out of my mouth, my eyes began to blur with hot tears. I looked down, embarrassed at my own emotionally-driven reaction, as the tears begin to spill down my cheeks.

Il'zaks surprised me again; he left his seat and swiftly knelt at my side. He placed his left hand, trembling as it was, on my arm, and I started at the contact. He had never touched me in any way, not even for a handshake.

"Can you forgive me?" he asked, and his voice was unable to conceal his pain.

I drew a breath, wiping my eyes roughly with the heels of my palms. I ventured to look up at him once more, noting how the light of the room danced across his silver irises, how his concern for me molded his features into a virtual mask of anguish. He was suffering and guilt-ridden because I had become upset.

"You only did what you thought was best," I managed finally. "Don't blame yourself…I think I would have done the same."

Il'zaks closed his eyes briefly. When he opened them again, he had regained his composure. He said nothing, and merely studied me carefully for a time.

"In all reality, I ought to thank you," I said after a moment. "You've shown me that there's more to this life than I had imagined, and that I'm not just another typical, average person. You have no idea what that means to me."

He shook his head slightly. "I deserve no thanks for all I have put you through already." He stood, the movement too quick for my eyes to follow; it was as if at one moment he were kneeling beside me and an instant later he was on his feet, as though he had never been kneeling at all.

"How did you *do* that?"

He managed a sad smile. "I have to make a conscious effort to move slowly enough that it will appear normal to you. When you finish your training, your reflexes will be just as fast as mine are, and you will also understand the rather unique challenge it presents."

I nodded. "Is there anything else I should be made aware of?"

Il'zaks sighed as he returned to his seat, and I was struck again by how graceful his simplest movements were. "The most difficult part of this training process for me is the uncertainty of its outcome. Most people who set upon the path do not see its conclusion. Some die, while others end up with a shattered mind and spend the rest of their days in mental health facilities. Few complete their training as a summoner."

"But, why?" I asked, unable to keep the question to myself.

"Some people have difficulty letting go of their preconceived notions," he replied. "I have bypassed some potentially talented humans in the past, because I knew they did not possess the open mindedness that is required to survive this training process. You struck me as someone who is in possession of an open mind—if you had not, we would not be sitting here tonight.

"Others have had misfortunes when trying to practice their summoning. Remember that I said it was important to know the words exactly, when I showed you how to call a *djinn*? There have been some students who were careless, mixing up their words, and most often that ends fatally. You especially need to be careful of this, since your summoning does not include speaking aloud in any way. I will not know if you jumble the words, and will be unable to stop you in time to prevent an accident."

There were so many things I had to be aware of, and so many risks involved. There was no way to dislodge myself from this track, as Il'zaks had mentioned before, so I was committed, regardless if I came to have any regrets.

"I must ask you, Chandra Grey—have you had any unusual dreams lately?"

I was immediately suspicious of his question, as I recalled the nightmare I had experienced the week prior.

"Yes," I replied slowly, glancing at him from the corner of my eye.

He appeared to be relieved at my response. "Your dreams are important indicators to how well you have mastered the summoning of various demons," he explained. "Most of the dreams will probably be very unpleasant—"

"You have no idea," I replied without thinking, cutting him off.

"Oh, but I do indeed," he contradicted me. "Tell me about them."

I told him of my nightmare and the shadowy figures within, trying to recall as much detail as possible. He listened intently, and when I had finished, he nodded.

"The shadow-people, as you called them, represent the *djinni*. The fact that there were three of them that came to you means that you should be able to call three of them at a time, so long as you concentrate enough on the task. Would you like to try it?"

I hesitated. "Will this give me nightmares again?"

Il'zaks chuckled. "No, you will not have any others due to our activities here until you are taught how to summon another type of demon. You should sleep perfectly well tonight."

Relieved, I stood up. "Alright then, I'll try it."

"Now that we know you can summon three *djinni*, all you have to do—besides concentrating on your words and movements—is to think of the number three. Do not be disappointed if it does not work the first time. I understand that it is quite a lot to focus on all at once. Your main concern should *always* be getting the words and movements correct each time."

I nodded. "I think I can do this."

I closed my eyes, which helped me to clear my mind and maintain focus. I had not yet been able to concentrate well enough with my eyes open to manage a summoning, and after our talk tonight, I knew it was safer to make certain I was focused when attempting such feats. The words came to my mind easily enough, and I danced—the steps had become more familiar to me over the last week and I no longer felt awkward when performing them. I managed to think of three *djinni* while I did this, imagining the number as an undercurrent to the main words I used to perform the summoning.

As had happened each time someone was near to me, I was bombarded with information as soon as I finished my dance. I had become accustomed enough to this that I immediately silenced the *djinni*. Only after I had done this did I realize that I could feel three separate entities connected to my mind, and startled, I opened my eyes to make sure I hadn't simply imagined it.

There were three softly glowing orbs floating in the air between Il'zaks and I. I grinned, unable to stop myself.

Il'zaks was smiling. "Very good, Chandra Grey. Continue to practice this. Tomorrow I will introduce you to Ke'tai and your defense training will begin."

"Thanks, Il'zaks," I said. "I'm glad you told me what you did tonight."

His smile faltered, and his expression became solemn. "I deserve no thanks." He sighed, then added, "Have Trey escort you home, just in case."

He didn't have to elaborate; I understood why he worried. If a hunter happened to be nearby, I was incredibly vulnerable.

"I will," I promised. "See you tomorrow."

# 5

# ATTRACTION

Trey bade me a good night at the base of the stairs leading up to my apartment, and informed me that he would meet me there the following afternoon at Il'zaks' request. I raised my eyebrows, but made no comment; I wished the big man a nice evening before I jogged up the steps, my keys jangling in my hand.

Xandra was still awake; she and Elliot were in the living room watching a movie I didn't recognize when I entered. Glancing at the stereo's clock, I noticed it was just after eleven.

"You're home early," Xandra said as I entered, her tone betraying her surprise.

I shrugged. "They didn't have much for me to do tonight. It sounds like tomorrow is going to be busy though."

"Join us for the movie," Elliot said. "We only started it ten minutes ago—it won't be a problem to restart it."

This certainly *was* a change for Xandra—a guy who actually had some form of manners and wasn't afraid to speak to me.

"Uh, sure," I said, trying to hide my surprise. "Let me go hang up my jacket, and I'll be right back."

The movie was nothing I would have cared to watch again, but what caused me to remember that night was Elliot. He seemed to genuinely care for my sister, and whether she consciously recognized that fact or not, I had never seen her appear so completely happy. While a part of me was pleased that she had finally found someone decent, another part burned with a jealousy unlike anything I had ever experienced. I was torn inside as those emotions battled within me.

My feelings escalated to the point that I was relieved when Elliot said his good nights to us and mercifully left the apartment almost three hours later. Xandra's face was flushed and she could not hide her smile as she closed and locked the door.

"So, what do you think?" she asked excitedly.

I managed a smile. "I think he will be good for you," I replied truthfully, but I was unable to maintain the charade of happiness. I looked down, breaking eye contact, and sighed.

"Chandra, what's wrong?"

*I'm crazy about your boyfriend,* I thought bitterly in response to her question. "I'm sorry, Xan, I'm just tired," I lied. I forced another smile. "I think you've found someone special with Elliot. I'll be honest with you—I was shocked when he asked me to join you two for the movie. Who knew men could actually learn manners?"

Xandra giggled. "Oh, he *is* wonderful. I don't know why I never paid attention to him before."

"Maybe you needed to learn what *not* to look for first," I replied, thinking of her latest relationship disaster with Dillon.

Xandra smiled knowingly. "Probably. But I think Elliot is *perfect*."

Perfect. I couldn't find it within myself to disagree.

The following evening, I practically fled the apartment as the sky began to darken. Xandra had the night off work, and she had asked Elliot over for dinner. Simply being in the same room with him was almost too much to endure. I decided I needed to start seriously looking for a boyfriend of my own; perhaps then these terrible pangs of jealousy—and the ensuing guilt they caused—would disappear.

Trey was waiting at the base of the steps as promised, and wordlessly we hurried the short distance to Chaos Rising. A cold drizzle was falling from the sky, and I silently cursed at myself for neglecting to grab my umbrella on my way out of the apartment. Trey seemed oblivious to the weather, marching along steadily without a word until we had reached the arcade.

At the base of the now-familiar concrete steps stood a man whom I did not recognize. He was average height and looked to be Hispanic in the failing light. His dark eyes were intelligent and alert, and he bore a thin, whitish scar near his left eye. He was dressed in a gray-brown trench coat and had the collar turned up to shield his neck from the rain.

"This is Carlos," Trey said by way of introduction. "He works for the summoner Ke'tai."

Carlos extended one leather-gloved hand, and we shook hands briefly. "It seems that Il'zaks has spoken very favorably of you, Ms. Grey," he said. "Ke'tai has been anxious to meet you."

I felt my face flush, and mumbled something in response that I could not remember only moments later as I stood just inside the door. The overhead lights were on in the room at the end of the corridor, and provided plenty of light for me to walk by.

When I reached the room, Il'zaks stood near its center with the summoner I recognized as Ke'tai from my work with the *djinni*. Ke'tai was considerably taller than his former mentor, and had a thin build but was wiry with muscle. He wore a thin cotton t-shirt that fit him in such a way that it accentuated the muscles of his shoulders and torso. His facial features were Asian, though I was unsure of where his ancestry was from, he was clean-shaven, and his white hair stood on end in an array of disorganized spikes. He was smiling as I entered, and his silver eyes glittered in the wash of fluorescent light.

"Good evening, Chandra Grey," Il'zaks stated, wearing a slight smile of his own. "I would like to introduce you to Ke'tai."

Il'zaks, as usual, was dressed impeccably, and his hair was combed to one side, not a strand out of place. Standing next to Ke'tai, Il'zaks reminded me of my high school librarian befriending a rebellious teenager. At first glance, they seemed to be polar opposites.

Ke'tai stepped forward and offered his right hand in greeting.

"Hello," I said, shaking his hand briefly. He had a surprising amount of strength in his hands.

"It is a pleasure," he said, never taking his eyes from mine. "Il'zaks has told me a lot about you. When he asked me if I was available to help with your training, I have to say I was excited. You've definitely got potential."

For the second time since I had arrived at the arcade with Trey, I felt my face turn crimson. "Thanks," I mumbled. I didn't think I would ever be able to get used to so much attention.

Ke'tai laughed good naturedly, and Il'zaks said, "I have some business of my own to tend to this evening, so I shall leave the two of you to your practice. I will see you tomorrow night, Chandra Grey."

"See you then," I managed to say in reply as Il'zaks began making his way out of the room.

Ke'tai waited to speak until Il'zaks had gone. "I thought it might be best if you knew a little bit about me before we start," he said. He sounded unsure of himself. "I know that Il'zaks feels that sort of information is better left until you're officially a summoner, but I'd feel better about myself if I told you now, since we'll be seeing a lot of each other from now on." He flashed a brilliant smile. "I'm pretty sure I can trust you to keep this information secret."

I nodded. "More than anything, I want to finish this training. I wouldn't do anything to compromise my situation."

He nodded knowingly. "I thought as much, from what Il'zaks had told me about you. I felt exactly the same way when I was in your position. That was quite a few years ago, but I am still considered very young for a summoner."

Based on what I had learned from the *djinni*, Il'zaks had trained Ke'tai over forty years ago. He looked to be perhaps a year or two older than I did, so I decided he must be somewhere around sixty-five years old. I had no inkling as to how old Il'zaks might be.

"How old are you?" I asked finally, after thinking over what he had said for some time.

He grinned. "Probably old enough to be your grandfather," he laughed. "In all seriousness, I am forty-three by the summoners' reckoning, but I've been on this earth for twenty-seven beyond that. I was born seventy years ago, but as a summoner, I will be considered young until I've lived at least a couple centuries."

I gaped at him. Il'zaks had told me that summoners did not age, but to hear it stated like this came as a shock. "How old is Il'zaks then?"

Ke'tai laughed again. "If he hasn't felt it necessary to tell you that piece of information, then it is not my place to say. I will tell you that he is *much* older than I am."

This revelation did not surprise me. The way in which Il'zaks dressed, how he spoke, his mannerisms—these all told me that he was from a bygone era. He was too *proper* to be from the same century that I had grown up in.

"Would you like to hear more, or have I shocked you too much already for one night?" Ke'tai asked, teasingly.

"Tell me more," I replied.

He smiled. "Glad to hear I haven't bored you yet," he said, laughing. "I was born and raised in San Francisco. I think I had a pretty average life, but I don't remember much of it. It's very hard to hold on to those human memories, once you aren't human any more."

He paused, and his gaze was unreadable. I had the distinct feeling he was trying to judge my reaction. I said nothing, but his words had made me stop to consider—how would it affect me if I were unable to remember my past?

"Now it's your turn," Ke'tai said after this relatively brief pause. "Tell me about yourself."

"My life has never been all that interesting," I replied. I hated talking about myself.

"Please, Chandra. It's important to me that I know."

I was startled by the sincerity of his words. "Alright," I agreed, not wanting to hurt his feelings. "I was born in Astoria. It's a town in northern Oregon, just south of the Washington border. I haven't really gone very far since then either," I laughed nervously. "I have a sister, Xandra—"

"Oh, yes, Il'zaks *did* tell me about that," Ke'tai put in.

"He told me she could be a hunter one day," I added, feeling rather self-conscious.

"It wouldn't be the first time something like that has happened," Ke'tai replied. "Don't worry; no one will think any less of you because of her. You have no control over your genes, or those of your sister."

"So, this ability we have, it's genetic?" I asked, surprised.

Ke'tai nodded, smiling. "There are rare genes—recessive is the technical term for it—that allow for a person to harbor the power of summoning, or of hunting. What we don't know about these genes yet is what triggers them to be one form as opposed to another. See, it's the *same* gene you have that your sister *also* has, but for some reason hers is tuned to being a hunter, whereas yours is for a summoner. I work with summoners Ai'zhanna and Te'moru off and on doing research on this gene and its functions. It's really fascinating stuff. If you like science, that is," he added.

Under normal circumstances, I would have found this conversation too technical of a subject, and one that held little interest for me. But these circumstances were altogether *not* normal, and what he was speaking of intrigued me, in spite of my dislike for anything that had to do with science.

"What do you know about it so far?" I asked. I realized that I *did* want to know.

"Well, first off, how much do you know about genetics?" he asked. "That will sort of determine where I need to start with my explanation."

I thought for a moment, remembering we had touched on the subject very briefly in my high school biology class, but I couldn't recall anything specific. I relayed this to Ke'tai.

He laughed lightly. "Alright, this could take a while to explain, then," he began. "Good thing we've got all night."

He paused a moment, thinking, and I noticed the way his eyes shone with excitement and perhaps passion. He was preparing to tell me about something he truly enjoyed, perhaps it was even something he loved. In that brief moment, I sat riveted, helplessly entranced by his mere presence. Even Elliot had not managed to have so profound an effect upon me—but in the end, the moment passed. I blinked in surprise, and with a little disappointment, when Ke'tai spoke again, shattering my brief daydream.

"Alright, so to start off with, you inherit one set of genes from your mother and another set from your father," Ke'tai began. "The gene that I help to study follows these rules, so you have one copy of it from each parent. In order for this gene to actually do anything, you have to have the recessive—rare—copy from both parents as well. The thing is, that doesn't happen very often. Most of the time people are born with at least one copy of the dominant—the more common form—of the gene, so they end up as ordinary humans.

"Now you and I—we were born with two copies of this recessive gene. So was your sister. The gene requires some sort of outside influence in order for it to change from the hunters' form of the gene to the summoners'. Well 'change' isn't really the right word to describe it…It's more like the gene is triggered by something—it could be an illness, or some sort of trauma—and part of it gets activated that was turned off before. We aren't sure what exactly causes this activation to happen, we just know that it does in a small number of people. That's why hunters—those who can seek demons, those who can seek summoners, or those who can seek other hunters—are so much more common than we summoners are. Well, that and the risk involved just to finish the training."

He was silent for a time as I tried to absorb the information. He had explained it in words that, for the most part, made sense to me, but the concepts were unfamiliar and complex.

"If this is something genetic, why is it that I have to finish all this training before the transformation happens? Why hasn't it happened already?" I asked.

"That's a good question," Ke'tai acknowledged. "We aren't entirely sure of that answer yet, but here's what we know: While the gene needs prior activation to turn into the summoners' form, it also requires some sort of other stimulus in order for it to fully turn on. Our theory is that the stimulus it needs comes from reaching your mental limit of control over a demon; when you learn to summon the most powerful demon you are able to control, the gene is fully turned on, and that's when the transformation will occur.

"The transformation happens because when this gene is fully turned on, it causes your body to start releasing a new sort of hormone in fairly high concentrations. Think of it like when you were going through puberty, only it happens much, much faster and hurts a hell of a lot more. The hormones cause your body to change, and that's when you truly become a summoner."

"So how do you know what the strongest demon you can call is? I mean, why is it different from one summoner to another? Il'zaks told me that you are much stronger than he is."

Ke'tai nodded, his eyes twinkling. He was enjoying this discussion. "The actual power of a summoner comes from an entirely different gene, and it's one that I don't know as much about. Basically, that gene works in tandem with the other, and certain mutations in this 'power' gene can give one summoner a significant advantage over another. It works the same with hunters."

I was silent for a time, digesting the information. Finally, I said, "So basically, I'm the same as Xan, only something happened to me that she didn't experience…If we'd had the exact same things happen to us in life, she could have been here too—or me not at all. Is that right?"

"Exactly," Ke'tai agreed, and his brilliant smile surfaced again. "For someone with a degree in economics, you're certainly taking an interest in all of this gene stuff. Either that, or you're just being polite and letting me ramble on about my research project. That could be dangerous, you know—I've been told before that it can be hard to get me to shut up about it."

I smiled. "No, I was actually very interested. Thank you."

He blinked, as though he had been surprised by my answer. "Really? Well, that's good to know." He laughed. "Well, we are here for a purpose today, and I wasted too much time rambling on about my research. Are you awake enough to learn some basic karate moves?"

When I nodded, he grinned. "Excellent. Otherwise, I think Il'zaks would be pretty angry with me for not having accomplished anything tonight."

The training session lasted for a few hours. I had no prior experience with martial arts of any kind, and I had never taken so much as a self-defense class. I felt awkward and clumsy at first, but it got better as the night wore on. Ke'tai was incredibly patient with me, continually encouraging me to keep on and not to give up when I struggled. He made an excellent teacher.

Just as I began to feel as though I'd begun making progress, Ke'tai stopped me, saying, "It's pretty late. You'll need to sleep sometime before tomorrow."

I was disappointed. I had been having fun, and I did not want this night to be over already. I had to admit that I was certainly attracted to Ke'tai; his manner was so open and friendly that I felt very comfortable around him. I liked that.

"But I was just starting to really get into this!" I protested.

Ke'tai laughed. "I noticed that. But there will always be next time."

I sighed dramatically, causing him to laugh again.

"Give me a second to get my things together, and then I'll be ready to take you home," he said, turning to walk towards the back door that led into the old employee break room.

"What?" I asked. I was sure I hadn't heard him correctly.

He bent just inside the door to retrieve a small black duffel bag, and carried it out to the collapsible table. "I'm going to walk you home. Il'zaks told me you usually walk here, and I'd feel better if you didn't walk alone."

Just when I thought that I understood summoners, I realized that, like ordinary humans, each one was different. "Il'zaks usually just has Trey do that," I replied.

Ke'tai smiled, but this time there was a quiet sadness in his eyes. "I will tell you something about Il'zaks. He had a student he was very close to fail, some years before he met me. That failure, it tore him apart, and he swore that he'd never again become too familiar with another student. By not walking you home, by keeping his distance, it puts his mind at ease."

Ke'tai pulled a black hooded sweatshirt out of the duffel bag and tugged it on over his head. He pulled the hood up in order to cover his white hair, and then began rummaging in the bag some more.

"I never knew that about Il'zaks," I said after a moment of silence in which I had simply been content to watch Ke'tai. "I thought that it was just some rule that summoners have."

Ke'tai pulled out a pair of sunglasses with blue lenses, and zipped the bag shut once more. "Let him keep thinking that you think that," he replied. "I wasn't supposed to tell you."

I nodded, and Ke'tai slid the sunglasses in place. The effect they had made it seem as though he had blue eyes, since the lenses weren't reflective.

"Like my disguise?" he asked with a grin.

I nodded again. "You look almost normal now." I walked over to the table and retrieved my coat, pulling it on.

"What do you mean by 'almost'?" he asked, feigning hurt.

What could I say that would not offend him? "Um, well—"

He laughed. "I know, blue eyes are pretty much unheard of for a Japanese guy. But it's dark—nobody will notice." He flashed a grin, and slung the bag over his shoulder. "Ready to go?"

"Yeah, I guess."

We walked in silence while we exited the building. I was feeling rather melancholy all of the sudden, though I wasn't sure why. Perhaps it was because I knew my time with Ke'tai was almost over for the night, but I shoved that thought aside. *Don't be ridiculous,* I chided myself. *He's not going to have* that *kind of interest in me. Just forget it.*

"I wanted to tell you that I enjoyed working with you tonight," Ke'tai said abruptly when we were nearly across the arcade's parking lot. "Thanks for allowing me to bore you with my science hobby."

I had been looking down, but I snapped my head up at his words. He was smiling. "I...ought to thank you, too," I managed before looking away again. I wasn't sure what to make of his words, and it made me uncomfortable. I only wished that I knew what he was thinking about me.

"What's wrong?" he asked. "You seem upset. Did I say something—?"

With a shake of my head, I cut him off. "I'm not upset. I'm just...Oh, I don't know how to explain it. I guess...I just don't know quite what to think right now. I'm sorry." I sighed, frustrated with myself for my inability to express my thoughts clearly.

Ke'tai appeared to be at once both concerned and bewildered. "As long as you're not upset, that's what matters to me." He sounded unconvinced by his own words.

"I'm sorry," I said again, keeping my gaze focused on the sidewalk passing beneath my shoes. "It's just...you're so different from Il'zaks that I don't know what to expect. He's so predictable, but you...you're not. I thought I knew what I was getting myself into, but now I'm not so sure. But, it's not a bad thing," I added, offering him a smile. "I think it could be very good. I just don't know for sure yet."

Ke'tai looked at me in a sideways manner, as though *he* were now unsure of what to make of *me*. I directed my gaze quickly back to the ground, frowning. The last thing I wanted was for him to leave this encounter thinking I was crazy.

We walked in silence for a few moments, and then Ke'tai abruptly stopped. "Chandra," he said slowly, "I really hope that I haven't left you with a bad impression, but now *I* hardly know what to think."

I bit my lower lip, internally cursing at myself for being such a pathetic fool. I stopped a few paces beyond where he now stood and turned slowly around to face him, feeling my face burn with embarrassment.

"Just forget what I said," I mumbled. "I get nervous..."

Ke'tai said nothing, but he continued to look at me in that same perplexed manner. Finally, after what seemed to me hours instead of the mere seconds it actually was, his face broke into a lopsided grin and he began walking again. When he came to the place where I stood, I matched his pace, feeling more than a little confused.

"You've got nothing to be nervous about, Chandra," he said quietly, smiling down at me. "Then again, the same should hold true for me, but I'm still nervous. So, let's forget the nerves altogether and just work at being friends for now."

If he hadn't been smiling as he was, I would have felt like a complete idiot—or rather, more so than I did already. The attraction was there, seemingly for the both of us, and I knew it would be stupid of me to deny it any further. I returned his smile, feeling better than I had for most of the walk, and nodded.

"That's probably the smart thing to do," I said. "Besides the fact that I feel like an ass, I should have realized that this is probably harder for you than it is for me."

Ke'tai chuckled. "I understand why Il'zaks keeps his distance, but at the same time, I've never been one to play by the rules. Maybe I'm being reckless, but we only get to live once. Might as well be happy while we're here."

We were now crossing the parking lot, heading toward the stairs that led up to my apartment. Ke'tai turned to face me just before we reached the steps and gave me a smile that could have illuminated even the darkest and dreariest of Seattle's nights.

"I will see you the day after tomorrow—Sunday night," he said quietly. "Il'zaks will meet you tomorrow. I cannot wait to see you again, so be safe."

I nodded, still feeling unsure of myself. "I'll see you on Sunday, I promise."

# 6

# NIGHTWING

It was almost noon the next day when I finally emerged from my room. I was feeling well, even though I was sore in my arms and legs from the three-hour karate lesson. I felt discomfort in muscles I had never known existed, but the pain was manageable.

Xandra was preparing to leave for work when I came into the kitchen area to find something for breakfast. She was making a ham and cheese sandwich to take with her for dinner, spreading crumbs of bread all over the countertop in the process.

"Oh, good, you're up," she said without looking at me. "I didn't want to risk waking you up to leave a note. Elliot's going to stop by tonight after I'm off work, and I just wanted to let you know."

That internal groan and jealous longing that I had grown accustomed to experiencing at the mere mention of Elliot's name was absent this morning. I smiled to myself, thinking of Ke'tai.

"That's fine," I replied. "I have to work tonight anyway."

She nodded, stuffing the now-finished sandwich into a plastic bag. "Oh, I almost forgot. You have a letter that was in the mail today. I left it on the stand by the couch."

"Thanks," I mumbled, pulling a blueberry bagel and some cream cheese out of the refrigerator. "I'll check it out once I get some food."

Xandra took her sandwich and headed for the door. "See you later."

"Later," I called, spreading the cream cheese carefully over each half of the bagel. Xandra left, closing the door softly behind her.

Setting the bagel on a plate and replacing the container of cream cheese in the refrigerator, I took my breakfast out to the living room to examine my letter. It was a simple white envelope, and at first seemed to be ordinary mail; after looking closer, however, two things caught my eye. There was no return address, and there was no stamped-on postmark. Immediately, I wondered if Xandra had noticed the lack of a postmark. It meant the normal mail carrier couldn't have placed the letter in our box.

My name and address were handwritten on the front of the envelope in a script that I didn't recognize. The handwriting was legible, but messy, and slanted slightly toward the left. Curious, I tore open the envelope.

Inside was a card. The front had a black and white picture of a bouquet of flowers on it, but there were no words. When I opened up the card, I was greeted with more of the same slanted handwriting that had been on the outside of the envelope.

*Chandra,*

*I wanted to thank you again for last night. I only hope that I haven't frightened you away. My thoughts get all jumbled up sometimes when I try to talk to attractive women—yes, even summoners have to deal with the consequences of hormones. I would like to think that what I was feeling last night will continue, and that maybe you feel the same way. I have never been a very good judge of people and what they are thinking/feeling. I think I may have been a little too forward with you about some things, and I hope that I'm not making a mistake by leaving you this note. After I left you here last night, I was unable to sleep, I couldn't get you out of my mind. I wanted you to know what I'm feeling, since I know we will be spending so much time together from now on. After your lesson tonight, you should be able to contact me at any time, and I hope you won't hesitate to do so. I will see you on Sunday evening.*

*Be Safe*
*K*

I read and reread the letter several times, as though if I stopped, the words would suddenly change. This letter was confirmation; what I had sensed about Ke'tai the night before was true—he *did* have an attraction to me. I felt both relieved and excited; now that I knew what he felt, I would be able to talk to him more freely. I would not be constantly worried of making an ass out of myself.

I found I was filled with nervous energy and unable to sit still. I wasn't certain that I would be able to concentrate properly when I met with Il'zaks that night. I decided to clean the apartment during the next few hours, just to pass the time, but my excitement did not abate. I read the card a few more times before finally stashing it inside one of my desk drawers, shortly before I left for the arcade's basement.

Trey met me in the parking lot just outside of my apartment as twilight began to fall. "Evening," he greeted me. He was wearing a heavier coat than his customary leather jacket tonight, for it was colder than was usual. The darkening clouds overhead threatened rain, possibly even snow, but for now the ground was dry.

"Good evening," I replied, zipping my coat up a little higher as the winter air enveloped me.

We walked in silence for a time, and then Trey said, "I should probably warn you that Carmine is here tonight also, and she seems crankier than usual."

I groaned. "What is her problem, anyway?" I wasn't expecting an answer, but Trey replied nevertheless.

"Don't take anything she says personally. She doesn't like anyone, unless they've got silver eyes and white hair, but she particularly resents you because you *can* become that, whereas she's stuck in humanity." He shrugged his massive shoulders. "Believe me, I wish most of the time that I didn't have to work with her. Be grateful that you don't have to see her every day."

"Oh, I am. I definitely don't envy you in that department."

We were walking across the parking lot toward Chaos Rising by this time, and I was attempting to prepare myself mentally for the inevitable remarks I would receive from Carmine. I could see the top of her lime green head before we reached the concrete steps that led to the basement beneath the arcade.

As I reached the top of the steps, Carmine scowled and yanked the door open wordlessly. There was a fire in her gaze that made me incredibly uncomfortable, all the more so when she refrained from speaking to me at all. I glanced at Trey, who merely shrugged and rolled his eyes skyward.

I decided the best course of action would be to go inside and leave Carmine alone. She slammed the door with more force than was necessary as soon as I was beyond the threshold, and I was left wondering why I was deserving of her anger. With a weary sigh, I headed down the dim corridor towards the brightly-lit main room beyond, having effectively forgotten about Ke'tai for the time being.

Il'zaks stood in the center of the room facing me when I entered. He was wearing a dark colored suit, so it took me a few moments to realize that there was a small, black, bat-like creature perched on his left forearm, which he held outstretched and motionless before him.

Il'zaks smiled, amusement dancing in his silver eyes. "Good evening, Chandra Grey," he stated. "I would like to introduce you to a creature we like to call the nightwing."

I came to a stop just in front of Il'zaks, and bent a little to examine the creature better. It was perched upright, unlike a bat, but from what little I knew about bats it resembled one closely. It was a brown-black in color and had wings much like a bat's, but I noticed that it also had a tiny pair of arms that it kept tucked beneath its wings.

"We use the nightwing primarily as a means of delivering messages," Il'zaks continued. "They can fly very quickly, and they also have the ability to camouflage themselves to keep out of sight. Much like a chameleon," he added.

Now I understood what Ke'tai had meant in the card he had left for me. I would be able to send him messages using a nightwing, and no longer would I have to wait until our designated meeting times to ask him questions. I resolved then and there to send him a message in return as soon as I was home.

The nightwing flew from Il'zaks arm and perched carefully on the wall in one corner of the room. An instant later, its body had changed color to match the dingy white paint of the wall, and though I struggled to focus on it, it was nearly impossible to see from our position at the center of the room.

"Another advantage to using the nightwing is that because it is such a benign demon, some hunters cannot track it," Il'zaks continued. "They are also fast enough that even if one were tracked, there is little chance a hunter would be able to intercept any messages it may be carrying. It is the safest and most secure method we have of communicating with one another; that is why I felt you should be taught about it so early in your training."

I nodded. "So, it's like the summoners' postal service," I said. "Do you use nightwings for anything else?"

Il'zaks smiled. "Postal service; that's a very good analogy. To answer your question though, most summoners use the nightwing exclusively as a messenger, and for nothing else. I have heard of some using them as a sort of decoy at times, to throw off hunters or some such, but it is quite rare. The nightwing does not have any extranormal powers, like many other demons do."

I nodded, already planning out what I would write to Ke'tai. It didn't matter that I would see him tomorrow evening; what I wanted to tell him could not wait, not after the note I had received from him this morning.

"Very well. If you have no more questions, I will demonstrate the summoning for you," Il'zaks stated, breaking apart my thoughts and forcing me to focus on the lesson at hand.

"Okay," I replied, and he smiled faintly in response, though his eyes seemed guarded.

"Listen carefully, Chandra Grey," he reminded me. "You will always need to be careful of your summoning practices while you are still merely human. I do not wish to see you fail."

I nodded again, focusing my full attention on Il'zaks for the first time that evening. Failing in a lesson could prove fatal; I was forced to push my thoughts of Ke'tai aside.

Il'zaks nodded then, seemingly satisfied. He stood up a bit straighter than he had been, and carefully closed his left hand into a fist. Closing his eyes, he rapidly shot his fist upwards into the air and said, "*Nacht vin sún vinte*," in that same commanding tone he had used when calling the *djinn*.

That same surprising instantaneous knowledge came to me as had also happened with the *djinn*. I was prepared for it this time, however, and did not gape at Il'zaks as I had during our previous lesson. Still, it came as a shock, and I blinked rapidly a few times to sort out my newly-gained intelligence.

A second nightwing had perched upon Il'zaks' shoulder, while the first had begun circling the room, still assuming the color of the walls.

Il'zaks smiled encouragingly. "Your turn, Chandra Grey."

I closed my eyes in order to focus my mind, thinking the words while I danced to a new set of simplistic steps. When I had finished, I could feel the nightwing with my mind, but it did not come as such a profound shock as calling the *djinn* had. The nightwing's temperament was docile and subservient, and it simply waited for my first command. It took me several moments to realize it had perched carefully on my right shoulder; it was such a light-weight creature that I hardly noticed its presence there.

When at last I opened my eyes again, Il'zaks was smiling. The pair of nightwings he had called were gone; I assumed he had dismissed them.

"As you have probably noticed, a nightwing will do anything you ask of it," Il'zaks said. "It is a completely submissive demon. There will be others that are not so cooperative."

I nodded; I realized that I had been thinking of Ke'tai again, and had only partially listened to what Il'zaks had said. Inadvertently, I sighed.

Il'zaks raised one white eyebrow, but his expression was unreadable. "I would wager that you have something on your mind," he said after a moment. "Why don't you dismiss that nightwing, and then we can talk."

I felt the blood rush to my face, and I bit my lower lip, embarrassed, but did as he asked and released the nightwing. I followed Il'zaks to the collapsible table and sat down across from him, feeling at once ashamed and terrified; I was uncertain if he would approve of my news regarding Ke'tai, but I knew I must tell him.

"You've been distracted this evening," Il'zaks stated, steepling his fingers before him. "I think I know why, but I'd rather not jump to conclusions. I would like to hear it from you."

I looked down, unable to meet his piercing silver-eyed gaze. "I...I can't stop thinking about Ke'tai," I mumbled the admission, certain that I had not spoken loudly enough for him to hear my words.

Il'zaks broke into an amused laugh, and I snapped my head up to stare at him. I had been certain the news would utterly disappoint him, and was caught unaware when he had laughed instead of scolding me. I blinked rapidly several times, unsure of what to say next.

"Ah, it's exactly as I thought," Il'zaks chuckled. "Ke'tai spoke to me after he left you that letter this morning. He acted much as you did, like finding that you fancy someone is a crime comparable to murder!" He ended with another laugh.

"So, you're not mad?" I asked, still feeling uncertain of myself.

"Of course, I'm not mad," he said, as though that fact should have been obvious beyond any doubt. "As I told Ke'tai earlier, I may not venture down the path that he has chosen, but I will not stand in his way, either. Nor will

I stand in yours. I only know from my past experiences what sort of pain is involved when you lose someone very dear to you to an unexpected tragedy, and I do not wish to experience that again. However," he added with some emphasis, "my past should not dictate the choice that others decide to make. I can see where you would be good for Ke'tai; he has been lonely since becoming a summoner, and I have never seen him as happy as I did earlier today." Il'zaks smiled, and his expression reminded me of my father when he was especially proud of Xandra or I. "I am happy for Ke'tai, but I worry how it would affect him if you should never complete your training...Promise me that you will be very careful. For his sake."

I hesitated before managing a nod. "I promise, Il'zaks. More than anything, I want to see this through to its completion."

I realized after I had arrived home that I had been consumed with my thoughts of Ke'tai—and before that the terror of Il'zaks' disapproval—that I had neglected to ask a crucial question of Il'zaks before I had departed the arcade with Trey. Would I experience another nightmare like the one I had endured after my lesson regarding the *djinni*? I sighed as this realization dawned on me, knowing that I would inevitably find out once I went to sleep for the night.

First, I had a letter to write. Thankfully, Xandra was already asleep when I arrived, and I had no reason to worry about her discovering my activities. I locked my bedroom door all the same, as an additional precaution.

> *Ke'tai –*
> *I received your letter this morning, and afterwards I could not stop thinking about you. Il'zaks had to stop me and make me focus tonight. I know, that's a bad thing, and I shouldn't let myself be distracted like that. But you're just amazing. I wonder how I am so lucky that you're even remotely interested in me? I don't think my letter is any way near as articulate as yours was, but I want you to know what you wrote made me very happy. See you tomorrow!*
>
> *Chandra*

I folded the note carefully. It was written on ordinary, lined notebook paper, and compared to his card, it looked very plain. I hoped he wouldn't think less of me for not taking the time to find something a little nicer, but I had been too excited to wait any longer; I had needed to write it *now*.

Once I had finished, I summoned the nightwing. I gave it the letter and asked that it take it to Ke'tai. Il'zaks had told me as I was leaving that the nightwing had an uncanny ability to seek out specific people, summoners in particular, and that by merely telling it who to locate, it would find its way. I had to open my window a few inches to allow it outside, and it quickly flew away, seemingly full of purpose.

I could sense it as it flitted through the night sky, darting between buildings where it needed to, but always keeping out of direct lighting. I could not tell the direction that it traveled, nor could I recognize any of the structures that it passed from the vague impressions I received, but I knew when it had finally reached Ke'tai and delivered my letter.

I dismissed it as soon as it had completed its task, and then went about the business of preparing to go to sleep, remembering at the last moment to unlock the bedroom door. If Xandra should need to come inside, I did not wish to rouse her suspicions.

I fell asleep rather quickly; it came as a surprise, considering my excitement regarding Ke'tai and the nagging worry in the back of my mind concerning the nightmare I was likely to endure. My last conscious thought before drifting off, was of anticipation for my next meeting with Ke'tai.

I found myself standing on a barren hilltop, the single high point amid an ocean of deciduous trees. It was well into the night, and I could see thousands of stars overhead, though the constellations were unfamiliar. There was no moon in the sky, but the starlight was adequate enough that I could see individual leaves on the nearest trees, and the blades of scraggly grass that dotted the hilltop in sparse patches. A soft breeze was blowing, just enough so that I could feel it move a few wayward strands of my hair, but otherwise the world was still and silent.

I do not know how long I stood there, simply content to do so. It was peaceful, calm; as I realized this, I knew that I would be happy to stay in this place indefinitely, gazing at the strange stars overhead. For the moment, all of my cares had been forgotten.

Presently, I heard a dry, fluttering sound overhead, like the movement of many wings. I glanced skyward, toward the zenith, and could just make out the shapes of half a dozen bat-like creatures, their black silhouettes only a shade darker than the sky itself. I watched them as they gracefully glided down to land on the hilltop around me. These were nightwings, I realized belatedly, but I felt none of the hostility that I had encountered when I had dreamed of the *djinni*. Nevertheless, I remained cautious.

The six nightwings began to hop from one foot to the other, each in succession. They made no sound beside that of the soft patter of their tiny feet as each made contact with the bare soil. I watched them with curiosity, feeling myself relax again—I was not being threatened.

After several minutes of hopping about, the nightwings suddenly flew upwards and towards me. Surprised at this sudden change in their behavior, I was too stunned to move out of their way. I found, once I had recovered from my initial shock, that there were three nightwings perched on each of my shoulders, seemingly content with their new roost.

I looked up again to see the first rays of an angry red-orange sun begin to stream across the horizon. The glare was blinding, and I was forced to close my eyes against it. When I opened them again, I was laying on my back, staring up at the familiar popcorn ceiling of my bedroom.

# 7

# HOLIDAY

Almost two weeks went by in which I saw Ke'tai almost every night, but I had no lessons with Il'zaks. Ke'tai had mentioned that the elder summoner had been called away on business of the Order, and would return some time after the New Year. Even though Ke'tai and I had been together so often, I still woke up most mornings to find messages awaiting me, sent from him, which I promptly returned. The more I learned about him, the harder it became for me to ignore the attraction he held for me, and to focus on my studies.

My last scheduled training session before the Christmas holiday was on December twenty-third, a Wednesday evening. Xandra and I had spent the afternoon gathering up gifts to take home to our family and packing our duffel bags—it was an expectation of our mother's that we stay overnight on Christmas Eve at our childhood home in Astoria.

Elliot had arrived mid-afternoon unannounced, pleasantly surprising Xandra. He was still there when it came time for me to leave, and I was pleased that Xandra would not be alone so close to the holiday; she and Elliot looked happy together, which is something I could not say regarding her past boyfriends.

When I exited the apartment, it was my turn to be pleasantly surprised. Instead of Carlos awaiting me at the bottom of the stairs as was usual, it was Ke'tai. He smiled that brilliant smile of his, and took my gloved hand in one of his own. My pulse quickened to the point that I was sure he could hear it thundering along in my veins in response to his touch. Ke'tai was wearing the now-familiar blue-lensed glasses, a light gray hooded sweatshirt, with the hood pulled up over his head, and a pair of dark colored jeans.

"I wanted to surprise you tonight," Ke'tai said, smiling, as we made our way across the parking lot.

Instead of walking toward the sidewalk on the far side, however, he led me to a burgundy SUV that was parked to one side of the lot, and opened one of the back doors. As I climbed inside, I noticed that Carlos was sitting in the driver's seat; Ke'tai came inside through the other back door so he could sit next to me. Again, he took my hand.

"This certainly *is* a surprise," I said as Carlos began backing out of the parking space.

Ke'tai grinned. "You haven't seen anything yet," he replied with a wink in my direction.

Carlos drove southeast, guiding us out of Seattle, through Tacoma, to an area within Mount Rainier National Park, while Ke'tai and I talked in the back seat. Carlos stopped the car on the shoulder of a narrow, two lane road that I did not recognize, and Ke'tai smiled at me again.

"Wait here a minute," he said. "I'll come back to get you, once I'm finished, um…setting up."

As soon as Ke'tai was out of the vehicle, I said, "Just what is he up to?"

Carlos laughed. "If I told you, it would ruin his surprise. But you'll like it, trust me."

Ke'tai was gone for less than a minute before he returned. He pulled open my door, and led me outside into the cool night air, then stuck his head back inside, asking Carlos to meet us again at midnight. As the SUV pulled away, Ke'tai took my gloved hand in his once more, and led me into the trees at the side of the road.

"Ke'tai, what—?"

"Ssh," he replied, grinning. "You'll see."

The curiosity was going to drive me mad; I was certain of it. Each time I tried to pose a question, he responded with vague teasing comments, or "you'll see," all the while leading me along what was little more than a game trail winding through the densely packed trees.

After only a few minutes, we came to a break in the trees, and the trail led into a grassy clearing. At its center crouched an enormous creature, unlike any I had ever seen. It was easily larger than any zoo elephant I had ever encountered, and had glossy black reptilian skin. My first impression was that it was an overly large lizard, but then it shifted slightly and I saw that it had a pair of massive wings folded along its scaly back. I stared at it for some time, unable to make sense of what I was seeing.

Ke'tai was grinning, obviously pleased with himself.

"Ke'tai, did you—?"

He laughed. "Of course, I did. This is my dragon… I know Il'zaks will probably not be thrilled with me for calling her out so early in your training, but I wanted to take you flying. It's not raining tonight—in fact, the sky is nearly clear—so I thought it would be a perfect night for it."

I gaped at him. "*Dragon?* But I thought those were only in fairy tales."

Ke'tai laughed. "There are stories about almost every kind of demon you'll learn to summon," he replied. "We use them for travel on occasion. It's faster than driving, and safer than going to an airport. Do you want to take a ride with me?"

He was smiling again; it would be impossible to refuse even if I had wanted to. Besides that, there was the fact that my curiosity was now in overdrive…

"Yes," I said, returning his smile with one of my own. "I'd like that."

Ke'tai had to help me up onto the dragon's back, and he assured me several times that it was perfectly safe. I knew he was in complete control of the creature, but its size—and its razor-sharp teeth—were still very intimidating. Once I was settled into place, Ke'tai sat down in front of me, and glanced back with a boyish grin.

"Hold on," he warned me, and without thinking I put my arms around his waist.

He laughed, and the dragon launched itself skyward, its enormous wings beating the air to either side of us in powerful, rhythmic strokes. My hair was streaming behind me, and the cool night air washed over me; it was exhilarating. Ke'tai allowed his hood to fall backwards, exposing his white hair. The short, stiff spikes he liked to keep it in didn't even seem to tremble at the force of the wind. Idly, I wondered how much gel he had to use in order to achieve such results.

I do not know how long our flight lasted, but I was sorry when I realized the dragon was preparing to land. Below was an exposed rock ledge toward the top of a nearly vertical cliff-face, nearly two-thirds of the way up the mountain. When the dragon had landed, Ke'tai slid expertly down its side, landing gracefully on his feet. He beckoned me to follow.

My own trip down the dragon's side was less than perfect; I stumbled awkwardly when my feet hit the ground, which had been rushing towards me altogether too quickly. I was certain that I was going to fall, but Ke'tai was suddenly there and I crashed clumsily into his arms.

"You made that look so easy," I grumbled good-naturedly as I worked to regain my balance.

He laughed, but said nothing. Instead, he took my hand and led me to a part of the ledge that faced northwest, stopping a few steps away from the edge. I noticed that the dragon was gone, and *then* I noticed why he had brought me to such a place. The ledge had a perfect view of the Seattle-Tacoma skyline, millions of twinkling lights covering the darkened landscape far below for almost as far as the eye could see in either direction. I could not make out individual buildings because of the distance, but it was beautiful all the same.

Ke'tai smiled slightly, disentangling his hand from mine, then he slid his arm about my waist. "What did you think of the flight here?" he asked quietly.

I looked up at him, and his eyes were focused solely upon me; he was not mesmerized by the spectacular view as I was. "I could *so* get addicted to that," I replied grinning up at him.

He smiled in such a way that I thought my heart would melt. "I thought you'd enjoy that," he said. "Just wait until you can summon your own dragon—that feeling is even more incredible."

I did not know what to say, so I said nothing, and turned my gaze back to the city lights spread out before us. It was colder at this elevation than it had been below, and I could feel the wind more strongly, but I was not uncomfortable. I was with Ke'tai, and that was all that mattered to me; I didn't want to be anywhere else, no matter how much more pleasant the climate might be.

"Il'zaks asked me to tell you that he'll be back in the area on the second of January," Ke'tai said quietly after a time. "I wish I could take sole responsibility of your training now, but I know Il'zaks is right. You need to learn the basics from someone with a little more experience than I have."

"And forty years isn't enough?" I mused.

Ke'tai managed a half-hearted chuckle. "It is nothing compared to Il'zaks' time as a summoner."

I shifted slightly to get a better look at him in the darkness. His gaze was fixed on the skyline below, and he appeared to be lost in his thoughts.

"I can't imagine some of the things he must have seen in his time," Ke'tai said after another lapse into silence. "Just thinking about that makes me wonder what I will come to see in my own time…And what you will. I want…I want to be able to share those experiences with someone. It sucks being so alone for so long." He looked down then, and closed his eyes, his expression pained.

"You don't have to be alone," I said. "I'm here."

Ke'tai smiled faintly, then brought his gaze up to meet mine. "I know, Chandra. I just…I worry about you. Until you've finished your training, you'll be in danger, and there's no real way that I can protect you from it. I feel so helpless…" He sighed and dropped his gaze once more.

I could only imagine what he must have been going through. "You told me once that we should be happy while we're here," I replied. "Torturing yourself about the what-if's isn't going to help anyone, especially not you. Ke'tai, I'm happiest when I can see you smile, when I can hear your laugh. I think… Oh, never mind." Now it was my turn to sigh and look away; I had almost said, "I think I'm in love with you." Wasn't it too early in this relationship—or whatever it was—to reveal something like that?

When I looked up again, Ke'tai's eyes were fixed upon mine. He had taken his glasses off, and his eyes sparkled faintly in the dimness. "What were you going to say, before you cut yourself short?" he asked.

I felt my face flush. I feared that telling him the truth might ruin what we now had.

I bit my lower lip, feeling suddenly indecisive. "It was nothing," I said quickly, automatically, and immediately I regretted it. Why did my brain have to choose this moment to go on auto-pilot? I was beginning to feel like an ass.

Ke'tai tilted his head slightly to one side. "You're not a very good liar," he teased. "Tell me what you were thinking…I may need to hear it."

"Why?"

He smiled, somewhat sadly. "I feel a little unsure of myself when I'm near you, and that feeling is altogether foreign to me. I've never really needed anyone in my life before, but since I've met you, I've come to realize just how alone I've been all these years. I need to hear what you were thinking—whatever it was."

My heart was pounding so loudly I was sure he would never be able to hear my voice over the racket it was making. I had to tell him the truth; there was no way around that. Either this would end very badly, or I would see him be happy—truly happy—for the first time since I had met him.

"I...I was going to say that..." I drew a breath, hoping it would give me the strength I needed to finish my faltering sentence. "...I think I've fallen in love with you."

He stared at me for a few seconds, as though he hadn't understood a word that I had said, and then his face broke into the most beautiful smile I had ever seen. He laughed and drew me closer, and I reveled at his warmth.

"Oh, Chandra, I had dreamed of this a thousand times, but I dared not even hope it could be true," he said. "I was afraid..."

"So was I," I replied. "It's nice to know it was pointless to even consider the reasons behind the fear. I'm...relieved."

We stood on the rock ledge for some time, talking sometimes and silent others, but I felt happy—and relaxed for the first time in a long while—just being with Ke'tai. I was disappointed when Ke'tai told me we had best go back, and it was one of the more difficult things I had done to block him out while he summoned the dragon once more. I knew he trusted me to wait until I was ready to learn this bit of my talent, and I was not about to betray that trust. I realized then that I would do anything he asked of me, no matter what that happened to be.

The flight down the mountain felt too short to me, but I felt any parting from Ke'tai would come too soon. I wished that I hadn't made plans for the upcoming holiday, so I would have an excuse to see him at least once more before Il'zaks returned and my regular training lessons resumed. I knew this wish was foolish; I could not risk rousing Xandra's suspicions. It was even more important now than at any time previously that I keep my promises to her.

After we had landed, Ke'tai took my hand and led me back to the game trail. Before we had walked more than a dozen paces, however, Ke'tai stopped suddenly and turned to face me.

"Chandra, I got you something," he said quietly, reaching into the right hip pocket of his jeans. He retrieved a tiny gift bag that was only slightly crumpled, and placed it in my left hand. "Do me a favor, and don't open it until Christmas." He was grinning, and I thought my heart would burst from the beauty of his smile.

"Thank you," I replied quietly after a moment. "I didn't get you anything though. I thought—"

"Summoners don't celebrate Christmas?" he laughed. "I don't believe in the religious aspect of it, but the idea of giving is something worth participating in. I *do* like Santa Claus."

I smiled. "Well, thank you for thinking of me."

He smirked, and his silver eyes danced with delight in the darkness. "How could I not think of you? You're too beautiful to forget, and besides, you had me hooked when you feigned interest in my genetics research." He took my free hand in his again, and began leading the way back to the road. "You know, I was almost afraid to even bring that for you tonight. I wasn't sure if it was the right time yet...but I think I would have been kicking myself right about now if I had left it behind."

Just then we emerged from the trees to find the burgundy SUV idling on the shoulder. Ke'tai helped me inside again, and once he had also been seated, Carlos began driving. I knew they were probably taking me back home, and though I was starting to feel drowsy, I still wished that this night could last forever. I did not wish to part from his side.

Xandra awakened me the next morning at just after ten. I had been sleeping very deeply and was less than thrilled at being roused.

"What do you want?" I demanded groggily, attempting to turn away from her so I could resume my disrupted slumber.

"Elliot's going to be here in twenty minutes," Xandra replied. "I thought I'd be nice and give you some warning."

"Why is he coming here?" I asked, sitting up finally. "Aren't we supposed to be driving to mom and dad's place today?"

Xandra bit her lower lip and looked away. This was her typical reaction when she had either done something wrong or had neglected to pass on some crucial information.

I stood and began straightening the sheets of my bed. After a lengthy silence, I said, "Are you going to tell me today, or next month?"

Xandra sighed. "Well, mom called last night while Elliot was still here. I was in the bathroom, so he answered the phone...She invited him to come with us for Christmas. Since his parents are out in Michigan, and he doesn't have the money to fly home to see them, he agreed." She kept her gaze fixed on the floor as she spoke, as though this were something she had been afraid of.

"Xan, that's great!" I replied. "You and Elliot seem right together. I'm glad you'll let him meet the parents."

Xandra snapped her head up, her eyes wide with surprise for the briefest of moments before she grinned. "Well, he'll be here soon, so I should let you get dressed." She walked to the door, then turned around once more. "I'm so glad you're okay with this, Chandra. I mean, Elliot's different than the other guys I've been with, and—"

"He's better," I finished for her. "Better for you, *and* a better person. He actually treats you decently, which is a huge improvement over Dillon."

Xandra smiled. "This will be a great Christmas," she stated before leaving the room so I could take the time to make myself presentable before Elliot arrived.

After dressing and running a brush through my hair, I double-checked the contents of my duffel bag to make sure I hadn't forgotten anything important. I also took the opportunity to stash the little gift bag Ke'tai had given me inside. I wanted to open it on Christmas day, as early as I possibly could, because the curiosity was gnawing at me. I had to know what was inside.

Elliot arrived right on time—another "new" thing for one of Xandra's boyfriends—and after only a few minutes we were packed inside Xandra's car, headed south from Seattle toward Astoria, Oregon. I sat in the back seat of the car, while Elliot rode shotgun and alternated between chatting with Xandra and asking me questions. It seemed that Xandra had not told him much about me yet.

"Xan told me you've been working nights at some marketing firm, is that right?" Elliot asked. "I always wondered why you had to leave in the evenings."

I nodded. "Yeah. I'm liking the job, even though the schedule is rough sometimes."

"That's cool," he replied, nodding. "So, are you single?"

Xandra shot him a glance, obviously embarrassed that he would ask such a question. I bit my lower lip, thinking over what I should say in response.

After a moment, I decided it was probably best to tell Xandra something; if she happened to see me open Ke'tai's gift I would be forced to tell her anyway. Better to do it now and save myself an awkward moment later on.

"Maybe," I replied. "There's a guy I met at work, Kevin—"

I saw Xandra's eyes widen in the reflection from the rearview mirror. "You didn't tell me about Kevin! I want details."

I laughed, feeling suddenly self-conscious, and very much aware of how careful I must be with the information I relayed. "Well, he's a little older than I am, and he's a few inches taller, and his parents are from Japan. He teaches karate in the mornings sometimes…um…we went out last night after work. It was fun."

"You didn't tell me you had a date!" Xandra exclaimed.

I laughed. "I didn't know about it before I went to work last night," I said, which had been true. "He surprised me. And you were so crazy about Elliot this morning that I didn't have the chance to tell you." At this, we all laughed. "He gave me something last night though, and made me promise not to open it until tomorrow."

"Oooh," Xandra said, grinning. "When did you meet him?"

"About a month ago. We were assigned to work on this portfolio project together…I think we both felt sparks almost immediately. He's really nice."

"That's so great," Xandra replied. I noticed she held onto Elliot's hand with her right hand, while her left remained on the steering wheel. "So, when can I meet him?"

I should have seen that question coming, but it took me by surprise nevertheless. "Uh, we'll have to figure out a time for that," I managed, hoping my shock wasn't coming through in my voice. "He's really busy. I honestly don't know when he finds the time to sleep."

Xandra nodded. "It's fine. There's no rush, right?"

"Right," I replied, relieved at the outcome of the conversation.

The car fell silent, and I found myself gazing out the window but I did not see what was passing through the glass. My thoughts had drifted back to Ke'tai, and then on to Il'zaks. I had meant it as a joke when I had said I didn't know when Ke'tai found the time to sleep, but I began wondering all the same. He and Il'zaks always seemed to be busy with tasks from the Order, yet they still had the time to train me in the evenings. If they did sleep, it had to be during the day, and was probably minimal at best. Just what *was* I getting myself into?

Christmas Eve came and went, and I gradually forgot about the awkward moments in the car. My mother was thrilled to meet Elliot—too thrilled, in Xandra's opinion; she had to tell our mother to let him have space to breathe several times during the evening. Elliot was a good sport about it, though, and didn't voice any complaints.

My father was cordial, but kept his distance, as was his way when getting to know someone for the first time. By the end of the evening, however, Elliot had succeeded in getting him to open up a little. To my eyes, this was his first sign of approval. I was happy for Xandra.

Our parents retired for the night at just after ten, our mother warning us playfully not to peek under the Christmas tree or else "Santa" wouldn't visit. We laughed and stayed up talking a while longer before trudging upstairs to bed ourselves. Elliot was staying in the guest bedroom that doubled as an exercise room, while Xandra and I were staying in the two bedrooms at the end of the hall that had been ours since childhood. Mother had insisted on keeping them as they were until we had finished school and "settled down".

There was a door between the two rooms that our father had put in place when we were about ten years old, so we could access one another's rooms without going into the hall. While we were in high school, that door had been seldom used; Xandra and I had fought frequently during those years and we'd had little reason to talk.

As I stepped inside my old room, I grimaced at the lavender paint on the walls. As a child, lavender had been my favorite color. Why that had been the case was beyond my reasoning now. Perhaps one day I would be able to persuade my parents that it was okay to repaint the room.

There were a few posters left on the walls, their edges brittle and beginning to curl or tear. I laughed, remembering how sophisticated I had felt by plastering my room with pictures of boy bands and actors, and at how ridiculous it all felt now.

There was a small chair in one corner of the room, and my duffel bag was tossed carelessly on top of it. The twin bed was covered in a hideous lavender and green floral print comforter that matched the wall paint; to my amusement, my mother had even found pillowcases to match. On the other side of the room, adjacent to the door, was a long dresser of dark wood with an oval mirror set atop it. On the wall opposite the door and above the head of the bed was a large window with sheer white curtains pushed open to either side.

I wandered toward the window. It was very dark outside, and I could just make out the black shapes of the conifer trees that grew thickly together between my parents' property and the next house, which was a short distance up the hillside. I knew the view from Xandra's room was better; her window overlooked the downward side of the hill and she could see the lights of Astoria spread out below, encroaching on the edge of the Columbia River.

I pulled the curtains closed, then went to the chair that held my duffel bag, unzipping the bag and rummaging through it to find my pajamas. As I did so, I heard a soft tap on the door leading from Xandra's room, and then the door eased open.

"Hey, it's twelve," Xandra said, closing the door softly behind her. "Merry Christmas."

I smiled. "Merry Christmas, Xan. Do you think mom will come wake us up at seven like she always used to do?"

Xandra laughed quietly. "Probably. Although she might be nice to you, since you've been working nights lately."

We looked at each other for a moment, then we both said, "Nah," breaking into quiet laughter.

It was now officially Christmas day. I glanced down at the duffel bag, wanting to open up the gift from Ke'tai more than anything else.

Xandra must have sensed this. "Hey, you should open up that present that…what was his name? That guy from your work, the one he gave you."

"Kevin," I said quietly, and dug my hand into the duffel bag again, quickly finding the slightly crumpled gift bag.

I sat down on the side of the bed, and Xandra quickly walked over to join me. "Oh, it's little… Maybe he bought you a necklace."

I couldn't help but smile. "Maybe," I said, opening the bag carefully. Inside was a red velvet jewelry box, which I drew out, setting the gift bag on the bed behind me.

"I bet it *is* a necklace!" Xandra exclaimed, grinning. "Open it!"

I laughed. She was just as excited as I was. I paused for a moment though, and looked at her. "Did Elliot get you anything?" I asked.

She shrugged. "Probably, but he hasn't told me about it yet. I'll find out in the morning." She didn't seem overly concerned. "Open it!"

I nodded, and pulled the top of the velvet box carefully open. Inside was a necklace with a gold chain, the pendant was in the shape of an eight-pointed star, and in its center was set a round ruby, one of the most beautiful gems that I had ever seen. There was also a folded scrap of paper tucked inside the box. I stared at the necklace for several moments, unable to do anything else; Ke'tai had outdone himself with this gift.

"Chandra, it's gorgeous," Xandra whispered. "I've never seen a ruby like that…it's amazing."

I drew out the bit of paper, carefully setting the box on the bed between Xandra and I. Xandra picked it up almost immediately, and began fiddling with the packaging around the necklace chain. I unfolded the paper and began to read Ke'tai's now-familiar handwriting.

> *Chandra,*
> *I hope you like this gift. I chose this for you because it is one-of-a-kind, and it is beautiful—just like you. You won't find another necklace quite like it anywhere. I want you to know that I love you. I hope this won't change anything between us, but will only serve to make it stronger.*
> *K*

Xandra had succeeded in freeing the necklace from its plastic prison while I read and then re-read Ke'tai's note. She held it up towards me as I finally tore my eyes away from the bit of paper, then carefully placed it around my neck. I stared down at it, this token of Ke'tai's love for me, unable to find the words to express what I was feeling.

"Can I see what he wrote?" Xandra whispered excitedly.

I laughed softly, and nodded, handing her the bit of paper. I felt as though I was in the most wonderful of dreams. The only thing that could make this moment better would be if Ke'tai himself suddenly appeared. I knew he would not; it would be a risk to both himself and to me, but in that moment I did not care. He was perfect, and I was…only human. I sighed, but not unhappily.

"Oh, Chandra, this is wonderful!" Xandra exclaimed. "It's like you've found the perfect guy. You two must have *really* hit it off, if he gave you this on your first real date."

"He is the most incredible person I have ever met, Xan," I said, finally breaking my long, stunned silence. "I don't know if I deserve this gift...but it makes me so happy, all the same."

"Of course, you deserve it," Xandra replied. "After all of the losers you've dated, you deserve one that's a real gentleman, and who genuinely cares for you. We have got to find a time when we get back to Seattle so that I can meet this man. I want to see for myself if he's as perfect as this little present makes him seem."

I nodded, but said nothing in response. If it were possible for Xandra to meet Ke'tai, I would be happy, but I knew that it would probably prove to be impossible. Ke'tai was a summoner, and Xandra might one day become a hunter. It was hard enough for me avoid rousing Xandra's suspicions, but if she ever happened to see Ke'tai—without his blue glasses and a hat—it would be the end of my charade. But still I wondered, might it actually be possible for a meeting to occur?

# 8

# ZOMBI CADAVRE

We arrived in Seattle late in the afternoon on December twenty-sixth. I was anxious to send a note to Ke'tai, but was forced to wait several hours until Elliot had gone home and Xandra had gone to bed. They had enjoyed a great Christmas together with our family in Astoria, and after Xandra had opened Elliot's gift to her on Christmas morning, they had been nearly inseparable. Elliot had bought a pair of teardrop-shaped sterling silver earrings with very clear and sparkling cubic zirconium set into their hearts. Xandra had loved them.

Once Xandra had gone to bed, and had been fairly silent for nearly an hour, I called a nightwing to take a message to Ke'tai. I could wait no longer.

> *Ke'tai—*
> *I wanted to let you know that I loved the necklace! I doubt if I will ever be able to reciprocate a gift like that, but it is very beautiful and I love it! I hope you had a good holiday, even if you don't celebrate it. When can I see you again? We are back in Seattle.*
> *Love*
> *Chandra*

I sent the nightwing off as soon as I had finished writing. I was anxious to see Ke'tai again, and hoped that he would be available to meet again soon. I had only five days until Il'zaks returned, and I wanted to make the most of that time, if possible. I had never truly been in love before, and the feeling was like nothing I had ever experienced. I did not want it to end.

I went about my nightly routine; washing my face and brushing my teeth in preparation for going to bed. When I returned from the bathroom sink, there was a nightwing fluttering at my window. I hurried across my room to open the window and allowed the little creature inside once my door was closed and locked. It dropped a single sheet of paper, folded in half, into my hands before flying back outside into the cold, misty night. I shivered, and quickly closed the window once more.

I was surprised to have received a reply from Ke'tai so promptly, and realized he must have been just as anxious to hear from me, as I had been to write to him. I smiled as I began to read.

> *Chandra,*
> *I am the happiest person in the world right now! I am glad you liked the necklace. I hope your Christmas went well; mine was uneventful, and to tell the truth, pretty boring. I thought of you often. Unfortunately, I have business to attend to tomorrow, but I should be able to see you on Tuesday (the 29th). We should probably work on your self-defense stuff first, but afterwards maybe we can do something else (if you aren't too tired by then). I would love to take another night just to be with you, and skip the combat training, but Il'zaks will be in town again very soon. I don't want to disappoint him. I hope you understand.*
>
> *Have a good night, and sweet dreams.*
> *I love you, Chandra.*
> *K*

I sighed. I would have to wait for nearly two full days before I could see him again. Two days seemed entirely too long, a virtual eternity. I went to sleep that night, restless with anticipation, and I knew I would remain in that state until Tuesday evening finally arrived. I hoped that I would not drive Xandra too crazy during that time, but shrugged that thought aside. Xandra could live with it.

When Tuesday evening did finally come, I knew Xandra was more than ready for me to be out of the apartment. She had been at work most of the day on Monday, and had missed a good portion of my pacing about and general excitement. Tuesday, however, she had the day off; after about an hour of my insanity, she shut herself up in her room and emerged only if it became necessary.

As I was on my way out the door she called, "Have a good time. Now maybe I can get some peace and quiet!"

As I was heading down the steps, running in my excitement, I nearly crashed into Elliot as he was making his way up. I laughed nervously, and mumbled a "Sorry," in his direction before hurrying on at a reduced pace. Elliot appeared amused, and merely shook his head before continuing the climb upstairs.

I was met at the bottom of the steps by Carlos. He smiled at me when he saw me, and said, "Ke'tai has been waiting all day for your lesson to start. I don't think I've ever seen him quite so excited about something so routine."

I reddened, and hoped he could not see my reaction in the waning dusk light. "Well, um, I best not keep him waiting then, right?"

Carlos broke into a laugh and we began walking toward the sidewalk on the far side of the parking lot. "Right," he agreed, unable to hide his smirk.

We walked quickly to the arcade's rear entrance; it was cold that night, and a fine drizzle had been falling from the sky. I was glad to be inside again, more so because I knew Ke'tai was there than because I was cold and damp. I practically ran down the corridor to the large, open room. I felt a bit childish, but I didn't care; I desperately wanted to see Ke'tai once more.

Ke'tai had his back to the corridor as I came into the room. He was bent over a small table, and appeared to be reading something that lay upon it. He turned around quickly as he heard me approach, and gave me one of his most brilliant smiles.

"Chandra! How are you this evening?" he asked.

I stopped a few steps in front of him and smiled. "I'm doing much better now," I replied. "I couldn't wait to see you again."

"I couldn't, either," he admitted. "Carlos was giving me a bad time about it earlier. I've never been so excited to see someone before. The way you make me feel…Ah, I must sound ridiculous to you."

"Don't," I told him. "I'm glad you want to see me."

He smiled, then looked down and sighed. "I suppose we had best do some self-defense work tonight. I just got a message from Il'zaks a few minutes before you came—that's what I was reading just now. He's going to be back here earlier than he anticipated, probably tomorrow sometime. He'll want to start back in on your regular training right away, so I think we've just got tonight. Tomorrow he will want to see you." He sighed again, and looked troubled.

"Ke'tai, what's wrong?" I asked.

He chuckled humorlessly. "I've got to figure out how to break the news to Il'zaks about you and I," he replied. "I don't expect that he will be too happy about it, but we won't be able to hide it from him. I'll have to tell him. It's not going to be easy."

I tilted my head to one side, recalling the conversation I'd had with Il'zaks several weeks past regarding Ke'tai. "You shouldn't worry about that," I replied. "I think he will be okay with it."

Ke'tai frowned, doubtful. "We'll see."

The lesson went fairly well, though we were both distracted. After three hours, Ke'tai called a stop to the training because he felt he wasn't being effective as an instructor.

"I'm sorry, Chandra, I just keep thinking about what I should say to Il'zaks. He was my mentor, and I learned so much from him... I would hate to disappoint him with something like this," he explained. "I—"

"Ke'tai, it's okay, I understand," I said, cutting him off. "Don't torture yourself. I probably should have said something to you sooner, but Il'zaks and I, we talked about you the last time I met with him. He was happy for you. He could tell you were happy, and he said he wouldn't interfere, even though he said he wouldn't put himself in the same position as you've put yourself in."

Ke'tai stared at me for several seconds, his face unreadable. After a moment I looked down, unable to meet his gaze. I hoped that I had not angered him by revealing this information, but I could not tell what he was thinking.

After a moment, he said, "I'm glad Il'zaks is happy for me, but from what you just said he doesn't exactly approve of it, does he? That's what I was afraid of."

I looked up to see him staring down at the floor. I didn't know what to say, and I now regretted that I had ever opened my mouth to tell him about the conversation with Il'zaks. He was miserable, and it was my fault.

"I guess I'll just tell him how the last few weeks went," Ke'tai said suddenly. "I'll tell him how happy I've been, for the first time in *years*. Even if he doesn't approve completely, I wouldn't change this for the world. No matter what the outcome might be."

I felt cold creep into the pit of my stomach as he finished speaking. I knew without asking what he referred to—the fact that there was a very good chance I would never live to finish my training as a summoner. That reality frightened me, but at the same time, I knew I had to try. If I completed my training, Ke'tai and I could be together. We could find true happiness, once such uncertainty no longer loomed above our heads.

I managed a smile for him as he looked up to meet my gaze. "I think that's the best way," I said quietly.

Ke'tai nodded, and walked towards me. "Let's forget about these worries we have, and just be ourselves. We've got to take the opportunity to be together when it presents itself. I'm tired of thinking about the what-if's, and the danger you're in. It's only just after nine—would you like to go flying again?"

I hesitated. It had been incredibly fun the last time we had gone, but after his reminder of the uncertainty in my future, I was feeling morose. I would not enjoy the flight, as I had on our last outing.

After a moment, I said, "Any other night, I would probably say yes to that offer, but I don't really want to do that right now." I sighed. "I'm sorry, Ke'tai."

He nodded. "I understand… I shouldn't have said what I did. I'm the one who should be sorry, Chandra. Not you."

"Maybe we could take a walk, or something? I…I just want to do something normal right now."

He smiled, though his eyes betrayed sadness. He nodded once, thoughtfully. "We can take a walk around the area. Maybe we'll talk a little, too—that might make the both of us feel better."

I waited while Ke'tai made his way to the breakroom to retrieve one of his now-familiar hooded sweatshirts and the pair of blue-lensed glasses. He didn't put the glasses on until we were nearly to the exit door. We did not speak until we had left the building and had begun walking through the misty night. I didn't have a plan in mind of where we might travel, I simply wanted to walk, with the hope that the activity might clear my head. Ke'tai seemed to choose a path, and I matched his steps. I wasn't paying attention to where we were going, I merely strode along at his side.

After some time—I do not know how long—Ke'tai finally broke the silence with a sigh and said, "Chandra, I…I hope you aren't upset with me."

I glanced in his direction, and I knew he was worried. "I'm not upset with you," I replied. "I'm just struggling with the unknown, Ke'tai. You happened to remind me of what might happen, and I've been doing my best forget about those possibilities. More than anything I want to see this through to the end. At first, I wanted to learn this path because it seemed like the right thing to do, but now I want to do it because I can be with you—and you won't have to worry about me any more."

Ke'tai managed a sad smile and looked away. I couldn't read his expression very well in the darkness, and I wondered what was going through his mind. "I will be more careful of what I say from now on," he said quietly after a moment. "I remember what it's like, being in the position you're in now, not knowing what the next day will bring. I'm sorry for bringing that reminder to you so unexpectedly tonight. I'm just…not quite myself when I'm around you. But I mean that in a good way," he added, breaking into a grin.

Seeing his smile was like seeing sunlight after spending weeks in the rain. I returned his smile, and on an impulse took his hand in mine. We walked in silence again for some time, but the mood was quite different. Taking in our surroundings, I realized we had walked several blocks past the apartment complex, but that didn't bother me. I wanted to be with Ke'tai right now, not at home and alone.

Thinking of home triggered my memory. I wondered again if it would be possible for him to meet my sister. I knew Xandra would continue to ask about him until either I gave in and asked Ke'tai, or I fabricated a story that might appease her. I frowned in thought for several moments, then decided it couldn't hurt to ask Ke'tai what he thought about the possibility.

"Ke'tai?" I asked uncertainly. I was nervous, though I knew I had nothing to fear from his reaction.

"Hmm?"

"Um, I had a question, but…I think I already know what the answer is going to be."

He looked at me in a sideways manner, a smile playing at the corners of his mouth. "How can you possibly know the answer to something if you've never asked the question?" he teased.

I sighed. This was harder than I had anticipated. "Well, last week when I was away in Astoria, I had to tell Xan something about you, because of the necklace. I...told her your name was Kevin, and I met you at work..."

He laughed. "Are you worried that I'll be mad? I was expecting you to come up with some reason for having acquired it. We've been monitoring your sister since you started training with Il'zaks, Chandra. I know how suspicious she can be, and how curiosity drives her—just as it does you."

"I know, Il'zaks said he was watching her," I replied. "I just didn't realize that you could know so much about her..."

Ke'tai laughed again. "Don't worry about it," he replied. "I know the secrecy is hard for any normal person, but for you I think it's even harder. She's your twin. I am glad that you can come up with these little stories to cover up some of what you've been doing; it makes Il'zaks' job a bit easier."

I wasn't entirely certain of his implied meaning, but I didn't press him on the point. "Do you know what we talked about on the way to Astoria, then?" I asked, unsure of the true depths of his knowledge.

He stopped and turned to face me. "Chandra, Il'zaks and I may have the ability to call various creatures to help us from time to time, but we do not possess the ability to become suddenly invisible and follow you about. I may know some important details about your sister, but we have only monitored her comings and goings, who she meets up with, et cetera. We know she has the potential to become a hunter, and that's why we have been monitoring her so closely. If she is recruited while you are still training, it's going to be a very bad situation for you."

I nodded. "I know about Xan, I just don't know enough about you to ask the question that I need to."

Ke'tai shrugged. "Just ask it. You shouldn't be afraid to talk to me, Chandra."

I sighed and looked down at the wet sidewalk between my feet. "Xandra asked if she could meet you," I said quietly. "I don't think it'd be possible, but I don't know how to tell her that without making it seem awkward."

Ke'tai was silent for a moment, then he said, "It's not *impossible*, but it's not a risk I think we should take, Chandra. It would be wiser if your sister never met me."

I nodded, and looked up again. "I guess I have to figure out a way to tell her we can't meet," I said. "Or maybe I just won't mention anything, and she'll forget..."

Ke'tai laughed. "Even I know that won't work," he said, and began walking again, headed back toward the apartment complex. "Come on, we should probably get you home, before it gets to be too late."

We talked about mundane things for a while; we had an unspoken agreement to avoid delving into any further discussion related to my training or Xandra. We had spoken enough about those serious matters for one night. As we came to the parking lot in front of my apartment building, however, Ke'tai returned to business.

"Il'zaks will be back tomorrow," he reminded me. "Be ready—he will probably want to teach you a new summoning. I will be there if I can, but I can't guarantee that he'll allow it."

"Even if he doesn't, can't I see you afterwards?" I asked.

Ke'tai grinned. "You bet. I'll stay outside in the rain with Carlos...and probably Trey or Carmine." He made a face. "You'll owe me big time if I'm stuck with Carmine."

I laughed but cut the sound short as he stopped suddenly, several paces away from the stairs that led up to my apartment. He turned to face me, a mischievous smile on his lips. I knew that if he were not wearing the glasses, his eyes would be sparkling silver and orange in the glow of the streetlights overhead.

"May I kiss you goodnight?" he asked quietly, the smile never leaving his face.

My pulse quickened, and my eyes locked onto his. I nodded, and never took my gaze from his, even as he drew me closer. As our lips touched, I was startled by how warm his were, in spite of the lengthy walk we had taken through the cold night air. I closed my eyes, savoring the moment, and did not open them again until our lips had parted. I no longer felt the drizzle or the cold; I was only aware of the beating of my heart, and the warmth of Ke'tai's right hand as it rested upon my left arm.

I looked up at him, thrilled to see that he was smiling; I wanted to remember that moment forever, and to relive it as often as I was able. I returned his smile as best I could, though I doubt my own could ever have matched the beauty that I beheld in his.

"Do you really have to go?" I asked him quietly, teasing. "You could stay here and kiss me like that all night, and I wouldn't protest at all."

He laughed. "You might not protest, but you would become cold sooner or later, and I think you would get tired before too long. But maybe we can do this again tomorrow night?"

"I wish it was every night," I replied, loath to part from him so soon.

He smiled. "So do I, Chandra. Soon, maybe, it can be."

I broke into a grin. "No maybes," I replied. "It will be. I'll get through this."

He nodded. "Okay, soon, then. Have a goodnight, Chandra." He was smiling as he turned away and began walking toward the sidewalk once more.

"Goodnight, Ke'tai."

I remained standing in the parking lot, several paces away from the stairs—and away from the roof, where I would have been protected from the cold drizzle falling from the sky—merely watching Ke'tai as he walked away. My heart was beating faster than was normal, and I could feel the residual warmth left over from his lips, where they had pressed against mine. I wished once more that we did not have to part. As he reached the sidewalk, he glanced over his shoulder toward the staircase. He shook his head slightly; I imagined that he was amused. He waved once in my direction, before breaking into a slow jog. I missed his presence already.

I sighed, and finally turned away as Ke'tai disappeared from view behind the next row of buildings. I made my way up the steps slowly, melancholy now that our evening was at an end.

When I entered my apartment, Elliot was still there; he and Xandra were watching a movie, a large bowl of popcorn sitting on the couch between them. Xandra turned around, startled, as I walked inside.

"You're home early," she stated. "It's not even ten-thirty yet."

I nodded. "Yeah, there wasn't much for me to do again tonight. I guess it's slow this week between Christmas and New Years."

"So, did you get to see Kevin?" she asked.

I grinned, in spite of myself. "Yes. He walked me home…"

Xandra turned her attention fully to me, and said, "You didn't invite him in? I could have met him!"

"I did, Xan. He said…he isn't ready to meet family yet."

She frowned for a moment, then shrugged and turned back to the movie. "Well, that's fine then. But you'll let me know when he *is* ready, right?"

"Of course, I will."

I hated myself for lying to her—again—but there was no other option. She could never know the truth, no matter how badly I wished I could tell her. I knew Ke'tai was right; it would be a mistake for the two of them to meet, even if she was never discovered by the hunters. I would simply have to continue prolonging this facade until I finished my training. Xandra could never know that I was on the path to becoming a summoner.

The next evening, it was Trey who greeted me in the parking lot below my apartment. I had become so accustomed to meeting Carlos that I was openly surprised to see the larger, bald man who worked for Il'zaks.

"I trust Ke'tai told you that Il'zaks would be back today?" Trey asked as we began walking across the lot toward the sidewalk.

I nodded. "He did, I just sort of forgot…"

Trey chuckled briefly. "I noticed that." We walked in silence for a time, then he said, "I hear you and Ke'tai got along pretty well…"

I felt my face flush, and I glanced at him from the corners of my eyes. He was smirking. "Yeah, we did," I said after a moment spent in flustered silence.

"Good for you," Trey said, his tone becoming serious. "Good for you."

The remainder of our short walk was spent in an awkward silence. As we came to the rear entrance of the arcade, I saw Carlos was standing near the door, and I nearly shouted in delight. Ke'tai would be within; Il'zaks had not forbade him from attending my training, as he had feared.

"Evening, Chandra," Carlos said as he pulled open the door.

"Good evening," I replied, unable to hide a grin as I darted inside. I heard Carlos and Trey share a brief laugh before the door closed behind me, but I didn't care; Ke'tai was here tonight, meaning that his talk with Il'zaks must have gone well.

The two summoners were seated across from one another at a table that had been erected near the center of the main room. There was an open chair halfway between them, and as I entered the room, Il'zaks indicated that I should sit there. Both were smiling, though Il'zaks' smile was one of pleasure at seeing me again after our lengthy break, while Ke'tai's was the brilliant, beaming smile he seemed to reserve only for me. Again, I was struck by how different the two men were. Il'zaks wore a gray suit, pressed and immaculate, his hair was combed carefully to one side, the image of perfection. In contrast, Ke'tai, wore blue jeans and a form-fitting black t-shirt that revealed the muscles of his arms and chest; his short hair, as always, was spiked every which-way.

As I sat down, Il'zaks said, "Ke'tai has told me that he would like to be present while you complete your training with me, and I see no reason to deny his request. My concern is that you may not be able to concentrate as effectively as you need to. I will trust you to tell me if you need a moment to refocus during our sessions; I cannot read your mind, and I do not want you to fail due to something that can so easily be prevented."

I blinked. I had expected a remark like this from Il'zaks, but not immediately. I had anticipated he would ask how the last month had gone, make mention of his trip, or even say "Hello" first.

"I'll tell you if I'm not able to concentrate," I assured him. "How was your trip? Or whatever it was?"

Il'zaks smiled, seemingly amused. "It went very well," he replied. "I was in Moscow for a few days, and then Boston. That is the extent of what I can tell you." He paused a moment, collecting his thoughts. "I have heard from Ke'tai that you've made progress while I was away, among other things. I am pleased with his report."

I glanced at Ke'tai; I wondered why Il'zaks seemed to be evading the topic that hung between the three of us like a cloud. Ke'tai smiled faintly and winked, a sign that he would talk with me later regarding his conversation with the elder summoner. I relaxed a bit, and turned to face Il'zaks once more.

"I believe it is time for you to learn to summon another demon," Il'zaks said once my attention was focused upon him. "In fact, it is quite overdue. Tonight, I wish to teach you of the *Zombi Cadavre*, or zombie, as it is referred to. While this demon is dangerous—the most dangerous you will have encountered so far—it is *not* the same as the creatures popularized by those ridiculous movies you may have seen."

He paused a moment before continuing. "Let me begin by speaking of the mythology behind the zombie. The most common legend comes from

Haiti, and those who practice voodoo; while it is a myth, some aspects of the story are true, while others are completely false.

"In voodoo practices, there is the belief in *corps cadavre*, or the physical body, which has both the *gwo-bon anj*—the 'animating' principle—and the *ti-bon anj*—the awareness and memory associated with someone who is alive. All of these things can be explained by looking at, say, Ke'tai; he has a physical body, able to move, breathe, et cetera, and he has an awareness of his surroundings and an impeccable memory. He is alive; according to this belief, he is *not* a zombie. A zombie is described as a physical body that retains its 'animating' principle, yet lacks the *ti-bon anj*—the awareness and memory aspect. This makes the creature seem as though it operates in a mindless trance.

"The myth goes on to say that a zombie is typically the body of someone who is deceased and has become reanimated. This dead body is then controlled by what the legend refers to as a 'sorcerer'. The notion is utterly ridiculous; there is no tangible way to resurrect someone after they have died. There are also those who believe that zombies are the bodies of people whose souls have been stolen by said sorcerers; this is also inaccurate. In my many long years of experience, I have found no evidence of the soul; therefore, it is impossible for someone to steal one. I believe the zombies described by these legends have a truly medical explanation to them—the description fits a person suffering from catalepsy, which makes them appear to be in a trance, and they often become quite rigid. It may also describe someone afflicted with paralysis. Either way, the condition can be explained in regards to human beings.

"As I said previously, there are some small grains of truth to this myth, however ridiculous it may seem. The mention of a sorcerer, for one, leads me to believe that the origin of this legend came from someone having witnessed a summoner working with one of these creatures. The basic description of a zombie is fairly accurate as well; they appear to be mindless creatures, and vaguely resemble a human in form. If a human were to encounter a zombie from a distance, they may mistake it for another human being, or a malformed corpse; at close proximity, however, there would be no mistaking it as such. Zombies are decidedly *not* human.

"Zombies are rarely called upon by summoners, in my experience, though at times they can prove useful. They are voracious eaters, and will eat anything they can get their hands on, if allowed to do so. Because of this, they are sometimes called upon to destroy evidence, particularly if it is known that there are hunters actively working in the area. They do a very efficient job of eliminating any sign that a summoner had been present, and can do it quite quickly. Otherwise, zombies serve little purpose for us."

I thought over his explanation for some time before speaking. "What makes them so dangerous?"

Il'zaks nodded, and smiled faintly. "I am glad you heard that part, Chandra Grey. Zombies can be difficult to control; they may become very willful and disobedient if left to their own devices for any length of time. There have been summoners in the past that failed to monitor a zombie appropriately, and that creature in turn destroyed them, or betrayed them to the hunters. It is imperative that you focus upon controlling a zombie once you have called it; do not become distracted, and do not allow it any measure of freedom. They may seem to be mindless drones, but do not let that deceive you; while their intelligence *is* limited, they will follow their instincts if left to do so. One such instinct is to destroy anything they happen to perceive as 'different'. You must remember that the realm of demons is not identical to the world which we inhabit, and when we pull a demon through from their world into ours, some do not react ideally to the change. Zombies are one such breed of demon, and we as summoners must take every precaution we can, in order to safely control them."

I recalled the other lessons I had received from Il'zaks as I pondered his words. Calling *djinni* was relatively risk-free, and those demons seemed quite useful. The same could be said for nightwings. Tonight's lesson would be the first true challenge presented to me during my training as a summoner, and I knew that I must be very careful. I must heed the warning present in Il'zaks' words.

"Let me see if I understand the main points correctly," I said after a moment. "Zombies can be difficult to control, and have been known to kill their summoners. They aren't very useful, unless you need them to eat something. Is that right?"

Il'zaks nodded, and looked thoughtful, though he said nothing.

"Why I am learning how to call one now, and not later on?"

Il'zaks broke into an amused smile, and nodded. "Most students have asked that same question when they are introduced to this demon," he said.

"The reason is simple: It is the *least* dangerous of the demons you will come to learn about, after the *djinn* and nightwing. If a student can learn to call a zombie successfully, then the next two or three demons in the line will be called much more easily. It is safer for you, this way."

I nodded, feeling a bit foolish for asking the question, now that the answer seemed so obvious. Il'zaks rarely did anything without having a sound reason behind it, and I understood this.

"Are you prepared to learn to call this creature tonight, or shall we wait for tomorrow?" Il'zaks asked after a moment.

I thought over what he had said once more while I looked down at my hands upon the table. After some time, I released a sigh, and said, "We can do it tonight. I feel like I'm ready for this, but I'm a bit nervous. The others so far haven't been dangerous—not like this seems to be, anyway."

"It's normal to be nervous when you come to this point," Ke'tai said quietly. "I know I was."

Il'zaks nodded in agreement. "Yes, it is normal, Chandra Grey. I would not have introduced this demon to you, if I did not believe you were ready for the challenge."

I nodded, and followed Il'zaks as he rose from his seat. He walked slowly to one side of the room, some distance away from the table. If Il'zaks felt I could do this, then I should be able to—he had not been wrong so far when it came to assessing my newfound skills. Yet I still wondered what would happen if I did fail in a summoning, and what that horrible event might do to Ke'tai. I shook my head to clear it of those thoughts, and focused my full attention upon Il'zaks. I had no choice but to succeed in this; dwelling on the less attractive possibilities would help no one.

I watched Il'zaks carefully as he called forth a zombie. The creature was vaguely shaped like a human; it had two arms and two legs, a torso and a head, but the similarities ended there. It was altogether grotesque, with oddly placed humps of green-gray flesh dispersed seemingly at random about its body, and its joints did not seem to bend the way that was expected. It moved one of its arms so that it stuck out straight from the shoulder socket, but at the elbow the arm bent awkwardly toward the outside and hung limply there, as though the joint were somehow broken. The creature's glassy eyes stared lifelessly forward toward the wall, as though it could see nothing of its surroundings. Its jaw was slack, and a thick rope of drool hung from one corner of its mouth, glistening silver in the bright light from overhead. It had too many teeth crammed into its mouth, and these jutted in a myriad of directions, crossing over one another. Its teeth were pointed and brilliantly white; the only aspect of this loathsome creature that appeared relatively clean. I shuddered involuntarily as I looked upon it, and quickly shifted my gaze to meet Il'zaks'.

"They are not the prettiest of creatures, are they?" Il'zaks asked as he met my gaze. "Now you see why I find it completely ridiculous that people would believe that this is a reanimated *human* corpse." He paused a moment, then said, "It is your turn to call one now, Chandra Grey."

I sighed and closed my eyes, thinking over the words Il'zaks had spoken. I had already registered the movements I would need to perform while I had observed my mentor summoning moments before. Once I had mentally prepared myself, I began to dance while thinking the words Il'zaks had spoken moments earlier.

I felt the zombie's presence before I opened my eyes. Its mind was dull, but Il'zaks had been right—it desired nothing more than to begin tearing apart everything it looked upon. I frowned, exerting my will over the creature and firmly restraining it. When I opened my eyes, I saw a creature very similar to Il'zaks' standing several feet away from me. It was staring blankly at the floor, apparently oblivious to its surroundings, though I now knew otherwise.

Il'zaks was smiling, and appeared to be relieved. I turned briefly to face Ke'tai where he stood near the table, beaming at me. I smiled faintly, feeling awkward, and shifted my gaze back to Il'zaks.

"Can I send him back now?" I asked without thinking. The zombie was disgusting, and I wanted nothing more to do with it.

Both summoners laughed, and Il'zaks nodded. "That is a common feeling, to want it out of your sight," he said. "I want nothing more than to do the same with the one I have called."

Relieved, I released the creature, glad to be rid of it. Il'zaks' vanished only seconds later.

"The real test will come tonight, when you sleep," Il'zaks stated after a moment. "The dream you have will likely be very unpleasant, but I believe you are strong enough to endure it. There is nothing I can say to help you prepare for it; each summoner has their own version of the dreams, and those tend to be vastly different from one to the next. My advice to you is this: Do what feels right to you in each moment, and nothing more."

# 9

# FLIGHT

After the lesson with Il'zaks—and the foreboding about the night to come that it had left me with—I simply wanted to go home. Ke'tai understood without question, and offered to walk me home. I accepted, though now more than ever before, I wished he did not have to leave; he would know what to expect when I awakened in the morning, how to deal with what was to come. Unfortunately, I knew the coming nightmare was something I must face on my own, and I was terrified. My brief mental link with the zombie had left me on edge; the creature was dangerous and deceptively malevolent.

We walked in silence for a time, and then Ke'tai said, "You did very well tonight, Chandra. I was surprised at how quickly you seemed to intuit what you must do. You've definitely got a gift for this."

I managed a faint smile. The encouragement was welcome, but my mind was preoccupied with the last of what Il'zaks had said, and I could not truly appreciate Ke'tai's words. As I glanced at Ke'tai, I noticed that he appeared worried; his jaw was tight and there was a slight frown playing upon his lips. Behind the blue lenses of his glasses, his eyes sparkled, but they were filled with concern.

"I know how hard this is, Chandra, believe me," he said after a moment. "What Il'zaks told you is true. He would never have proposed tonight's lesson, if he did not feel you were ready for it. I know it's scary as hell, but you'll get through it. And once you do, the next few trials will be nothing. You'll see."

"From what it sounds like, 'scary as hell' is an understatement."

Ke'tai chuckled briefly. "That depends. Every summoner has a different experience, and yours might not be as bad as some others' have been. I know only what I've been through, and my experience with the zombies was one I'd rather forget."

"You are very reassuring," I replied sarcastically.

Ke'tai shrugged. "I don't know what else to tell you, Chandra. What you come up against tonight might be very different from my own experience. Nobody can predict what you will encounter."

I sighed. "I know, I'm just…scared."

He nodded. "I know. I wish I could be there for you tonight, but it goes against our rules. It's like a rite of passage…you have to get through it alone, to prove your worth to the Order. I don't know why we operate that way, but it's expected." He sighed. "I think tonight is going to be just has hard for me as it is for you, Chandra. I won't know if…if…you get through it…until the morning. Promise me you'll let me know, as soon as you're awake."

We had made our way into the parking lot, and I sighed again. I was terrified of what the night would bring, worried about Ke'tai, but most of all, I was disappointed that I would have to leave him in only a few short moments. He was the one person in all the world that was keeping me sane as I battled internally with my fears.

"I promise, Ke'tai. I know we didn't schedule anything for tomorrow yet, but…can I see you then?" I looked down at the pavement as it passed beneath my feet. "I…I just want to be with you again."

When I looked up once more, he had stopped at the base of the steps and was smiling, though his eyes betrayed his worry. "I'd like that," he said, and bent to kiss my forehead as I stopped to stand before him. "But first, get through tonight. I'll be waiting to hear from you."

I nodded, looking down. "I wish—"

Ke'tai suddenly moved away, faster than my eyes had been able to follow. "Your sister's coming down the steps. I've got to go, Chandra. I'm sorry I have to leave you like this…"

I nodded, disappointed, and watched as he jogged across the parking lot at a more normal speed. I turned away and began heading up the stairs, when Xandra came bounding down. She was grinning.

"Hey, Chandra," she said when she saw me. "Elliot just called—I'm going over to his place for a while. I'll see you in the morning!"

"Sounds good," I replied, secretly thankful that she would be out of the apartment, at least for a few hours.

"Are you feeling okay?" she asked as she took a better look at me. "You look upset…"

"I'm just tired, Xan," I replied. "Work was rough tonight."

She nodded. "Well, call me if you need anything. I…might not be back tonight." She grinned again, and jogged down the remainder of the steps. "Catch you later."

"Later, Xan," I replied, and continued up the steps to the apartment we shared. A cold feeling crept into my gut as I realized it may have been the last time I would see Xandra. As I unlocked the door, I found I was silently crying.

I stood in the basement room beneath Chaos Rising, the arcade where I had been meeting Il'zaks and Ke'tai for my training. This time, however, I was alone.

Faintly, I could hear music and various digitized sounds drifting down through the floor above. The basement itself was silent and the air around me was oppressive and stiflingly hot. I felt sweat beading on my forehead, and decided that I ought to go outside where the air was cooler.

I hurried out of the practice room, and down the dimly lit corridor that led to the exit. The door was ajar, and I could feel a cool breeze wafting inside as I neared. I could hear nothing but the frantic sounds drifting through the floor from the arcade above, and this began to alarm me. I should have been able to hear cars driving on the street outside, at the very least. Something was amiss.

I hesitated, my hand resting lightly on the door handle. Through the gap between the door and its frame, I could see it was early evening; the sky was clear, and I could make out a few stars. As my gaze drifted toward the western horizon, I noted the sky was a pale yellow-green, as though the sun had recently disappeared beneath the horizon. I waited, straining my ears to detect any shred of sound coming from the world outside. My apprehension increased as the unnatural silence ensued.

Slowly, I opened the door and stood on the threshold for several moments, evaluating my surroundings. Five steps away from where the stairs led up to the parking lot, but I could see nothing beyond the low concrete retaining wall and the sky above. As quietly as I could manage, I made my way to the top of the steps.

Directly ahead was the parking lot. I had always assumed it was reserved for the employees of the arcade; it was generally almost empty in its location at the rear of the building. Tonight, it was entirely devoid of anything that marked it as a place of human habitation; there was not even an errant piece of garbage or a dropped coin to be seen.

I turned to my right, my gaze sliding along the side of the building toward the visitor parking area and the strip mall that surrounded it. The other buildings appeared as they always had; windows lit from within by bright fluorescent lights, the neon signs above doors and in windows advertising the businesses within. The visitor parking held perhaps a dozen cars, parked at various intervals. A group of three people crouched near the center of the lot.

I could make out very little of their features; it had grown too dark to see them from a distance. They were gathered around an object that lay upon the ground, each in turn reaching down to grab hold of the thing and tear large chunks away. I was unable to tell for certain, but it seemed that when one took a piece from the thing that lay between them, they then began to eat it. The behavior was strange, and I found it both disturbing and disgusting. Though I wished to tear my eyes away, I stood riveted in abhorrent fascination.

I continued to watch the three figures for a time, while the darkness intensified around me. The stars above still appeared faint, and there was no sign of the moon. I do not know how long I watched them, but after a time I realized that it must have grown very late. I decided I should try to make my way home, though my subconscious balked at the very idea of crossing the parking lot and risking detection by those strange beings.

I took less than a dozen steps along the side of the building when one of the figures snapped its head up and stared in my direction. I could not see its eyes, but I had the distinct feeling that it glared at me, harboring a malice unlike any I had experienced previously. This figure turned to its companions and appeared to speak, though I could not hear it from my place along the wall. The other two figures then turned in unison, the perceived hatred in their glances a palpable force. The three figures stood erect, abandoning the object that had captured their attention.

I stood immobile near the arcade, afraid to move toward them, yet equally afraid to take my eyes from them to attempt an escape. At that moment I understood what a rabbit must have felt, trapped in the headlights of an oncoming car, frozen in place by fear.

I blinked, and suddenly the figures were only a few paces away. It was as though they had not moved, but had simply transported themselves closer; they stood in the same rough configuration, but were now at the front of the building, rather than the center of the parking lot.

I was now only a few short yards away, and I could see them more clearly. They were not *people* as I had assumed, but something else entirely. Their bodies were twisted and humped in a bizarre and grotesque manner, while many of their joints did not appear to hinge correctly.

I recognized them from my lesson with Il'zaks as *Zombi Cadavre*, and my terror intensified. My heart raced and I could not catch my breath, a cold sweat had broken out across my brow, while my arms and legs felt leaden. Had I the presence of mind to turn and run, my legs would not have cooperated. I stood rooted in place by fear, staring in horror at the repulsive creatures looming before me.

I blinked again, and the creatures shifted closer. They were now near enough that I could see the grayish tint to their skin even in the darkness, and the glassy, unseeing stare of their eyes. I could sense that those eyes masked a hideous and malicious intelligence, one which wished for nothing more than to kill me. Panicked, I was still unable to move. They were too near for me to attempt an escape; I was trapped.

I glanced past them toward the parking lot, hoping desperately that someone or something would suddenly appear, distracting them long enough to allow me to escape. There was nothing but the strange object near the center of the lot, clearly visible in the orange glow coming from the streetlights above. I felt my bile rise as I realized the body of a woman lay there, and that she had been what these grotesque creatures had been feasting upon. I tore my eyes away from the spectacle and focused again on the three beings surrounding me, certain they would lend me the same fate, if given the opportunity.

One of the three had broken into a twisted grin; chipped and yellowed teeth were visible between its cracked and peeling lips, a thin line of drool hung glistening from one corner of its mouth. The other two simply stood nearby, silently observing what was to happen next. My heart was pounding so loudly it had drowned out the sound coming from the arcade, and I began to hear a ringing in my ears as the grinning zombie took one lurching step toward me.

I swallowed hard, unable to take my eyes away from the creature. A certainty came over me then; this was how I would die, at the hands of this demon from my nightmare, unable to move or make a sound. The world around me abruptly became clearer, and I realized I could make out the most minute details of my surroundings. I could see every leaf on the tree that was growing at the far end of the parking lot, I could make out the chips and cracks in the brick wall next to me, I could see clearly the face of the dead woman at the center of the parking lot. Her face was my own.

I began to scream, finally released from the paralysis that had taken over my body. The three creatures shuffled backwards, seemingly startled. I could sense they had not expected this turn of events, and were now uncertain of how to proceed.

I took the opportunity to fight back, kicking and punching, blinded by sudden rage. I knew Ke'tai would never approve of my fighting in this manner, without inhibition or control over my emotions, but I knew a strange certainty that it must be done. Two of the creatures cowered against the wall after a few moments, seemingly terrified of the fury they had unleashed within me. The third suddenly shifted backwards and stood at the center of the parking lot near the mutilated body that lay there.

I blinked, unable to comprehend the change in its tactic. The zombie, inches away, prepared to strike at me while its companions cowered nearby. It had moved in that instant to the center of the lot, where it stood menacingly over the body. I shuddered to think of it as my own dead body.

It never occurred to me that what I had witnessed was impossible; it simply served to fuel a sudden and unexpected anger. I sprinted toward the single creature, ignoring the other two as they crouched near the building; as I bolted past them, I caught the pungent odor of fear. I had no plan, but I knew I must strike the creature down. I was not prepared for what happened next.

The creature stood unwavering until I was within arm's distance, and then moved its disjointed arm so quickly I could not avoid its attack. I felt a sudden excruciating pain in my right arm. Glancing down, I noted that it had gripped my wrist in its deformed hand, and was twisting my arm viciously. The pain was such that I fell to my knees as my eyes stung with unwanted tears.

The zombie bent down, pressed its forehead against mine, and stared into my eyes with sadistic glee. Its breath smelled of rotting meat, and I was forced to swallow another wave of rising bile. My anger had dissipated, leaving me drained. The creature increased the pressure on my arm, and I cried out in anguish. Feebly, I aimed a kick at its groin, but it shuffled away, avoiding the blow.

I choked out a sob as it twisted my arm further. I knew my arm would break if it continued its assault, and the pain was becoming unbearable. "What do you want from me?" I managed in a hoarse whisper.

It erupted into a hideous laugh, and opened its mouth wider. I was dimly aware that its teeth were razor-sharp, but I was unable to look away from its glassy, hate-filled eyes. I could sense nothing but the pain it was inflicting upon my arm and the rancid odor of its foul breath. I screamed again as darkness enveloped me.

I opened my eyes to gray daylight. It took me several moments to register my location; I was laying on my back, in bed, the apartment around me silent. I was not in the parking lot of Chaos Rising, and it was no longer the middle of the night. There were no zombies here, only the horrific memory of the worst nightmare I had ever experienced. I sighed, relieved.

I was drenched with sweat, and felt as though I had been run over by a large truck repeatedly during the night. My body ached and every joint was stiff and sore. I sat up slowly, and as I did so, my head began to pound. I raised one hand to my forehead, wincing, but realized belatedly that I had survived the night. My sudden joy at that revelation blocked out some of the pain, and I managed to stand up. I made my way to the bathroom to locate the bottle of ibuprofen stored in the cabinet.

After swallowing two of the pills, I returned to my bedroom and set about writing a message to Ke'tai. I knew he would be anxious to hear from me. I kept it short, stating that I was awake and that I would not care to repeat the experience of such a nightmare again. Within ten minutes, a nightwing was fluttering outside my window carrying his reply.

I smiled and retrieved the message, pausing to observe the little creature as it flew away.

*Chandra,*
*I am so happy you are ok! The later it got in the day, the more I was worrying about you. I am glad that my worries were pointless. I told Il'zaks as soon as I received your letter, and he was pleased. I think he was worried about you as well, but he doesn't like to share that sort of info.*

*I would like to see you as soon as possible, if you feel up to it. Please let me know.*

*I love you. Always.*
*K*

I smiled again after reading his reply. I was starting to feel better as the ibuprofen began to alleviate my aches, and decided that I would love to see him "as soon as possible". I sent him another brief message, then returned to the bathroom to shower and dress while I awaited his response.

I was surprised, however, when the doorbell rang only a few minutes after I had finished showering. I was dressed, but my hair was still damp and uncombed as answered the door.

I was surprised to see Carlos. "Morning," he said cheerfully as I opened the door. "Is your sister here?"

I shook my head. "She stayed at Elliot's last night."

Carlos looked relieved, then said, "I can wait a few minutes while you finish getting ready. Ke'tai sent me here. He wants to see you…I don't think he slept at all last night. He looked like hell this morning."

I bit my lower lip, and softly closed the door behind Carlos. He took a seat at the end of the couch while I headed to my room to finish brushing my hair. When I returned a few minutes later, pulling my jacket on, Carlos was already standing near the door, ready to leave.

"I know it's none of my business what went on last night," Carlos said as we left the apartment, "but I don't think I've ever seen Ke'tai so worried before. I talked with him after he came back from your lesson, and it just wasn't like him."

I looked down, unable to meet his dark-eyed gaze. "I think last night was sort of a milestone for me," I said after a moment's pause. "They were both worried—Il'zaks and Ke'tai, I mean. I think it was my first real test, and neither one of them were sure I would make it through."

Carlos was silent for a moment, then said, "That makes sense. It was difficult for him, when he couldn't be there for you during the night." I must have looked surprised, because he chuckled and said, "I have been trained in the rules of the Order, Chandra. I know they aren't supposed to be around one of their students when it comes to these things."

By this time, we had come to the burgundy SUV I had seen Carlos driving previously. He opened the passenger side door for me, then went around the front of the vehicle to let himself in.

"I'm supposed to take you to Ke'tai's apartment," Carlos said slowly as he started up the car. "I hope you're okay with that."

I couldn't help but smile. "Of course, I am," I replied.

Carlos laughed, and shook his head slightly in amusement as he backed out of the parking space. "The two of you are so funny… But I'm glad Ke'tai has finally opened up to someone. I think he was very lonely before, but he didn't realize it."

"Can I ask you a question?"

Carlos glanced over at me briefly before returning his eyes to the roadway. "Sure."

"How long have you known Ke'tai?"

Carlos nodded slightly, that amused smile resurfacing across his face. "Long enough that I can say I know him pretty well, but not long enough to know all there is. I've been working for him for almost fifteen years."

"How did you meet?" I asked.

"From what I understand," he said slowly, "Ke'tai had been following me for some time. He knew I had a gift, but naturally, I didn't. There was a woman working for him at that time, and it was she who first met with me. She called me, pretending that she wanted to meet me for a job interview." He smirked. "I guess that's really what it was, even though this is unlike any job I'd ever imagined." He paused a moment, contemplative, while he steered the SUV through a left turn onto a narrower and quieter street. "She came right out and told me what I was capable of. I thought she was out of her mind, *loco*. After she began to show me a few things, I started to believe her. I was working with her for almost two weeks before I was finally introduced to Ke'tai. The rest, as they say, is history."

"What exactly can you do, Carlos?" I asked. "I mean, what is your ability? If you don't mind my asking."

"I don't mind," he replied. "I can track hunters, that's my specialty. That's why I asked about your sister this morning… She makes me nervous."

I laughed. "Ke'tai says that she hasn't been found out yet. She isn't a threat, is she?"

Carlos shifted uncomfortably in his seat. "Once you've had a couple encounters with hunters, anyone who has that ability feels like a threat."

We drove on in silence for a few minutes before Carlos turned into a parking garage. We were somewhere downtown, only a few blocks away from Columbia Tower, Seattle's tallest building. I had not been paying attention to the route he had taken to travel there. He pulled into one of the first open spaces he came across, and cut the engine.

"His apartment is in the building to our left," Carlos said as he got out of the car.

I scrambled to follow him. We took the stairs down to the ground floor, and walked along the damp sidewalk a short distance before coming to an ordinary glass door that led into the lobby of what appeared to be an office building. Carlos led me to the elevators, and pressed the button for floor thirty-two.

"There are some businesses on the lower levels of this building," he explained, "but above the twenty-fifth floor, it's all condos. I still think Ke'tai is taking a risk by living here, but both he and Il'zaks have told me it's safe. For now, at least, there aren't any hunters in the area."

Once the elevator had stopped, I followed him down one of the hallways, to a wooden door near its end. Nearby was a large window overlooking the street far below.

"Well, here you are," Carlos said, knocking loudly on the door. "I'm not going to stick around—I have some other things to do today—but you two have fun." He winked knowingly, and without another word, turned to walk away.

Ke'tai opened the door a crack. I smiled at him as he suddenly threw the door wide, grinning, and led me inside. Carlos had been right; Ke'tai *did* look tired. There were dark circles beneath his silver eyes, and his hair was flatter than usual, as though he hadn't taken the time nor had the energy to gel it that morning. As he closed the door quickly behind us, I took a moment to look around.

We were standing in a small tiled entryway that led into the kitchen on one side, and into a living room directly ahead. To the right was a large picture window, but the curtains were drawn and very little daylight seeped in around the edges. The kitchen was small, very organized, and nearly spotless; I had the impression it was rarely used. On the far end of the kitchen was an open space where a small round table stood with two chairs. The living room was furnished with a matching couch and loveseat covered in a light gray fabric, a wall-mounted stand bearing a television and DVD player, and a small square coffee table littered with various books and magazines. On the near wall of the living room was another door, which I presumed led into a bedroom.

"I hope you don't mind that I asked you to come here," Ke'tai said quietly after a moment. "It's just the safest place for me to be during the day—inside, where no one can see me."

I nodded. "I understand, Ke'tai. I'm just glad that I can spend some time with you today. It doesn't matter where." I glanced around again, then said, "You have a nice place."

He chuckled. "I rented it with all the furniture already in place," he replied. "Don't give me the credit for decorating." He paused a moment, then said, "Would you like to watch a movie or something? I...didn't really think about what we should do."

I shrugged. "A movie is fine," I replied, and he led me into the living room area.

As I sat down on the couch, he looked thoughtful for a moment, then said, "Have you eaten yet today, Chandra?"

I shook my head. "Why?"

"You seem a little pale," he replied. "It's probably from the ordeal you went through last night... I thought Il'zaks would have told you it's important to make sure you eat after enduring one of those episodes."

I took a moment to consider all that Il'zaks had discussed with me, but could not recall if he had mentioned anything of the sort. Finally, I said, "No, I don't think he did. Why is that so important?"

Ke'tai sighed wearily. "It's important because each time you get through a stage like that, your body changes. You won't notice yet, because you haven't come far enough along in your training. What I'm trying to say is that because of the changes, your body needs more energy than it might be used to…The best way to get that energy is to eat something." He shook his head. "I'm sorry if I'm rambling a bit today, Chandra. I didn't sleep well."

"Carlos told me," I replied softly. "So, what have you got to eat around here?"

Ke'tai smiled and stood up. "I'll order a pizza," he said. "I don't cook very well, and I'm not here often enough to worry about groceries. When it comes, you'll have to answer the door though."

I nodded. "That's fine. I think I can handle that much."

We ate our pizza in the living room, and Ke'tai found a movie to watch on cable—some mid-1990's disaster thriller about a meteor impact. I remembered very little of the film; I fell asleep not long after I had eaten a couple slices of the pizza.

When I awoke, I was laying on the couch and the room was lit only dimly by a small lamp in one corner. The apartment was completely silent, and I knew within an instant that I was alone. Confused, I sat up, rubbing the sleep from my eyes. It was then that I noticed a scrap of paper had been placed on the coffee table next to my cell phone. It was a message, scribbled somewhat hastily by Ke'tai.

*Chandra,*

*Two things.*

*1. Your sister called earlier. I spoke to her briefly (I hope you don't mind, but you were asleep). She is staying w/ Elliot tonight.*

*2. I received a call from Il'zaks. Something has come up, and I had to meet w/ him ASAP. I will be back before 10pm. We may have to leave quickly.*

*I hope you slept well. I love you.*

*K*

The first portion of his note I dismissed quickly. I was not surprised that Xandra was staying at Elliot's place again, and I was somewhat pleased that

Ke'tai had finally been able to speak with her. It should ease Xandra's mind, and she would stop asking to meet him, if I were lucky.

The second part of the note worried me. Whatever had happened, it was something important and had to be dealt with very quickly. Though I did not know the reason for Ke'tai's sudden and inexplicable disappearance, my thoughts sprang immediately to the worst conclusion I could imagine: hunters had arrived in Seattle.

I stood up and located my shoes. Whatever was happening, I had to be ready to leave when Ke'tai returned—that much was clear from his message. I located a clock on the cable box after a moment, and noted that the time was nine twenty-two. Ke'tai would be returning any time, and I had slept most of the day away.

I sighed and looked around me, hoping to find something with which I could occupy myself while I waited. I searched the room for a few moments, unable to locate the remote for the television successfully, and finally resigned myself to flipping through one of the magazines from the coffee table to pass the time. Fortunately, I did not have to wait long.

At just after nine-thirty, I heard the sound of a key turning in the door of the apartment. Moments later, Ke'tai rushed inside, closing the door behind him quickly. I was on my feet and in the entry way before he was fully inside. He had a dark blue hooded sweatshirt on, the hood pulled up to cover his head, and the familiar blue-lensed glasses were perched atop his nose. He managed a smile when he saw me, but his expression was anxious. There was an urgency behind his actions that I could sense, but could not place.

"Chandra," he said quietly, "we have to leave town tonight. There is very little time to explain it to you now, but please understand that if we don't, we will be taking a very great risk. We have time to take you to your apartment so you can gather some things to take with you, but after that we must go."

I stared at him for several seconds, unable to comprehend what he had said.

"Chandra, please, we don't have time!"

There was a tremor in his voice that I had never heard before; Ke'tai was afraid. This realization woke me up more fully than if I had been doused full in the face with a bucket of ice water.

When I nodded, he took my hand and pulled me toward the door. There was a thunderous shock within my mind when his cool skin touched mine, not unlike the sensation I had come to expect when Il'zaks taught me new means of summoning. Yet this was different, and altogether unique; as I hurried to keep up with Ke'tai as we raced down the corridor towards the elevator, I realized I could sense Ke'tai's power. I noted with surprise that I could measure it against my own, and I now understood why he and Il'zaks had been so impressed with my "potential". I swallowed hard, wondering how I was going to tell Ke'tai this news in the midst of what was obviously a crisis.

As the elevator doors closed behind us, Ke'tai said, "Chandra, I'm very sorry about this sudden need to get you away from Seattle, but it is the only way. What you need to know now is that there are hunters on their way here—they haven't arrived yet, but they will within a day. We need to be as far away as possible before that time comes."

My heart sank. Somehow, I had known all along that it would be hunters causing this trouble, but I did not understand why Ke'tai was so terrified. He was a summoner; I had foolishly believed that he and Il'zaks could defend themselves easily with the assistance of their collective trackers.

"Ke'tai, I—" I began, but he held up a hand for silence as the elevator stopped and the doors slid open. We had arrived on the ground floor.

We hurried through the lobby, and I could see the burgundy SUV that belonged to Carlos parked outside at the curb. Behind it was a black Mustang with tinted windows.

As we climbed into the back seat of the SUV, Ke'tai said, "Il'zaks is in the car behind us, with Carmine and Trey. They will follow us to your apartment, where you can gather your things. While you are inside, Il'zaks will come to this vehicle, so that the three of us can talk on the way to our next destination."

"And where is that, exactly?" I asked, finally able to put together a complete sentence for the first time since Ke'tai had returned.

"We will be heading south, that is all I really know," Ke'tai said softly. "Il'zaks is waiting for news from the Order... Until we receive word, we will not know where they expect us to go. But we must leave Seattle tonight, before the hunters arrive."

I sighed and dropped my gaze. If hunters were coming to town, that meant they might find Xandra. Nothing would ever be the same again between us, even if I were to stay. As sudden and terrifying as it all seemed, I resolved that I would remain with Ke'tai, no matter where he happened to be going. If it meant I must leave my sister behind, possibly forever, then so be it. I knew I was leaving everything I had ever known and had become accustomed to; though the realization was daunting, I would not give up on my chosen path.

I sighed again, and shifted slightly so I could gaze out the window. The tall buildings of downtown passed in a blur, their neon signs flashing briefly before my eyes as the burgundy SUV sped past them. I did not know how fast Carlos was driving, but I could tell that it was well beyond the posted speed limit. I prayed that he would not be stopped by a police officer; any delay could prove devastating to our sudden escape.

I was so absorbed with my thoughts, my fears, and the "what-ifs" that streamed through my mind that I did not realize the vehicle had stopped in the parking lot outside my apartment. I was staring out the window, no doubt with a bleak look upon my face, when Ke'tai reached across the seat and took my hand in both of his. Startled, I turned to face him, only then realizing where we were.

"Chandra, there is no way I can apologize enough for what we must do tonight," he said. His silver eyes sparkled in the orange light coming through the windows from the parking lot, but they were anguished, and he did not smile. "It had always been our plan to let you prepare for this departure yourself, to allow you the time to say goodbye to the things you have always known. These hunters...They've come at a bad time, and I'm so sorry. I—"

"Ke'tai," I said, squeezing his hand gently, "I understand. I know that this has to happen. I'll be fine."

He frowned, skeptical, but nodded. "It doesn't make me feel any better about this," he replied softly, and looked down. "I wanted the best for you, and this isn't it."

I sighed, feeling suddenly tired even though I had slept for the majority of the day. "I'll be fine, Ke'tai. Let me just go get this over with... I promise I'm not going to run away."

He managed a faint smile, then nodded. "I'll be waiting for you."

I drew an unsteady breath, then pushed open the car door with an effort of will to find myself standing outside in the cold Seattle drizzle, possibly for the last time. I sighed, bracing myself for this last, brief trek to the apartment. There were so many memories there, and I did not feel ready to leave them yet—but I had been given no choice. Completing my training was imperative; if I did not go with Ke'tai tonight, not only would I lose him forever, but the hunters would undoubtedly track me down and kill me. I would be seen as a threat to them, something corrupt and utterly *wrong*, something that must be destroyed.

I found myself walking purposefully across the parking lot. As I approached the stairs, I noted that Xandra's car was parked nearby, and internally I groaned. She was home, rather than at Elliot's as she had mentioned to Ke'tai. I would be forced to conjure another lie, on the last night I was likely to see my sister.

I trudged up the stairs, stalling a little to give myself the time to prepare a strategy. Before I had reached the top, I knew what I must say to her, though I was concerned that I would become emotional and ruin my plans. As I put my key in the lock for the final time, I steeled myself, and hardened my heart. She could not know that this would be our last encounter.

As I pushed the door open, I was greeted by the sound of her laughter, mingled with the lower tones of Elliot's voice. They were seated on the living room couch, and were taking the time to talk and enjoy one another's company. The television was turned off, and the apartment was otherwise silent.

"Hey, Chandra," Xandra called as I entered. "I was wondering if I'd see you tonight."

"Uh, yeah," I managed, looking down and smiling a little, trying to act embarrassed. "I was, um, just stopping by to get some things for tomorrow..."

She grinned. "Are you staying with Kevin tonight, then?" she asked, although she obviously knew the answer. "You know, I talked with him on the phone earlier. He seems like a nice guy."

I smiled. "Thanks. He's, um...waiting downstairs. I'll just be a minute, and you two can get back to talking."

I hurried out of the room, terrified that Xandra might suspect something already. I hoped that my performance had been believable.

I dug through the bottom of my closet for a moment, searching for my duffel bag amongst the shoes that littered the floor. As soon as I found it, I began stuffing it with a few articles of clothing and my daily necessities. I was nearly finished packing when there was a light tap on the door frame, and I looked up to see Xandra.

"Elliot just reminded me that we were supposed to have been at his place tonight, according to the message I left you," she said, biting her lower lip and looking somewhat sheepish. "We had to change plans... His downstairs neighbors decided to throw a party, and, well, we both kind of wanted to be somewhere quiet."

I laughed. "Xan, you worry too much," I replied. "I figured something must have come up, and that's why you were here. No big deal."

She nodded, smiling before she turned away, and returned to the living room. I did not take my eyes off her until she turned the corner and disappeared from my view. I was going to miss her; the short temper, the awkwardness, and everything else in between. I sighed, tossing the last of my things in the duffel bag, and zipped it closed. It was time to say goodbye.

I slung the bag over my right shoulder and exited my room, taking a brief moment to look around at all of the mementos I would never see again. As I flicked the light switch off, it felt as though I were at both the end and the beginning of two very important stages of my life. I turned my back on the room, and walked down the hallway, doing my best to appear casual and at ease. I was terrified of my uncertain future, and felt sick to my stomach as I made my way through the apartment for the final time.

I paused near the door to say good night to Xandra and Elliot. As I made eye contact with Elliot, however, I nearly gasped in shock. I was once again experiencing that strange sensation, as I had previously with Ke'tai while we fled from his apartment. Elliot possessed the summoner's talent.

"Chandra? Are you alright?" Xandra asked.

I had been staring at him, dumbstruck. *Great.* I had intended to make my exit without garnering their suspicions, but my sudden revelation had derailed all of my plans.

"Uh, yeah, sorry," I managed, shaking my head as though to clear it. "I just... Elliot reminded me of something I have to tell Kevin, that I forgot to mention earlier."

Xandra nodded, a knowing smirk appearing on her face. She brushed a strand of her dark hair away from her eyes and said, "Well, you'd best not keep him waiting down there too long. You two have fun tonight." She gave me a knowing wink.

I laughed, relieved, and Xandra joined in. "You two have a good night also, Xan. I'll see you tomorrow."

I pulled open the door to leave, and heard her call, "Don't come back too early, we might not be ready for you yet!" Elliot said something in reply to her which I could not hear, and she laughed in response. I closed the door behind me, and took the steps rather quickly, leaving the apartment—and my sister—behind forever.

Il'zaks was seated in the front passenger seat of the SUV when I climbed inside. I tossed my duffel bag on the floor, noting that Ke'tai had not moved an inch while I had been gone. I knew that they both wanted to speak with me about our future, but as soon as I had the door closed again, I told them what I had learned about Elliot. My words came out in a torrent; I spoke so rapidly, that Ke'tai had to ask me to repeat what I'd said. Both summoners looked surprised at my revelation, and Il'zaks frowned deeply, turning around to stare out the windshield while he contemplated the news.

"Why didn't you tell me you could sense that?" Ke'tai asked after a moment. "You must have been very excited to discover this new ability."

I nodded. "It just happened, when you came back for me tonight," I explained. "I *was* excited, and I did try to tell you in the elevator, but... There was too much going on." I sighed and my face fell. "I thought it was important that you knew about Elliot, though. Will he be okay with the hunters here?"

"He will be fine," Il'zaks replied, and I noticed he had turned to face us once more. "There are stages to gauging the level of ability within yourself and others, Chandra. You have just come to realize that you can sense the ability, and that is the starting point. The more time you spend with others like yourself, the farther this ability will develop. You will eventually be able to distinguish between a summoner who is fully trained, and one who is still in training, as well as one who has not been trained at all. Those rare hunters who can track summoners, and not just their demons, can distinguish those things as well. The hunters have a rule that they will not harm any person who does not yet know of their summoning ability. Elliot has nothing to fear."

I nodded, relieved. Elliot was a good person, and he was a great match for Xandra. I did not wish to see anything bad happen to him, if I were in a position to prevent it.

"You, on the other hand, would have been hunted down," Il'zaks said after a moment, "the same as Ke'tai and myself would have been."

While I had known this indirectly based upon Ke'tai's earlier words, it still came as a shock when stated so matter-of-factly. My attention was now fully upon the elder summoner, and he gazed steadily at me with his strange, silvery eyes.

"The hunters can distinguish between someone who has not been trained, and someone who has," he continued. "Their rules dictate that they treat those who have had any amount of training the same as they would a full-fledged summoner. Had we left you here, you would have been killed."

I nodded, feeling suddenly numb. "I know."

I felt Ke'tai take my hand in his, but it did little to dispel the melancholy that had fallen over me. At that moment, I wanted nothing more than to break down and cry, but I stubbornly kept my composure. I knew that crying would not improve the situation, and that Il'zaks' words had been for my benefit. Before we had reached my apartment, I had known I would never return, never see Xandra again. It remained difficult news to digest. I sighed heavily and stared down at the floor.

"We learned that the hunters were coming just this evening," Il'zaks stated after several long moments of silence; the only sounds that could be heard were the tires on the wet pavement and the swish-click of the windshield wipers as they cleared away the steady drizzle. "The Order discovered that they are holding a convention of sorts here in Seattle, and that there will be a great number of them in the city. We have no other choice but to leave here. The first group is scheduled to arrive tomorrow morning."

"Do you think they'll find Xan?" I asked, surprised at how lifeless my own voice sounded.

Il'zaks sighed. "I cannot say for certain, Chandra Grey," he replied, "but it is a possibility. It is better that you are away from her now."

I was defeated; in one evening, I had been forced to flee from everything and everyone I had ever known, with only these three strange men for company. I had been forced to leave my twin sister behind, because she was a threat to my very existence. Dwelling on this was beginning to give me a headache, and I felt heartsick.

"Where are we heading to?" Ke'tai asked, voicing one of my many unspoken questions.

"For now, the safe house in northern California," Il'zaks replied. "It is hidden far inside the forest there, and is inaccessible to most humans," he added for my benefit.

I nodded dully, and turned my gaze out the window. We were on the freeway now, passing through part of Tacoma, but it was dark and there was little to see other than lighted advertisements and the headlights of the north-bound vehicles. After a moment, I turned back to Il'zaks.

"What is going to happen now?" I asked. "I mean, with me."

"You will remain with us," Il'zaks replied.

"We'll be with you full time," Ke'tai said at the same time, giving my hand a slight squeeze.

"We will continue with your training," Il'zaks continued after a brief pause. "This will give us the opportunity to measure your progress a bit better as well. You will be safer this way, and perhaps, may learn faster."

"Speaking of learning," Ke'tai said, "I think you may have forgotten to mention to her about making sure to eat in the mornings after important lessons."

Il'zaks sighed, and closed his eyes briefly. "I more than likely did forget," he admitted. "I have become too forgetful, when it comes to students, Ke'tai. Perhaps I should—"

Ke'tai shook his head. "No, not yet. You are a better teacher when it comes to learning the basics than I am, and she's going to need that." He disentangled his hand from mine, and slid his arm about my shoulders. "Besides, I may be too much of a distraction when it comes to her lessons," he added playfully.

I glanced over at him, and he was grinning at me, eyes sparkling faintly in the darkness. I managed a smile in return, grateful that he was here with me on this wretched night.

“Anyway,” Ke’tai said after a moment, “we should stop somewhere along the way and get something to eat. It’s been almost twelve hours for me, and I know I’m hungry.”

Il’zaks nodded. “Let us get across the border into Oregon first, and then I will feel better about stopping, even if it is only for a short period of time.”

I settled back against the seat, as close to Ke’tai as the seatbelt would allow, and gazed out the window into the dreary darkness. My mind was blank, and I simply watched the cars go by on the other side of the freeway; I could think of nothing. Too much had transpired in the past few hours, and I could not fully comprehend the situation, even now. I wondered if the morning would feel as surreal as the night seemed, or if my experiences would seem nothing more than a troubled dream produced by a feverish mind in the bright light of day.

# 10

# PERFECT

I awoke to the sound of a car door slamming. Sunlight was streaming through the tinted windows of Carlos' SUV, and I was stiff from having slept in an awkward position on half of the back seat. I rubbed my eyes and sat up, somewhat disoriented.

Ke'tai was sitting next to me, his head tilted against the opposite window; he appeared to be sound asleep. Il'zaks was awake, however, and had turned around to face me as I sat upright and stretched as best I could.

"We are in Albany, Oregon," he said quietly. "Carlos and Carmine stopped here to go into the grocery store and pick up some items. If you need to get out of the vehicle to stretch, or use the restroom inside the store, Trey is outside and can escort you."

I glanced outside, noting the big bald man leaning against the car parked next to the SUV. The surreal feeling I had experienced the night before returned, but was muted by the daylight. I remembered everything that had happened the previous night with the unusual clarity that comes from experiencing an event that is both terrifying and exhausting. I sighed, resigning myself to this new life, most of which I knew would be spent on the move or in hiding. I doubted that I would ever have a place to call home again.

"I'll be back soon," I told Il'zaks quietly, and climbed out of the SUV as soundlessly as I could, hoping that I would not wake Ke'tai.

"Good morning," Trey said. He sounded more cheerful than I believed the situation allowed for. "Need to go inside?"

I nodded, and followed his lead into the store. We were only inside for three or four minutes, but by the time we had returned to the parking lot, Carlos and Carmine were back, packing sacks of groceries into both the back of the SUV and the trunk of Carmine's black mustang. Trey immediately went to help Carmine with her task, so I decided to help Carlos. I noticed through the open back hatch of the SUV that Ke'tai had awakened; he was sitting upright on the seat, and had pulled the hood of his sweatshirt over his head. Il'zaks remained in the front seat, facing forward and out of view of anyone who might peer inside. I could see only the outline of his thin shoulders.

Once we had finished, Carlos and Trey took the shopping carts back inside, and Carmine strode over to hand me a sack of warm breakfast burritos. "These are for you all," she said, without her usual brand of animosity. I noticed that dark circles had formed beneath her eyes, made to seem even darker by the contrast of her pale skin and her hair, which she had dyed black since I had last seen her.

"Thanks," I said, managing not to sound overly surprised at her uncharacteristic civility.

She nodded and turned away to climb into the driver's side of the black car without another word. I took the opportunity to take my seat next to Ke'tai again, setting the burritos down on the middle console between Il'zaks and the empty driver's seat.

Ke'tai grinned. "Breakfast!"

I laughed, and Il'zaks chuckled as he took three burritos from the sack and passed one each to Ke'tai and I. The last he kept for himself. At that moment Carlos returned, and he took out a burrito and unwrapped it, setting it on the console next to the bag. The SUV was moving again before we had begun to eat.

I had not realized how hungry I was, until I had taken a bite from the burrito. It was warm, packed full of eggs, sausage, and melted cheese, and tasted delicious. The vehicle was silent for some time as we ate.

"We'll be having lunch on the road," Il'zaks said after a time. "There are plenty of things in the back there to choose from, so do not hesitate to get something if you become hungry again."

"How long will it be before we get to…wherever it is we're going?" I asked.

"It will be around seven hours of driving, and then an additional two or three of hiking in to the safe house," Ke'tai replied. "It'll be dark by the time we get there."

"That is only if we do not receive word from the Order first," Il'zaks added.

"Is this…Is this something that happens often?" I asked. "I mean, having to move suddenly and all."

"It happens sometimes," Ke'tai replied with a shrug. "It isn't something that happens frequently. Had it been just one or two hunters, we would have stayed in Seattle, but this is different."

I frowned and released a frustrated sigh. "How many *are* there?"

The car was silent for several seconds, before Il'zaks said, "The convention being held was open to every hunter that was available. The message I received yesterday from the Order stated that there were over three hundred hunters planning to be in attendance. Ke'tai and I together could keep you safe from a dozen or so, but not three hundred."

"They'll find Xan," I said quietly, more to myself than to the two summoners.

"You don't know that," Ke'tai replied firmly.

"If they do find her, what will happen to Elliot?"

"We went over this last night," Il'zaks stated. "They will not harm Elliot unless he has begun training, which he has not."

"But Xan will know!" I burst out. "She'll…" I was unable to finish the sentence. Everything that had transpired during the last twenty-four hours suddenly came crashing down upon me, and I was unable to withstand the barrage of emotions any longer. I covered my face with my hands and began to sob; hard, racking sobs filled with pain, frustration, fear.

Il'zaks said something, and Ke'tai replied, but I did not know what either had said. A moment later, I felt Ke'tai take my hands in his, but I refused to open my eyes to look at him. I wanted nothing more than to find a dark room to lay down in and cry until my tears were spent.

"Chandra, listen to me," Ke'tai said gently. I found the sound of his voice soothing. "I am so sorry that we brought this upon you, but we had no other choice. Had Il'zaks and I left without you…" his voice cracked with emotion, and I heard him swallow hard. "Had we left without you," he repeated, his voice steady once more, "we would have lost you. Please believe me when I say that I could not bear to see that happen."

I drew a shaky breath, and ventured to open my eyes. Ke'tai's face was inches from my own, and it was drawn with concern. His eyes sparkled in the light, not only because of their color, but because they were filled with tears. I felt my heart breaking as I saw this; I felt horrible for having caused him such suffering.

"Ke'tai, I'm sorry," I whispered, feeling fresh tears spill down my cheeks. "I'm just… I'm just scared. I don't know what is happening, and I don't know what to expect. I just walked away from everything I've ever known… I know it's necessary, I know why you asked me to do this, but knowing that doesn't make it any easier."

He nodded, and managed a strained smile. "I am here for you, Chandra. No matter what happens, I'll be here."

It is amazing how exhausting the act of riding in a car for a full day can be. When we finally stopped, somewhere deep within the redwood forests of northern California, it was just after four o'clock. Because it was early January, the day was already fading into twilight. I was glad to leave the car, to stretch, to walk around a bit, but I felt drained. Perhaps it was from the car ride itself, or perhaps it was due to the emotional roller-coaster I had spent the last two days riding upon.

The groceries that Carmine and Carlos had purchased earlier in the day were packed into two fairly large wooden crates. Il'zaks and Ke'tai went off into the trees some distance away while the rest of us filled the crates, in order to summon demons to help with moving the load. They returned not long after; Il'zaks with a shadow demon trailing in his wake, but Ke'tai appeared to be alone.

Ke'tai flashed one of his brilliant smiles in my direction as he approached. "How would you like to go flying again?" he asked in a low, excited tone.

If nothing else, the suggestion of flying took my mind away from other matters. I returned his smile and nodded. "I'd like that."

"I thought you might." He grinned, and motioned for me to follow him. Once we were away from the others, he said, "Il'zaks' demon can handle those crates easily. We both thought—Il'zaks and I—that it might be good for you to do something fun, to take your mind off all that happened yesterday. We know how hard it is, Chandra. It's probably the worst part of becoming a summoner."

I nodded. "I'm sorry about earlier. It felt like the whole world was falling down around me… But I'm a little better now."

Not far from where we had left the others, we came to a small space within the giant trees where Ke'tai's dragon stood majestically, its tail curled about its taloned feet. He had to help me up, as he had before; that night at Mount Rainier seemed like a lifetime ago. So much had happened since then, but it had only been just over a week.

Ke'tai kept the dragon low, beneath the canopy of the trees, and had it fly slower than he had on our previous outing in order to avoid running into the massive branches. It was less exhilarating, yet it served its purpose, allowing me to clear my mind.

"I wanted to explain a couple things while we were away from everyone else, Chandra," Ke'tai said over his shoulder after a few minutes.

"What's that?" I asked.

"Well, first of all, Il'zaks only has a couple more lessons to teach you. He'll be moving on to other things pretty soon."

"But you said last night—"

"Yeah, I know," Ke'tai said. "What he has left to teach you is still part of the basics I was referring to. You *do* need to learn that from him—he is much more experienced than I am."

"How long will it be?" I asked. I was saddened that my time with Il'zaks would soon be over, but I was thrilled at the prospect of working exclusively with Ke'tai.

Ke'tai was silent for a few seconds while he thought over his response. "Well," he said slowly, "that is going to depend on what we're told to do next. We don't yet know where we will be going. If we were to stay in one place, however, my guess would be around two weeks. But don't worry; you'll have plenty of opportunity to see Il'zaks once you're done with your training. This won't be the end."

"How does the Order work?" I asked. "I mean, you tell me that you have to wait for news, or orders, or whatever, but I don't understand it yet."

Ke'tai chuckled. "Sometimes, neither do I." Then, in a more serious tone, he said, "There's a hierarchy of summoners, based on ability and age. The leader is the Master Grand Summoner, Te'chok. The leader of the Order is decided by the power present in the name, and experience is not taken into account for that position. However, the Grand Summoner isn't all-powerful and can't do whatever he pleases. He must go through the Board of Elders before most things can be decided. Most of our orders come from the Board of Elders, and not the Grand Summoner." He paused a moment, then added, "Think of it sort of like the Grand Summoner is the Queen of England, and the Board of Elders is the Parliament. Parliament ultimately makes the laws; the Queen is just a figurehead."

I nodded, and then felt a little silly for doing so. I was sitting behind Ke'tai, and it was growing dark; he would not have been able to see my action. "So, the Grand Summoner is chosen by their name?" I asked. "I know Il'zaks told me that the names are powerful words, but..."

"Our names are part of what determines our ranking within the Order," Ke'tai replied. "Each summoner has a different name, and each name is uniquely powerful in its own way. The more powerful the name is, the higher the ranking. Usually. Some summoners have a higher ranking than those with a more powerful name, because they have been with the Order for so long, and usually they're part of the Board of Elders. There are seven summoners on the Board of Elders, but I am guessing Il'zaks may be joining them soon as the eighth."

Again, I wondered how old Il'zaks must be, though I knew asking Ke'tai would be futile. He had told me previously that Il'zaks would tell me when he felt the time was right for me to know.

"What sort of name do you think I will have?" I asked.

Ke'tai laughed. "It is very hard to tell, Chandra," he replied, grinning as he glanced over his shoulder at me. "Judging from your ability so far, it will be more powerful than my name is. But, I will miss calling you Chandra. It's a pretty name."

We flew on in silence for a time, and my thoughts returned to a conversation I'd had with Ke'tai some time ago. He had told me that he remembered very little of his life before becoming a summoner; I wondered how much of my past I would ultimately forget.

"Ke'tai?" I asked after a time.

"Yes, love?"

"Will I remember all of this, after...I change?"

He was quiet for several moments, and I began to wonder if he would answer the question. Finally, he sighed, and said, "I don't know, Chandra.

Some summoners remember parts of their lives from before, and others remember nothing at all, not even their training. Those summoners can turn out to be completely different people than they were prior to the change. It's rare for that to happen, though. As for me, I forgot many things, but I remember bits and pieces, like snapshots, if you will. It seems that Il'zaks was the same way, based upon what he has told me."

"I don't want to forget you," I whispered, hanging my head. I was uncertain if he had heard me over the rush of the air around us. If he had, he made no reply.

We landed not long after our conversation had ended. There was a clearing in the trees, and at the center was a two-story log cabin. There were no paths leading away from the cabin, nor were there any markers pointing toward it; you would have to know its location in order to find it. The windows were dark, and it looked as if no one had been to the place for quite some time; dried leaves had drifted thickly against one side of the cabin and cobwebs clung thickly to the siding.

"The others should be here any time," Ke'tai said as he led me to the front door of the cabin. He pulled up a plank of wood from the porch, and felt around in the hole beneath. "There's supposed to be a key here…" he said, making a face, which quickly turned into a smile. "Found it," he grinned, springing up to unlock the door.

I stayed near the door, while Ke'tai ventured further inside. The interior of the cabin was dark, and I was unfamiliar with its layout; I did not wish to fall over a piece of furniture and make a fool of myself. After a few moments, a light blazed on the far side of what I now could see was a living room; Ke'tai had found a propane lantern in the darkness and was holding it up so that I would have enough light to navigate through the room.

"I'm afraid the cabin doesn't come with electricity," he said as I entered, closing the door behind me. He set the lantern carefully on top of a stone mantel that was situated above a fireplace on the far side of the room. "Just give me a few minutes to get this fire going, and then we can talk a little more. There's something else I need to ask you about." He headed back out the door.

I nodded, and while he was busy, I took the opportunity to acquaint myself with the new surroundings. The living room was furnished with two wicker couches and a matching table, and these had been placed to face toward the fireplace. To the left was a small kitchen, with a sink, and a propane-powered camp stove which had been placed on the counter. None of the usual appliances were present, though there was a sturdy set of table and chairs to one side. Along the right wall of the living room was a wooden staircase that led up into the darkened second story.

I dropped my duffel bag on the floor as I sat down on one of the wicker couches, and a cloud of dust erupted from the cushion. I sprang to my feet, coughing as Ke'tai returned from his errand outside. I was futilely waving away the motes of dust that had billowed into the air.

He laughed, pausing a moment to watch me, an amused smile on his face. He had an armful of split firewood, which he stacked neatly inside the hearth.

"You know, sometimes you can be pretty funny," he said, striking a match and tossing it quickly amongst the firewood.

"Well, the same thing would have happened to you, had you been the first one to sit down," I replied, feeling my face flush.

He chuckled. "I doubt anyone has come here since this place was built," he replied. "It must've been twelve years ago, at least."

I nodded, and ventured to sit down once more. This time, only a small puff of dust rose from the cushion.

Ke'tai rose and turned away from the fire, which was beginning to smolder nicely. "Chandra, I needed to talk with you about something else, before the others arrive," he said, a hint of worry in his tone.

"What is it?" I asked, immediately concerned.

"Well, there are six of us, and only four bedrooms," he began, staring down at the wooden planks of the floor rather than looking at me.

I cocked my head to one side, unable to stifle an embarrassed laugh, and said, "So…what are you trying to say?"

"I was wondering if you'd be okay with sharing a room," he mumbled. "With me."

I thought over his proposition for less than a second. "Sure," I replied. "I mean, they're probably going to expect anyway, right?"

He looked up at me then, and nodded. "Actually, it was Il'zaks that asked me if we were, and I had to tell him I didn't know." He glanced down for a moment, and then his silver eyes met mine once more. "I'm not used to this uncertainty I have when I'm around you," he said quietly. "I love you, and I don't want to be the one that hurts you." He sighed. "I guess I just wanted to make sure you were okay with it before I gave Il'zaks an answer."

I smiled at him, and said, "Thank you. That means a lot." I had dated men in the past that could care less about what I felt or thought, and it was nice to have someone who genuinely cared about me as a person. More so, Ke'tai was beautiful and intriguing, and I had fallen completely in love. I was about to say more when the door opened.

"I see the two of you made it here safely," Il'zaks said as I turned around to face him, trying not to let my disappointment at his arrival show. "I have yet to receive any word from the Order, so we may be here for a few days. Make yourselves at home."

The room we were to share was at the end of the second-floor hallway. The room was not large, and was furnished only with a full-sized bed and had two small windows. Thin floral-print curtains hung limply over the windows, but the bed was bare of any covering.

Carmine found a small closet that contained sheets and quilts for the beds, each set enclosed in a zippered plastic bag to keep them free of dust. It appeared that all of the beds had been left in the same barren state.

Ke'tai helped me with the task of putting sheets on the bed we were to share, then left to speak with Il'zaks. I was left alone for the first time in over twenty-four hours. I finally had the opportunity to sift through my jumbled thoughts, to determine what I felt about the situation I'd found myself in.

I missed Xandra terribly, that was undeniable. We had been together nearly every day of our entire existence, and now that I knew we would be separated forever, I felt as though I had lost half of myself. I hoped that she would be happy in whatever she chose to do with her life. I wanted to believe that she would not be discovered by the hunters that had converged upon Seattle and forced my premature—and permanent—departure.

I was uncertain of what to feel when it came to the hunters themselves. From what I had learned during my time with Il'zaks and Ke'tai, I knew they were dangerous and would try their best to kill me if I were discovered. Though they believed they were doing the world a favor by hunting demons and those that controlled them, I knew that their belief was wrong and based on nothing but old stories and folly. Leaving Seattle had been my only option; even if I had resisted the plan Il'zaks and Ke'tai had contrived, I was certain that Ke'tai would have done anything in his power to protect me—even if I needed protection from myself.

Ke'tai... I had never felt so strongly about anyone before. I never wanted to lose that feeling, and would do anything to preserve it. Yet I was nervous tonight; the others—Il'zaks in particular—had assumed we would be sharing a room. That assumption irritated me, but I knew that from an outsider's point of view, it was a logical conclusion. Ke'tai and I had grown very close, but I was unsure if I was ready for that next step in our relationship.

I wondered how he felt about the matter. I settled into the bed, after turning off the propane lantern that was sitting in one bare corner of the room. It was not long before my emotional exhaustion took over, and I was soundly asleep.

I awoke the next morning, feeling rather comfortable despite the unfamiliar surroundings and all that had happened. The sun was streaming in through the small windows of the bedroom, and I was pleasantly warm beneath the blankets. Ke'tai's arm was draped around my waist, and he was laying perfectly still behind me; my back was to him as I lay on my side. I stared across the empty room toward the door for several moments, not wishing to move and wake him, savoring the moment. I wondered what time he had come into the room—I had not heard him enter, nor felt him climb into the bed. So much for my being nervous the night before.

I turned over slowly, trying my best not to disturb him. I was surprised to see his silver eyes open and alert, as though he had been awake for some time. He was smiling, and the expression he wore was one of supreme contentment. I felt as though my insides would melt in that instant.

Wordlessly, he moved his hand up to touch the side of my face. The sheet fell down, revealing his shirtless and sculpted torso. He simply stared into my eyes for countless seconds, smiling all the while. The sun shone down on him from behind, illuminating the white, somewhat flattened spikes of his hair. I was captive to his gaze, unable to look away from those glittering silver eyes; he had never appeared so beautiful, so *perfect* before.

"Chandra Grey, I love you," he whispered.

I smiled. “I love you, too, Ke’tai.”

I wished that moment could have lasted for eternity.

# 11

# MISTAKES

Unfortunately, the moment was abruptly cut short by a loud knocking on the door to our room. I sighed, disappointed, as Ke'tai disentangled himself from the sheets and rose to see what the commotion was. He was wearing a loose pair of black sweat pants and nothing more, and I was unable to tear my eyes away from his half-naked form.

When the door was opened a crack, I could see Il'zaks standing in the hall outside, dressed impeccably as usual, not a hair out of place on his head. He smirked as Ke'tai opened the door, and put one pale hand over his mouth in what I assumed was an attempt to hide a laugh.

"Good afternoon," Il'zaks said after a moment, amusement in his tone.

"What?" I asked, rubbing my eyes.

Il'zaks chuckled, glancing past Ke'tai briefly to make eye contact with me. "It is ten minutes past noon, Chandra Grey," he replied. "I came to tell you that I've received word from the Order. We have another lengthy drive ahead of us, and I would prefer to start as soon as possible, since we still have to hike back to the vehicles before we can begin."

"So, uh, what's the news?" Ke'tai asked. To me, he sounded groggy still.

"We are to go to the headquarters," Il'zaks replied. "As I said, it will be a lengthy drive. I trust you can fill Miss Grey in with the details while the two of you gather your things to leave."

Ke'tai nodded, and closed the door as Il'zaks turned away. I sighed.

"Where is the headquarters?" I asked once he had turned around.

"In Boston," he replied, then leaned his head back against the closed door and stared up at the ceiling for several moments. He sighed, and dropped his gaze back down to meet mine. "I haven't been there in years. Il'zaks was just there in December, when he left Seattle the last time. It is the one place we have always been safe, Chandra. By ordering us to go there, they must believe we were followed, or are in danger somehow."

A cold fear gripped my insides, and I looked down. "It's because of me, isn't it?"

Ke'tai moved so swiftly I didn't realize he had; he seemingly appeared at my side, kneeling next to the bed. "Why would you believe that, Chandra?" he asked, gently taking my hands in his own.

"Xan would be worried about me," I replied with a shrug, unwilling to look up at him. "She's probably filed a missing persons report. They'll be looking for me, Ke'tai."

"Knowing how the police run in this country, I doubt they will be looking for you so soon," he replied. "Usually, they'll wait a few more days before they start looking into it. You have only been 'missing' for just over a day now, you know."

When I didn't respond or look up at him, he sighed. "I'll admit I think you may be right as to why they've told us to go to Boston, though I don't believe there's any threat to you yet. It's probably just a precaution, Chandra."

I sighed. "It will be on the news, eventually. I have to hide forever now, don't I?"

Ke'tai nodded, and his expression was sad. "Yes, but only from the rest of the world. You won't have to hide from anyone affiliated with the Order, and you won't have to hide from me."

I knew he was trying to make me feel better about the situation, but I was feeling so helpless that his words did not improve my mood. "Ke'tai, I…I don't know what to say. You're always there to protect me, to look out for me, and I'm…not able to do the same. I feel so useless."

He touched the side of my face, softly, and finally I gathered the nerve to meet his gaze once more. "Chandra, you are not useless," he said evenly. "One day, you'll be able to do for me what I've been able to do for you." He managed a sad smile, then added, "I wouldn't change this for the world, you know. Even though I've had to up and move twice within as many days, I'm with the one person I love more than life itself, and that's the important part. Nothing else matters, Chandra, just you."

After nearly a week spent riding in the back seat of Carlos' burgundy SUV, eating whatever foodstuffs Trey and Carmine had picked up at the grocery store in Albany, Oregon, and sleeping only fitfully during the drive, we arrived in Boston. Carlos and Ke'tai had taken turns driving the SUV, and I assumed Trey and Carmine had driven in shifts in the other vehicle.

The only stops had been at gas stations to refill the fuel tanks and to venture inside to use the restrooms. I was now forced to join Ke'tai and Il'zaks in the game of disguise; while we had heard nothing yet of my disappearance on the radio or from the Order, we knew that it must be inevitable, and none of us wanted to take the chance of someone recognizing me and reporting it. If I had to go into one of the gas stations along the way, Ke'tai made me wear one of his hooded sweatshirts and sunglasses, no matter the time of day.

When we finally had reached Boston, I was ready to be done with the marathon car trip, even if it meant I was forced to stay within the headquarters of the Order. I did not wish to spend any more time crammed inside a car, at least for a while.

The headquarters of the Order was located below ground, and the entrance was inside what appeared to be a dilapidated warehouse building a few blocks from the wharf. There was a man dressed in a blue work uniform outside of the warehouse, who opened up one of the shipping bays after speaking to Carlos and Ke'tai for a moment. Carlos drove inside the building, which I realized had been converted into a two-story parking garage. The bottom floor held perhaps a dozen other vehicles besides the two our group had arrived in. The shipping bay door rattled closed as Carmine's black mustang entered. I was out of the SUV as soon as Carlos had parked, far too restless to remain in the car any longer.

The warehouse was lit dimly by orange lights hanging from the ceiling above. On the side of the building opposite the shipping bay we had come in through, there was a concrete staircase that led downward. Once everyone had exited the vehicles and gathered what belongings we needed to take with us, Il'zaks led the way towards the staircase. It felt wonderful to be walking again.

"We will be expected to meet with summoner Te'chok as soon as we are inside," Il'zaks explained, primarily for my benefit. "It looks as though not many others are here, which means things must be going well for us in the world, and there have been few altercations with the hunters."

"This is our safe haven," Ke'tai whispered as we approached the stairs. "It's also the place we gather for big meetings, and special occasions. But, mostly, it's our refuge when things go badly. The hunters know our domain is in this area, and because of that, they usually do not wander into Boston."

I nodded as I followed Il'zaks down the steps. The staircase was relatively short, only ten steps, but led to a downward sloping ramp that ran through a concrete corridor. The only illumination came from small red-orange lights along the floor, reminiscent of those found in a movie theater. At the end of the corridor was an elevator with an "Out of Order" sign tacked across the doors. Another workman in a blue uniform was lounging in a camp-style chair next to the elevator, and he snapped to attention as we approached, having recognized the two summoners in our group.

"Go on down," he said waving his hand at the elevator. "The sign's just there for show," he added with a grin.

Il'zaks nodded once, and pressed the button to open the doors. "Thank you," he said to the workman as the doors slid noiselessly open.

The elevator was quite large, and easily held our entire group with room to spare. The interior was lit with a bright white light, while the sides of the elevator were metallic with a highly mirrored surface. The floor was covered in plush red carpet. My first impression of the headquarters was one of decadence.

I was nervous, uncertain of what to expect. I knew that it was very rare for someone not yet finished with their training to be allowed inside this place, according to what Ke'tai had told me during our trip from California. We were expected to meet with Master Grand Summoner Te'chok upon arrival. It was not because of policy, but because our safety was of concern to him. Beyond that, I knew nothing else about the headquarters, and very little about the Order.

The elevator descended for perhaps thirty seconds before it stopped and the doors slid open once more. We stepped out into what appeared to be the lobby of an upscale hotel, perhaps; there were many chairs and couches arranged in groups around the room, centered about low wooden tables. Each piece of furniture appeared expensive to my eye. Several corridors branched away from the lobby in all directions, leading to destinations yet unknown to me. I could hear classical music playing, the sounds floating down from speakers built into the ceiling above. At the center of the room was a square, polished marble desk, behind which a dark-haired woman dressed in a business suit was standing. She wore wire-framed glasses, and her hair was pulled up in a tight twist. She looked to be in her mid-forties. She was the only person inside the room, apart from our group.

"That's Adele," Ke'tai whispered to me as Il'zaks led the way toward the desk. "She works for Te'chok and pretty much runs the business end of this place. I haven't met her myself, but Il'zaks has."

Adele smiled warmly as Il'zaks stopped before the desk. "It's a relief you have arrived here safely," she said with a distinct British accent. "Te'chok's been waiting to speak with you. Come with me, I'll take you to him."

"Te'chok stays here most of the time," Ke'tai told me as we began walking again, following Adele down one of the corridors. "I guess he's pretty busy with keeping the Order organized and making sure everyone gets equal share of the funds. See, they run some night clubs in the major cities on the east coast, and a few in Europe; that's how they have the money to keep us going. Like I said, Adele takes care of most of that business, but Te'chok is always busy with his own agenda. I've met him twice before this, but he seems to be a very interesting guy."

I nodded, swallowing my anxiety; I felt decidedly out of place. I noticed Adele had stopped in front of a pair of wide double doors with panes of etched and frosted glass set within them. Though I could not see through the glass, a warm yellow light emanated from within the room on the other side of the doors.

"Wait here a moment, and I will tell Te'chok that you have arrived," Adele said briskly before letting herself into the room.

"Ke'tai, what should I expect from this meeting?" I whispered. "I don't know—"

"Don't worry about it, Chandra," he replied with a slow smile. "Il'zaks will probably do most of the talking. You shouldn't have to say anything if you don't want to, unless he asks you a question directly."

I nodded, though I remained unconvinced.

Ke'tai chuckled. "He isn't scary, Chandra. Relax."

I frowned, annoyed that I had allowed my fear to overshadow my rationality. I was about to reply, when Adele returned through the doors. "You may go inside," she said, holding one door open. "I will be in the lobby, should you need anything after your meeting."

Il'zaks was the first to enter the room, followed by Ke'tai, and then myself. Carlos and the others followed behind, but stood near the doors once we were inside. The room appeared to be a library; shelves of books lined the walls, though there was an open space directly across from the door with an empty fireplace and a large flat-screen TV mounted on the wall above it. The TV was tuned to a news station, though its volume had been muted. The floor was made of polished wood planks, and tall lamps at the corners of the room provided a soft light. The center of the room held a cluster of large, comfortable chairs, which were situated to face the fireplace and TV. Upon one of these chairs sat the summoner Te'chok.

Te'chok appeared to be twenty, perhaps, though I knew from conversations with Il'zaks and Ke'tai that he had been leading the Order for over a century. He had very fair skin that was dotted lightly with freckles, and I immediately had the impression that prior to becoming a summoner, he must have had red hair—his complexion reminded me in some ways of Teddy. His white hair was curly, and was just long enough to fall over his eyes as he turned his head to peer in our direction. I was startled at the power I could sense within him, and I knew without a doubt why he had been named the head of the Order. He stood up as we approached, and I realized he was only slightly taller than I was at five feet five inches.

He smiled warmly, and made a welcoming gesture with his hands. "Il'zaks, it is good to see you again," he said. "And you as well, Ke'tai. Please, come sit down. It seems that you are just in time." He bent to retrieve a remote from the arm of the chair he had been sitting in, and pressed a button to unmute the television.

Il'zaks took a seat across from Te'chok, while Ke'tai took one in between the two. I stopped still in my tracks as I heard what was being spoken of on the TV, and I simply stared up at the screen in horror.

"...missing persons case from Seattle, Washington," the female reporter on the screen was saying. "It appears to be the case of a relationship gone wrong, according to sources who know the missing woman, twenty-three-year-old Chandra Grey. Authorities are investigating..." My picture flashed onto the screen, taken a few months ago by Xandra at our birthday party.

She said more, but I did not hear it. I felt the room start to spin, and I grabbed onto the back of Ke'tai's chair in an attempt to steady myself. While I had expected Xandra to go to the police, I had not expected it to be on national news so soon, if ever.

Ke'tai turned around to face me, clearly concerned. "Chandra, are you going to be alright?" he whispered.

I stared at him for several seconds, uncomprehending, before I finally looked away and nodded. "Yeah, I…I think so."

I heard a soft click as the TV was turned off, and looked up again to see that all three of the summoners were watching me with concern in their eyes.

"I apologize," Te'chok said after a moment. "This was just beginning to air when Adele was leaving the room, and I believe you needed to know what was happening. You will no longer be safe in the world outside, as you once used to be, Miss Grey."

I nodded, and forced my unsteady legs to carry me to the chair between Ke'tai and Il'zaks, which I promptly collapsed into, rather ungracefully. "It's so unreal, to see something like that," I murmured after a moment.

"I understand," Te'chok replied in a soothing tone. "Now you know why you must remain here until your training is completed. Not only will people be on the lookout for you as a missing person, but cases like that also draw the keen interest of many hunters."

"Hunters realize that some of the missing persons cases in the news are actually people who have disappeared to join our Order," Il'zaks added. "They will have your picture now, and until the story dies down in the media, you must remain in hiding."

"And this is the safest place to be," Te'chok stated, gesturing widely. "It is our refuge from danger, our safe place where no hunter dares enter."

The talk of hunters roused a question in my mind, one I had wanted an answer for since we had fled Seattle a week earlier. "Did they find Xan?"

Te'chok shook his head. "Your sister is yet undiscovered," he replied. "Once the hunters' gathering had concluded, I sent summoner Kai'lind to the area to keep a watch on her, as well as Elliot Thompson. Kai'lind will be working with Mr. Thompson as his teacher in the near future."

"Elliot's agreed to be trained then?" I asked, hopeful.

Te'chok nodded, smiling faintly. "Yes, he has indeed, though I fear it will be difficult for him to keep his doings a secret from your sister." He looked away from me to Il'zaks then. "Tell me all that has happened since you left Seattle."

Il'zaks launched into a detailed explanation of what had occurred in the past week, though it was of little interest to me. I was still reeling from the shock of seeing my picture flashed across the national evening news. I was only half-listening to the conversation, until Te'chok turned to Ke'tai and asked, "Would you be willing to abdicate your training position with Miss Grey to another?"

My attention snapped to Te'chok, and I stared at him, wondering what he was planning, outraged at the thought that he would ask such a thing of Ke'tai. Without thinking, I blurted, "What do you mean by that?"

Te'chok smiled knowingly, and appeared amused. "I have been told of the growing relationship between yourself and summoner Ke'tai. While it pleases me to see that Ke'tai no longer needs to face the world alone, it also worries me greatly. When it comes time for you to train under someone other than Il'zaks, it will be too much of a distraction for you to safely learn what you must in order to complete your training, should your next teacher be Ke'tai, as we had originally planned." He paused a moment, looking first into my eyes, then shifting his gaze to study Ke'tai. "I know you want to do what is best for her, Ke'tai. It would be the wiser choice to allow someone else to do the training. I have no problems with you helping her practice what she has already learned, but for the new summoning techniques, I feel it would be best if you were not the primary teacher."

Ke'tai looked down, and his jaw was clenched; he was obviously disappointed. He swallowed once, and said, "While I know you are right about this issue, I don't want to agree with it."

"Do not let your emotions cloud your judgment," Te'chok replied smoothly. "I know you have been waiting for this opportunity, but perhaps postponing it until the next apprentice is ready for your guidance would be best."

Ke'tai sighed, the sound full of frustration. "Fine. Whatever. Who's going to train her then?"

I closed my eyes briefly, and sighed. I had hoped he would fight the proposition; I wanted more than anything to train with him, be with him in all aspects of my life. And now this, another wrench thrown into the gears.

"I will," Te'chok replied simply, and I brought my gaze up to look at him, feeling rather angry. "She will need to work with me anyway, once her training is finished." He turned his gaze back to me, and his silver eyes were unreadable. "Your own ability surpasses mine," he stated. "Should your training finish successfully, you will become the next head of the Order, and there will be many things you will need to learn from me before that occurs. A summoner with your gift is very rare, and I have no interest in seeing you fail. This Order needs a new leader; my time has been long—too long, perhaps—and fresh ideas will be most welcome."

I found myself looking down at the wooden planks of the floor, feeling confused and overwhelmed. "That's not possible," I whispered after a moment, though I knew he was not lying to me. I simply did not want to accept what he had told me.

Te'chok laughed softly. "I assure you, Miss Grey, it is not only possible, but a very probable reality. *If* you complete your training, you will take my place. There is no denying that."

"He is right, Chandra," Ke'tai said softly, his voice resigned. "You should trust him."

I didn't want to trust him, didn't want to listen to him. I had been anticipating being able to learn from Ke'tai more than mere combat skills. The sheer disappointment of Te'chok's assessment left me irrationally angry. Coupled with our initial meeting and my story on the news, I was less than happy about the new teaching arrangement.

I sighed angrily and crossed my arms defiantly. "What if *I* don't want to accept this?" I asked, my voice coming out in a heated whisper. "First you show me this news message, and if that isn't enough to freak me out, then you decide Ke'tai isn't good enough as a teacher. I am not willing to accept that sort of judgment from *anyone*. Ke'tai is...I love him. And if he won't stand up for himself, I'll do it for him."

Te'chok blinked, startled by my outburst, and leaned back in his chair. He appeared surprised and wounded, as though he had been slapped. The air was heavy with tension, and the room had become suddenly stifling. I bit my lower lip, wondering if I had gone too far, and now I regretted my angry words toward the leader of the Order.

Ke'tai took one of my hands, and I glanced over at him, terrified of what I would see. He was smiling faintly, though he seemed uneasy. "That was probably not the best way to go about relating your feelings on this issue," he whispered, his smile widening slightly, amusement shining in his eyes. "I think that what Te'chok has said is right, though. If I were to pursue this track, and train you...Not only would you be distracted, but so would I. And I would probably screw something up, and then...I don't want to think what would happen to you, Chandra. I don't want to lose you. As disappointing as it is for both of us, it's the right thing to do. For you."

I nodded, feeling badly about what had just transpired between us. I turned back toward Te'chok, nervous and uncertain, the combination of which forced my stomach into knots. "I...I'm sorry."

Te'chok was gazing down, and as I spoke, he closed his eyes, drew a breath, and then brought his head up slowly to look at me once more. "I will not hold that outburst against you," he said evenly. "You must understand that I do not suggest things such as this without good reason. The original plan we came up with was for Ke'tai to finish your training once Il'zaks had completed his part; however, none of us ever anticipated Ke'tai falling in love with you, nor you with him. Please understand, I am attempting to look out for the welfare of you both, Miss Grey. Should either of you become distracted or careless with the training, there is a very high likelihood that you will not survive to see its completion, and that does not bode well for either of you."

I nodded. "I can see that, now," I replied hesitantly. "I'm sorry."

Te'chok chuckled, and did not appear to be upset, merely amused. I felt the tension that had grown in the air melt away, and I managed to relax slightly. "It is not unusual for someone in your position to react as you did," he stated with a shrug. "I am sure that the last week has been very trying, and you would welcome some rest. It is late regardless; I will show you to the guest apartments. As I am sure you noticed while you were making your way inside, there are not many others here at present; you may occupy the rooms of your choice."

Te'chok led us back to the lobby, then down one of the other corridors that branched away from it. Along this hallway were many doors, most of which were open, revealing the insides of fully furnished small apartments.

"There are enough apartments built into this complex that every summoner and each one of their assistants may have their own," Te'chok explained. "It was constructed that way as a precaution, should our long war with the hunters escalate to the point where we are all forced into hiding. In any case, there are enough apartments for each of you, and you can take your pick."

Il'zaks and the three trackers quickly disappeared into rooms on either side of the hall, while Ke'tai moved to stand near an open door. I lingered outside, feeling obligated to say something to Te'chok, but unable to find the correct words to amend the situation any further. Ke'tai's eyes were locked upon me, but he said nothing and merely watched.

"I'm really very sorry about what I said earlier," I mumbled after an awkward silence. "I know that my apology is not good enough, and that you are probably thinking I'm an insensitive, unthinking asshole—"

I had been staring down at the carpeted floor, afraid to look up to make eye contact with Te'chok. I was startled when he reached forward and put a hand on my shoulder. "I do not think any of that nonsense you just spouted, Miss Grey," he said quietly, his tone earnest. "We have both made mistakes today, and I must apologize for the stress I caused you between the news bit and my request that Ke'tai does not train you. I will accept your apology, should you also accept mine."

I ventured to look up at him, and his expression was genuine and expectant. I nodded, and said, "Yeah, okay."

He smiled then. "Let's forget about what happened between us today. We will be working together in the very near future, and I should like to look forward to that time, rather than dread it. You and Ke'tai have a good night."

# 12

# DISTRACTIONS

The next morning, I awoke alone and felt immediately disoriented. The bedroom of the apartment was cool and very dark, since it was below-ground and had no windows. I clutched the bed sheets around me, attempting to preserve some of the warmth left in them as I rose to find my duffel bag and some clean clothes. I stumbled through the dark room and over the scattered garments I had been wearing the day previously. After a few moments, I located the light switch near the door and flicked it on.

After I had dressed and made myself look presentable, I left the bedroom and found myself in the living room. There was a couch near the door to the bedroom, and an entertainment center with a television across from it. To my left was the door leading into the rest of the compound, and to the right a small kitchenette with a sink, mini fridge, microwave, and a handful of cabinets. The tall lamps in the corners of the room had been switched on, which I was thankful for; I had already stubbed my toes enough for one day in my attempt to find the light switch in the bedroom.

There was a small table next to the exit door, where a phone and extra keys to the apartment were kept. Ke'tai was standing at the table, the phone to his ear, speaking in a low tone. It looked as though he had just stumbled out of bed himself; he was wearing nothing but his boxers, and his spiked hair was rather flat. I wondered what had happened that required such an early morning phone call.

I made my way to the couch, and waited for him to finish his conversation. As I sat down, he turned around to face me, mouthing the word "sorry" while he listened to whomever was on the other end of the line. I shrugged; I knew by now that it was most likely business of the Order he had been called to discuss.

After a few more minutes, I heard him say, "Okay, I'll see you later then. Yeah, thanks. 'Bye." His tone was one of anger, the words coming out short and sharp. He hung up the phone with a soft click and walked over to where I was sitting. "I hope I didn't wake you," he said softly.

I shook my head. "No. What's going on?"

"Oh, that was Il'zaks," he replied with a frown. "He's wanting to train with you today, whenever you are ready for it. I wanted to come along..." He sighed, clearly frustrated.

I suspected that his frustration was related to our conversation with Te'chok from the night before. "Ke'tai, what's wrong?"

"Il'zaks was against it, based on what Te'chok said last night," he replied. "Apparently, I'm too much of a distraction to even stand back and observe now." He sighed, and ran his hand through his hair. "I'm sorry, Chandra. I'm just pissed."

I nodded. "I know. We'll be together often enough now, so missing out on a training session isn't that bad, is it? We both understand their reasons for it, even if we don't like it. I mean, it's only training. It's not that big a deal."

"It *is* a big deal, Chandra," he replied. "If something goes wrong, I don't want to be the second person to know; I want to be there, to know right away, to help if I can."

I looked down and sighed, disliking the reminder of the risks involved with this type of training. "From what I have been told, most of what can go wrong will happen when I go to sleep," I replied. "You'll be there, Ke'tai. I know that it doesn't make you any happier to hear that, but what choice do we have?"

He sighed, and when I looked up at him, his jaw was clenched stubbornly. "I'm coming with you today," he said after a moment. "Il'zaks will have to deal with that."

I sighed. "Ke'tai, don't turn this into some sort of battle with him. I like him, and I love you. I don't want to be caught in the middle of something like that."

"I'm still going with you," he replied stubbornly before vanishing into the bedroom to get dressed. "I'll prove them both wrong," he added loudly from the other room.

I rose from the couch and moved to stand in the doorway of the bedroom. "What is really going on?" I demanded. "This isn't about me, is it?"

He was silent for a time as he tugged one of his thin t-shirts over his head. "They think I'll be too much of a distraction for you, and that something bad will happen. I know better," he stated. "And I'm tired of them telling me that the next new person found with the summoning ability will be the one I am finally allowed to train. Then nothing comes of it! I'm tired of these broken promises, Chandra."

"Last night, you said yourself that Te'chok was right," I reminded him. "Besides, if you do come with me today, I'm not going to be able to do anything, knowing how pissed off you are at Il'zaks. You'll have to calm down before you join me today. A lot."

He frowned, and nodded. "Okay. I'm sorry. I just wanted to be there for you."

"I know, Ke'tai. I wanted that too, but…we can't always get what we want, you know?"

Ke'tai made a non-committal sound, and turned to face the mirror hanging on the bedroom wall to my right. There was a small table beneath the mirror, and he took up the half-empty bottle of hair gel he had placed there the night before. Pouring a little into his hands, he began running his hands through his hair to reform his customary spikes. I could tell he was thinking by his expression in the mirror, but he did not say anything until he had finished with his hair.

Turning around to face me once more, he said, "Chandra, I…I want the best for you, and…I know that what Te'chok said last night is the best path forward. But…I'm selfish, and I don't want to share you, especially knowing what your next lesson entails." He chuckled dryly but did not elaborate. He looked down at the carpeted floor between us. "I guess that's why I've reacted so badly to all of this change."

I looked down, uncertain of how to respond to this latest confession. Did he think I would be interested in Te'chok, for whatever reason? That was utter nonsense, but I wondered if he knew that for sure.

I was frowning in thought when his hand touched the side of my face. I looked up, startled, having failed to hear him walk across the room.

"I'll settle down, and I'll try to stop being angry," he said softly. "I promise."

I smiled up at him. He returned the gesture, and the smile he gave me was so beautiful it nearly took my breath away. "Ke'tai, you should know by now that you'll never have to 'share' me," I whispered after a moment. "I'm yours, and only yours, forever."

He grinned, and the familiar happy sparkle returned to his eyes. "Let's go catch some breakfast. Il'zaks is probably tired of waiting already…I, uh, forgot to tell you we were supposed to go and meet him."

I laughed, relieved that he had finally relaxed, and took his hand. "To breakfast it is, then."

There was a large cafeteria in the compound, where we met with Il'zaks that morning. Il'zaks occupied a seat near the center, but otherwise the big room was empty with the exception of the two cooks working behind the ordering counter. There were dozens of tables in the room, though it appeared as though they had seldom been used in the past.

We joined Il'zaks once we had placed an order for our breakfasts; I requested an egg and hash browns, while Ke'tai got a stack of six pancakes drenched in maple syrup. He had already devoured a large forkful, unable to wait, by the time we reached the table where Il'zaks was sitting.

"Hopefully Ke'tai has relayed my message to you, Chandra Grey," Il'zaks said as I took the seat opposite him. Ke'tai sat to my left.

I nodded. "You wanted to train today."

"Yes," he replied. "However, I have been thinking over the situation. I spoke with Te'chok again, after I spoke to Ke'tai over the phone. I believe I may have caused some unwarranted tension."

Ke'tai grunted, and focused intently on his pancakes. I sighed, and rolled my eyes. "Yeah, I think so," I replied.

"I apologize for that, Ke'tai," Il'zaks said evenly. "After I spoke to Te'chok, he felt that what I had said to you was taking things a bit too far, perhaps."

Ke'tai glanced at him, his expression one of displeasure.

Il'zaks sighed. "I think that it will be safe enough for you to attend Chandra's lessons. Te'chok agreed."

"I'm glad I have his blessing, then," Ke'tai replied sarcastically. "I was planning to come anyway, whether or not you agreed with it."

I was disappointed with how Ke'tai was handling the situation, though I did not know what had been said over the phone earlier. I had hoped he would forget his anger, as he had promised me, but it seemed that was not the case.

"It does not surprise me that you should react in such a way," Il'zaks replied smoothly, as though Ke'tai's words had no effect upon him. "You must promise me one thing, however, before we begin today."

Ke'tai looked up at the elder summoner again, but this time his silver eyes were wary. "What is it?"

"As I informed you previously, today's lesson covers the incubus and succubus," Il'zaks stated. "I do not want you becoming irrational based on what the incubus may say. Promise me that you will keep your wits, Ke'tai."

I glanced first at Il'zaks, and then at Ke'tai, confused.

Ke'tai snorted a laugh. "You think I'd get, what? Jealous?"

"That is exactly what I am concerned about," Il'zaks replied. "You know how these demons can be."

"Well, yeah. He won't be able to do anything during the lesson, though."

Il'zaks gazed steadily at Ke'tai, his expression unyielding. "I'm not concerned about the lesson itself, Ke'tai. I am concerned about what may be said—and you know how the dreams following usually turn out to be."

Ke'tai looked down at his plate, crestfallen, as though some terrible realization had just dawned upon him. "Yeah…I didn't really need that reminder, Il'zaks. I'd rather not think about it."

Still perplexed, the cryptic conversation before me only served to deepen my confusion. "Can I ask something?"

Il'zaks nodded. "Of course."

"When are you going to explain to me what is going on?"

Ke'tai burst out laughing, and Il'zaks chuckled. "We'll cover the details once you have finished eating," Il'zaks replied. "Sometimes we tend to forget that there are others around that do not know what we are speaking of. You will understand, one day, when you have reached the same age as I."

I finished eating quickly; my curiosity was burning and eager to be fulfilled. It had been over a week since my last training session, and even though that one had proven unpleasant, I was excited to be learning something new once more.

After we had finished eating, Ke'tai and I followed Il'zaks down another of the corridors that branched away from the lobby. This one led to a series of vast, empty rooms, furnished only with overhead lights. The rooms had very high ceilings, which caused our footsteps to echo as we stepped inside the one that Il'zaks had chosen for our lesson. Ke'tai closed the door after we had entered, and sat down with his back to the wall not far from it. I followed Il'zaks to the center of the room.

"There are two demons I will teach you about today," he began. "They are of the same type, but are of different genders, and that is an important aspect of this lesson. Both are experts at seduction and temptation."

Il'zaks paused, appearing thoughtful for a moment. "We will begin with the succubus—the female of the species. I could try and describe what their specialty is, but it is usually best to see for yourself. You have shown good intuition when it comes to understanding the demons you can summon, Chandra Grey, and I feel this will be no different."

"What do you mean by experts at seduction?" I asked, even though I had a good idea of what he was speaking of. "Do you mean…these demons can seduce *people*?"

Il'zaks chuckled, and nodded slightly. "You will see what I mean in a moment. Listen carefully as I call my succubus."

I heard Ke'tai snicker behind me, and wondered briefly what he thought was so amusing about the situation. As Il'zaks began his summoning, I was forced to ignore Ke'tai, and focused my attention solely upon my mentor. As had happened each time previously upon hearing the words needed to call the demon, I knew immediately the steps I must perform in order to summon the creature myself.

I was startled by the appearance of the demon that materialized once Il'zaks had finished. She appeared nearly human, though she sported a pair of black, bat-like wings that were folded neatly over her back. Her body was perfectly formed, and slender, yet curvaceous enough that I knew most men would have had their jaws hanging open if they gazed upon her. She was several inches taller than Il'zaks. She wore a short black skirt that looked to be made of leather, and a bikini-style top of the same material. Her hair was pale blonde, falling in soft waves to her fair shoulders. Her eyes were closed, the dark lashes long and slightly curled. I glanced at Ke'tai after a moment, and was relieved to see his eyes were fixed upon me, rather than the female demon.

"The succubus is very useful in extracting information from men," Il'zaks said after a moment. "She is also quite the resourceful assassin. However, their main talent is seduction, and even the most stoic of male hunters may have a difficult time resisting a succubus' charms."

Il'zaks' succubus smiled knowingly then, and opened her eyes, which I was shocked to see were a bloody red in color. "Many summoners cannot resist us either," she purred, glancing sideways toward Il'zaks.

I gaped at the pair for a moment, astounded that she would flirt with him so unabashedly.

Il'zaks appeared unaffected by the comment, and said, "They also have a mind to speak what they will. This is something that cannot be controlled, even though it is up to the summoner to dictate their actions. They are intelligent, and if you were to give them a task, they will successfully complete it without requiring guidance for their every movement."

"So, she said that on her own?" I asked, realizing now some of what had been suggested during breakfast.

Il'zaks nodded, and the she-demon replied, "Of course, I did."

Il'zaks chuckled. "Go ahead and try this for yourself, Chandra Grey."

I nodded and closed my eyes, clearing my mind in preparation for my dance. Once I was mentally prepared, I began moving, thinking the words Il'zaks had spoken in my mind. As I completed the motion, I could suddenly sense the mind of the she-demon I had called.

I opened my eyes to see another very much like Il'zaks', though she had very dark, almost black hair falling in a mass of curls, and olive-toned skin. Her thoughts focused upon her lust for the two men in the room, and a number of sexual activities she could perform with them, some of which I had never imagined possible.

"Oh my god," I said automatically, gaping at my succubus with a combination of disgust and surprise, which caused both Il'zaks and Ke'tai to laugh.

"Now you see why I mentioned that you must see for yourself," Il'zaks replied. He had released his demon, and was watching mine with unconcealed interest.

She had turned her red-eyed gaze upon Ke'tai, who was still sitting on the floor. "He's cute, can I have him?"

"Absolutely not!" I cried without thinking, which caused the two summoners to laugh again. However, the succubus' mind had instantly changed focus, and she was now gazing lustily in Il'zaks' direction.

"What about this one?" she asked, her eyes never leaving Il'zaks'.

I was flabbergasted. Nothing Il'zaks had taught me had prepared me for something like this, and I did not know what to do or say. Coupled with the deviant thoughts I was receiving from the she-demon, I felt incredibly awkward and out of my element. There were images I was glimpsing from her regarding Il'zaks that I would rather not have had in my head. Involuntarily, I grimaced.

Il'zaks chuckled. "Go ahead and release her, Chandra Grey. I will have you call her again once we have finished your lesson on the incubus; there is one aspect of these demons that you must become accustomed to, at the very least, and that will have to wait for the end."

Again, I heard Ke'tai snicker from his place near the door. Once I had released the demon, I glanced questioningly in his direction, and he gave me a knowing and mischievous smile.

"Another item that I should perhaps mention is that these demons will react a bit differently if you call them to interact with humans," Il'zaks stated. "Around summoners, they are flirtatious, but not malicious. The incubus and succubus are rather disdainful towards ordinary humans, however, and if you allow them to have free reign to do as they will, they will first take their pleasure, and then they will kill their victim. It is in their nature to murder, if left unchecked."

I nodded, thinking over his words carefully. "What you're telling me is that I need to be careful with these, and how I use them?"

"Yes, Chandra Grey." He paused a moment, then asked, "Are you ready for the second portion of your lesson today?"

When I nodded, he was silent for a moment, and then began the second summoning. The words were nearly identical, yet there was a subtle difference at the end. The movements required of me were the same as those used to call the succubus.

Il'zaks' incubus was tall and broad-shouldered, shirtless, with perfectly sculpted muscles. He had the same dark, bat-like wings the succubus had sported, though his were proportionally smaller than hers had been, and did not appear large enough to allow him to fly. His skin was bronzed, as though he had spent weeks at the beach tanning, his hair was cut very short and was a tawny color. As with the succubus, his eyes were a deep crimson. Had he been human, he would have been gorgeous; one of those men featured on the covers of magazines or in advertisements. He wore a pair of dark colored pants, either black or dark brown, I could not tell which.

I turned my attention to Il'zaks as he said, "Now, it's your turn."

I nodded, closed my eyes again, and began to dance. When my own incubus was called forth, I knew immediately, and I was repulsed by what I sensed within his mind. His thoughts, naturally, were focused on the only female present: me. The imaginary scenes I was receiving featured the both of us naked, and the myriad things he wished he could do with me in that state. I felt my face flush, and my stomach clench into knots.

When I finally opened my eyes, forcing the demon's thoughts into the background where they were not so distracting, I ventured to study him more closely. He had a physique almost identical to Il'zaks' incubus, and he was dressed in a similar fashion. He had raven-colored hair that was just long enough to cascade over his forehead.

His lips twisted into a deviant smile, and he glanced backwards over his shoulder towards Ke'tai. "Your girlfriend's hot," he said, grinning. "Too bad I have to share."

My jaw dropped, and I stared incredulously at the incubus as he turned his handsome face in my direction. Ke'tai had risen to his feet, but appeared nonchalant, as though he had been expecting this outcome.

"You can't do anything I don't want you to," I said after a moment.

"Not right now, I can't," the incubus replied, and glanced back toward Ke'tai once more. "But tonight…That's another story."

I was furious. I heard the incubus laugh wickedly before I abruptly released him, but I had squeezed my eyes shut, and was unable to see his expression. I realized after a moment that I was standing very rigid, shaking from my sudden rage.

Ke'tai was suddenly there, his hands resting gently on my shoulders. "Chandra, are you alright?" he whispered, his tone concerned.

I swallowed hard, and nodded. "Yeah, I just...wasn't expecting that. I lost my temper." I opened my eyes then to meet his gaze, and he looked relieved. "Tell me, though—does every man have thoughts like that?"

Ke'tai blinked, surprised by the question. "Uh...I, um...can't say that for sure, but, uh...I can tell you that most don't think like that *all* of the time."

I wanted to ask him if *he* harbored such thoughts, but I was afraid of what the answer might be. I kept my mouth shut, instead, uncertain if I truly wanted to know that piece of information.

I turned to Il'zaks after a moment. "Is there any way to control what comes out of their mouths?" I asked, my tone pleading.

Il'zaks shook his head. "I told you earlier, they will say what they wish. You can give them tasks, which they will complete for you successfully, but they possess more free-will than most other demons do...which is a blessing in some cases."

"What do you mean by that?" I asked.

Il'zaks smiled ruefully. "Do you actually want to be in control of an incubus' actions while he is having sex?"

My jaw dropped open again, and I stared at the elder summoner for several seconds in shock. Not only had that thought never occurred to me, but to have something of the sort come out of Il'zaks' mouth was surprising. "Oh," I said after a moment, "I hadn't thought of that."

Ke'tai snickered. "You made that pretty obvious," he said.

I frowned in his direction, and he laughed.

"There is one more aspect of these demons that you will need to become accustomed to, as I said earlier," Il'zaks said after a moment. He appeared amused by my reaction to his last question. "You will need to summon your succubus again."

I nodded, and I heard Ke'tai chuckle again. It was clear that he knew what was about to happen, and though I had my suspicions, I was not completely certain of Il'zaks' intentions. Pushing my questions aside for the moment, I focused on calling the succubus once more. This time, I was prepared for the barrage of lewd images I knew would be seeping into my mind through our mental link, but I was pleasantly surprised when the succubus paid no heed to Ke'tai whatsoever.

"Have your demon follow me, Chandra Grey," Il'zaks said quietly after a moment. "Allow her to have her way with me, once I have led her back to my apartment."

I stared at him in disbelief, struggling to comprehend what I'd just heard. "What?"

"It is the only safe way to learn what it is like to have a succubus' or incubus' thoughts in your head, when they are at the height of passion," he explained. "Sending them with another summoner means they will not harm their target; sending them with a human would be dangerous, and the human would likely wind up dead. This is something you must learn, if you plan to successfully complete your training."

I bit my lower lip, uncomfortable with the outcome of this lesson. Finally, I nodded, reluctantly informing the succubus of what she must do. *Go with him. Do what you will once you're in his room.*

I felt her thrill of excitement as she walked toward Il'zaks. She smiled enigmatically and swayed her hips in an overtly provocative manner. I felt ill.

Il'zaks made his way out of the practice room, and I simply stood where I was for several moments, unable and unwilling to comprehend what had just occurred. Ke'tai made his way toward me, gently taking my left arm in his right. He led me back the way we had come.

When we were nearing our own apartment, Ke'tai said, "I probably should have warned you how this would turn out. I'm sorry."

I shook my head. "Don't be sorry, Ke'tai. He's right, though, isn't he?"

Ke'tai shrugged. "I guess so, but…Il'zaks kind of has a fetish with succubus. Every person he's trained on this, he does the same thing. There are other summoners who would warn you to be prepared for what these demons will do, but won't force you into acting with them in such a way. It's strange, but I think what Il'zaks does actually prepares you better for what to expect, even though it's a bit unorthodox."

We had reached the door to our apartment, and Ke'tai led me to the couch in the living room. I collapsed onto it rather ungracefully, both because I was still in shock, and because I was beginning to receive images from the succubus as to what she was currently doing with Il'zaks. I made a face, betraying my disgust.

"Are you okay?" Ke'tai asked.

I nodded. "Yeah, but…there's a new scary place inside my head regarding Il'zaks, and it's kind of hard to ignore it." I sighed. "I don't know if I'll ever be able to look at him the same way again, Ke'tai."

Ke'tai sat down beside me, and offered up a sad, yet knowing, smile. "If it makes you feel any better, I went through the same thing with him. It's not pleasant, and I don't think he will blame you if you decide to start working with Te'chok from now on. It's a risk he's willing to take with every one of his students."

I had to concentrate hard on Ke'tai's words in order to understand what he was saying. The succubus' thoughts were difficult to ignore, and were growing increasingly more sexual in nature as she toyed with Il'zaks. I sighed.

"He'll be upset if I released her now, wouldn't he?" I asked Ke'tai.

Ke'tai nodded. "Not only that, but your demon would be upset as well, and that could prove badly for you when you go to sleep next. Let her finish, and come back to you afterwards, before you release her. I know what is playing in your mind right now can't be pleasant, Chandra, but Il'zaks was right—you do have to learn to live with it if you plan on becoming a summoner." He paused a moment to study me carefully. "I worry that you may have dismissed your incubus too soon, love, but I suppose only time will tell."

I scarcely heard his words. "I hope she finishes soon. I'd like to be able to think straight again."

Ke'tai chuckled. "It will get easier with time," he promised. "Practice with these demons makes you better able to ignore distractions, no matter what you're doing. Believe me."

"Can you distract me from her?" I asked after a moment.

He grinned, and kissed me. "I thought you'd never ask."

# 13

# CONTROL

I awoke the next morning after a night filled with one very long and unpleasant dream in which the incubus played a rather disturbing role. He had made good upon his promise to Ke'tai the day before; he'd had his way with me during the night, repeatedly, and without regard to my well-being or emotional state. All the while, the succubus had stood by, watching, at times silently, though for the greater part of the ordeal, she made lewd comments or laughed mirthlessly. They were a breed that cared nothing for others, and sought only the pursuit of their own twisted and deviant pleasures. Even now, many years later, I do not wish to speak of the details concerning that particular nightmare.

When I finally surfaced from the dark and disturbing dream that had tormented me all the long night, I was sore in every muscle of my body, as though the ordeal had been more than a mere figment of my warped imagination. This was not the first time such physical manifestations had come to me after a night's worth of dreaming; I recalled I had felt much the same way after my first summoning with the *Zombi Cadavre*.

I rolled over onto my back, and stared up at the ceiling of the dark room for some time after I woke. Ke'tai was laying on his side next to me, propped up on one elbow, watching me silently. I could see him in the periphery of my vision, and his brow was creased with worry. When I made no further movements and said nothing for several minutes, he took it upon himself to make something of a conversation.

"Chandra, are you feeling alright?" he asked softly.

I turned to face him slowly, feeling each muscle protest as I did so. "Not really," I replied. The darkness was nearly absolute in the windowless room, but there was enough light cast from the digital clock on the nightstand behind me that I could just make out his features. I caught a glint of green light reflected in his eyes for the briefest of moments before he dropped his gaze and nodded.

"He was none too gentle with you, was he?"

I clenched my jaw and winced involuntarily. I did not want to remember what I had endured during the night, but at the mention of it, the horror of it all came flooding back into my mind. I closed my eyes, unable to make an answer for the knot that had suddenly formed in my chest. Hot tears squeezed from between my closed eyelids, and I simply shook my head.

I wondered just what I had gotten myself into, and not for the first time. I knew there was no way I could return to the innocent girl that I'd been before that first strange meeting with Il'zaks; on that night I had unwittingly agreed to leave everything and everyone I had ever known behind in order to become something other than a mere human. It had seemed so appealing then, that offer of power; so tantalizing, so alluring, I had been unable to stop myself from going down this path that would more than likely end in my very destruction. And yet, I was eternally grateful to Il'zaks for having shown me down that very pathway; I had met Ke'tai, I had fallen in love—truly in love for the first time in my life—and I would not change that for the world. No matter how difficult this path may become, I would remain steadfast and see it through to the end, if for no other reason than I knew I was meant to be with Ke'tai.

Ke'tai reached toward me with trembling fingers, and touched the side of my face lightly, brushing away the tears he encountered there. "The incubus are usually not so rough with their summoners," he said softly after a moment, and his voice cracked with emotion. "Chandra, I'm so sorry...It's my fault."

I moved my head only slightly, and opened my eyes so that I could meet his gaze. "That's not true, Ke'tai."

He shook his head, his expression tormented. "No, it really is my fault," he insisted. "It's because I was there at your lesson yesterday. Sometimes, they feel threatened if someone you love is in the room, and then they'll show you no mercy. I should have listened to Il'zaks. I should never have gone with you yesterday. I was too proud, too pigheaded, to do the right thing."

I made no reply. Somehow, I knew in my heart that Ke'tai was right, but I did not want to believe it. I wanted to think that what had occurred during the night was only due to the demons' lust, and there was nothing more to it.

"That was probably the worst thing I could have done," Ke'tai went on, and his voice was raw and pained. "Somehow you made it through the night... They would have killed you, Chandra. I...don't know why they didn't."

I closed my eyes again, and fresh tears escaped from the corners of my eyes. He was right, and I knew that. This training was going to kill me, before the end, but I didn't want to put voice to my concern. He was distressed enough as it was by this apparent near-miss.

"I...I think they came very close," I whispered into the darkness, without opening my eyes. It hurt to move even the tiniest amount, and despite having slept the whole night through, I felt exhausted.

He was silent for a while, and then he sat up slowly, carefully, as though he were trying not to cause the mattress to shift even a millimeter as he did so. "I love you, Chandra," he whispered. "And I've been stupid, really, really stupid. I hope you can forgive me."

He sounded as though he were the one in pain. I opened my eyes once more, seeking him in the darkness. He was staring down at his knees, which he had drawn up to his chest, his arms circling them, hugging them to himself. His jaw was clenched, and his face had become a mask of agony. I felt my heart breaking to see him in such a state.

"Ke'tai, there's nothing to forgive," I said softly after a moment, and closed my eyes again. "There was no way to know that he'd react like that...And even if there was, I don't want to hear about it. I wanted you to be there with me, and I'm glad you were."

Ke'tai swallowed hard, and released a pained sigh. "I didn't want to think Il'zaks and Te'chok were right," he said after another moment of silence. "I wanted to believe that I could still train you just as effectively as they could, or even better because I do love you. But, they were right, Chandra. I'd make a mess of things, and I'd hate myself afterwards."

"You don't know that, Ke'tai."

He swallowed again. "No, I do know that. I...I nearly killed you because I couldn't bear the thought of you facing these things alone. Had you failed to awaken this morning, I wouldn't have been able to bear that pain. Il'zaks would have come in to find two dead bodies instead of just one."

My eyes snapped open, and I stared up at him through a mist of tears. "Don't say that," I managed after a moment, my voice strangled due to the growing knot that had formed in my throat.

He turned his head slightly to look at me, and his eyes glittered with unshed tears. "I'm only telling you the truth, Chandra," he replied. "I couldn't live without you."

I forced my left arm to move, despite the ache in the muscles and the leaden feeling that remained in the limb. I touched the side of his face gently. "I'm still here, Ke'tai. Let's not think about what might have happened, and focus on what is."

He nodded and dropped his gaze, though he still wore that same agonized expression.

"I love you," I said to him. "We'll get through this, you'll see." I tried to sound cheerful, though I felt that I was lying to him, instantly hating myself for it. I couldn't stand to see him in such pain any longer, and I hoped my words would do something to improve his mood.

Finally, he sighed. "I should call Il'zaks, and let him know you're awake," he said quietly. "I'll have him bring us some breakfast...you'll need to eat."

I dropped my arm back to my side, and simply lay there with my eyes closed. I had never been so thoroughly exhausted before, nor had I ever experienced such pain, caused only by the slightest of movements. I simply wanted to sleep, forever if need be.

Ke'tai rose carefully, then quickly dressed, not bothering to take the time to style his hair, which was the flattest I had seen it yet. He turned on the little lamp near the door before he exited the room. A moment later I heard his voice, muffled as it came through the wall, speaking with Il'zaks on the phone. I was unable to hear what he said, but after a short time he returned, pulling one of the wooden chairs from the other room behind him.

He set the chair beside the bed near where I lay, and sat down heavily. "Il'zaks will be here soon," he said softly. "Try to stay awake, Chandra.

Sleeping now could prove to be dangerous; you have to eat something first, and Il'zaks will probably want to ask you some questions."

I sighed, knowing as always that there was some deeper reason behind his words than simply having to answer a few questions and eat. "Tell me why, Ke'tai," I whispered, opening my eyes a fraction.

"Why, what?"

"There's always a reason, I'm finding, when you or Il'zaks say I need to do something. Always a reason…Why can't I sleep now?"

"You're vulnerable, Chandra," he replied. "If you fall asleep now, you will only descend back into that nightmare, and this time, he'll finish what he started. I think that's what he wanted all along—for you to wake up, so that I would believe everything was fine. He could make what he sees as his triumph all the more devastating for me. He sees me as a rival, Chandra."

"Why wasn't this something that came up before?" I asked. I closed my eyes again; I was so incredibly tired.

"Chandra, stay awake," Ke'tai pleaded.

I opened my eyes again, but it was a struggle. "Tell me why, Ke'tai. I need to know."

"The other demons all obeyed you automatically, and they saw you as their master," he said. "It was obvious, from watching you, that you were in complete control. We had no real worries about you not waking the next day with those, but yesterday…" He sighed painfully, and trailed off.

"What happened yesterday that was different?" I asked, my words coming out in a mere mumble.

"Yesterday, you weren't in complete control," he replied. "It's always difficult with the incubus and succubus, because they will say whatever comes to their minds, and the summoner has no control over that. But you lost your temper, and sent the incubus away before you probably should have. It was a natural reaction, given what he said, but I think it angered him. It doesn't matter to him that you are training to be a summoner; last night, he saw you as his next human victim, but he also had the additional motivation to make you suffer so that I would as well. This wouldn't be the first time something like this has happened, and the only way to make it safe for you is to have you regain some of your strength and summon him again. Otherwise, he will be waiting for you the moment you drop off to sleep, and then he'll finish what he's started. He only let you awaken to put me at ease, just so my pain at what he plans will be that much greater. He knows you sent him away because of what he said to me."

I thought back to the previous day's lesson. It seemed as though it had been ages ago, and I was having difficulty remembering the exact words he had spoken. I could see the incubus standing there, glancing back towards Ke'tai, who had been standing near the door of the practice room. I had said he couldn't do anything I didn't want him to, and he had replied with a smirk.

*"Not right now, I can't. But tonight...that's another story."*

And he had laughed. I had been furious, thinking only of Ke'tai in that instant in which I dismissed the incubus. Il'zaks had not said anything to me about dismissing him prematurely, but now that I began to think about it, Il'zaks had been a bit preoccupied with his own desires as well. Images floated into the forefront of my mind unbidden of Il'zaks and the succubus, and I squeezed my eyes shut tightly in a futile attempt to ward them off.

"Are you alright?" Ke'tai asked uncertainly.

I managed a tired laugh. "Sorry. I just thought about Il'zaks and...what he did yesterday. And now those pictures are in my head again."

Ke'tai laughed, a genuinely happy and amused sound. Hearing him brightened the world around me significantly, and I suddenly felt as though some weight had been removed from my body. I was able to move freely again.

"You aren't the only one with X-rated pictures of Il'zaks floating around in your head," he replied with a smile. "Remember, I've been there too."

I laughed, but was cut short due to a rapid knocking at the door of the apartment. Ke'tai smiled, sadly now, and stood up. "That will be Il'zaks," he said before disappearing out the bedroom door to allow the elder summoner inside.

I stared up at the ceiling, imagining pictures within the popcorn texture in an attempt to force myself to remain awake. It was only a few brief moments before Il'zaks arrived, but my struggle made it seem an eternity. Il'zaks wore a concerned frown and quickly took the chair Ke'tai had vacated. I could hear some noises in the kitchen, presumably made by Ke'tai.

"Ke'tai has told me you are not well this morning," Il'zaks said. His voice was quiet, subdued, and his silver eyes were solemn. "He is looking for a tray for the breakfast I've brought you. I am worried, Chandra Grey."

I nodded slightly. "So is Ke'tai. He told me—"

"Good," Il'zaks replied, cutting me off. "I should have been more careful yesterday, and I should have warned you. I apologize for my lack of foresight—again. I have made one mess after another of your training, it seems."

He sighed, and ran a hand through his perfectly combed hair, disheveling it some. It was apparent that he was frustrated about the situation. He sighed again, then looked into my eyes.

"There is something I must tell you, Chandra Grey," he said softly. "I am usually much more attentive to my students than I have been with you. I have been asked to join the Board of Elders within the Order, and the preparations for that position consume much of my time. I was offered this opportunity only sixteen days before I first encountered you in Seattle, and between the excitement of discovering someone with so much potential and the time and mental resources that I must put into my preparations for joining the Elders, I have been a very poor teacher to you indeed. I am going to put my preparations on hold for the next few weeks, while I help you complete this stage of your training."

I gazed at him, but made no reply. Ke'tai had mentioned something about Il'zaks possibly joining the Board of Elders, but I had no idea what that involved, nor that it had consumed so much of his time. Only now did I understand some of what he had done, and the purpose of his trip away from Seattle a few weeks ago.

"I should not have told you what I just did, Chandra Grey," Il'zaks said quietly after a moment, "but I feel it was something that you must know. Traditionally, those in training do not learn the internal workings of the Order until they have completed said training, but you have become an exception to many of the rules we have in place. It is not only because of your great potential as a summoner, but because a summoner has fallen very much in love with you. It is a rare occurrence that we find love, and Te'chok himself was the one who issued the orders that some rules may be broken for you. We must see you through to the completion of your training, for your sake and that of Ke'tai."

At that moment, Ke'tai appeared in the doorway bearing a thin metal tray with a plate of fruit, some scrambled eggs, and two pieces of toast. Slowly, I forced myself to sit up, feeling every joint, muscle and tendon scream in protest.

"There's some orange juice too, if you'd like it," Ke'tai said, setting the tray down carefully in my lap. When I nodded, he headed out of the room once more.

The aroma of the food caused my stomach to growl, and despite the aches and pains I was feeling, I realized that I was very hungry. I began to eat before Ke'tai returned with the glass of juice, and Il'zaks sat beside me silently for a time. Almost immediately, I began to feel better. The exhaustion that had plagued me since I had awakened slowly began to dissipate.

"Tell me something, Il'zaks," I said after a moment. "Why is it rare for a summoner to find love?"

Il'zaks chuckled briefly, and nodded. "I suspected you might ask about that," he replied. "There are not very many of us, compared to the number of humans there are on this world, and there are very few women amongst our Order. Why that is, I do not know."

He paused a moment, and glanced toward the doorway. Following his gaze, I noticed Ke'tai was standing there, smiling wearily. He held a glass of orange juice in his hands, and was leaning casually against the doorjamb. "Go on," Ke'tai said after a moment, rousing himself and coming toward me to set the juice on the tray along with the rest of my breakfast. He sat down on the bed beside me, carefully, so that he did not tip the tray—or cause me any further discomfort.

"What I was trying to say is that the chances we have to find someone to fall in love with are very limited," Il'zaks said. He looked down at his hands, and appeared sad, yet thoughtful. "There have been those who fall in love with a tracker—someone in the position of Trey or Carmine, for example. While those relationships may flourish for a while, it is always painful for both in the end; the summoner does not age, and usually we outlive those counterparts who choose to assist us. It is painful seeing the one you love grow old before your eyes, while you remain forever young."

I looked upon Il'zaks with a new admiration, as the realization dawned on me. "You've been there, haven't you?"

He smiled, but his eyes remained sad. "Yes, Chandra Grey, I have. You and Ke'tai are very fortunate, indeed."

The room fell silent for a time, and I continued with my breakfast. Ke'tai slid his arm around my waist after a few moments, and I glanced over to see him smiling, his silver eyes twinkling. I flashed him a grin before returning my attention to the food. It seemed that every bite I swallowed made me feel better; already the aches had faded to a much more tolerable level, and the fatigue was nearly gone.

"When you have finished, you must summon the incubus again," Il'zaks said quietly after the silence had stretched for several minutes. "When you do so, you must keep control of your emotions, Chandra Grey. You cannot release him at the first inappropriate comment that comes from his mouth—and I know from past experience that there will be several of those. You will have to bend him to your will, and task him to do some menial things. He will dislike it, but he will see it as a just punishment for his behavior last night. Such is the way of these matters. Until your dominance is made clear to him, you will be in danger, so it is best to set things straight now, while we have the opportunity."

"What sort of menial things?" I asked, hoping with every fiber of my being that he did not want me to send the demon off to seduce another person within the compound. I'd had enough of that experience yesterday, and did not want to go through it again so soon.

"Have him take your breakfast dishes back to the kitchens, or wash your laundry," Il'zaks replied. "Very menial things such as those, things that would normally go against his nature. He will resent it at first, but make it clear that it is his punishment for what occurred overnight. Once he has submitted to your will—and you should realize when this has happened—he will no longer be able to drag your conscious mind into his realm while you sleep."

I narrowed my eyes, contemplating his words. "Is that what happens?"

Il'zaks nodded. "That is yet another aspect of our kind that we do not fully understand," he replied. "We have determined that the trainee's consciousness is somehow lured away while they sleep, and pulled into the demons' plane, or dimension, whichever it happens to be. We refer to them as dreams, for that is what they appear to be. The demons will choose to submit to you, or in some instances, they will not. The times in which the demons do not submit are those in which the summoner-in-training forfeits their life. You have had a very close call this time around, Chandra Grey, and I do apologize again for my lack of foresight. I am thankful beyond measure that you have made it this far today."

"Is that why sometimes, like today, I wake up and I feel like what had happened had been real?" I asked. "It's because it *was* happening, on some plane."

Il'zaks nodded again, and said, "You feel as though it actually happened, because it *did* happen. Not to your physical body, but to your conscious mind; the mind is a very powerful force, Chandra Grey, and it can manifest many things that your physical body never encountered. You felt weak and injured because your consciousness had been, even though your body was wholly untouched."

I swallowed hard, trying to wrap my head around what he had said. I felt as though I had walked into a bad science fiction movie half way through and was completely lost as to what was happening on screen.

"So...you're saying that...the mind can become separated from the body?" I asked, my disbelief evident in my tone. "I thought that was impossible."

Il'zaks chuckled. "It is not impossible," he replied, "but it does take a great force of will to do so. I have never met a person who could do so of their own will, though there are stories—myths, you might say—that speak of just such a feat. What happens to us during our training is not done because we wish it to be; it is done because that is what the demons themselves wish for. It is a two-way street; you summon them, and when you are less aware—usually when you drop off to sleep—they reciprocate the action. Only after the summoning has gone successfully in both directions will the demons truly become loyal to you. But in some cases, the summoner must call a demon a second time in order for things to be finalized."

I nodded thoughtfully, and finished off the last of the eggs on my plate.

"If you want to know more about the mind-body thing, you should talk to Te'chok," Ke'tai said after a moment. "That's his area of interest. He's done some really ground-breaking research the last few years."

I drained the glass of orange juice, then sat back and sighed. I was feeling infinitely better than I had been, but I was afraid to face the incubus again. The room was silent for a long moment before Il'zaks spoke once more.

"We should get this summoning finished," he said quietly. "I will wait in your living room while you dress and make yourself ready, Chandra Grey."

I nodded as he swiftly rose from the chair and left Ke'tai and I alone in the room. Ke'tai lifted the tray of dishes and set them at the end of the bed before he also stood and went to close the door.

"Are you going to be alright?" he asked softly, returning to sit at my side.

How was I supposed to answer such a question? I wondered. Physically, I was feeling much better, as though the pain I had experienced earlier had been nothing more than a mere figment of my imagination. But I was terrified. I knew that I could not afford to make any further mistakes, and yet, I didn't know exactly what I was expected to do, or how I was to know when the incubus had been sufficiently "punished" with household chores that he would no longer be a threat to my life.

I sighed, feeling weary. "I don't know, Ke'tai," I said finally.

He managed a strained smile, his silver eyes filled with unspoken concern. "Are you still in pain?" he asked.

I shook my head. "It's not that…I'm feeling much better than I was," I replied, deciding that I needed to attempt an explanation for what was running through my mind. "It's just…how am I supposed to know when it's safe for me again? Il'zaks said I should feel something, but what should I expect to feel?" My voice broke with emotion, and I turned my face away to hide the tears that had come unbidden to my eyes. "He almost killed me, Ke'tai," I finished in a hoarse whisper. "I…I don't want to die."

Ke'tai's arms wrapped around my shoulders, and he pulled me into his embrace. "I don't want that either, Chandra," he said thickly after a moment. "We've got to trust Il'zaks in this; he's been down this pathway before, and he's gotten others through it. He'll get you through it, too."

I desperately wanted to believe him, but I simply couldn't make myself do so. I attributed that feeling to the dread I was experiencing, the sick—yet irrational—certainty that I was not going to make it through the day. After several long minutes, in which we simply sat there clinging to one another, I finally raised my head from where it had been resting upon Ke'tai's shoulder.

"Il'zaks is right," I said wearily, "I have to do this. I can't spend the whole day hiding in here with you—even though I'd prefer that."

He smiled, but the expression was sad. "Let's get through this, then," he replied, and rose from his place on the bed. He walked toward the little table and the mirror that hung above it, stooping down to pick up my duffel bag and its dwindling supply of clean clothing. I mustered the strength required to haul myself out of bed as Ke'tai found a clean pair of blue jeans and a plain black long-sleeved t-shirt in the bag. He tossed the items onto the bed, and said, "That's all the clean stuff you have left," before attending to his morning ritual of gelling his hair into its usual mass of untidy spikes. With my back to him, I changed from my rumpled pajamas into the clothing he had found in my duffel bag, only turning to face him once I had finished dressing.

"I need to do laundry," I complained, walking to the table where he stood to retrieve my hairbrush.

"Well, let's have your demon work on that once you've brought him back here," Ke'tai said. "That should be a task he'll dislike; even *I* don't like to do laundry."

I managed a half-hearted laugh, and nodded. "I'll see what Il'zaks has to say first."

I brushed my hair quickly, and pulled it up into a high ponytail. Ke'tai cocked his head to one side as I set the brush down on the table again.

"You look good with your hair up like that," he said after a moment. "You should do that more often, instead of always leaving it down."

I shrugged. "Maybe I will," I replied, and walked towards the door. "Let's get this over with, shall we?"

Il'zaks was sitting, patiently as always, on one end of the couch when we emerged from the bedroom. He stood swiftly, almost too quickly for my eyes to follow the movement, his expression grave.

"You should have no trouble summoning the incubus here," he said as I came to stand near him. "Be aware that he may attempt to disobey you when he first arrives. You *must* put all of your focus into breaking his will so that he will do your bidding. This is going to take every ounce of concentration you can muster, Chandra Grey."

I closed my eyes briefly, and swallowed hard, before nodding. I drew a shaky breath, and said, "I'm as ready now as I ever will be. I need to do this, and be done with it."

"Before you call him, let Ke'tai and I summon something first," Il'zaks said quickly. "We should be prepared for anything. I am not about to lose you, after you have already come so far."

I bit my lip, and looked down nervously. I heard Il'zaks' powerful, commanding tone begin almost at once with the summoning of his succubus, and a moment later Ke'tai's voice joined in. I had never been present as Ke'tai summoned before, and I couldn't help but raise my head to watch him, staring in awe-struck silence. He sang the words in a soft tenor, calling to him a pair of *djinni*. I had not realized that his singing voice would be so beautiful.

He caught my gaze as he finished, and his face flushed slightly, as though he were embarrassed. He smiled uncertainly before closing his eyes to work with the two demons he had called.

"Go ahead with your summoning now, Chandra Grey," Il'zaks said, breaking me from my daze.

With some effort, I pulled my gaze away from Ke'tai and turned away, so I was facing in another direction. I could not afford to become distracted at all during this process. I drew another unsteady breath, and began to dance.

As soon as I had finished, I could feel the incubus' presence in the room. His burning desire to possess me again as he had during the night was coupled with a cold fury that was directed at Ke'tai. His raw emotions were unlike anything I had experienced previously. His goal had been to finish what he had started during the long nightmare, just as the summoners had suspected; I could feel his bitter disappointment when he realized that I was not alone. Slowly, I opened my eyes to look upon him, determined to set things right.

He stood within arm's reach of me. His muscular arms were crossed before his chest, and his chin was held high in defiance. His scarlet eyes were cold and unreadable; his lips were drawn into a sneer.

*You cannot get away with what you did to me last night,* I thought to him, my anger rising as I looked upon his face once more. *And you* will *not.*

The vehemence I encountered within my own thoughts surprised me, and the incubus blinked and appeared uncertain for the briefest of moments before his handsome face twisted into hate-filled leer. "You can't win," he stated.

I clenched my jaw, my ire rising. I would not stand for his insubordination any longer; I would force him to obey. I had no other choice, if I wished to survive this encounter.

I drew myself up as straight as I could, though he still towered over me by several inches, and I looked up squarely into his eyes. "*I* am the one in control here," I said, my voice coming out in an angry whisper. "*You* are going to listen to me, or face the consequences."

His eyes narrowed, and he raised his right arm as though to push me away. I sensed his intent, and immediately I forced my will upon him. "You will not touch me again."

He staggered backwards, as though he had been dealt a heavy blow. His arm remained in the same reaching position, though the contact he had sought to make never occurred. His eyes were wary now, an expression of uncertainty upon his face.

I was not about to relax my guard, though I could sense as he began to realize my words were true: I *was* in control. I instructed him to collect the breakfast dishes from the bedroom and take them to the kitchens through our mental bond. As Il'zaks had predicted, he was loath to perform such a trivial task. He found it demeaning.

"I am not some errand-runner," he replied haughtily. "I am an incubus. These tasks are better left for some other, lesser demon, like your boyfriend's *djinni*." He practically spat the word boyfriend, as though simply acknowledging Ke'tai left a bad taste in his mouth.

"Not today," I replied as icily as I could. "You've got to learn who is in charge, and whom to respect. After last night, you're lucky I haven't tasked you to scrubbing the floors with a toothbrush."

He winced, as though he had been slapped. "Fine," he replied sulkily, glancing toward Il'zaks with a resentful glare before disappearing into the bedroom to do as I had commanded. A moment later he emerged bearing the tray of dishes, and then stalked out of the apartment without another word.

As soon as he had gone, I released a shaky sigh, relieved that things seemed to be going according to plan. I knew I could not allow myself to relax; the incubus was still very angry, and did not want to admit his defeat. I continued to focus on his every movement as he traversed the hallways to the compound's kitchen, unwilling to relinquish an ounce of the mental grip I had upon him. I could not, until I was completely certain that it was safe to do so.

"It is going better than I had hoped it would," Il'zaks said after a time. "You are a strong summoner, Chandra Grey, but I still feared the worst." He glanced at Ke'tai and said, "I do not think we will need our demons for this. The worst of his insolence is most likely spent."

Ke'tai nodded and closed his eyes briefly. I watched as the pair of dancing blue lights faded from my sight and disappeared. Il'zaks' succubus blew a kiss towards each of them in turn before she suddenly winked out of existence. I refocused all of my energy on the incubus once more, noting that he was returning to the apartment.

A moment later he stalked through the door, stopping just inside. He crossed his arms, emanating displeasure. "You send me out there, and the only person I encountered took no notice of me," he said acidly. "Do you know how disappointing that is?"

I could sense his thoughts and feelings all too well, and I knew that he was only voicing this complaint in an attempt to anger me. "Well, we can't always get whatever we want, now can we?" I replied. "Besides, I can't control who might be walking through the hallway." I paused, and glanced toward Il'zaks, who nodded in encouragement. "By the way, I need my laundry done today. And Ke'tai's as well."

The incubus narrowed his eyes and clenched his jaw. "I'm finished with your errands," he replied, unable to conceal his anger any longer. "And I am not about to do any task that will help *him*," he added, his eyes flashing in unadulterated rage as they darted briefly in Ke'tai's direction.

"You aren't finished, and you will," I replied, closing my eyes in order to better focus my thoughts. With a force of will, I pushed him toward the bedroom, where he collected the basket heaped with clothes in need of washing. I hoped that I would not have to battle his will much longer; it was beginning to wear on me, and a headache was building from the mental exertion.

The laundry facilities were in a part of the compound that I had not yet been to; I was forced to command the incubus to follow me while Il'zaks led the way. All the while, I could sense his resentment and his utter disdain at being ordered to perform a task that would "help" Ke'tai.

Once we had arrived, I had him sort the clothes out before placing anything inside the washing machines. He did so, albeit grudgingly, though he kept his complaints to himself. I could sense that his resolve was beginning to crumble, but he had not yet completely given up on his cause. I believed that it would take only another small push, and my battle with him would be concluded. I was unsure of what more I ought to have him do while we waited for the washing machines to finish their cycles.

After we had stood silently for a few moments, the incubus' handsome face twisted into a frown. "What other ridiculousness do you have in store for me today?" His tone was bitter, yet somehow resigned. I wondered at this sudden change.

"Um..." I racked my brain for some other task, but could think of nothing. Annoyed with myself, and afraid of hesitating too long, I glanced toward Il'zaks where he was standing in the doorway. He merely shrugged in response, and I began to become frightened again. He was so close to giving up on his conquest, but my mind was devoid of any further ideas.

Ke'tai took a few steps toward me, and then bent to whisper in my ear. "I'm feeling a little hungry, Chandra," he said, and I could hear mischief in his voice. "Why don't you have him go get me something from the kitchen? You know what I like."

I bit my lower lip to keep from laughing, and then informed the incubus of his next task. He responded with a sullen look, but went about the task and left the room without a word.

"Much more of this, and he will give way to you," Il'zaks commented once the incubus had departed. "I think he was a bit surprised a few times this morning, Chandra Grey. When you stopped him from striking you, that was a major victory on your part, and did much to get him this far so quickly."

I nodded, reluctant to relax the hold I had managed on the demon thus far. Until I was certain he would cause me no further trouble, I would retain my mental grip. "I was angry," I admitted to Il'zaks. "He did enough damage last night that I'll be coping with it for a lifetime. I wasn't about to let him do any more." I glanced at Ke'tai. "He's almost to the kitchen. Do you want pancakes again?"

Ke'tai laughed, though the sound was strained. "See, I knew you'd know what I wanted."

When the incubus returned to the laundry area, he handed a plate of pancakes to Ke'tai, before sitting down on one of the chairs with a loud sigh. "You're going to keep torturing me, aren't you?" he practically whined. "We like working with summoners because they let us be ourselves, but this—this isn't what I was made to do!"

"I know what you were made to do," I replied evenly, "but I'm not going to allow you to do that until you acknowledge me as your summoner."

I contemplated his emotions; he was torn between obstinance and surrender, though neither of these emotions, nor the conflict I could sense within him, were evident upon his face. The room was quiet for several long minutes, the silence broken only by the buzzer of one of the washing machines as its cycle completed.

"You'd best get that into the dryer," I said to him, and received a look that was almost a pout.

He rose and did as I ordered, then sighed heavily as the dryer was started. He turned around to face me, his hands at his sides. "Can I speak with you alone?"

I felt Ke'tai tense at my side, but Il'zaks said from behind me, "We will go out into the hallway, and await you there, Chandra Grey."

I nodded, instantly nervous. Ke'tai wore a worried frown as he carried his half-empty plate of pancakes outside and Il'zaks closed the door behind them.

"I didn't want *him* in the room," the incubus said after a moment of awkward silence. I was uncertain of what his decision had been, but the fact that Il'zaks had so readily left us alone spoke volumes; it seemed that he was finally willing to submit to my authority.

"Why do you hate him so?" I asked without thinking.

The incubus smirked, and his crimson eyes glittered strangely in the light. "You really are new to all this, aren't you?" he asked condescendingly. "You became angry with me yesterday, after our very first meeting, and you sent me away because of *him*. I know you love him, but all I told him was the truth about what would happen last night, and he knew that. But you sent me away, and you were angry—it is one of the greatest shames to my kind to be scorned by a summoner, or even a would-be summoner as is the case here. I cannot be shamed like that again."

He said all of this without looking at me directly, but I could sense that his words were truthful. He had endured a great deal of emotional pain at my expense, and now I was beginning to feel rather badly about the whole ordeal. I wanted to apologize, but I feared that it would ruin everything I had worked to achieve this morning, so I tried a different track.

"So you tried to kill me?" I asked incredulously.

He shrugged, his expression weary. "It seemed like the only option I had at the time," he replied. "I…I apologize for that, because I think now that I was mistaken. You are far stronger than you appear to be."

In that instant, I felt all of his defiance disappear, and I could see his mind more clearly than ever before. I stared at him, unsure of what to say, and his eyes rose to meet my gaze and held it for several seconds.

"You're more powerful than I had expected from a woman," he said slowly after a moment. "I realize now that it was foolish to fight you. Instead, I would like to serve you, as others of my kind serve your friends out in the hallway. But you must promise me something in return."

I nodded, dreading what he would ask of me.

"Please never make me do chores like this again! It is torture."

I laughed, somewhat nervously. "I can agree to that," I replied.

He smiled, his expression suddenly seductive. "Is there any chance I could tempt you away from *him*? I can guarantee you I'd be much better between the sheets."

I felt my face flush, and I dropped my gaze. "I'm afraid not," I said once I had regained some of my composure. "I'm sure there will be others in the future though."

"That will have to suffice, I suppose," he replied, falling into the same teasing, seductive manner he had assumed when I had first summoned him the day before. "I will not cause you any more trouble, and that is a promise." He turned slightly, then looked at me from the corners of his eyes. "Is there any chance I could have a go at that secretary in the lobby?"

# 14

# SURPRISE

Four days had gone by since the morning in which I had been forced to tame the incubus, and life in the compound had gone on without incident. Il'zaks had been kept busy with his business of joining the Board of Elders, but Ke'tai had no such preoccupations and he took the time to show me around more of the compound. We even had the opportunity to practice some more karate skills. I was grateful that Ke'tai had been allowed to continue helping with that aspect of my training.

On the fifth morning, I awoke to the sound of the phone ringing in the other room. Ke'tai was sound asleep, and was oblivious to the noise. I was forced to rise to answer the call, noting that clock revealed it was just after eight o'clock. Our early morning caller proved to be Il'zaks.

"Good morning, Chandra Grey," he said. "Would you and Ke'tai like to join me soon for breakfast? I would like to teach you for the last time today, and Te'chok would like to meet with you when we have finished."

I heard the bedroom door open on the other side of the room, and glanced over my shoulder to see Ke'tai standing in the door frame, rubbing the sleep from his eyes. "Uh, sure, we'll be there soon," I replied as Ke'tai sauntered toward me with a yawn. "It's Il'zaks," I whispered to him.

He nodded. "Let me talk to him for a minute."

I handed him the phone after informing Il'zaks that Ke'tai wanted to speak, then made my exit from the room to quickly dress. I was sitting on the end of the bed, tying my shoes, when Ke'tai reentered.

"Il'zaks was originally planning to teach you twice more," he said with a slight frown, "but he said this is going to be the last lesson he will perform. It makes me wonder if something came up, since he's cutting this a little short."

I gazed up at him, trying to make sense out of his puzzled expression, before I understood the true import of his words. This would be my last lesson with Il'zaks, and after today I would be working primarily with Te'chok. I had not encountered the Grand Summoner since we had arrived in Boston, with the exception of that first, troubled night in the library. I was uneasy around Te'chok, in spite of Ke'tai's assurances that I had nothing to fear from him.

With a sigh, I looked down and finished tying my shoes. "I'd rather not have to train with Te'chok," I mumbled, mostly to myself, though Ke'tai had heard the words clearly enough.

"There isn't much we—or anyone else, for that matter—can do about it," he replied gently. "Te'chok is probably the only one that is truly qualified to train you, anyway," he added somewhat grudgingly. He turned toward the small closet the room sported to find something more than his boxers to wear.

I made no reply, but simply watched him for a few moments as I perched on the end of the bed. I loved to watch the movements the muscles of his back underwent as he reached into the closet and pulled out a thin, close-fitting t-shirt, pulling it on over his head. The shirt accentuated his shoulders and biceps, and I believed he must be the most beautiful man alive.

He pulled on a pair of loose-fitting blue jeans, and turned around to face me with a strange expression upon his face. "Did you hear what I asked you, Chandra?"

I felt my face redden as I shook my head. "Sorry, I was...daydreaming."

Ke'tai laughed. "Obviously. I said that Adele told me yesterday she is planning on a shopping trip this afternoon. If you're up for it after your lesson, she asked me if you'd be interested in going with her. Did you want to go?"

I did want to; it would be a nice change of pace to get out of the compound. I hesitated, however, recalling the television broadcast we had been witness to on the night of our arrival. I was afraid of being recognized by someone on the street.

Ke'tai's eyes narrowed in concern, and he came to sit alongside me on the end of the bed. "Chandra, what's wrong?" he asked gently, and he ran one of his hands through my loose hair.

I sighed, and dropped my gaze. "I...I just worry that it isn't safe for me."

He laughed, which startled me, and I snapped my head back up to meet his twinkling silver gaze. "You'll be safe enough," he replied with a grin. "You won't be leaving here without some sort of disguise—we know that would be a risk, and Te'chok would probably wish he could disown me for even thinking of letting you do so. Don't worry, Il'zaks had Carmine arrange something for you."

I gaped at him. "Right, don't worry. I know what Carmine's taste in clothing—and hair, for that matter—looks like. Hah!"

I stood up, meaning to head for the door, but his arms went about my waist and he pulled me back down playfully. "I was only teasing about that last part," he said, his lips very close to my ear. He kissed the side of my neck once, and then a bit reluctantly, he released me.

I grinned at him. "But you do have something in mind, I take it?" I asked him, taking one of his hands in both of mine and pulling him to his feet.

"Of course," he replied. "It's a surprise though, so you'll have to wait until you're finished with Il'zaks this morning."

After we had finished breakfast, Il'zaks led the way to the same empty room we had held my last lesson in. Before we began, he stopped in the center of the room and turned to face me squarely. Ke'tai took his place next to the door, sitting on the floor while leaning his head against the wall.

"There are some things we must discuss before we can begin, Chandra Grey," Il'zaks began. "As you know, this is the last lesson I will be giving you, and from this day forward, you will be training under Master Te'chok. I know you have spoken to him very little since the night we arrived here, but do not let the events of that night color your assessment of him entirely. His is a good person, and he will teach you well."

I nodded, and dropped my eyes to the floor. "We'll still see you, though, won't we?" I asked. My voice trembled, betraying my emotions. I had come to like Il'zaks, despite his old-fashioned mannerisms and his disturbing fetish with the succubus. I knew if he were forced to leave, I would miss his company.

Il'zaks chuckled briefly. "Of course, you will still see me, Chandra Grey. I will be within the compound for at least another two months, while

I finish my work to become part of the Board of Elders. After that, I cannot say; however, there are periodic meetings of the Order held here, and sometimes at some of the other facilities we possess. We can always meet up again at those times."

I nodded again, and raised my eyes to meet his once more. "It's just hard for me, Il'zaks," I said. "You and Ke'tai are the only people I know from before we had to leave Seattle. Everyone else was left behind, and sometimes I feel a little homesick… I don't want to have to say goodbye to you, too."

Il'zaks smiled warmly. "You won't need to, Chandra Grey."

The room fell into silence for several moments while we each became tangled within our own web of thoughts. I remembered the last time I had spoken to Xandra; Elliot had been with her and they had seemed so happy together. She had been excited for me, believing that I was leaving to spend the night with "Kevin". I wondered now if that name had come up in the ongoing police investigation regarding my "disappearance", and what Xandra believed regarding what had happened that night. I also wondered how things with Elliot were progressing, and if he had a difficult time keeping the secret of his training from my sister. I wished that I had a means of knowing how far he had come, or if he would live to see the end of his training, as so many others did not.

After several moments, Il'zaks broke the silence and brought me out of the whirl of my thoughts. "The other matter I needed to speak with you about is something I should have gone over with you sooner, and I apologize for not doing so," he said. "Within a month, perhaps, maybe six weeks, depending on the pace Te'chok sets, you will complete the path to becoming a summoner. I want you to be aware of the changes you will undergo at that time."

His silver eyes met my dark ones, and I stood riveted in his gaze. I knew some of what to expect, but my information was vague.

"You and Master Te'chok will know immediately upon the end of your final lesson—whichever lesson that may prove to be—that the change is imminent. You may not feel any different at that point, Chandra Grey, but you will likely lose consciousness as the transformation begins. Within the hour, the change will begin in earnest. You will be in a great deal of pain, pain of a magnitude that you cannot fathom right now. The pain is caused by the very DNA within your cells, as parts of it awaken that have lain dormant for your entire life. During this process, you will cease to age and your reflexes will be greatly increased, but it will hurt more than you can imagine. Most who undergo this change only remember pain and darkness, for your mind cannot withstand what your body must endure, and your consciousness will drift. You must be aware of what awaits you. I do not want you to live through any more unpleasant surprises, due to my negligence."

I had been aware that the transformation would be painful, but Il'zaks' description left me worried and afraid. I simply nodded, feeling somewhat numb, uncertain of what to say in reply.

Il'zaks sighed. "Once you do awaken, things will be very different for you," he continued. "Most summoners cannot recall much of their past, prior to their training, and this has much to do with the physical changes we undergo during the process I just described. Our past memories may be obliterated during the change, and some summoners awaken and know nothing of who they had been. I want to emphasize that losing all memory of one's past is incredibly rare. Most remember snapshots of their prior life, and most remain relatively unchanged when it comes to personality. There is one other thing that may prove very different when you awaken from your change, and this is something that you must remember."

I nodded for him to go on as he paused, and he said, "When you awaken as a summoner, you will not be able to recall your name as it is now. You will no longer be Chandra Grey, and that name will be lost from your memory entirely. You will know yourself by the name that is yours as a summoner. It is customary that we ask your name, soon after you awaken. If you remember my words, do not become angry at us when this question is posed, and know that we will not know you by your true name, until you speak it."

I swallowed hard. "I won't remember my name at all? How does that work, exactly? I mean, how am I supposed to know my name if I can't remember it?"

Il'zaks broke into a knowing smile. "I believe we all ask similar questions when this information is brought to our attention," he replied. "You may have guessed this by now, but the name of my birth was not Il'zaks. I do not recall what it was, nor can I, but when I awoke as a summoner many years ago, I immediately knew myself as Il'zaks. I am no brain scientist, Chandra Grey, so I cannot tell you the workings of the mind when it comes to these matters. You will learn for yourself, soon enough."

The rest of the lesson went by relatively quickly. Il'zaks taught me how to summon a tiny demon called *Vysposidae*, a creature that looked somewhat like a cross between a spider and a hornet. Its body was much like that of a spider in shape, but it had the black and yellow markings of a hornet, and the translucent wings to match. Its temperament was much like that of the nightwing, which I was silently thankful for after what had occurred during my last two lessons. The summoners seemed to use these creatures primarily for spying on the hunters. They were so tiny they were easily overlooked, but they had excellent hearing, and because they could fly, they were able to travel quickly.

After the lesson had ended, Ke'tai led me to the lobby, grinning all the while, obviously pleased with himself. He would not tell me anything more about his surprise, although he could hardly contain his own excitement. I was unable to learn what he was scheming, and I had no success with my attempts to coax him into giving me hints. He would grin and say, "You'll see."

Adele was on the phone at the desk in the lobby when we arrived, but Ke'tai did not stop to wait for her. He ushered me toward the elevator leading up to the warehouse-turned-garage, informing me that Adele was planning to meet us there once she was available.

As soon as we had exited the elevator however, Ke'tai stepped swiftly behind me and placed one hand over my eyes, while the other rested on my right hip. "I told you I had a surprise for you," he whispered excitedly. "I'm going to take you to it now."

He guided me down the corridor, and carefully led me up the flight of concrete steps that ascended into the summoners' parking garage. Our footsteps echoed hollowly in the nearly empty space.

Ke'tai stopped me after we had walked some distance away from the stairs, and said, "You'll probably want to practice a little with this first, before we take it out, but here's your surprise, love."

He dropped his hands, and I opened my eyes, blinking to adjust to the sudden brightness of the overhead fluorescent lights. Before me were a pair of motorcycles, sleek black and chrome machines. Upon each seat was a black helmet with a darkly tinted visor. I simply stared for several seconds, wondering what had possessed Ke'tai to buy these. I had never driven a motorcycle, let alone been riding on one.

I turned to face him, and he was grinning. "I know it's probably not what you were expecting," he admitted, "but I thought maybe it would be a good way for the two of us to get around unnoticed. Especially after…you're finished training." He paused a moment, then added, "After what you told me when I took you flying—about how you loved the rush you felt—I thought you'd like this, too."

"You're probably right," I replied. "I've just never even been on one of these before. You'll have to help me learn how to drive it."

He grinned. "See? I *can* teach you something, and Te'chok won't have any gripes about it." He glanced behind his shoulder suddenly, and said, "It looks like Adele is here to take you shopping. I gave her permission to use part of my monthly allowance so you can buy some new clothes. I know that little duffel bag worth of stuff isn't going to last you long."

I threw my arms around him, and smiled. "You're the best, Ke'tai. Did I ever tell you that?"

# 15

# SHOCK

Two days later I found myself in an empty room alone with summoner Te'chok. Ke'tai had left early in the day to check in at the genetics lab where he worked periodically. It was near the headquarters; he had taken one of the two new motorcycles, which I had only attempted to drive once around the interior of the warehouse at a very low speed. I had seen him off, watching him rocket outside with a wave of his hand, while I wished that he were not going to his lab today. I didn't want to face Te'chok alone after how poorly our first encounter had gone.

My only consolation was that Te'chok appeared to be just as nervous and uneasy as I was. Neither of us had managed to say more than a brief "hello" in the corridors since the night of my arrival; I continued to feel badly about losing my temper with him, even though he had stated he harbored no ill will over what had been said.

He had been standing near the door when I had entered to room, and we stood in awkward silence for several long moments before either of us ventured to speak.

"Uh, hi," I said almost at the same time as he said, "Where is Ke'tai?"

I bit my lip, wondering why Te'chok didn't know of Ke'tai's departure earlier. "He said he wanted to go to his lab," I replied. "He left a couple hours ago."

Te'chok frowned, and his expression was one of frustration and hurt. He sighed. "I asked him if he would accompany you today," he said after a moment. "Apparently he is still angry with me. I am sorry you have been pulled into the middle of this, Chandra."

"Into the middle of what?" I asked. Ke'tai had been angry the morning after we had arrived at the headquarters, when Il'zaks had advised him to stay away from my lessons. I had believed he was over his anger, once Il'zaks had relented and changed his stance.

"A few days ago, Il'zaks and I spoke regarding what had happened to you with the incubus," he began slowly, "and I made the comment that perhaps it was dangerous for you and Ke'tai to have become so close so quickly. I didn't realize that Ke'tai was within hearing distance until he was suddenly behind me. I have never seen him so angry before, and frankly, it frightened me. I know I would be no match for him if it came to a physical confrontation." He looked down at his wiry frame, and shook his head.

"He never said anything about that to me," I admitted, surprised. "When did you say this was?"

"Three days ago, in the cafeteria."

I nodded, realizing I knew exactly when it had occurred. "He went to get something for breakfast that morning, and he came back and was pissed off about something," I said, mostly to myself. "He wouldn't tell me what was wrong."

Te'chok managed a strained smile. "Yes, well, he seems very protective of you, and he definitely didn't like the fact that I seemed to disapprove of your relationship. In reality, Chandra, I do approve of it; as I'm sure you know, it is very rare for one of our kind to find true love. I meant nothing by the comment, except that it was dangerous for you both, because you have not yet finished with your training. I swear to you, I will do everything in my power to see that you *do* finish, because I do not relish the thought of having to deal with Ke'tai's temper and whatever else he might do should you fail."

"I'm sorry he was angry with you," I replied quietly. "I'll talk to him later, and maybe he'll calm down a bit."

"One can only hope," Te'chok replied dryly. The room descended into another strained silence, and then Te'chok said, "Well, let's get started, shall we?"

When I nodded, he said, "Today you will learn of the creature we call the shadow demon. I believe you have seen it before, once, when you first met Il'zaks in Seattle."

I thought back to that night, which seemed like it had been years ago rather than a mere three months. Il'zaks had called me in the earliest hours of the morning, and I had recklessly agreed to meet with him at the entrance to a night club downtown. Trey had been there to escort me from the arranged meeting place to Il'zaks' location, and Carmine had been standing at the door when we arrived, ready with one of her customarily condescending and snide remarks. Il'zaks and I had spoken, and then he had said something in a strange language that I could not comprehend. A monster had suddenly appeared at his side. I felt my face flush with embarrassment as I recalled how I had fallen backwards out of my chair while frantically scrambling away from the creature.

That monster had been a shadow demon. I remembered that it had been built somewhat like a human, though it had large leathery wings not unlike those of the incubus and succubus. Its skin had been a dark gray in color, and had been marred by many scars. What I recalled most from that memory were the demon's eyes; they had been a vibrant red, with vertically slit pupils.

Il'zaks had apologized profusely for having frightened me so, and I had eventually agreed to learn from him what I could. Thinking back on that night now, I would have been less frightened if he had summoned any of the other demons I had learned about so far, and yet, none of the others would have been as impressive as his shadow demon. Had he called the nightwing, or the *Vysposidae*, I would have believed he was joking, and I now understood from experience that it would have been extremely unsafe for him to have called a *Zombi Cadavre* or an incubus. That would have left the *djinn*, which would have begun my training prematurely. His only option had been to call the shadow demon, for he had fewer of the creatures at his disposal than a summoner such as Te'chok possessed.

All of these thoughts passed through my mind in an instant, and I nodded to Te'chok. "Yes, I do remember that one."

Te'chok nodded, looking pleased. "The shadow demon is the most powerful demon many summoners are able to call," he said. "There are a few of us—very few—that can call some others. That is why your training now falls to me, because this is the last demon Il'zaks would have had the ability to teach you of."

I knew there was a great difference in ability between Il'zaks and Te'chok, and so I merely nodded. Il'zaks had told me early on that he would not be able to train me to my full potential, and that others would have to complete the task; at the time, we had believed it would be Ke'tai, but things between us had changed rapidly since the holidays had come and gone. I nodded to Te'chok, indicating that he should go on.

"The shadow demon is a warrior," Te'chok said, seeming to choose his words carefully. "It is often the demon many summoners call upon when they are forced to confront a hunter face to face. Thankfully, those circumstances have been very rare for the past decade, but we can never truly be safe as long as the hunters still exist in great numbers. Most are unwilling to understand our place in this world, and refuse to listen; the majority of hunters do not simply wish to kill the demons we are able to summon, but they want to destroy every last one of our kind as well." He sighed, and said, "Ours is a life of secrecy, and sometimes of deception. It will not be easy, Chandra, and it will only become more difficult as you continue down this path."

His talk regarding the hunters caused me to think of Xandra again, and what she would ultimately become: a hunter. I fervently hoped she remained undiscovered indefinitely, though that was a fool's wish if ever there was one, and I knew it. Without meaning to, I sighed.

"Chandra, what's wrong?" Te'chok asked uncertainly.

I shrugged. "I was thinking about Xan." I looked away, and sighed again. "I'm actually afraid of what could happen if she became a hunter and I had to face her. My wish is that she's never found by them, but based on what everyone has told me, that's unlikely. She's my sister, my *twin sister.*"

Te'chok nodded, as though he understood very well what I was going through, but I doubted that he did. "I am still puzzled by the fact that the two of you have opposing talents," he said, "but be that as it may, you will have to come to terms with it eventually. And…there is always the chance that you may not even remember her once you have undergone the transformation."

I knew his words were meant to encourage me, but they left me feeling almost sick to my stomach instead. Somehow, I knew, even then, that I would never be able to forget Xandra and what she was to become.

While I was working with Te'chok, I focused all of my energy on learning what I could about the shadow demon and how to summon it. It was a creature of great physical power, and I knew as soon as I had called mine for the first time why Te'chok had mentioned that many summoners preferred to use it as a sort of warrior. This demon could withstand severe injury, while still remaining strong enough to defend itself and its summoner.

Once we had concluded the lesson, however, my thoughts drifted back to my sister and what seemed an inevitably wretched future for one or both of us, should we ever be forced to meet again. Every summoner I had spoken with had a distinct fear of the hunters, and I was not entirely sure as to why. I knew that hunters had the ability to track demons, and some could even track summoners; they were often guided by some religious belief, and thought that what they were doing was divine will. What I did not understand was what hunters were truly capable of. I made the decision as I was walking back toward my apartment to seek out Te'chok again and ask for more information.

I returned to the room we had used for the lesson, but as I had expected, he had already departed. Frowning, I decided to speak with Adele; if anyone knew where Te'chok had gone to, she would. She was typing into her computer when I came to stand in front of her desk in the lobby, but she stopped her work abruptly. She looked up at me expectantly.

"What can I do for you, Chandra?" she asked in her British accent.

"I was looking for Te'chok. I mean, we just finished a lesson, but then I came up with a question. He was gone when I got back to the room."

Adele looked over my shoulder as I finished, and I turned to see Te'chok standing a few paces away. "Let's talk in the library," he replied. "The chairs are more comfortable there, and I sense your questions may take some time to explain."

"I have a good idea of what you intend to ask," Te'chok said after we had seated ourselves in the library. "Il'zaks has told me that he did explain to you the basics of what the hunters stand for, and why they believe what they do, but I think your question goes beyond what you have been told. Am I right?"

I nodded. "I understand why they believe what they do, as you said, but I want to know what they're actually capable of. Everyone here seems afraid of them, even though you are all so powerful. I want to understand why."

Te'chok nodded knowingly. "I suspected as much. The answer to your question is not easily explained, but I will try my best. Can I ask you something first, though?" When I nodded, he stated, "I'm wondering why you did not ask this of Ke'tai."

I felt my face redden; in actuality I had not thought to ask Ke'tai, and now that Te'chok mentioned it, I was uncertain of my reasoning.

Te'chok chuckled after a moment, and said, "You don't have to answer, Chandra, and I did not mean to embarrass you like this. As I said earlier, I will try to answer your question as best as I can." He was silent for a time, collecting his thoughts, then said, "Like summoners, there are different ability levels within the ranks of the hunters; some are stronger than others when it comes to their specific seeking capabilities. We worry over your sister because, like you, she is very strong in her ability.

"There are a few different types of people who are often recruited to the ranks of the hunters, Chandra. There are those who can seek out demons, which are the most common sort—you look as though you have heard this already, no?"

I nodded. "Ke'tai told me some of it, but go on."

"Okay," he replied. "Well, your sister has the ability to track demons. Then there are those who can track summoners—these are much rarer, but much more dangerous for us. A hunter who can seek out demons is problematic enough, but releasing a demon will cause them to lose their trail. However, one who can track a summoner is a much greater threat, as you can imagine. There are also some who can seek out other hunters—they have the same ability as Carmine and Carlos do—and they are primarily used for locating new hunters among the populace. The last sort of hunter is one who can use ether stones; these are by far the rarest sort, probably about as common as we summoners are. These hunters have the ability to use various items to not only track summoners and demons, but to also see what their fellow hunters have seen in the past or present. I am not completely sure how this process works, but I do know that these people are often selected as leaders amongst the hunters, because of what they are capable of. I have even heard reports of these people using ether stones to see the last moments of a comrade who has died. It is very important that you always know if one of these sorts of hunters is in the area in which you are staying."

"So, they can track us, or our demons, but what makes them so dangerous?" I asked, still having difficulty with the concept. "And what is an ether stone?"

Te'chok laughed. "I'll answer your second question first. Ether stones are simply objects used by certain hunters...I know they are required for those hunters to be able to see and track as they do, but without them, those hunters cannot do anything overly remarkable." He sighed before continuing. "The answer to your other question is that one cannot simply walk up to a hunter and ask to negotiate. The hunters are taught that demons, and those who command them, are abominations that do not have the right to exist. They will shoot first and ask questions later—*if* they even come to think of questions in the first place. In order to *exist*, Chandra, we are forced to hide. To make ourselves known to the hunters is to ensure our certain deaths. Secrecy is our greatest ally."

I felt weak, and was glad I was seated for this discussion. "And Xan...she'll be like that if they find her?" I was surprised at the tremor in my voice as I asked the question, and even though I knew what his answer would be, I dreaded hearing it. I did not want to have my sister destined to be my enemy, let alone a threat to my very existence.

Te'chok was silent for some time before he made any reply. Finally, he said, "You know the answer to that question well enough, Chandra. I'm afraid that my telling you otherwise would be the greatest of lies. If they do find her, she will become just as I have described."

My heart sank, even though I had been expecting this response, and I dropped my gaze to the polished wood floor with a sigh.

"I know it is not easy news to take, Chandra," Te'chok said quietly after a few moments. I did not look up, and could not have if even Ke'tai had suddenly walked into the room.

The room was silent for a long moment, and then Te'chok sighed. "You should not give up all hope yet, Chandra. There are accounts I have read, from the past, in which some hunters were made to see that we are not evil, and that we simply just want the right to exist. Such accounts state that those same hunters allied their forces with ours, bringing a time of peace for both sides. I do not know what occurred to destroy that peace, nor do I know how it was forged in the first place, but I do know that it happened. There is always hope that it may happen again."

"How likely is that?" I asked without looking at him.

I heard Te'chok release another sigh, this one sounding frustrated. "Not very," he admitted after a moment's hesitation.

I frowned, having known that would be his response, and stood up to leave. "I need some time to think," I muttered as I walked away, glancing only briefly at Te'chok's youthful countenance as I passed. My thoughts were troubled, and I clung desperately—and foolishly—to the hope that Xandra would never be discovered by the hunters. The other alternative was too disturbing for my mind to accept.

It was well into the evening hours before Ke'tai returned to the compound, and I had spent most of my afternoon pacing aimlessly through the myriad hallways desperately hoping—and failing—to find something to occupy my thoughts. I wished to forget the conversation I'd had with Te'chok regarding my sister.

I was on the far side of the compound from our apartment when Ke'tai suddenly appeared in my field of vision, some distance down the hall. He glanced in the opposite direction from where I was walking, then turned his head quickly toward me; the relief in his expression was unmistakable.

"Chandra!" he called, breaking into a jog to meet me that much faster. He stopped only a step or two away, and he studied me for a time before speaking. "Chandra," he said again, "you had me worried. You were gone from the apartment when I came back, and no one seemed to know where you were. After I spoke to Te'chok…Damn it, but I wish he had not told you what he did today. It's bad timing."

I frowned. "Why is that?" I asked.

He narrowed his eyes in concern. "Have you not heard, then? I came back as soon as I saw it myself…" He sighed, and seemed frustrated. I did not understand what he was referring to, so I simply waited expectantly, hoping that he would elaborate.

He took my arm gently, and sighed again, leading me down the hall. "There's been more on the news relating to your disappearance," he said quietly. "I assumed that you had seen it, and that's why you were off on your own."

I shrugged. "No, I haven't seen it, or heard about it," I replied, "and frankly, I don't care to. I've been trying to deal with the fact that my sister is likely to become my greatest enemy, if what Te'chok told me is true."

Ke'tai looked uncertain and continued to steer me toward some unknown destination. "I…I think you'd best see what exactly is on the news, Chandra," he replied very softly after a few moments of silence. "And there's another thing you ought to know, regarding all of this; Kai'lind was asked to bring Elliot here almost two days ago, and I think that's what this news report was really about."

I stopped walking suddenly, startling Ke'tai, and stared at him for a few moments as I battled with a swirl of emotions. "Why didn't you tell me?" I demanded, feeling rather hurt as I finally broke the silence.

He shook his head. "I only just found out from Te'chok myself, while I was searching for you," he replied curtly, annoyed that I would believe he had kept it secret from me. "The news report I saw while I was at the lab…Well, it's best if you see it for yourself, Chandra, but it's not going to be easy news to take."

I looked down, unwilling to follow him; I did not want to witness this thing that had him so concerned for my welfare. I was scared and frustrated. I felt tears sting my eyes, and I simply shook my head. "I don't want to see it, Ke'tai," I whispered. "If it's bad news, I don't want to see it."

He was suddenly at my side again, in that startling manner he had when we were alone and no one was present to see his extraordinary reflexes in action. He took my hands in his, and when he next spoke his voice was quiet, soothing. "Chandra, I know it will be difficult, but you simply cannot run away from this. It is something that we are all going to have to live with—but for you it is going to be the most painful. I know that, and I want you to know that I am here for you, any time you need me, no matter where you are."

I raised my eyes to meet his, feeling the hot tears that had been threatening finally spill down my cheeks. "She's gone to them, hasn't she?" I asked in a choked whisper, finding some difficulty in forcing the words through the lump that had suddenly formed in my throat.

Ke'tai looked down, and nodded. He gathered me into his strong arms as my anguish overwhelmed me and I began to sob in earnest. I do not know how long we stood there in the hallway, he holding me close to him while I cried and clung to him as though he were the last pillar of safety in a rising flood. After an interminable amount of time, I finally regained some control over myself, and I drew a shuddering breath. When I ventured to look up at him once more, blinking the last of the tears out of my eyes, his expression was one of compassion.

"I think…I can go watch that news clip now," I said quietly.

He nodded. "Te'chok said if you hadn't seen it yet that he would have it ready in the library for you," Ke'tai replied, circling an arm about my waist and guiding me once more toward our destination. "Like I said earlier, his chat with you today came at the worst possible time imaginable. I…I should have been here with you today, Chandra, and I'm sorry I wasn't. I was avoiding Te'chok, and being an ass about it, and now I feel really horrible for leaving you alone."

I shrugged. "Te'chok told me why you weren't there this morning," I replied wearily. "I think I would have been angry too, if I were you, but I don't think he meant anything bad by it. He apologized, if that means anything to you."

Ke'tai managed a small, tired smile, and nodded. "He told me as much earlier, when I was looking for you."

We walked along in silence for a time, until the door to the library came into view. I sighed, tired and resigned, and yet determined to see what had caused such a stir amongst the summoners. Ke'tai glanced down at me, a look of concern on his face, but he said nothing and merely held me closer.

When we entered, Te'chok was on his feet and speaking, standing near the soft chairs at the center of the library, the television remote in one hand while he gestured with the other. Il'zaks occupied one of the chairs, and his familiar countenance was drawn with worry. The television was turned off, though it was apparent that it would soon be switched on.

"…I'm sure they'll be here any time. I told you, he went off a while ago looking for her," Te'chok was explaining. "Adele told me she did not leave the compound, though there are any number of places where she might be hiding inside. Ah, you've found her!" he exclaimed as he took notice of our arrival. He appeared genuinely relieved.

"I need to see the news report," I stated before anyone could say a word more. "If it's about Xan, I need to see it."

The room was silent for several long moments. Il'zaks turned in his chair to study me; his expression was unreadable, but I thought I could detect some sort of pity within the depths of his silver-eyed gaze. Te'chok stood unmoving for several long seconds, before nodding quickly. He spun around to face the television and work the remote.

"I recorded the initial broadcast," Te'chok said quietly, "though I missed the first few seconds of what was said in my shock. I think you'll see more than enough as it is, however."

I simply nodded, and watched as the news story unfolded.

On the screen was a middle-aged man, reporting for CNN in his crisp navy business suit and burgundy tie. "…sister, Xandra Grey, gave a brief statement today, pleading for her sister's safe return." The screen flashed to a video clip of Xandra, who looked as though she had been crying. She was standing in the rain outside of the police headquarters in Seattle, surrounded by uniformed officers and several others who were not in uniform. I could not identify any of the people surrounding her. To one side stood our parents; both appeared weary in the clip.

Te'chok paused the video just before Xandra began to speak, and walked to where the television was on the wall. He pointed to several of the figures in the picture, most of whom were men, and said, "These people are known to us as hunters from the Seattle area, Chandra." He indicated one man in particular, who stood just behind Xandra in the image; a thirty-something brown-haired man with rugged features. "This man is Thaddeus Taylor, the leader of the Seattle area hunters. He is one of those whom I spoke of with you earlier today, one who can use the ether stones." He pressed a button on the remote, and the video began to play once more.

Xandra glanced at the man Te'chok had identified as Thaddeus Taylor, and then nodded briefly before returning her gaze to the cameras and the other on-lookers. "I just wanted to say to whoever kidnapped my sister that we'd really like her to come home safely. And whoever Kevin is, please come forward; we need whatever information you might have on my sister's whereabouts."

The image flashed back to the CNN newsroom and the middle-aged anchor at his tidy desk. "Authorities state that this Kevin who was mentioned is a person of interest in the case, but is not a suspect at this time. No other information has been released about him, but CNN will continue to report as more information becomes available." He paused, and in the space beside him a picture of me suddenly appeared. "Chandra Grey went missing after a night out with the man she had been seeing, this unknown Kevin, just over three weeks ago. There have been very few leads in the case, but investigators are following each one they have very carefully in the hopes of finding Chandra alive. Her family asks that your prayers be with Chandra as the search continues."

The image beside the anchorman's head changed suddenly to show a picture of Elliot. "In related news, the boyfriend of Xandra Grey, one, Elliot Thompson, was found dead earlier this afternoon in his Seattle-area apartment. Authorities were called in to investigate the report of a strange odor coming from the apartment, where they found Mr. Thompson's remains. A note was found at the scene, and police state that this is an apparent suicide. It may be connected with the disappearance of Chandra Grey, based upon the contents of the note, which has not yet been released to the press."

I stared at the screen, not wanting to believe what I had just heard. The anchorman said more, but I did not hear it in my shock. When Te'chok switched the television off once more, I managed to shift my gaze in his direction. "I thought Elliot was coming *here*," I said.

Te'chok nodded. "He is, Chandra. The suicide was staged; Kai'lind left a *djinn* behind to act as Elliot's body, though the note was real enough, and was written by Elliot himself as part of the ploy. They should be here within a few days."

I felt relieved at this bit of information, but I still had many questions that needed answering. "I need to know... When did the hunters find Xan? And do they know about *me*?"

"As far as we can determine, it was two days ago when they first made contact with her," Te'chok replied. "I believe she was discovered because of the publicity surrounding your disappearance; she has been on the local news in Washington much more frequently than she has been on the national stage. As soon as we learned they had made contact, we sent word to Kai'lind to move himself and Elliot away from the area as quickly as possible. Kai'lind had already set in motion the staged suicide scene by that time, so Elliot should remain safe. As for your second question, we do not believe the hunters know where you are, or what you will become. For now, your secret is safe."

While I was relieved that the hunters did not know about me, and that Elliot was alive and unharmed, I was disappointed that my fears about Xandra had come true so quickly. It made sense, however; they would have had an easier time finding her with all of the news appearances she'd been a part of. I also understood now why Ke'tai had been so worried about me having seen the news clip earlier—if I had thought Elliot was dead without the explanation Te'chok had given me, I would have assumed it had been the work of the hunters in the area. Perhaps I would have even jumped to the conclusion that they were following my trail as well.

"No matter what comes of this, Chandra Grey, we will be here to help you," Il'zaks stated after a momentary silence had settled over the room.

Te'chok nodded in agreement. "Yes, we will. Never forget that."

# 16

# ELLIOT

I found myself back in the practice room with Te'chok three days later, this time with Ke'tai in attendance as well. The two summoners seemed to have put their differences aside for the time being, and for that I was grateful. We were still receiving news reports from Seattle and the national scene almost daily, and having both Ke'tai and Te'chok in agreement eased my mind significantly.

Te'chok was smiling as I entered the room with Ke'tai, who took up his customary position near the door. "I think you'll find today's lesson is one you have been waiting a long while for," he said as Ke'tai closed the door quietly. "I know that you have been around dragons before, Chandra, and Ke'tai has told me of your love of flying already."

I broke into a grin. "Finally!"

Ke'tai laughed from behind me. "I told you yesterday she'd be excited."

Te'chok nodded, seemingly amused. "Yes, well, let's get started, shall we?"

The lesson seemed to go by quickly, which turned out to be for the best in the end. Te'chok had just finished explaining to me some of the other things summoners often used dragons for besides travel—the great beasts had incredible strength, and were sometimes used instead of the shadow demon when it came to defense—when there was a rapid knock on the door. I paid little attention to the noise, so enthralled was I with the green-scaled, golden-spined dragon that was mine to call. It took me several seconds to realize that Te'chok had asked me—twice—to release the creature so that Ke'tai could open the door. It would be best to attend to the interruption without the added distraction of having the demon present. I sighed regretfully, but did as he asked.

Te'chok laughed as the dragon vanished from sight, but his amusement dissipated as soon as Ke'tai had opened the door. Adele stood in the hall, looking rather impatient and did not seem to be happy that she had been kept waiting.

"Summoner Kai'lind has just arrived with his charge," she said in her rapid British accent. "They are waiting for the lot of you in the library." She turned on one black stiletto heel, and strode away, the click of her heels on the tiled floor echoing in the empty corridor.

Te'chok bit his lower lip and appeared annoyed about something. "She's not happy about something," he said once she was out of hearing range. "I'll have to talk with her later. But first, we should go see Kai'lind and your friend, Elliot."

I made a face and followed Te'chok into the hallway. "He's not really my friend," I said quietly. "I hardly know him."

Te'chok shrugged, as if to say that it wasn't important, and continued on. "I just assumed he was, since you asked about him so often."

I sighed. "It's not that simple," I replied. "I wanted him to be safe, because I knew how it would affect Xan if something happened to him. But now…everything's changed. I know why you had them leave Seattle, but I think the loss of him is something she'll never recover from."

Te'chok glanced over his shoulder to look at me for a moment before he spoke again. "That statement seems very ominous to me, Chandra."

Although I didn't understand the meaning behind his words, I did not press him on the subject. I had only said what I had because I knew my sister; she had *finally* found a guy she was happy with, after countless failed relationships, and now she believed he was dead. I knew how Xandra would have reacted, and it would devastate her for many years to come.

As we entered the library, I saw Elliot standing near one of the cushioned chairs, looking rather nervous. Across from him and seated was the summoner I assumed must be Kai'lind; he was very tall, well over six feet, and had the appearance of being in his mid-thirties. His head was completely shaved, his skin was tanned, and he had the appearance of one who often went to the gym; had it not been for the silver irises of his eyes, I would not have known he was a summoner at first glance. He was dressed casually in blue jeans and a plain black t-shirt.

Te'chok introduced himself to Elliot and welcomed Kai'lind to the compound in much the same fashion as he had done for Il'zaks and Ke'tai upon our arrival. Elliot was focused primarily on Te'chok at first, and then his focus shifted and he caught my gaze. He managed a somewhat strained smile while worry crept into his dark eyes.

"I am glad the two of you made it here safely," Te'chok said once the introductions were finished. "Things in Seattle seem to have become rather tense for our kind lately."

Kai'lind nodded knowingly. "That they have," he agreed. "I am glad to see Miss Grey is still here, and safe as well." He turned to face me, and then said, "The news in Washington State has been focusing on your supposed disappearance altogether too much, if you ask me."

I looked down, feeling suddenly uncomfortable under his intense gaze. "I'm sorry if Xan's caused you any trouble," I mumbled. I doubted that Elliot had heard my words, though I knew Kai'lind and the other two summoners had.

"You can't go apologizing for what your sister may or may not have done, Chandra," Ke'tai whispered in my ear.

Te'chok sighed, and Kai'lind stood, rising suddenly to his full height. "You have nothing to apologize for. We came here safely, and that is all that matters now." I had the distinct impression that Kai'lind could become quite intimidating if he wanted to be, due in part to his height and physical appearance.

The talk shifted to the trip from Seattle to Boston, and while Kai'lind and Te'chok did most of the talking, Elliot walked nervously towards where I stood beside Ke'tai. "When we're finished here, I need to talk with you," he whispered. "About Xandra, and…other things."

I nodded, and Ke'tai whispered, "I want to be present for this talk, if that's okay with the two of you."

I glanced at Elliot briefly, and we both nodded. We stood quietly, listening to the conversation as it wound to its conclusion. Once Te'chok had satisfied his curiosity, he excused himself, mentioning that he needed to speak with Adele. I had the impression he was concerned regarding her apparent displeasure from earlier. Kai'lind followed a moment behind, pausing to inform Elliot he would be expecting him for a lesson in the morning, before he exited the library.

"Well, let's sit down," Ke'tai said after a moment of awkward silence. "I'm sure we have a lot to talk about."

Once we were all seated, Elliot looked straight at me and said, "Kai'lind didn't tell me you were alive, that he knew what happened, until last night. Xandra was worried sick, and I…I did my best to comfort her. It was so hard; the police told her that since you hadn't turned up yet, you were more than likely dead." He sighed and ran a hand through his dark hair. "I understand why you left as you did," he said after a moment. "Kai'lind told me about the hunters, too."

I nodded, feeling little better than wretched. "I'm sorry, Elliot, for everything. I wish I could have said something, but it would have been impossible with Xan as she is."

Elliot smirked. "As soon as Kai'lind found out she had met with Thad Taylor, he was banging on the door of my apartment practically shouting that we had to leave *now*. God, I've never been so scared in my life."

I nodded, understanding well what he had likely gone through.

"For the both of you, it was a dangerous game you were playing, being so close to Xandra," Ke'tai said quietly. "I think it was probably necessary while it lasted, but it was very risky. I'm surprised that Te'chok let it go on as long as he did."

"There weren't any other hunters there at first, though," I reminded him. "It wasn't until recently…"

Ke'tai nodded. "I know, but all the same, it was bound to happen eventually."

"So, Xan, she thinks you're dead, and probably me as well?" I asked Elliot uncertainly. When he nodded, I looked down and sighed. I wanted to cry, but I held the tears at bay. In a wavering tone, I said, "I know that there is no way I could be…but I wish there were some way I could be there for her. We weren't always close, but that changed during the last few years. And she's my *sister*."

Elliot looked down at the wood-planked floor, his dark eyes betraying his grief. "I was going to propose to her, before this all happened," he said quietly. "Before you went away, I mean. And then I was forced to fake my own death because I was no longer safe around her, the one person in all the world that I wanted to be with more than anything." He raised his dark eyes to meet mine again, and there were tears there. His next words came out in a pained whisper. "Do you have any idea what that is *like?*"

I gazed at him, and felt tears sting my eyes. I could only imagine what he was going through. "I'm so sorry, Elliot," I whispered. "Had we just left that night, and I hadn't stopped by the apartment to get some things, no one would have learned of the ability you have. You could have still been there for her."

His face twisted into an expression of anguish, and he closed his eyes. The room was silent for several seconds while Elliot regained his composure, and when he spoke again, his voice was raw. "I loved her, Chandra. But if she were ever to have found out about me, even if I never was trained, she would have left me. Because of what we are, the relationship was doomed no matter what. I knew that within a few days after you disappeared…It was one of the first things Kai'lind explained to me. And yet, I still tried, because I loved her so very much."

"But you were there for her, when she needed you," I said softly. "I'm sure my turning up missing was hard news for her to take."

He nodded, his eyes locked upon the floor once again. "At first, she was angry…You know how Xan is, that's always her first reaction whenever anything goes wrong. She blamed the mysterious Kevin—who I assume is Ke'tai?" When I nodded, he went on. "I guess in that sense she was right, in a way. You did run off with him."

"I didn't have much choice in the matter, though had he simply asked me to leave with him, I would have," I admitted. I glanced at Ke'tai who flashed one of his beautiful smiles in my direction, and I felt my face flush as I turned back to face Elliot. Elliot was still looking down, and I did not think he had seen the brief exchange.

"Well, anyway, she was angry," Elliot continued. "After two days, when you didn't show up, she called the police to report you missing. At first, they didn't want to treat it as a case—they thought you would still turn up at any moment and announce you had been to Vegas or something to elope, since there was a boyfriend involved. They told her to wait another few days, and then if you still didn't show, to call back." He sighed, and finally raised his eyes to look into mine. "I've never seen her so furious before. I thought she was going to bring the building down around her—she was throwing things, and screaming and crying, and…and I didn't know what to do."

I raised my eyebrows at this news. "I don't think I've seen her like that before, either. What did you do?"

Elliot's mouth twisted into a worried frown. "I left her there," he said. "I went out and sat in my car, but I didn't drive away. I didn't want to leave her, but I was afraid of staying and getting hurt. She was crazy." He sighed. "In the end, I sat there for maybe thirty minutes, and then I went back up to the apartment. She was calmer then, but the apartment was a mess. I helped her clean it up again, and we talked for a long while."

"That day should have been near the end of the hunters' convention," Ke'tai said. "It was about three weeks ago, then?"

Elliot nodded. "That seems about right, yes. And Xan, she did as the police asked and waited those few days before she called them again. This time, they actually took her seriously, because by then you had been gone for a week, and no one knew anything about it. There happened to be a news reporter at the police station when she went in to make the official report, and he overheard the story. Naturally, it was all over the local news within a couple of days, and when you didn't turn up, and the police found nothing to move the case along, it started to appear nationally. It was one of those times where the reporter was in the right place at the right time and got hold of a story no one else had yet. Xan was happy about the publicity, even though I think it made it harder for her to deal with some of the things the police said to her."

"Like what?" I asked.

"Well, about three days before I had to leave, they told her that since they couldn't find anything, you were either not going to turn up by your own choice, or you were dead," he replied. "She didn't believe the first part would hold true, but the thought that you might be dead…Let's just say she didn't take that news very well." He sighed. "I think it must have been the day after that when she first met with the hunters, from what Kai'lind has told me."

"There must have been a group of them that decided to stay in Seattle after the convention was over," Ke'tai said thoughtfully. "That's probably why Te'chok chose Kai'lind to approach you about training…Kai'lind can blend in with a crowd better than most of us can."

Elliot managed a strained smile, and nodded. "That's probably true." He sighed. "One of the hunters approached her when she was at work," he said after a moment. "He gave her a business card, and said he'd offer her a better job if she called the next day. I know Xan wasn't happy working at the grocery store, so it makes sense that she called them." He looked down and was silent for a time, and then he looked up again and said, "The day after her first meeting with them, Kai'lind came and told me we had to leave. I hadn't seen her since she met with them, but...I think they knew about me, based on something she must have told them. Or if they didn't know, they suspected it."

Ke'tai frowned. "Do you think the suicide ploy actually worked to fool the hunters?"

Elliot shrugged. "Kai'lind said if the police were the only ones to investigate, there would be no trouble. He was worried about the hunters investigating though, and that's what made me think they must have at least suspected something. If they did investigate, they'd know that wasn't a real body in my apartment, and Xan would know soon afterwards that I wasn't really dead, but something far worse, according to their thinking." He swallowed hard, and said, "If they do find out, and they tell her what they know about me, she'll hate me. Not because of anything I did to her, but because of what I *am*. I was always told that 'life's not fair', but this...This is torture. I *love* her."

"I can relate to what you're saying," I replied quietly. "If Xan knew about me, she'd react the same way. It wouldn't matter that we're sisters, that we're family; when she gets it into her head that something is true, there is no dissuading her, no matter who you are or how ridiculous her claims might be."

"She'll fit right in with the rest of them, then," Ke'tai said dryly.

I sighed. "So I've been told. But it doesn't make it any easier, Ke'tai."

The room was silent for a few moments, and then Elliot sighed heavily. "There's something else you should know, Chandra," he said, uncertain.

"What is it?" I asked, turning my attention fully upon him once more.

"It's something Xan said, a few weeks ago," he replied. "We were talking—she was having a bad day, because the police investigation into your disappearance wasn't going well, and she was frustrated. I asked her, based on some of the things she had told me about your childhood, if it was really worth getting so worked up over. And she looked at me and said, 'I know you don't get along with your siblings, Elliot, but that isn't how it works for everyone else. Chandra and I have had some rough spells, but the last few years have been the best. I'd do anything just to know she was alive, and safe'." He sighed. "That was before she met up with the hunters…and I've wondered since then if she would have said something differently if that conversation had occurred afterward."

I looked down, unable to respond. A wild, desperate hope had seized me; just a few days prior, Te'chok and I had spoken of the possibility of an alliance between the summoners and the hunters, unlikely though it was. Maybe Xandra would prove to be the key to such an occurrence? Moments later, my sense of reason returned, and I sighed, knowing well that what I had hoped for during those few fleeting seconds was nothing short of wishful thinking. I had just mentioned that Xandra was stubborn when it came to changing her way of thinking, and I knew that it would be nearly impossible to convince her that what she was now being told by the hunters was false, little better than propaganda. There was no truly safe way to even make contact with my sister, and I knew this. Te'chok's words came back to me then: *"They will shoot first, and ask questions later."*

I looked back up to meet Elliot's dark-eyed gaze, and said, "Had it been after she'd met with the hunters, I think that conversation may have been very different—if she knew the truth about what I am."

Elliot nodded. "You do have a point, there," he conceded. "As far as we could tell—Kai'lind and I, that is—Xan didn't suspect anything about your disappearance, besides that it had something to do with this 'Kevin' person you had been dating. I think…I think your secret's still safe."

"Besides," Ke'tai put in, "if the hunters had any idea where you really had gone, Chandra, Te'chok would have told us something. As aggravating as he can be at times, he's a good guy for the most part."

Elliot yawned, and then shook his head while blinking several times, as though to clear his head. "Sorry, I'm really tired. I have trouble sleeping in moving cars, so the trip here was pretty exhausting. Do you know where my room is?"

"No, but I know someone who will," Ke'tai replied, quickly rising to his feet, and beckoning the two of us to follow him. "We'll go ask Adele—she should be in the lobby, unless Te'chok is still speaking with her."

Elliot nodded, stifling another yawn. "It just hit me all of a sudden," he said. "I must have been running on adrenaline or something, and it finally wore off."

When we reached the lobby, Adele was indeed at her station as usual, and Te'chok was nowhere to be seen. Ke'tai explained Elliot's request for a room so he could catch up on his sleep. Adele nodded briskly, rose from her desk, and motioned for Elliot to follow her down the corridor toward the apartments.

"So, I finally meet the mysterious Elliot," Ke'tai said once they had gone. "You know, in a way, I'm kind of glad he's here now—he can help you get through this mess with your sister. He understands what you're going through all too well."

I managed a smile. The lengthy discussion regarding Xandra had caused me to feel melancholy, and I didn't feel much like talking any more. "I suppose he does. But I'd rather just do something to forget about her for a while…It's depressing."

"Let's go for a ride," he said after a moment. "We'll take my bike, and just drive for a while. That always helps me take my mind off things—maybe it'll help you, too."

I nodded in agreement. "Let's do it. I don't care where we go—let's just go."

# 17

# CHIMÆRA

The next morning, I awoke to the sound of the phone ringing. Ke'tai rose and was already at the door by the time I had managed to sit up. He glanced over his shoulder as he heard my movement. He smiled and said, "I was just getting the phone. I'll be back in a moment."

He disappeared through the doorway. A few seconds later the phone stopped ringing and I could hear him talking quietly in the other room. I rose and began to dress, feeling rather well this morning in spite of having a dream the night before; the dragon in the dream had not been threatening in any way, and we had been flying through the sky of another world for what seemed to have been many hours. My body did not ache as it had with so many of the other dreams, and I welcomed this change, however brief it may have been.

Ke'tai appeared in the doorway as I was pulling on a shirt, the phone in his hand. "It's Elliot," he said, sounding a bit mystified. "He wants to talk to you."

I nodded, taking the phone from him as he went about his morning routine. "Hey, Elliot," I said into the phone.

"Uh, hi." He sounded nervous on the other end of the line. "I was wondering if you and Ke'tai would care to join me for breakfast? There was something else I wanted to talk to you about, that I forgot to mention last night."

"I don't think it'll be a problem," I replied, "but let me check with him." I put my hand over the receiver and said, "Do you feel up to breakfast this morning, Ke'tai?"

He chuckled. "You ought to know me well enough by now, Chandra. They serve pancakes. I'm there."

Laughing, I put the phone back to my ear. "We'll be there in a few, Elliot."

"Great. See you there."

"What did he want?" Ke'tai asked as soon as I had hung up the phone and returned to the bedroom. He was now standing before the mirror, spiking his hair as usual.

"He just wants to talk some more, I guess," I replied with a shrug. "It didn't sound serious."

A few minutes later we were in the cafeteria; I had settled at a table with a bowl of hot oatmeal, while Ke'tai was standing at the counter awaiting his customary stack of pancakes. Elliot arrived not long afterwards, taking the time to place his order for scrambled eggs and toast before coming over to join us. As Elliot seated himself across the table from the two of us, the summoner Kai'lind entered the room, and Elliot sighed.

"What's wrong?" I asked.

"I was hoping to have a little more time to talk before I was dragged off for more training," he replied, frowning slightly. "Now that he's here, I know that's not going to happen."

"Have him join us," Ke'tai offered.

"No, I—"

Ke'tai stood up without waiting for Elliot to finish, and strode to where the much taller Kai'lind stood near the counter. Elliot hung his head and sighed again. The two summoners talked for a moment, and then Ke'tai returned, flashing us both a grin.

"He'll be over as soon as they have his food ready," Ke'tai stated cheerily. "You know, Kai'lind and I finished our training about the same time, and I taught him a bit of karate awhile back. He's a good guy."

"So, you didn't just invite him over to give Elliot more time to talk then?" I asked, amused. "You wanted to talk to him yourself."

Ke'tai shrugged. "Well, yeah. We've become pretty good friends over the years."

Elliot looked between us as though he weren't certain of how to respond. At that moment, Kai'lind set his tray down and took the open seat next to Elliot.

"You know, I was glad to see you here this morning," Kai'lind said to Ke'tai as he speared a fried potato wedge with his fork, "it's been a while since we last could to talk face to face."

Ke'tai nodded. "It seems that things in Seattle have made it possible for us to work together again, at least for a time."

The two chatted for a while, sometimes speaking of our current situation, and other times about things from the past. Elliot picked at his breakfast and said little; he looked rather disappointed at the turn of events. I felt sorry for him, and a bit guilty; he had asked us here to speak privately, and Ke'tai had ruined his opportunity.

I was about to say something to Ke'tai, when he turned his attention to Elliot. "I know you wanted some time to talk this morning, and I'm sure all of this catching up Kai'lind and I have been doing is boring for you. Why don't we let you say what you came here to?"

I was pleased, to say the least; Ke'tai had been more perceptive than I had given him credit for. Elliot looked a bit uncomfortable, however, and I wondered why that was.

"Well, I...I feel like I need to let Chandra know about what I wrote to Xan, in that infamous 'suicide note'," Elliot said haltingly. "I wanted you to know what I wrote and what the truth of the matter really is...in case you ever happen to see a copy of it."

Kai'lind nodded knowingly, and rose from his seat, having finished his breakfast already. "I'll catch up with you when you're finished," he said to Elliot. "Meet me in the lobby." Elliot nodded, but said nothing until the tall summoner had exited the room.

"The note was pretty lengthy," Elliot said quietly, "and I tried to make it as detailed and as realistic as possible—something that Xan would believe. I mean, the hunters already suspected something by the time Kai'lind and I staged my apartment, and I didn't want there to be anything she would question. But you have to know, Chandra."

I nodded uncertainly, a myriad of questions swirling through my brain.

"I told Xan that I didn't love her," Elliot continued in a choked whisper. "That was the greatest lie I've ever told, and I never want to be forced to tell another like it again." He was silent for a time, collecting his thoughts, before he continued. "I told her that after I had met you, she was only the sister that I had settled for—that I was actually in love with you. Now, I'm *not*, Chandra, but that's what I wrote, because I knew she'd believe that."

I stared at him, uncomprehending for several long seconds. "Why on earth would Xan believe *that*?" I demanded.

Elliot looked down and mumbled, "She was very insecure when it came to comparing herself to you. She always thought you were the prettier one, and that no matter who she dated, there was always going to be the chance he'd leave her for you."

I gaped at him. "Xan never told me any of that!"

He managed a sad, half-smile. "She was afraid to. When she was telling me this, she said she was terrified that you would find out, and think less of her. She had you on this pedestal…She thought you were perfect, and that she'd always be second best."

I sighed and looked away, shaking my head. "I've never been perfect," I replied. "I know when we were out together, I was usually the first one the guys would try to speak to, but I never thought anything of it. I never realized how it would affect Xan."

"Well, it did," Elliot stated, sounding weary. "I'm a horrible person…I used one of her greatest fears to make her believe something that was a complete lie. But…I couldn't have stayed there, pretending that everything was fine, and just waiting for my own execution. Please understand, I had to do something—and a mere disappearance would have only roused the hunters' suspicions even more."

I wanted to be angry with him for causing my sister so much pain, yet I couldn't bring myself to do so. I knew he had done what any other would-be summoner would have, had they been in the same position. I simply couldn't find it within myself to hate him for it. I sighed.

"You did what you had to," I conceded, "and I understand that. Honestly, I'm no better—from what you said last night, she probably thinks I'm dead, too."

Elliot's gaze met mine, and he seemed somehow surprised. "I was anticipating that you'd be mad at me," he said after a moment. "I just thought you would be…Xan's always getting angry at the least little thing, and this isn't really a little thing."

I managed a half-hearted smile. "I'm not Xandra."

He nodded and stood to leave. "Yeah, I know."

After a few moments of staring down at the tabletop, I sighed, and turned my head to meet Ke'tai's gaze as he sat beside me. "Is it right that I feel so numb to all of this?"

His eyes narrowed in concern, but he shrugged. "I don't know, Chandra. I can't say I've ever met another summoner who has gone through quite what you have to get where they are. Maybe what you feel isn't numbness, exactly, but something else? Perhaps shock?"

It was my turn to shrug. I honestly didn't know how to describe what I was feeling.

"Hey, maybe we can see if Te'chok wants to do a training session with you today," Ke'tai suggested after a moment. "It might help to take your mind off everything else that is going on." When I nodded, he gestured toward the door of the cafeteria and said, "He's here."

I lifted my gaze to see where Ke'tai pointed, and simply nodded again, unwilling to make the first move today. Ke'tai waved to Te'chok, and the other summoner came over a moment later, worry tracing lines in his brow. I frowned, not having wanted to alert him that anything was wrong.

"Is everything okay?" Te'chok asked as he slid into the seat across from me.

I sighed and frowned at Ke'tai in annoyance before I nodded to Te'chok. "I'm fine, nothing went wrong last night," I assured him, knowing well that was what had been in the forefront of his mind. "We were just talking with Elliot, and he told me some things about what happened between he and Xan...But I'll be fine."

Te'chok's gaze was unreadable, but he nodded.

Beside me, Ke'tai shrugged. "I thought you might be able to help, if you weren't too busy today..."

Te'chok nodded briefly, understanding. "Yes, of course. The next one will be a little more difficult, and I would advise at least a couple days' worth of rest between this and the next, but today should work out fine." Te'chok glanced behind him to check the clock on the wall above the door. "Meet me in the usual training room in an hour. I have an appointment in a few minutes, and then I should be free for most of the day."

An hour later, I was standing in the center of the training room while Ke'tai stood sentinel near the door. Te'chok had just entered, apologizing for keeping us waiting, though he had been punctual, as usual. I had recovered somewhat from the shock I had been given by Elliot earlier in the day, though the knowledge of what he had written to my sister still tore at my heart.

"How are you feeling?" Te'chok asked as he approached me.

I shrugged. "I'm fine. Better than earlier."

"I am sorry you have had to go through so much so quickly," he said softly. "If there is ever anything I can do, all you have to do is ask."

I nodded, wishing that I could convince both he and Ke'tai that there was nothing to be concerned over. How many times did I have to reassure them that I would be fine, that nothing was wrong? I simply wanted to complete my training, in the hope it would distract me from my sister and Elliot, if even for a short while.

When I said nothing in reply, Te'chok nodded and glanced uncertainly at Ke'tai, before he turned his attention back to me. "Well, I suppose we should get started, then. I wanted to teach you of the demon called chimæra today." He paused briefly, gathering his thoughts, before continuing on. "The chimæra is an interesting creature, one you may have heard mention of before, if you studied Greek mythology."

I shook my head. "I think we looked at a couple myths when I was in high school, but that one doesn't sound familiar."

"The chimæra, according to some sources, was a three-headed creature, part goat, part snake, and part lion. In the Greek mythology, a chimæra could breathe fire, but the actual demon does not. The demon we call chimæra is an altogether different creature, and its true form is one that is difficult to look upon; the chimæra is a shape-shifter, and in its native state can appear as either a conglomeration of many different creatures, or as a shadowy form with no definitive shape. Each summoner's chimæra seems to appear slightly different. I suppose the Greeks' version of the chimæra may have assumed the form it did because it is difficult to describe the creature's true shape…

"Anyway, we typically summon the chimæra when we are in need of something that can easily blend in with its surroundings," Te'chok explained. "Because it can take on the shape of nearly any living creature, it is very difficult for the hunters to detect. The chimæra has some limitations, however; it cannot assume the form of a human being, nor can it take on the form of something significantly larger or smaller than its native state. Some summoners have used them as assassins when the need has arisen, for the bite of the chimæra is highly venomous and can incapacitate a human being within minutes."

I nodded, having some difficulty in picturing the creature that had just been described to me. I wondered just how often I would actually have the necessity to call such a creature.

Te'chok's mention of the hunters, although involuntarily, had caused me to think once again of Xandra and what she soon would become. I frowned, hoping I would never have to call such a creature—or any creature, for that matter—to defend myself against her. If it were any other hunter, I doubted that I would hesitate, but Xandra was my sister...

"Chandra?" Te'chok asked in concern.

I sighed. "Sorry, I was just thinking," I replied evasively.

Te'chok nodded once, but appeared unconvinced. "About what, I have no doubts. Are you in the proper state of mind to continue, or shall we postpone the rest of this until later?"

His tone was genuine, but I found the remark somehow grating. I felt the irrational need to lash out at him, but instead I shook my head in an attempt to clear my thoughts. I closed my eyes for a few brief seconds, attributing my anger to the fact that my sister had unwittingly joined forces with the very people who would kill us, given the chance.

"We can continue," I replied after several moments of silence, and then I finally opened my eyes again. "I'll be fine...I just had to refocus."

Te'chok's silver eyes scanned my face for a time, and then he nodded as though satisfied. "Very well, then. I will summon a chimæra to me, so please do focus. I would hate to see you make a mistake at this stage, Chandra."

I nodded, glancing briefly at Ke'tai before Te'chok began. Ke'tai was still leaning casually against the wall, though his gaze was riveted upon me. I could see that he was worried in that instant when our eyes met, but I quickly diverted my gaze to focus upon Te'chok. I hoped I had not given away any of what had been running through my mind in that brief moment of contact. As Te'chok began to call his demon, I heard Ke'tai sigh and I knew that he would be expecting to talk with me once the lesson had concluded.

Pushing my thoughts aside, I focused my full attention upon Te'chok, memorizing and internalizing the words he was speaking prior to the appearance of the demon called the chimæra. I had a difficult time looking directly at the creature; it was at once amorphous, and yet seemed to be on the verge of taking one of a thousand different shapes in the same instant. The creature's outline seemed to flicker and distort if I focused directly upon it. I found if I stared at the wall beyond, the flickering seemed to lessen, and I could pick out individual shapes for the briefest of instants before it abruptly morphed into something else.

After nearly a minute of trying to distinguish what exactly the chimæra appeared to be, I frowned and looked away. The constant shifting was beginning to give me a headache.

Te'chok chuckled, and I turned my gaze toward him. "Not all chimæras appear as mine does. I must admit that mine is quite difficult to look upon, unless I order it to take on a specific form and remain that way."

"No kidding," I replied.

He smiled. "Why don't you try now? Let's see if yours is any easier on the eyes."

I required no further encouragement; I closed my eyes and began to dance to the cadence of the summoning words. As I finished, I opened my eyes to take a look at the chimæra I had called. This one did not flicker as Te'chok's did, but it was equally difficult to discern its form; it appeared as a faint shadow with no determinable shape, so faint that it could have been attributed to a trick of the light. I knew it was there and what it was, because I could sense its presence within the room, its precise location, and its bond to my mind.

Both Te'chok and Ke'tai appeared frantic. "Chandra?" Ke'tai asked from his post near the door. He was now standing fully upright, and looked poised for a fight. At the same time Te'chok asked, "Did your summoning fail, Chandra?"

Confused, I shook my head. "What are you talking about? It's right *there*," I said, pointing at the vague shadow. "Aren't you able to tell when I summon a demon?"

The two summoners looked at one another, and then both shook their heads. "Why would you think we could sense that?" Te'chok asked after a moment. "I can tell when other summoners are nearby, but I cannot sense their demons. Your chimæra, it is here then?"

I nodded. "That shadow, there," I said, pointing again. "It's hard to see…should I make it change?"

Te'chok nodded as the color drained from his face, and I had the distinct feeling that neither he nor Ke'tai believed anything was there. I frowned, frustrated that even Ke'tai had failed to listen to me, and ordered the chimæra to change forms. Because I was upset, the first creature that came to mind was a tiger—a creature that was both powerful and dangerous. The chimæra shifted and became visible to both summoners while it bared its teeth, sensing my mood.

The expression of relief upon Ke'tai's face was unmistakable, and he leaned back heavily against the wall. I frowned at him again, though he didn't react. Te'chok drew a breath and released it slowly, seeming to relax.

"I have never seen a chimæra quite like yours, Chandra," Te'chok said after a moment. "I apologize for not believing you when you said it was here, but I could not see the shadow you were speaking of. To my eyes, there was nothing there…and then suddenly there was an angry tiger."

I managed a small smile. "I think it sensed that I was frustrated," I replied. "I told it to be a tiger, but I didn't tell it to act like that."

"I am interested in your chimæra's native state," Te'chok said thoughtfully. "Can you have it return to that? I want to see if I can make out anything of its form."

I nodded and complied with his request. Te'chok frowned as the chimæra seemed to disappear from his view, and then he walked to where I was standing. "Interesting," he muttered to himself, and then walked to another angle, nodding all the while.

"What is it?" I asked.

"It seems that your chimæra is only visible if someone is standing very near to where you are," he said, "and even then, it is very difficult to see."

Ke'tai pushed away from the wall and made his way over to where I was standing. "Oh, I do see it now," he remarked to himself. "Huh."

I frowned at him again. "We'll talk about this later," I hissed into his ear before he wandered back towards the door. He turned around to face me, obviously confused, which only served to frustrate me all the more. How could he feign innocence, when he had failed to believe me? He ought to have known me well enough by now to discern when I was telling the truth, especially when it came to a matter such as this.

"Have it change again," Te'chok said, breaking my train of thought.

I nodded, tearing my gaze away from Ke'tai. I asked the chimæra to shift forms, to become a wolf with silver-gray fur. It bristled in Ke'tai's direction, releasing a low growl. I restrained it, and refused to allow it to do anything more than threaten. Ke'tai raised his hands, palms upward, in a gesture that seemed to say, "What did I do?"

"I want you to look carefully at the chimæra's eyes, Chandra," Te'chok said after a moment. His voice sounded uncertain, and I turned to look in his direction, ignoring Ke'tai for the time being.

"I'm not angry with you," I told him, "so there's no need to be worried about it. Besides, I'm not actually going to let it do anything to him, and he *ought* to know that."

I crossed my arms and shot Ke'tai another angry glare before turning my attention back to the chimæra. I knelt down as the chimæra turned and padded silently across the floor to my location. It stood still as I looked into its eyes, and I noted what Te'chok had been wishing me to see. The demon's eyes had a faint, grayish-black swirling pattern that traced its way through its pupils; the pattern was very subtle and would be almost impossible to detect if one did not know what to look for.

"There's a swirl," I said, standing up again.

Te'chok nodded. "Yes. When a chimæra takes on the form of another creature, that swirl, as you termed it, is the only indicator that it is something other than what you see. The phrase we use to describe it is *ocular scieropia*, which means roughly that we see a shadow over its eyes." He hesitated a moment, then said, "I believe that is all I had for your lesson today, so you may release the creature if you would like to."

I nodded and did so, refocusing my gaze upon Ke'tai.

"I will contact you in two or three days for your next lesson, Chandra," Te'chok said as he strode towards the door. "I hope you have a pleasant afternoon."

"You also," I replied without looking at him, causing Ke'tai to frown as Te'chok left the room.

"What is wrong with you?" Ke'tai demanded as soon as the door had closed again. "I don't understand!"

"Yeah, I noticed that," I replied dryly. "You didn't *believe* me, Ke'tai. Why do you think I would risk lying to you about something like this?"

He sighed, looking suddenly weary. "I didn't think you were lying, Chandra. I—"

"What was it then?" I demanded. "You were just as freaked out as he was, even after I told you right where the demon was. You thought I had failed…"

"I didn't want to think that, Chandra," Ke'tai replied softly, walking towards me from his post by the door. "Believe me when I say that. It's just…"

"Just *what?*" I demanded, my anger slipping away as Ke'tai placed his hands on my shoulders. I felt tears began to threaten.

"I've seen others fail, and deny that they have because they fear the outcome of such a thing," he replied quietly. "Il'zaks once told me a story about one of his former students, and I've never forgotten it; I think I ought to share it with you. Would you like to take a walk and hear it?"

I nodded, feeling like a fool for having been so angry with him. "I'm sorry, Ke'tai. I just thought you should have known me better than that by now…"

He smiled sadly. "You are right, Chandra, but sometimes when I'm afraid for you, I let that cloud my judgment. And I *was* afraid, when you had finished dancing and I could see nothing there. I feared that I was going to lose you. I don't want to think about what I would do if that were to happen. I know it would not be pretty."

"I'm not going anywhere," I assured him.

He managed another sad smile, and nodded as he pulled open the door to the training room. "Il'zaks told me once about a student of his, one who had great potential, much like you do. This man, he was of noble birth, and had been brought up in a manner that had left him very arrogant and confident in his own abilities to a fault—"

"Noble birth?" I interrupted him. "Does that mean Il'zaks was in Europe then? And when was it?"

Ke'tai chuckled and took one of my hands in his. "He never told me when it was, Chandra, nor where, though my guess runs along with yours. I think it must have been somewhere in Europe, probably one of the western countries, and I also think that it must have been at least a couple hundred years ago, though I do not know exactly."

I nodded, and he continued. "Anyway, Il'zaks saw this man's potential for greatness, and offered to train him in the ways of the summoner. Even though this man treated him as one of his servants, and expected to be able to learn everything as soon as he was taught, Il'zaks attempted to teach him. People like that don't usually survive the training…Il'zaks knew that, and yet, he hoped that he would be able to change this man's attitude somehow, to guide him through the training process safely."

"He didn't, did he?" I asked.

Ke'tai shook his head. "No, but that's not my point here. During one of this man's lessons, he went through the process of summoning, and nothing appeared for him. Since it was one of the less powerful demons, Il'zaks knew immediately that he had failed—not only did nothing come, but Il'zaks had noticed the man had mispronounced one of the words he had spoken. The man tried to make up a story that his demon was right there in front of him, and that Il'zaks simply did not see it. Il'zaks is generally a gentle person, and will avoid conflict if at all possible, so he went through the rest of the lesson pretending to believe this man even though he knew it was a hopeless case. That man left and went home afterwards…Il'zaks heard the next morning that he had died in his sleep, apparently of a heart attack."

"What happens to people when they fail a summoning, exactly?" I asked in a near-whisper. "I know they die…but what *happens?*"

Ke'tai shrugged and appeared uncomfortable. "We don't know, Chandra. Most of the people who don't finish the training die in their sleep, usually of an apparent heart attack, even if they seem completely healthy. What happens during that time is something no one has ever been able to learn. I mean, there are some speculations, but we don't know anything for sure."

"What do you think happens?" I pressed, curious.

"I think they die in one of those dreams," he said quietly, his gaze focused downward. "But instead of the demons submitting to them, I think the demons attack… When those dreams happen, you're in *their* world—or at least your consciousness is—and you're very vulnerable. A wrong move, even if the initial summoning was successful, and they could turn on you. I think a failed summoning is almost like an insult to them, and they react badly…Sort of like what happened with your incubus. Thankfully we were able to fix that situation," he added as an aside. "I don't think I've ever been so scared before."

"Ke'tai, can I ask you something else?"

He nodded. "Of course, you can. You know that."

"How many more demons are there for me to learn?"

He hesitated a moment, looking torn, and then sighed. "I'm not supposed to tell you that," he replied. "It's part of the rules the Order has in place. But, they've already broken so many of them for you—and now for Elliot—that I don't see Te'chok getting angry if I told you…But, I don't want him pissed at me again either, so I'll check with him first. Okay?"

I nodded. "Okay."

He smiled, one of those brilliant smiles I had come to love so much, but which had been scarce during the past few days. "What I *can* tell you is that you're much closer to finishing than you were when you started all of this."

I laughed. "Oh, that is *so* helpful, Ke'tai."

"Yeah, I know," he said with a grin. "But you love it all the same."

# 18

# CHANGE

It was another four days before Te'chok contacted me about our next lesson. I knew I was nearly finished with the training, based on what Ke'tai had hinted at, and by the time Te'chok finally called to speak with me, I was anxiously awaiting the next step of my training, and what it might bring.

"I don't think I've ever seen you so excited about a phone call before, Chandra," Ke'tai teased as we left the apartment to go to the training room Te'chok liked to use.

"Had you called me instead of writing a letter when we first met, you would have seen me even more excited about a phone call," I replied.

He laughed and took my hand in one of his while we walked along in a blissful silence.

The last few days had been pleasant ones; there had been no more news stories from Seattle regarding my disappearance or my sister, I hadn't had the occasion to see Elliot as a reminder of those events, and I had been able to spend plenty of time with Ke'tai. He had taken me to see his laboratory, just outside of the Boston city limits to the west. Although most of what he tried to describe to me about his work there made little sense, it had been nice to finally see the place where he spent so much of his free time. Like the headquarters, the lab had been built beneath a warehouse building, the interior of which served as a sort of parking garage. When we had been there, only one other vehicle had been present besides the two motorcycles we had driven ourselves, though whom it had belonged to I did not know. We had not met its owner during the tour Ke'tai had given me.

"You aren't going to do any unnecessary worrying today, are you?" I asked him as we approached the door to the training room. "I'm going to be fine."

He smiled. "Yeah, I know. I'll pretend I'm not worried, but I can't promise that I won't be. You mean too much to me, Chandra; I'll always worry."

"I'll be fine," I told him again as I entered the room.

Te'chok was already inside, standing in the center of the room with his back to us. Ke'tai gave my hand a final squeeze before he released it to take his place near the door and I made my way to where Te'chok was standing. He turned around slowly as I approached, and nodded in greeting.

"It seems I've kept you waiting," he said, a bemused smile surfacing on his apparently young features. "You sounded very excited on the phone."

I felt my face flush, but nodded. "I was. I am."

"Good! That's wonderful, because you are nearly finished with the training, and I want you to be aware of a few things before we go on to the real reason why we are both here." He paused a moment, then said, "I know you have been made aware of what the change will be like, but I want you to know that both Il'zaks and I—as well as Ke'tai—will be at your side when it begins, and we will all be there when you awaken again. A summoner undergoing that process is never left alone."

I nodded, relieved at the news. While I had known Ke'tai had no intentions of leaving me alone during that time, I had been uncertain if he would be the only one allowed to attend me while I underwent the painful transformation. I was glad he would have the others with him, if for nothing else but company.

"When you awaken from your transformation, Chandra, one of us is going to ask you a question. At that time, it may sound absurd to you. During my many years of experience, I have learned that by telling those nearing their change that we will ask, it has lessened the confusion later on. One of us will ask you your name; when you awaken, you will not know yourself as Chandra Grey any longer. You will in all probability remember us, and wonder what must be wrong, that we should ask you what your name is after all the time we have spent together. Right now, you understand why we will be asking, but later, you may not."

Again, I nodded, making a mental note that they would be asking this question. I also began to wonder if today would be my last training session, since Te'chok was taking the time to go over this topic with me once more.

"The last thing I wanted to mention is that once you awaken again, you will be working with me full time," Te'chok said. "You will need to know the full workings of the Order, its rules, its people, and its history. You will take over my position within eight weeks of your transformation, and in that time, you will have much to learn." He paused a moment, and then added, "At the end of the eight weeks, there will be a ceremony held here by the Board of Elders, and during that ceremony they will name you as my successor, and I shall step down."

I looked down. I did not feel at all ready to assume so much responsibility within an organization that was still such a mystery to me. Perhaps my insecurity would dissipate once I had finished my training, though I doubted it. I could only hope that Te'chok would help me learn what I needed to in that short eight weeks so that I would be able to take over his role and do well in it.

I felt a hand on my shoulder and looked up to see Te'chok's earnest face just inches from my own. "You'll do well, Chandra; I promise you that. I know exactly what you are feeling now, and I will admit that I had the same sort of misgivings you must be having now. We'll get you through it, and it will be easier than you are imagining. Trust me."

When I nodded, he stepped back and dropped his arm to his side. I hoped what he said was true.

"Ke'tai asked me a few days ago if it would be okay for him to tell you how long you had left in training," Te'chok said after a moment. "I declined that request, solely on the basis of our traditions. However, I've given it some more thought, and I think we may as well tell you. You are here, in our headquarters, which had been unheard of before now, and I do not believe you knowing will change the outcome of anything we do from here on."

My gaze was riveted upon him. I was torn between a dozen different emotions all at once; excitement at knowing, trepidation, fear that I may forget so many things, joy, anxiety, hope… In that moment when Te'chok paused, it felt as though time had stopped and the whole world awaited his next sentence.

"After today, you will have one more training session before the change occurs."

Time suddenly began to flow again, and I felt myself draw an unsteady breath. “One more?” I asked. “That means…”

Te’chok nodded, but his face was grim. “Two more demons, one of which will be unique to you. I will explain more about that at our next session, Chandra. Today I wanted to share with you the knowledge I have of the demon we call the Dreamweaver. This would have been the final demon Ke’tai would have been able to show you, so you would have had to come to me to learn of your final summoning had circumstances not brought us together earlier.”

I glanced over Te’chok’s shoulder to meet Ke’tai’s gaze. He nodded, as though in affirmation of Te’chok’s words, and gave me a somewhat sad smile from his post near the door.

“The Dreamweaver is an interesting sort of demon, unlike any you have studied so far,” Te’chok continued after a moment’s pause. “It is a female demon that possesses the ability to influence a person’s dreams while they sleep. I believe it was the summoner Nae’leil who found a possible reference to these demons in some eastern European folklore; the people called them *Al basti*, and claimed they were responsible for nightmares. Under the command of a summoner, the Dreamweavers can cause nightmares of the worst sort, but they can also cause the most pleasant dreams a person could ever hope to have.

“During the time of the American Civil War, there was a great deal of conflict going on between the Order and the hunters as well. We often used the Dreamweavers to obtain information from those people who were helping the hunters, but who were not hunters themselves. Most hunters would know the instant a demon of any sort came near them, and to be effective, the Dreamweavers must be within arm’s distance of their target. We have also used Dreamweavers to draw out information from prisoners when the need arises, though I am sure there are other uses for these demons as well.”

“How do they influence someone’s dreams?” I asked, unable to visualize such a scenario.

Te’chok appeared thoughtful for a moment before he said, “It’s difficult to say, exactly, because we don’t know how they do it. It seems that their presence near a sleeping person is enough to cause minor disturbances in the normal dream patterns, but if they concentrate on the person enough, they can change the dreams entirely. How these demons do what they do is actually an area of active research the Order is pursuing. If you ever have the chance to meet summoner Nae'leil, which I am certain you will one day, you should ask him what he knows concerning the Dreamweavers."

I nodded, though I wished he could have answered my question more adequately.

"I will show you how to summon a Dreamweaver, though you will not know their full range of capabilities until you summon yours near someone who is asleep," Te'chok stated after a brief pause. "If your training had been more typical, we would have had this session at night, and would have gone somewhere so that you could see for yourself how a Dreamweaver may manipulate a person's dreams. We cannot do that with you, however, because your face has been plastered all over the national news, thanks to your sister."

I frowned and looked away, unhappy with the reminder of my sister and her doings. If only I were finished with this training, perhaps I wouldn't have to remain hiding in Boston any longer under the protection of the summoners...

"I'm sorry, Chandra," Te'chok said quietly. "I know how difficult it has been for you since you left Seattle, and I didn't mean to bring that up about your sister."

I shrugged, and raised my eyes to meet his once more. "It's hard for me to accept what she's done lately," I replied. "I keep wondering, what will happen if I ever see her again? What would I do if I had to fight her? I know she's joined the hunters, but she's still my sister. I don't know what I'd do."

Te'chok's expression was troubled, and he said, "Why don't we work on the summoning, and forget about her for a while?"

"Yeah, sure," I said automatically, at once relieved for the change in subject, yet annoyed by it as well.

Te'chok nodded, though he still appeared uncomfortable as he began to summon the Dreamweaver. I pushed all my other thoughts aside and concentrated on his words carefully, ignoring the urge to continue the conversation about Xandra. That could wait for another time.

When Te'chok had finished, I could see a very faint outline of what appeared to be a woman standing several feet away from him. The figure was translucent, and I could make out very few details of her being.

"Ke'tai, can you turn off the lights?" Te'chok asked. Ke'tai nodded and reached across the closed door of the room to flick the light switch off.

In the sudden darkness, I could see very little—with the exception of Te'chok's Dreamweaver. The figure was indeed that of a woman, perhaps no more than five feet tall. She had hair that fell to her waist in a tangle of curls, and wore a long white dress, the hem of which seemed to disappear before it reached the floor, giving her the appearance of floating. Her entire form was pale, and I had the feeling I was looking through her, rather than at her. I was immediately reminded of the ghost stories I'd heard over the years.

"Dreamweavers are much more difficult to see under the lights," Te'chok said from somewhere in front of me, near to where the ghostly form of the she-demon was currently standing.

"She looks like—"

"—a ghost?" Te'chok asked, humor in his tone. "I would agree, based on the stories I was told as a child about them. I believe that many of the 'ghost sightings' you hear about are actually of these demons; it seems they are more capable of coming across to our realm than any of the others are, though very few of us can actually summon them."

There was a pause, and then the lights came back on, causing me to blink several times in the sudden brightness. It seemed that in the darkness, Te'chok had signaled to Ke'tai to turn them on again, though I had not been able to see the exchange for myself.

"In the daylight, as you can see, the Dreamweaver is nearly invisible," Te'chok continued.

I interrupted him before he could say more. "Can I ask you something that is totally off-topic?"

Te'chok nodded uncertainly. "Yes…"

"Are you able to see in the dark? Because when the lights came back on, it looked like you had motioned to Ke'tai or something, but I couldn't see it."

Ke'tai laughed, and I turned my head to look at him. "We can, Chandra, though I think it's something we've all forgotten to mention to you."

Te'chok shrugged as I turned back to face him. "The ability to see in the dark is not really that important in the grand scheme of your training," he explained. "It is usually something that is overlooked, and comes as a bit of a surprise to new summoners—though they all seemed to have enjoyed that new ability as far as I have seen."

I nodded. "I was just curious how you two managed that…"

"A couple of the things that will change—besides your hair and eye color—will be enhanced eyesight and very fast reflexes," Te'chok replied. "Additionally, you will also be able to summon demons without fear of them—they will obey your every command without question or hesitation, once you have undergone the change. There are also a small group of summoners who have dedicated their free time to studying ancient lore in the hope that they will discover the correct word combinations to summon other types of demons than those currently known to us. Before the change, that sort of research is nothing short of asking for death, but afterwards, it can be done without fear of dire consequences." He paused, then said, "Enough about that. Now it's your turn to call forth a Dreamweaver."

The rest of the lesson went by quickly and without incident. Te'chok left, warning me that my dreams would likely be unpleasant that night. He promised to visit Ke'tai and I for breakfast the following morning—to check up on how I had fared during the night, I presumed.

That night, my dreams were indeed troubled, and the faint, ghostly form of the Dreamweaver haunted them throughout. I awoke, feeling slightly nauseous, disoriented and drenched in sweat, sometime the following morning. Ke'tai was not in the room when I finally found my bearings, but I could hear his voice coming from the living room in low tones. I assumed he must be on the phone with Te'chok.

I sat up slowly, feeling my head spin, and simply sat on the edge of the bed for several seconds while the dizziness receded. I stood unsteadily and began to gather some of my clothes, anticipating that I would have time to shower before we met up with Te'chok for breakfast.

After a few moments, I realized that the other room had gone silent. I turned around to see Ke'tai leaning against the doorframe, smiling, and watching as I picked out some clothes.

"I'm glad to see you're awake," he said quietly. "That was the fourth time Te'chok had called this morning, even though after the first time I told him that I'd call once you woke up. I think he is almost as excited as you must be."

I smiled. "I'm not quite awake enough to be excited, yet," I replied. "Let me get a shower and some food, and maybe then, that will change."

Twenty minutes later found me standing just inside the door to our apartment, waiting while Ke'tai finished up yet another phone conversation with Te'chok. Ke'tai seemed amused at the other summoner's unconcealed excitement, though he was all smiles and full of energy himself.

As he hung up the phone, he flashed me a grin and sauntered over, wrapping his strong arms about me and looking down into my eyes. "I'm excited for you, Chandra," he said softly, pausing to kiss me firmly on the lips. "But you know what? I'm going to miss gazing down into those beautiful brown eyes of yours. I'm sure your eyes will still be beautiful, but they'll never be the same after today."

I looked down as I felt my face flush crimson, but I was unable to conceal the grin that quickly spread across my face. I was excited and scared, nervous and happy all at once. "Yeah, I know," I whispered, venturing to meet his gaze once more, "but I don't think I've ever been so excited about something in my entire life. Well, besides when I hooked up with you, but there's no comparison to that."

He laughed and we kissed once more before he dropped his arms and turned away to open the door. "I can guarantee you that Te'chok is in the cafeteria already, even though I just got off the phone with him. Again," Ke'tai added with a grin. "We shouldn't keep him waiting like this."

Ke'tai was proven correct when we arrived at the cafeteria; Te'chok was indeed there, pacing across the middle of the nearly-deserted room in a rare show of impatience. Il'zaks was there as well, but he was seated at one of the tables calmly sipping coffee from a white mug, dressed impeccably as always. In one corner of the room sat Kai'lind with Elliot, though neither turned in our direction as we entered.

"Were you planning on keeping me waiting all morning?" Te'chok demanded of Ke'tai, though he was grinning all the while.

"Actually, we were thinking about keeping you waiting just a bit longer, to see what you'd do," Ke'tai replied with a mischievous glimmer in his eyes.

"We came as soon as I was ready," I assured Te'chok. "Can I get something to eat before we leave?"

He nodded. "Of course. And I'm sure your significant other would be upset if he missed out on his pancakes…We'll just be sitting here, while you get your breakfast," he said, taking the seat across from Il'zaks.

"I wouldn't be upset," Ke'tai replied, "just not happy."

We all shared a laugh as Ke'tai and I made our way up to the counter to order our breakfasts from one of the cooks. When we returned to the table where Il'zaks and Te'chok were already seated, I was surprised to see Carlos and Trey had appeared to join us as well. Sitting next to Carlos was a man I did not recognize, tall and broad-shouldered with a head as bald as Trey's was, and blue eyes that danced as though he were privately laughing at some sort of joke.

As we approached, Carlos stood to shake Ke'tai's hand once he had set down his plateful of pancakes. He gestured to the newcomer who had stood alongside him and said, "This is Marek Vanderhaas. I was waiting to introduce him to you until we knew for certain that his services would be needed."

Marek nodded, and extended one big hand in my direction. "You must be Ms. Grey," he said in a low voice. "I hear that I'll be working for you within a few days, doing about the same thing Carlos does for Ke'tai. It is a pleasure to meet you."

I took his offered hand, and managed a nervous smile. "It's nice to meet you also, though I'm a little surprised. Nobody told me about this."

Marek shrugged, as if to say that it didn't matter, and took his seat once more. "Don't worry, I've been trained in the workings of this business, and I'll make damned sure nobody messes with you without going through me first."

I raised my eyebrows, uncertain of how to respond, while Ke'tai chuckled and said, "It sounds like you'll be in good hands, love. Sit down and eat, before Te'chok starts pacing around again."

After we had finished eating, Te'chok led the now-sizable group toward his preferred training room. Everyone, including Ke'tai, remained outside in the hallway, and only Te'chok and I entered the room. The room felt much emptier without Ke'tai standing near the door as I had become accustomed to, and I wondered why he had opted to remain outside today.

"There have only been eight summoners, including you, who have been able to call forth a demon stronger than the Dreamweaver in the entire history of the Order," Te'chok stated once the door had been closed. "Only eight, in our nearly twenty-five-hundred-year history. That ought to tell you something of your abilities, Chandra."

I nodded, curious to see where this would lead.

"The man who founded the Order, summoner Ae'tama, was the first; he was also the first summoner to realize his powers. Ae'tama passed away several hundred years ago, but his teachings did not die with him. What I am going to show you today is a part of those teachings—how to summon a unique demon.

"The demon you call today will be one of a kind, bound to you alone. No others will be capable of summoning one exactly like it. Ae'tama, after years of study, told the Elder Nae'leil that he believed these unique demons are attuned to specific summoners' calls; they would complement the summoner's own strength, either at the time of the summoning, or sometime in the future. In truth, we do not know why certain unique demons seem to bind themselves to the summoners they do, but what Ae'tama said appears to be true—either now, or sometime in your future, this demon will be a great asset to you."

"So, there's no way to predict what it will be like?" I asked.

Te'chok shook his curly head. "I'm afraid not, Chandra. The only way to find out what yours will be is to call it. If you react as all others have before you, simply calling the demon here will trigger your change. I want you to know this, so that you are truly ready."

I looked down for a time, thinking over his words carefully. Finally, I drew a breath and raised my head to meet his gaze once more. "When the change begins, what exactly is going to happen to me?"

Te'chok nodded, as though he had been expecting that question. "Most people black out as soon as the change begins. For most, it does not start until after the summoner falls to sleep the night after their final summoning. For those of us like you and I, however, it begins as soon as we call our unique demons. The reason for this seems to be that these demons are so powerful, they take a great deal of our strength simply to call them here. That exertion seems to trigger the change immediately.

"To answer your question simply, you will call your demon. You will likely black out immediately, or very soon after you summon it. When that happens, I'll have Ke'tai come in and take you back to your apartment. Il'zaks, Marek and I will stay there as well, and await your awakening. During that time, your demon will remain present here in our realm, and will not be able to return to its own until you have completed the transformation."

"Why can't Ke'tai be in the room with us?" I asked, finally putting voice to the question that had been nagging me since we'd entered.

"It is our tradition, Chandra," he replied with a shrug. "I do not think it would have hurt anything to have him here, personally, but with so many others waiting outside for you, I felt it was best to follow that tradition. I didn't enjoy the thought of answering questions regarding my reasons for deviating from the expected path."

I nodded, dropping my gaze to the smooth, tiled floor. I was unsure if I was truly ready for this day, even though everything I had done for the past three months had been preparing me for these next few moments. It would be wonderful to be able to go about life without Ke'tai constantly fearing for my safety, and I was looking forward to learning more about the Order. I was terrified, however; there was a chance I would forget everything I had ever known, and I did not want that to happen. There was also the grim possibility that I would never wake up once the change had begun. Everything I had been taught by Il'zaks and Te'chok, all of my concentration, would have to go into this next summoning—and I could not fail now.

Finally, I tore myself away from my questions and doubts, deciding that I had but one option. I looked at Te'chok, holding him steadily in my gaze, and said, "I'm ready."

He nodded once, and began to summon his unique demon. I focused upon him more intently than I ever had in the past, determined to succeed.

His demon was a very large wolf-like creature with orange-yellow eyes that seemed to harbor a keen intellect. Its coat was a sleek silver-gray, and as it sat down on its haunches by his side, its head came nearly to his shoulder.

"This is Gwyllgi," Te'chok said by way of introduction. "As you know, Chandra, I dislike conflict and would rather avoid it, if possible. This demon allows me to strike such fear into those who would fight me that I am able to escape them without the need for physical confrontation. Gwyllgi can create an aura about herself that makes those near to her experience an overwhelming sense of dread; it is so strong, that in most instances, they turn around and flee." He smiled faintly, then added, "Your demon will likely be very different than my own. Let's see it."

I suddenly felt incredibly nervous, and swallowed hard, closing my eyes in a futile attempt to calm myself down. I had to get this right; I would not get a second chance as I had with the incubus. I must *do* this—I had no other choice.

I drew a shaky breath, and began to dance with my eyes still closed. The movements were more complicated than any of the others I had learned so far, but my body found its rhythm and my feet picked out the steps flawlessly while the cadence of the summoning words ran through my head. As I finished, I opened my eyes long enough to take in the creature I had called; it was shaped like a human, with two arms, two legs and a head, but was draped from head to toe in a heavy, black robe-like garment with a deep hood. The hood was drawn up, casting its face into deepest shadow.

I shifted my gaze from it to Te'chok as a fuzzy darkness began to encroach on my vision from all sides. Although I knew what was happening, I felt a sudden, blinding panic envelop me as the darkness obscured my world and I began to fall. Abruptly my fall was stopped, and though I wanted to open my eyes to see how that had happened, I was unable to do so. I heard, as though from a great distance, Te'chok's voice shouting, though I could not make out his words. Moments later, I could hear the sound of running feet racing towards me.

I felt as though I were being lifted up by a pair of strong arms, and though there were voices around me, I could not decipher what was being said. Suddenly, I felt pain unlike anything I had ever experienced—I felt as though my body were being torn in a thousand pieces by angry claws, while I was simultaneously subjected to powerful electric shocks, and stabbed by hundreds of blades that twisted in the wounds. I seemed to hear from a distance one long, anguished cry; I believed it was my own voice, screaming in agony, but I could not be certain. I had a single, fleeting thought that this must be what it felt like to die.

Through the haze of pain and confusion, one voice made it through, crystalline, cutting through the darkness that had become my world. I knew immediately that it was the voice of my demon. *My name is Alastor, and I look forward to the time when we can work together. I am pleased I have found such a strong summoner once more. I shall be awaiting you when you awaken.*

The words brought me hope; I was not dying, I was simply on the verge of unconsciousness and in a great deal of pain. I let go of the tenuous thread of awareness that had tethered me to the world, and fell into an agony of darkness where I knew no more. The transformation was upon me.

# PART TWO

# DEVASTATION

# 19

# MIRROR

My head was throbbing, and I felt as though I had picked a fight with a professional boxer and had lost that battle miserably. My entire body felt bruised and battered, and I was certain that if anyone had touched me—regardless of the location—I would have cried out in pain.

I was laying in bed, that much I knew. I remained motionless with my eyes closed for some time, wondering how much agony it would cause me to open them. What had happened overnight to leave me feeling so utterly wretched? Try as I might, nothing came to mind.

Slowly I opened my eyes. The room was dark around me, though I could still see everything clearly, as though it were illuminated by the light of a full moon. I knew that was impossible, because the bedroom of our apartment did not have windows. Carefully, I sat up, and as I did so I noticed Ke'tai was dozing in a folding chair to one side of the bed, his chin nearly touching his muscular chest. Why was he sleeping there, and not at my side?

"Ke'tai?" I asked uncertainly.

He startled awake, and blinked furiously. Then as he became aware of his surroundings, he broke into a relieved grin and leapt from his chair, knocking it over in the process. In one swift motion, he was at my side, and I realized a little belatedly that I had been able to follow his movement even though I knew it should have been too fast for me to do so.

"You're awake," he breathed, taking my hands gently in his. "Oh, thank goodness... We were beginning to worry."

I closed my eyes, feeling disoriented. "What? Why?"

Ke'tai bit his lower lip and a look of concern appeared on his face. "Let me go tell Te'chok and Il'zaks that you've awakened," he said softly.

"They're in the other room." He rose, and exited the room, closing the door quietly behind him.

Te'chok...Il'zaks...Then I suddenly remembered why I was here, and what had occurred. Alastor had come, and then my world had vanished beneath an ocean of pain. I was...a summoner now.

Alastor was still present, looming ominously in one corner of the room. As I turned to look at him—for Alastor was a male demon—I again heard his voice within my head. *I am pleased you have survived. I will help you with your revenge, when the day comes that you seek it. I am tired now, and wish to return to my home.*

I nodded, and released him, turning around again as I heard the door opening. Te'chok entered first, looking somewhat hesitant, followed by Ke'tai, and then Il'zaks, who was unable to hide his joy at seeing me awake. Both Te'chok and Il'zaks wore clothing that looked as though it had been slept in, rumpled and creased as it was. I found that strange, particularly for Il'zaks, who was always dressed to perfection. Even his hair, usually combed so that no strand was out of place, seemed disheveled. How long had they been here, and how long had I been unconscious?

Te'chok stopped at the foot of the bed. "I'm glad you are awake," he said. "Do you remember that I said I would ask you something when you first came to?"

I searched my memories, though it was difficult to concentrate on any one thing for more than a nanosecond. "I...don't know," I said slowly after some time.

Te'chok sighed, and then nodded, the curls of his hair bouncing slightly. "Tell us your name," he replied evenly. "It will be different now..."

I frowned in confusion. They all should have known my name, and asking for it was nothing short of nonsense. Or was it?

Then a memory came to me, drifting as though through a thick fog. "*...One of us is going to ask you a question. At that time, it may sound absurd to you... One of us will ask you your name...*" Te'chok had said that, though there had been more to his words than I was currently able to recall.

"Ji'anne. I am Ji'anne."

Te'chok's face broke into a smile. "You do remember some things, don't you?" he asked. "It was not all destroyed."

I nodded slowly, moving my head only slightly so that I did not aggravate the headache that was still thundering within my skull. "I remember all of you," I replied, "and…coming here. Elliot's here, too. And Xan…" I sighed, hanging my head, memories of my sister coming unbidden to my mind.

Te'chok appeared disappointed. "I was actually hoping you'd have forgotten about her," he said mostly to himself. He straightened then, and strode abruptly out of the room, his expression troubled.

Ke'tai made his way to the side of the bed, and sat down carefully beside me. He was smiling, and his silver eyes seemed to dance. "Ji'anne is a beautiful name," he said softly, taking one of my hands in his. "I'm glad you remember me…remember us."

I nodded, offering him a smile of my own. "So am I, Ke'tai. I love you." I paused, then asked, "How long was I out?"

It was Il'zaks who answered, from the doorway. "Three days, and nearly eighteen hours. Yours was a very difficult transformation, it seems."

"We were beginning to worry," Ke'tai admitted. "It usually doesn't take so long."

"Ke'tai never left your side, during the whole process," Il'zaks added. "I am happy that you did not lose your memory completely. It would have pained me to see him so distraught over losing what the two of you have."

Looking up at Ke'tai, I could see unshed tears in his eyes. "We don't have to worry about that any more," he replied to Il'zaks, though his eyes never left my face.

"That's right," I assured him, offering up a smile.

Te'chok reappeared in the doorway then, brushing past Il'zaks. "I hate to interrupt the reunion, but I have a meeting to go to very soon and there are some things I am going to need to know before I leave, Lady Ji'anne."

I blinked, surprised by his sudden formality.

"I need to know about your demon," he continued, ignoring the apparent confusion on my face, "the one that was here when you awakened. Did it say anything to you? And what is it?"

"Um…His name is Alastor," I replied. "Why do you need to know this for your meeting?"

Te'chok sighed. "Three of the Elders arrived late last night, and I promised them I would speak with them as soon as you had awakened. They will be wishing to speak with you in the near future as well, but you are probably going to need a little more rest before then." He frowned, and said to Il'zaks, "Zy'driks is one of them, which puts me in a less than stellar mood."

Il'zaks raised an eyebrow, but said nothing in response.

Sensing that Te'chok was impatient and frustrated, I said, "Alastor did tell me one thing before asking to be released. He said he is there to help me with my revenge, whatever that is supposed to mean. I don't have any reason for revenge."

Te'chok nodded and looked thoughtful for a time. "Perhaps yours is a demon that chose you because of some future event," he replied guardedly. "Anyway, I need to be off. I'll return here once I'm finished with the inquisition." He turned and was quickly gone from the room. Just before I heard the door to the apartment close, the lamp in the other room turned on, casting a faint yellowish light on everything in the bedroom.

"I take it Te'chok doesn't much like this Zy'driks person," I remarked.

Il'zaks chuckled. "Zy'driks was the former Master Grand Summoner, and he does not like Te'chok's avoidance of conflict. We have lost several very good summoners within the last few decades due to Te'chok's desire to run away from a fight rather than do something about a bad situation. To say the least, the two often disagree."

"And Zy'driks doesn't have much in the way of patience," Ke'tai added. "If he doesn't get the answers he's looking for, he'll drill you with questions until he does. That's what Te'chok meant about the inquisition," he finished with a laugh.

There was a knock at the door then, and Il'zaks glanced behind him for a brief second before nodding. "Marek will get that," he said. "I must say, your Carlos chose a very good tracker to pair with Ji'anne."

Ke'tai grinned. "I told Carlos to settle for nothing short of the best."

I looked down, trying to recollect this Marek the two spoke of, but failing to do so. I remembered Carlos, and what he did for Ke'tai, and assumed that Marek must have been brought here to do the same for me. Try as I might, I could not remember him.

A moment later a tall, muscular man appeared in the doorway behind Il'zaks, his bald head shining faintly in the lamplight coming from the other room. "Elliot is here to see you," he said quietly to me in a low tenor. "Are you up for a visit?"

I nodded, sitting up a little straighter as the man turned away. I turned to look at Ke'tai. "Was that Marek?" I asked, feeling horrible that I could not recall having met him.

Ke'tai smiled faintly, and nodded. "Yes. You met him not long before the change happened—it is no wonder you don't remember him."

"Will you be able to tolerate some light in here?" Il'zaks asked. "Your friend Elliot will not be able to see in the darkness as well as we do."

"Yeah, I think so."

Il'zaks nodded and turned to flick the light switch just as Elliot appeared in the doorway. He paused, his hand hovering near the switch, and said, "You must remember that Ji'anne will not be quite the same as when you last saw her, Elliot. I will turn on the light now, so you can see."

I winced as the overhead light blazed suddenly on, causing the fading ache in my head to redouble its efforts to torment me. When I opened my eyes again, Elliot was standing at the end of the bed, simply staring at me, though his gaze was unreadable. I wondered what he must be thinking, but I could not bring myself to voice the question.

Finally, he shook his head, closing his dark eyes briefly. "You are…so different, yet so much the same. It's a little weird, but I'm sure I'll get used to it."

"Different, how?" I asked.

Ke'tai rose from the bed and, standing near the side, offered his hand to me. "I think it's time you look in the mirror, love. You'll understand what Elliot was talking about once you do."

I nodded, taking his hand, and slowly rose to my feet while my every muscle and joint protested at the movement. "When will I stop hurting?" I asked of no one in particular, looking down at my unsteady feet.

"It will probably take some time, maybe a day or so," Il'zaks replied. "This is a normal reaction, but it will pass with time."

Nodding, I allowed Ke'tai to guide me toward the mirror, his strong arms supporting me more than I was able to support myself. Each step I took sent a shock of pain throughout my body, and I was tempted just to crawl back into bed. However, that same curiosity that had led me so far along this path to becoming a summoner was now pulling me toward the mirror—I must see what had Elliot so troubled.

I raised my eyes slowly to look at the reflection as Ke'tai stopped, holding me up gently with his arm about my waist. I could do nothing but stare for several long moments; the person I had been was gone, replaced by this beautiful summoner at Ke'tai's side. I remembered my hair had been a dark brown, almost black, and now it was snow white. The brown eyes that I recalled Ke'tai having loved so much were gone, replaced with the same eerily silver ones that he possessed. My face was the same, but with those features altered, I looked like someone else entirely. I simply gazed at that strange reflection of myself in the mirror, unable to speak for the barrage of thoughts that were swirling through my mind.

"I know it is unsettling, the first time you see yourself after the change," Il'zaks commented quietly from behind me. "The mind struggles to replace that mental self-image we all have of ourselves. Ke'tai and I have been down that path; we know what you are feeling right now."

Ke'tai's arm tightened about my waist briefly, and I saw him turn to face me in the mirror's reflection. "I am here for you," he whispered into my ear, "and I always will be. I promise you that things will get easier for you from now on."

I nodded and closed my eyes with some effort, turning away from the mirror with a sigh. I looked at Elliot when I opened my eyes again. "You were right—it is going to take some getting used to. And it is very, very weird."

Elliot nodded, though he still appeared troubled by something. "Kai'lind told me that I won't be that far behind you," he replied. "I'll know what you just went through soon enough, and then I'll have my own mirrors to contend with."

# 20

# COMPLICATED

Two days later, I found myself following Te'chok down the long corridor leading from the lobby to the library on our way to meet with the Board of Elders. My presence had been requested by the summoner Zy'driks, whom Te'chok seemed to dislike more each day, but neither Te'chok nor myself had been informed what the meeting would entail.

As we approached the door to the library, Te'chok paused and sighed in frustration. "I've told you what I know about each of the Elders, and I hope that will help this meeting go a little more smoothly. Zy'driks has been a thorn in my side since he arrived here three days ago, and I doubt this little meeting of his will make it any better."

I shrugged, determined not to let his preconceptions cloud my first impressions of the Elders. "Let's go inside and get this done then, so you can get it over with quicker. Stalling outside in the hallway is only going to postpone the inevitable, you know."

Te'chok glowered at me, but I did not let it bother me. Since the pain had faded away and I had been able to function normally again, nothing was going to get in the way of my happiness. For the first time, I had seen Ke'tai *truly* happy; he was free of the worries that had plagued him during my training. Seeing his joy enhanced my own.

"Fine," he said, his voice disappointed as he realized his bad mood wasn't having any effect on me. "Let's do this, then."

As we entered the library, the seven summoners that made up the Board of Elders rose from their seats in greeting. They had gathered near the center of the room where the couch and cushioned chairs were located.

Te'chok introduced me first, and then began the introductions of the Elders. Of the seven, two were women—Ai'zhanna and Al'ora. The others introduced to me were Il'koru, Yai'venne, Nae'leil, Te'moru, and lastly was Zy'driks, though he was the first to speak once Te'chok had finished.

"So, you are to replace Te'chok in a few weeks?" he asked, unable to hide a smug smile. He was dressed in a long black trench coat, black denim pants, a white t-shirt, and black combat-style boots. His hair was spiked in much the same fashion as Ke'tai's usually was, and he had a single diamond stud in his left earlobe. "I am pleased to meet you, and I am glad you were able to attend this little gathering on such short notice."

I had been notified of the meeting the night before, and did not consider it to be short notice in the least. "You gave more than enough time for us to come," I replied, "though I am curious to know what exactly you wanted to see me for."

Zy'driks nodded once. "Straightforward and to the point, I like that. What I don't like is trying to decipher the point of a statement when it is clouded by flowery words that mean nothing," he stated, giving Te'chok a pointed glance. Te'chok returned the comment with a heated glare, but said nothing in his own defense.

"We have asked you here today simply to get to know you, Lady Ji'anne," Al'ora broke in. She was a tall woman with a graceful demeanor and a kindly face. Her dark skin contrasted sharply with the curly white hair that framed her face and the pale, silvery color of her eyes. She wore a long wine-colored dress with an A-line skirt that looked more like something I would have worn to a holiday party than to a simple meeting.

I nodded to her. "Alright, what would you like to know?"

"Let's start off with what we already know about you," Nae'leil stated. "Sometimes that is easiest, and then you can fill in the gaps of our knowledge." Nae'leil was the first summoner I had encountered who actually *looked* old; I assumed this must have been because he had remained undiscovered until he was in the later years of his life. What hair he had was thin and wispy atop his head, and he was dressed in a pair of khaki slacks and a blue-and-white plaid button-down shirt.

"We have been told of your flight from the Seattle area, at the start of January," Zy'driks said. "We also know of your sister, and the troubles she has already caused for the trainee Elliot Thompson." He paused to gaze into my eyes for some time, as though he were searching for something, before he continued. "We know about you and Ke'tai, and all that has gone on during your training sessions with both Il'zaks and Te'chok. And now that we have had the privilege of your presence, we also know the power you have as a summoner."

"We have been told that you remember much of what occurred from the time you started your training until the time you began the change," Nae'leil said. "I was pleased to hear that, though I know some others had hoped you would forget certain things—namely, your sister."

I sighed and shot an angry glance toward Te'chok before responding. "I was hoping that I would not forget her, even though she has caused some trouble for me already. The thing is, she *is* my sister, and there is no point in denying it. And one day, sooner or later, I'm probably going to have to deal with her and those hunters working with her. When that day comes, I'll deal with it. Forgetting would have only complicated matters, I believe."

"If it makes you feel any better, Ji'anne, most of us had hoped you would remember her as well," Zy'driks put in, though his smug look was directed at Te'chok. "Knowing your enemy when it comes to battle is an advantage—and in the case of your sister, one we will be grateful to have. You know her better than anyone else in the world."

I nodded. "I am glad that at least somebody agrees with me on this," I replied. I had grown weary of Te'chok's complaints over the past two days when it had come to the topic of Xandra. While I did not care for Zy'driks' pointed smugness and aura of superiority, I felt that my viewpoints tended to coincide more with his than they did with Te'chok's.

"Tell us of your final demon," Te'moru said, changing the subject. He appeared to be in his mid-twenties, as the majority of summoners did. He was soft-spoken and had a strange accent that I could not place. He was dressed in an immaculate pin-striped suit with polished black shoes. His hair was cut very short, in a style reminiscent of the military. He reminded me somewhat of Il'zaks.

"My final demon is…interesting," I replied, uncertain of how to phrase it. "It is a male demon, and goes by the name of Alastor."

Ai'zhanna stood suddenly, her eyes wide with surprise. "Alastor, you said?" she asked. She was a small woman, not even five feet tall. Her hair was straight and long, falling nearly to her knees as she stood. Her features were Asian, and I recalled that Te'chok had told me she had been born in Thailand many years ago.

I nodded in answer to her question.

"You are not the first summoner Alastor has chosen," she replied. "His first master was also the leader of the Order, long ago."

Nae'leil was nodding, as if he knew what she were speaking of, though most of the others seemed to know nothing of this history.

"Tell us what you know, Ai'zhanna," Zy'driks stated. "I am curious to know which leader it was whom this demon chose before."

"Alastor was the unique demon of Ae'tama," she said with some significance. "Most of you did not join the Order until long after he had passed away."

I remembered from one of the lessons Il'zaks had given me early on that Ae'tama had been the very first summoner, and the man who had eventually founded the Order. Ai'zhanna must have been with the Order for a very long time, indeed—perhaps a millennium, at the very least.

"Alastor specializes in helping his summoner seek vengeance upon those who have wronged them, which I find very interesting," Ai'zhanna continued. "You do not seem to have anything to seek revenge for at present, which seems to indicate Alastor chose you for some event that has not yet come to pass."

Zy'driks turned his head to look in my direction. "Interesting, indeed," he mused. "I think with this bit of knowledge, we should expect a change in the way certain things are handled within the Order, once you are officially in charge. A change for the better, I should say," he added, giving Te'chok a meaningful glance.

I shrugged, uncomfortable with the fact that he was assuming such things so soon after having met me. I did not even know what I expected to do yet myself, and I was coming nearer to that point every day. I had only seven weeks and five days left before I was placed in charge of so much, and I had only just begun to learn the workings of the Order.

"It is always a change when a new summoner takes over leadership of the Order," Nae'leil said, easing the tension that had begun to grow between Zy'driks and Te'chok. "No matter what the person's beliefs are, or what demons they are able to call, it is always a change for everyone, and we have been surprised in the past when our initial assessments are proven wrong. Jumping to conclusions now will not do us any good."

Zy'driks nodded. "You are right, Nae'leil, and I am prone to getting ahead of myself. However, I must say that it has indeed been a pleasure to speak with you today, Lady Ji'anne, and I look forward to working with you in the future. Now, I believe it is time to have some lunch." He paused and strode to where I was standing. "Would you care to join me? You may have Ke'tai join us as well, if you'd like, for I have enjoyed his company in the past."

I knew it would be perceived as an insult if I turned him down, and so I accepted the invitation, awkward as it made me feel. As we made our way out of the library, I turned briefly toward Te'chok and mouthed to him that I was sorry. He simply shrugged, and then held up two fingers, indicating that I should meet him again at two o'clock. I nodded, and followed Zy'driks from the library.

"Officially, there is no single leader of the Board of Elders," Zy'driks said once we were in the hall. "However, I have assumed that role on many occasions, simply to get things moving. I will say this to you—I personally think you will be a good replacement for Te'chok, based on what I have seen of your personality so far."

I nodded, uncertain of what to say in reply. Zy'driks seemed the type who liked to be in control, and I wondered if this lunch invitation was nothing more than a power play of sorts. My instincts told me to be wary of his motives.

"I know that you have been bombarded with information since you awakened, and I hope that this is not going to overwhelm you," Zy'driks continued. "But I did feel there are a few things you ought to know—things which Te'chok will probably gloss over if he even sees fit to speak of them at all to you in the next eight weeks. His nature has always been to run away and hide, rather than face his problems, and while that may have worked for him, it does not help the Order."

As we entered the lobby, I began walking in the direction of the desk at the center where Adele was seated. "I would like to call Ke'tai, and let him know of the lunch invitation. He was planning on being around here today…"

Zy'driks nodded. "You do not need to explain yourself to me, Ji'anne. I assumed that is why you were going this direction, and as I said earlier, Ke'tai is a good man and I enjoy talking with him."

I spoke briefly with Adele, who promptly punched in the four-digit number that would call our apartment. She immediately handed me the phone receiver; the phone rang twice before it was picked up by Ke'tai.

"Hello?"

"It's me," I replied. "Are you available for lunch today? Zy'driks has invited us..."

There was a pause on the other end, and I wished I could have been there to see his expression and at least have a guess as to what he was thinking. "Of course, I'll be down in a minute or two," he said finally, his tone indicating he was wary of the Elder as well.

Handing the phone back to Adele, I said, "He'll be there."

Zy'driks nodded once, smiling with satisfaction. "Excellent," he said as we began walking in the direction of the cafeteria. "As your partner, I am sure he will be rather influential with some of the decisions you make in the future. There is no point in speaking to you of business without him being present, as far as I am concerned."

As we neared the doors of the cafeteria, I could see Ke'tai striding down the corridor toward us. His smile was warm as he shook the Elder's hand in greeting, though his eyes betrayed some level of uncertainty.

"I am pleased you were able to join us," Zy'driks stated as he led us to a table in one corner of the room, which was far busier than usual. Several summoners, in addition to the seven Elders, had arrived at the compound within the last five days, and from what Te'chok had told me, more were expected to appear in the days to come.

"I wouldn't miss it," Ke'tai said lightly.

Zy'driks indicated that we should sit down as we came to the table in the corner, and he motioned for one of the people working the counter to come to us. Since I had arrived at the headquarters, we had always gone to the counter to place our orders, and I found his action unusual. However, a woman of perhaps thirty made her way over to us, a pad of paper and pen in hand.

"What can I get for you, sir?" she asked of Zy'driks, without paying much attention to Ke'tai and I.

Zy'driks glanced in my direction. "Is pizza alright with the two of you?" When I nodded, he placed his order for an all-meat pizza and requested a pitcher of ice water be brought with it. The woman did not seem the least put off by his having called her over to take the order, and I wondered what he had said or done around the cafeteria staff to make them so amenable to his wishes. Perhaps it was the mere fact that he was an Elder, but I could not be certain.

Once the woman had gone, Zy'driks folded his hands on the tabletop and leaned toward us. "I have no doubt in my mind that you are wondering just why I asked to speak with you alone right now," he said. "There are two reasons—first, Te'chok would object to what I'm about to tell you, and second, he's at the end of his reign anyway, and this is something that concerns the future rather than the present. Besides that, the little twit annoys the hell out of me."

"I'd have to say that last sentiment is shared by the both of you," Ke'tai remarked dryly.

Zy'driks laughed. "Yes, I know that. If it weren't for his tracker, that Adele, I doubt anything would ever get done between us. She has worked as a sort of go-between for a few years now, and that arrangement has been quite nice. But I did not come here to discuss Te'chok; I came here to speak of other matters."

The woman who had come to our table earlier returned then with three empty glasses and a pitcher of water that had a smattering of ice cubes floating at the top. Condensation ran down the sides of the pitcher and it made a ring on the table as she placed it in front of us. "Your pizza should be ready in a few minutes, sir," she said, again speaking directly to Zy'driks.

He nodded. "Thank you, Lynne."

"I haven't seen her around before; does she work for you?" Ke'tai asked as Lynne strode away.

Zy'driks shook his head. "No, she is one of Nae'leil's trackers. I think she started working for him about eight months ago. She's a little unnerved by being here, around so many summoners, but I think in a few days she will settle in just fine." He paused, taking a moment to glance about the room before he continued. "What I asked you here for is a continuation of our earlier meeting, but as I said, Te'chok would have objected and I do not want to deal with him right now."

I wanted to ask him what he wanted to know that he didn't already, when Lynne returned carrying our pizza and a hot pad to set it upon. I glanced at Ke'tai while Zy'driks thanked Lynne; Ke'tai looked about as uncertain as I felt. I could sense that Zy'driks was not a man to be crossed, nor would he allow himself to be ignored if he felt his cause was important. As the "unofficial" leader of the Board of Elders, I knew I would have to work with him more often than not once I took over Te'chok's position within the Order, and at this point in time I was not sure if I should be looking forward to it or dreading it. Zy'driks, and his motives, were a mystery to me.

As Lynne turned away to leave us to ourselves once more, Zy'driks helped himself to a slice of pizza and said, "What I want to know is this: If it came down to it, would you be able to fight against your sister?"

I had just picked up the spatula to take a slice of the pizza myself, but as the question left his lips, I let go and it clattered to the table. I raised my eyes to meet his intensely scrutinizing gaze, and said, "I think it will depend on the circumstances. Xan and I got along well, for the most part, but we did not always. If you are asking if I would be able to fight against her, I think the answer would be yes. If you are asking if I would be able to kill her, I don't think so."

Zy'driks nodded, his expression unreadable. "What circumstances would sway you one way or the other?" he pressed.

I clenched my jaw, balling my hands into fists under the table, angry that he would ask this of me. Ke'tai must have sensed my mood; he took one of my hands in his own, gently, in an attempt to ease my sudden frustration with the Elder.

"You have some nerve," I muttered angrily. "I don't *know* what circumstances, but I won't rule out the possibility of anything when it comes to her. It's going to depend on what she does, what events happen…And until something *does* happen, I cannot answer your damned question!"

Zy'driks cocked his head to one side, an amused sort of smirk surfacing upon his face. "You are quick to anger," he stated, "and that may help us, or hinder us, depending on what transpires. I did not mean to make you mad, but in a way, I am glad I did—now I see another side of your personality that the meeting earlier did not show me."

I glared at him, tempted to stand up and walk away, even though I had not eaten anything at all.

"I understand now why Te'chok would have objected to this," Ke'tai murmured, his voice weary. "She's been awake for just over two days, and you are already pressing to see where her stance lies when it comes to the hunters—"

"Not just any hunters," Zy'driks interrupted. "I am concerned about only one in particular—this Xandra Grey from Seattle, our Lady Ji'anne's twin sister."

"Look," I said evenly, trying to control my voice despite the hot anger coursing through my veins, "I told you that I don't know what I will do yet. Xan might be my sister, but if she does something to piss me off, she will have to deal with that—as will you, and I don't give a damn if you're an Elder or not."

Zy'driks raised his eyebrows, but did not look in the least offended by this latest outburst. "You are angry, and rightly so," he replied. "I only sought to find out the answers, as it is a very unique situation you are in, unlike anything this Order has ever been faced with. I am not the only Elder who is curious to see what you will do when it comes to your sister, though I think you will find I am one of the least difficult to talk with about such things."

After several seconds of silence, Ke'tai said, "He's right about that, Ji'anne. Some of the others are probably wishing you are a weaker summoner about now, so that they will not have to be pulled into this unknown territory."

"Well, I'm *not* a weaker summoner, so they'll have to deal with it just as I will," I replied, my gaze fixed upon Zy'driks. "Since I was told of Xan's abilities—before she was even approached by the hunters—I haven't been overly thrilled with the prospect of what might happen if I am forced to face her. When I learned she had joined with the hunters, I was upset—because I knew then that one day, I would *have* to face her. It will not be easy for me, and I hope you understand that, but I'm not afraid to do it if the time comes."

Zy'driks nodded, his features softening somewhat, and I was struck momentarily by how attractive he was. "Now I have my answer," he replied quietly, taking another slice of pizza from the otherwise untouched pan. "Eat. Enjoy your lunch. We'll talk about other things now."

The rest of the lunch meeting was spent speaking of mundane things, but I did learn much about Zy'driks that I would have never guessed had he not spoken of them. He was a classically trained pianist, and also played the cello—very well, according to Ke'tai—but his current favorite instrument was the electric guitar. Not only was he a musician, but also a painter, and he was a voracious reader of non-fiction—anything from how-to books to medical and law school texts to biographies. Zy'driks had a brilliant mind hidden behind his mysterious and difficult demeanor. In spite of our earlier disagreement, I found that I had enjoyed talking with him by the end of our meal.

It was five minutes past two o'clock before I realized what the time was. Zy'driks was in the midst of explaining how he wanted to form a band to perform at gatherings and big events of the Order, when I happened to glance up at the clock above the door.

"Oh no, I'm late," I said with a shake of my head. "I'm sorry, but I was supposed to meet Te'chok a few minutes ago, and I almost forgot."

Zy'driks smiled, seemingly amused, and stood from his seat as I did so. He offered his hand, and we shook. "I am glad we had this opportunity to get to know one another better," he said. "I think we can work well together."

I nodded, relieved by his words. "I think so, too." I turned to face Ke'tai, who had remained sitting. "I'll see you this evening."

He smiled and nodded. "I may go into the lab for a couple hours this afternoon while I'm waiting, but I'll be here when you're finished with Te'chok's business."

I returned his smile before turning away to head toward the library. Te'chok was pacing around the center of the room when I arrived, and though he said nothing at first, he appeared wounded.

"I'm sorry I'm late," I said after a moment of uncomfortable silence. "I lost track of time..."

He sighed and nodded, but said nothing for several long, awkward seconds. He kept his gaze focused upon the floor. Finally, he looked up, and said, "I have a good idea of what Zy'driks wanted to speak with you about, and while I think it was ill-timed on his part, there isn't much that I can do about it now, is there?" He sighed again, running one hand through his mop of curly hair. "He doesn't like me, and I definitely don't like him. I'm sorry that you are getting pulled into the middle of our feud."

"It was probably bound to happen sooner or later, Te'chok. I'd rather have it happen now, instead of later when something important is happening, you know?"

He frowned slightly. "Right, whatever. The thing is, he's very interested to know more about your relationship with Xandra, and I don't think it's any of his business."

I leveled my gaze at him, and said, "Te'chok, she's joined the hunters. She's become *everyone's* business."

Te'chok sighed and hung his head. "Fine, you're right. But I still don't like the way he went about talking to you, subverting me in the process. He's a manipulative prick—"

"I understand the two of you don't get along," I replied, cutting him off. I didn't really want to hear more of this than I already had today. "Can we just get back to work and forget it for a while? I told him earlier—and now I'll tell you—if it comes down to it, I'll do what I have to regarding Xan. Until something happens, I don't want to be forced into thinking about it. So please, can we just do something else now?"

Te'chok stood motionless for a time, and then finally he nodded and looked up once more. "Yeah, okay. I'm sorry...I'm just frustrated."

The rest of my afternoon was spent going over lists of known hunters and the areas in which they frequented. Te'chok stressed the importance of knowing which hunters were able to use ether stones, because these were generally the leaders of regional groups. He showed me how to use the database they had set up specifically for tracking hunters; it included information such as age, family status, where they worked, their exact abilities, and most entries even included photographs. By the time we had finished, it was nearing seven o'clock, and my brain was feeling rather numb and over-taxed.

Te'chok remained in the library when I left. As I entered the lobby on my way back to the apartment I shared with Ke'tai, Zy'driks appeared, walking toward me from the direction of the cafeteria. He smiled as we approached one another. "I believe you'll find Ke'tai in one of the training rooms," he said. "That Elliot asked him for some lessons in karate this afternoon."

I nodded. "Thanks." I went to move past him, but he stepped sideways to block my path.

"I spoke to Ke'tai about Elliot earlier. We know he left Seattle because of the hunters and your sister, but Ke'tai would not tell me the specific details. He said he didn't know all of them, but that if Elliot would not share them with me, you might."

I sighed. "Elliot and Xan were dating," I replied quietly. "He was going to propose to her…before all this happened. Don't pester him about it, if you have any shred of compassion—what he had to do when he left her scarred him pretty badly, and I don't know if he will ever fully recover. He really did love her, and probably still does, so please leave him be."

Zy'driks stepped aside, appearing thoughtful. "I had no idea things would be so complicated," he remarked, mostly to himself. "Have a good evening, Lady Ji'anne." He strode away, leaving me alone in the lobby to contemplate his motives further.

I stood there for a few seconds longer, before turning to head in the direction of the practice rooms, where I hoped to find Ke'tai. I wanted nothing more than to be at his side, happy and oblivious to all the troubles and tension that had suddenly developed in our lives. I wanted to focus all of my attention on him, to forget the conflict brewing between Zy'driks and Te'chok, but most of all to forget about Xandra—if only for a short while.

# 21

# ALONE

The next few weeks flew by in a blur. I spent most of my time each day with Te'chok, learning the workings of the Order and any other pertinent information he felt necessary to share with me. Most evenings were spent with Elliot and Ke'tai in the practice rooms, refining my karate skills, and before I realized it, my eight weeks of preparation were almost over.

During the seventh week, Elliot was scheduled to complete his final lesson with Kai'lind, and Te'chok made it a point that he and I both be present. "You must know what goes on during the change," he had said to me. "This is the perfect opportunity for you to see that in person, and it could not have come at a better time."

Elliot's final demon was the chimæra, for he was not strong enough to call a Dreamweaver or a unique one. I observed quietly near the door to the practice room, while Kai'lind instructed Elliot on how to summon the creature; like Te'chok, Elliot's chimæra seemed unable to settle on any one shape and shifted incessantly between a hundred different forms. Kai'lind's chimæra appeared as an amorphous, smoky presence until he willed it to change its form. Te'chok stood beside me, arms crossed over his thin chest, watching intently.

"His change will not start quite as suddenly as yours did," Te'chok said in a low whisper. "He will have the opportunity to dismiss his demon first, but upon the breaking of that contact, it will begin. He will have a little more time to prepare himself than you did."

I nodded, and continued to watch as Kai'lind explained to Elliot some of the reasons summoners had for using a chimæra, and what some of the limitations of the creature were. He paused and glanced toward Te'chok and I, where we stood near the door.

"Ji'anne, would you mind calling your chimæra? I've been told it has an unusual form. Telling a student that each summoner's demon is going to be slightly different is one thing, but actually seeing that is another experience entirely."

I nodded to Kai'lind. "Of course."

I closed my eyes and began to dance, knowing exactly which steps to take without having to concentrate on anything but the words of the summoning. It was much easier for me now than it had been when I was in Elliot's position. When I opened my eyes again, Elliot was gaping at me, and Kai'lind appeared rather confused. It took me a moment to realize that neither of them could see the chimæra until I told it to take on another form; I had forgotten that only Te'chok and Ke'tai had been present to see this particular demon of mine.

I pointed to the faint shadow to my left that was the chimæra. "It's very difficult to see, unless you are at the right angle," I explained. "Here, I'll make it change."

As the chimæra morphed into the form of a house cat, orange striped with green eyes, Kai'lind said, "That is an unusual one. I could see that particular form being advantageous in some situations. Interesting."

Elliot was still staring at me, and did not seem concerned about the chimæra. "You just dance, and it works? How is that possible?"

"Every summoner has their own method of calling demons," Kai'lind stated. "Most have to speak the words, or vocalize them in some way, in order to summon their familiars. Ji'anne's way of doing things is uncommon, though there are others in this building at present that summon in a similar fashion." Kai'lind's gaze left Elliot and fell upon me. "You still have to *think* the words correctly, am I right?"

I nodded. "Yeah. At first, Il'zaks was very careful with my training because he could never tell if I had the words right. I got through it, though," I added with a shrug.

Kai'lind explained a few more items to Elliot, and then finished the lesson by saying, "There isn't anything else I can teach you about this demon, Elliot. You know what will happen when you release it, so if you need to take some time to prepare yourself, go ahead. We will be here to help you through this."

Elliot nodded and looked away, silent for some time. When he raised his head once more, his gaze met mine, and he walked slowly toward me from the center of the room. "I know I might not remember some things when I wake up again," he said quietly, "but I don't want to forget Xan, no matter what some of the others might say." He reached into the left pocket of his jeans, pulling out a small green velvet jewelry box. With a sigh, he flipped the lid open, revealing a simple gold band with a square-cut ruby inside. "This is the ring I was going to give her," he said, his voice thick with emotion. "I want you to give this to me when I wake up again. If I remember her, I will understand…If I don't, maybe it will help me remember. No matter what happens, she did make me very happy once, and that's something I never want to forget."

I nodded; I understood exactly what he was going through. I took the box in my hands. "I'll do it, Elliot. Don't worry. I think everything is going to be okay."

His dark eyes betrayed an unspoken fear, but he simply nodded. "Thanks," he said as he turned back toward the center of the room, making his way to Kai'lind. "I'm ready now."

Kai'lind nodded, and Te'chok pushed away from the wall where he had been leaning to my right. Elliot closed his eyes, and the chimæra suddenly winked out of existence. In the same instant, Elliot toppled over, but Kai'lind was there to stop him from falling to the floor. Kai'lind picked up the thinner Elliot in a fireman's carry, and began to head toward the door purposefully.

I followed him into the hallway along with Te'chok, as Elliot began to convulse, his body wracked by violent spasms. We followed the corridors through a circuitous route to the apartment Elliot had been given, avoiding the common areas of the compound such as the lobby and the cafeteria in the process. As we neared the apartment, Elliot began to scream as though he were in terrible, excruciating pain.

Te'chok must have noticed my troubled expression, for he said, "You went through a similar ordeal. It is a blessing that we awaken without any clear recollection of the pain we had to endure. Watching others go through the same process is difficult, but it is also important to know exactly what goes on."

I followed the two other summoners inside the apartment, where Kai'lind laid Elliot down on top of his bed without bothering to pull down the sheets. Elliot continued to spasm and scream intermittently, so loud that I was positive everyone in the compound could hear them. Had I screamed, as he was doing now?

"The pain is a reaction to the body's cellular reorganization," Kai'lind stated calmly as he sat down in a chair near one wall of the room. "Some small part of our brain is altered during that last summoning, and with that comes the transformation. That event causes a fundamental change to occur within every cell in the body. I don't know much of the details about it. I just know it happens."

"Ke'tai could fill you in on the details, if you are interested in them," Te'chok added, as Elliot let out another anguished scream.

"Isn't there anything you can do to ease his pain?" I asked.

Both men shook their heads, but it was Te'chok who answered. "No, I'm afraid not. As I told you earlier, it is a blessing that we black out and cannot remember this part of our lives..."

The room was quiet for a moment, and only the sound of Elliot's rapid breathing as he writhed atop the bed could be heard. Then Kai'lind spoke in a subdued voice.

"The pain alone has been known to kill summoners before they even finish their transformations. That's why we always have someone there with them for the change—" He was cut off by another of Elliot's screams, and then said, "There may not be anything we can do to prevent their death, but at least they were not alone when they died."

I looked down at the green velvet jewelry box I still held in my hands. "Elliot will make it through, won't he?"

Te'chok shrugged. "It's difficult to tell, so early on, but most who get this far do. You'll just have to remember that he won't be Elliot any more when he wakes up."

I nodded, managing a strained smile. "Yeah."

At that moment, a loud knocking at the front door interrupted our conversation. "I'll get that," I said, and left the doorway where I had been standing. It was difficult to watch as Elliot endured his painful transformation, and someone at the door was a convenient excuse to step away, if only for a few moments.

Zy'driks was standing in the corridor as I opened the door, his hands clasped behind his back. He was wearing a black trench coat as usual, paired today with blue jeans and a black Metallica band t-shirt.

"We could hear screaming, down the hallway," he said. "Is it Elliot…?"

I nodded. "He's going through his change." I looked down briefly, shaking my head. "It's hard to imagine that I just—"

"Experienced that?" Zy'driks asked with an amused grin. "Yes, it always is, and it's truly remarkable that we do not remember a thing from it. But back to the point—I came here to make sure everything was alright. Now that I know what—" here he was forced to pause while another scream issued from the bedroom, "—the cause of the commotion is, I'll leave you be. Tell Te'chok he has eight days; he will understand the meaning."

I nodded, closing the door as Zy'driks strode quickly away. When I returned to the bedroom, I noted that Elliot had begun another set of violent convulsions. I quickly averted my eyes, unsettled by his suffering.

"Who was at the door?" Te'chok asked. When I told him, and relayed the cryptic message Zy'driks had ended the conversation with, Te'chok crossed his arms and scowled.

"What does it mean?" I asked.

Te'chok snorted in anger. "It's his countdown for the day I'm no longer in charge of things," he said bitterly.

"Oh." I looked down, not having realized that it was *only eight days away*. Eight days until I was named as the new head of the Order, and I still didn't feel like I knew my role adequately enough to help Te'chok with his duties, let alone perform them solo.

"Hey, you'll do great," Kai'lind said in an attempt to cheer me.

I shrugged. "I don't know. I don't think I'm ready for this yet."

"You're more ready than you know," Te'chok assured me. "We all feel that way, when we first start out. I know I did, and I'm sure Zy'driks did as well, though he'd never admit that fact."

I shrugged again, unwilling to acknowledge that he was probably right. Elliot thrashed atop the bed and let out a low moan.

"There won't be any visible changes for some time yet," Te'chok murmured. "We can take turns sitting in with him, but we should all stay near the apartment in the event something unexpected happens."

"I'll take the first shift," Kai'lind offered, settling back into the chair.

Te'chok nodded, and motioned for me to follow him as he left the room. We went only to the living room, and sat opposite the coffee table from one another, he on the couch and me on the over-stuffed chair.

"How are you holding up?" he asked after a moment's silence.

I sighed; I had anticipated the question. "I...don't know. I keep wondering, was it like that for me? Shouldn't I have remembered it? You would think that going through so much pain would be something you would remember afterward. And Elliot...He's already been through so much, just to get here..."

"You shouldn't worry about it so much," Te'chok replied. "No one, as far as I know, has ever remembered their transition, until they awaken afterwards. I know it's hard to believe, but I think there's some biological reason why we don't recall the pain we experience...Perhaps if we did, we would never approach others to follow us down this path. I know it's difficult the first time you see the change process taking place, but it's something you need to see first-hand, too. Especially since you are going to be leading the Order soon."

I sighed again. "I know why you want me here, but...I just wish there was something more we could do for him, to make the transition easier."

Te'chok smiled knowingly and nodded. "Yes, I understand. I feel the same way... But after so many years, and seeing so many of these changes occur, I've become numb to it. You will come to expect it, and it will become easier with time."

I frowned; I doubted that I would ever be able to "become numb" to bearing witness to such an event. "If you say so."

Eighteen hours and forty-some minutes later, I was taking my turn at Elliot's bedside. By this time, his hair had gone from dark brown to white, and the screaming and spasms had completely stopped; he'd had no more episodes since the night before. He no longer appeared to be in any pain, and seemed to be sleeping peacefully.

I was reading through a history of the more important summoners, some who were still alive, and others who had been long dead, when I heard Elliot stir. Looking up, I was relieved to see he was sitting upright, though he was hunched over, his hands gripping the sides of his head. His eyes were shut tightly as he grimaced.

I was on my feet in an instant. "Are you alright?" I asked, moving quickly to the side of the bed.

He turned his head slowly, and opened his eyes a sliver. I could see a hint of silver glinting between his narrowed lids. "Um, I think so. My head is killing me... Where's Kai'lind?"

I smiled, relieved that he was awake and seemed to be remembering some things. "I'll go find him. Just stay here, and try not to move. It'll hurt more if you move."

He nodded without looking at me, and I strode out of the room. Te'chok was asleep on the couch in the other room, and Kai'lind was sitting on the chair working through a crossword puzzle.

"Is everything okay?" Kai'lind asked in a whisper as I came into the room, though he did not take his eyes from the puzzle.

"He's awake," I replied. "He asked for you."

Kai'lind was on his feet and in the doorway of the bedroom in less than a second, the puzzle he had been working on lying discarded on the floor near the chair. Te'chok sat up, blinking the sleep from his eyes, the sudden movement having awakened him. I motioned for him to follow me to the bedroom.

Kai'lind was standing to one side of the bed when I reentered the room, and was bent down to look our newest summoner in the eye. "How are you feeling?" He asked.

"I already told Ji'anne that my head hurts," he replied. "Other than that, I suppose I'm okay. I feel like I got hit by a bus or something."

Kai'lind smiled faintly. "It's more of an 'or something', but we can talk about that later." He paused, looking down at his hands, then said, "I told you a few days ago that when this happened, and when you woke up again, I'd ask you a question. Do you remember what that was?"

"Yeah, my name...because before it was something else wasn't it?"

Kai'lind nodded, glancing up toward Te'chok who was standing beside me at the end of the bed, his eyes betraying some level of uncertainty. "I'm actually surprised you remember that, to be honest with you," he said. "Anyway, we need to know your name. Can you tell us that?"

He nodded, a nearly imperceptible up-and-down movement. "My name is Xen'din. And I remember a lot more than just that."

I went to the table that was on the opposite side of the room from the chair and Kai'lind, where I had left the green jewelry box several hours before. I picked it up and returned to the bedside, offering the box to Xen'din—and struggling to remember he was no longer Elliot Thompson.

"You asked me to give this to you, when you woke up," I said softly. "You said you would understand, if you remembered..."

He took the box gingerly, tears forming in his now-silver eyes. "I'll never be able to explain it all to her," he whispered, flipping the lid of the box open with his thumb. "Now that this has happened, I'm always going to be alone."

# 22

# CEREMONY

I awoke one morning nearly a week later, knowing exactly what day it was without having to consult Ke'tai or a calendar. It was March twenty-ninth, a Friday, and the day Te'chok had set aside for the Transition Ceremony.

When I awoke, I knew it was early in the day even though there were no windows in the compound. It was strangely quiet, and this sense was bolstered by Ke'tai's rhythmic breathing as he continued to sleep beside me. I rose carefully, hoping I did not wake him; I knew it would be futile for me to remain in bed. I was filled with a nervous energy that would not dissipate, and would not, until the ceremony had been completed.

I dressed quietly in the darkness, able to see well enough without turning the lights on. I still marveled at my newly heightened senses, two months after the transformation. I smiled briefly at this; today marked two months to the day.

Ke'tai continued to sleep, undisturbed, as I slipped out of the room, closing the door softly behind me. I turned on one of the lamps in the living room, then sat down on the couch with a sigh, retrieving the stack of papers I had left there the night before. These contained instructions regarding the ceremony today, and I skimmed over the pages for at least the twentieth time in an attempt to reassure myself that I was truly ready for this new chapter of my life. I remained unconvinced.

Less than an hour later, Ke'tai emerged from the bedroom already dressed, his hair spiked up into his version of perfection. I was still re-reading Te'chok's notes, and received an amused look accompanied by a shake of the head from Ke'tai.

"You're going to get through today just fine," he assured me, making his way around the couch to drop onto the cushions beside me. "Re-reading this stuff for the millionth time is not going to make any difference."

I sighed, knowing well that he was right, and dropped the papers back onto the coffee table. I sat back, leaning my head against his shoulder, and gazed up into his silver eyes. "I don't feel ready for this."

His lips brushed my forehead in a brief kiss. "Ji'anne, that isn't going to matter. Today is the end of your eight weeks, and regardless of how ready you think you are, you've got to accept what is coming. Besides, if you make mistakes at first, Zy'driks will probably convince the other Elders it's Te'chok's fault anyway."

I nodded. "I don't want to make mistakes, though…and if something is my fault, I don't want Te'chok getting blamed for it just because Zy'driks doesn't like him."

Ke'tai shrugged slightly. "I think you will do just fine, love. Relax."

I shrugged noncommittally; I knew I could not relax.

Ke'tai must have sensed what I was thinking, because he said, "Okay, don't relax. How about we go grab some breakfast, and maybe take your mind off all this for a while? I know it's early yet, but maybe it will help."

I nodded slowly. "Sure, why not?"

Ke'tai sighed as he pushed himself up off the couch, offering one hand to me. I took it, and allowed him to pull me to my feet. He did not let go of my hand until we stood in line at the cafeteria and he needed to balance his tray.

I was surprised at the number of people present so early in the day. It seemed the entire compound had arisen before the sun had, unable to continue their slumber due to excitement or nerves. There were many summoners present whom I did not yet know, and scattered amongst them were their various trackers and assistants. The room felt to me much like a bee hive, thrumming with activity and pent up energy.

While we stood in line, one voice rose above the drone of conversation in greeting. I glanced in the direction of its source, noting Zy'driks was making his way around the crowded tables toward where we stood. Several of the summoners I was unfamiliar with paused in their conversations as they heard my name uttered above the din.

"Ji'anne, Ke'tai, hi," Zy'driks said again as he finally reached us. "I'm glad you're here so early."

"Why is that?" I asked, turning away briefly to order a bagel with cream cheese and a glass of orange juice.

Zy'driks looked down, appearing somewhat uncomfortable, which was unusual for him. I glanced at Ke'tai, who simply shrugged.

"Uh, something happened, late last night," Zy'driks replied. "I know Te'chok will probably try to avoid telling you before the ceremony at noon, but I really think you ought to be informed. It's about your sister."

I turned to face him fully, ignoring for the moment the breakfast counter. "What about her? What's happened?"

Movement caught my eye behind Zy'driks and I noticed Te'chok had just entered the room and was attempting to make his way towards us.

Zy'driks sighed. "Te'chok sent summoner Ly'dritz to the Seattle area several weeks ago in an attempt to monitor the hunters there. Ly'dritz was chosen for the task because he is not a very powerful summoner and it would be more difficult for the hunters to discover his presence nearby—"

"Ji'anne!" Te'chok called, now only several steps away from where I stood with Zy'driks. Zy'driks scowled at the interruption, and turned his head to glare in Te'chok's direction. I took the opportunity to gather my bagel and juice, which were now ready, and led the way to one of the few empty tables in the room. Ke'tai and the other two followed quickly in my wake.

"As I was saying," Zy'driks continued as we sat down, he taking the seat directly across from me, "Ly'dritz was dispatched to Seattle. We received word from him very late last night; both of his trackers have been killed, and we assume it was the hunters at fault—your sister among them."

Te'chok sighed and dropped his gaze to the tabletop, his expression conveying his disappointment with the Elder. "I wish you would have waited until this afternoon—" he began, only to be cut off by Zy'driks.

"I know that's what you wanted," Zy'driks spat angrily. "I don't care if you think you are protecting her—it doesn't help matters within the Order when you withhold information, especially if you are withholding it from our leader!"

Te'chok's jaw clenched, his pale face flaring crimson. "I am still the leader for now," he replied in a low voice, the tone threatening. "You may be an Elder, but your actions this morning are flawed, Zy'driks, and I'm not afraid to tell you that."

I sighed, wishing I could be anywhere else but at the table with these two argumentative men. "Who cares? He told me. So what? I'll manage." I shook my head in frustration. "What I would like most this morning is some peace and quiet from the both of you. Please."

Zy'driks nodded once, his expression unreadable. Te'chok sighed, mumbled an apology, and pushed away from the table. "I'll see you at eleven, then?" he asked, sounding weary. When I nodded, he managed a faltering smile and strode away.

Once Te'chok was gone, I said, "Thank you for telling me about the trackers, Zy'driks. Even though it killed my mood, I'm glad I know about it—regardless of what Te'chok might think."

Zy'driks appeared thoughtful for a moment before he replied. "I have wondered for some time now if your views on things did not mesh more closely with mine than they did with Te'chok's. I think now I have an answer. I will be awaiting your appearance at noon, Ji'anne. Until then, enjoy your day." He nodded once as he rose and turned away.

I turned to Ke'tai, who had been quietly picking at his pancakes the whole time, though he had not managed to eat much. "What do you suppose that meant?"

"I think Zy'driks believes he will agree with you more often than not, that's all," Ke'tai replied tiredly. "I'm glad you put a stop to their argument. It will be a blessing when all this ceremonial crap is over and done with, and Te'chok and Zy'driks are able to part ways again. I don't know how you can tolerate the two of them together."

"I don't, as you saw," I replied with a shrug. "They give me a headache if they go at it for too long."

At eleven o'clock that morning, I met Te'chok in the library to finalize his preparations for the ceremony that was set to begin at noon. Ke'tai accompanied me, which I was grateful for, although Te'chok was less than pleased at his presence simply because it did not follow typical protocol.

Most of what was said was a reiteration of what he had already covered in the days prior to this, and for my part I nodded often but said little. The review of my part in today's ceremony was boring and tiresome, particularly since I had expended the remainder of my patience that morning during Te'chok's spat with Zy'driks.

After about thirty minutes of pointless review, Te'chok paused and looked thoughtful for a moment. "Well, I believe I've told you everything I was going to today," he remarked after a time. "Now, we wait."

I nodded, glad he was finally finished, and turned to face Ke'tai. "I'm glad you'll be with me for this," I said softly. "I know it's just a ceremony, but I'm nervous…"

He smiled. "You have nothing to be nervous about, love," he replied, taking my hands in his. "You'll do a great job as the head of the Order, and for the first few months you'll probably get more offers for help than you can possibly use…so if you do need advice or assistance, it'll be there. Besides, I'm always going to be here for you, no matter what."

I returned his smile and nodded, his words easing my tension. Nothing of import was said during the next half hour; we passed the time with idle chat that held little meaning. Te'chok paced impatiently from one end of the library to the other, checking his watch every few minutes. He appeared nervous as well, though I could not fathom why he should be. He had said little of what part he would play in the ceremony, mentioning only that it was a minor role.

Time seemed to drag by slowly, but finally as the clock reached five minutes to noon, there was a knock upon the library doors. Ke'tai and I rose from our seats quickly while Te'chok collected himself and strode purposefully to the door. In the corridor outside stood Il'zaks, dressed immaculately as usual, though more formally than I was accustomed to.

His gaze swept quickly past Te'chok to where Ke'tai and I stood. "I was selected to escort you to the grand ballroom, Lady Ji'anne," he said, beaming. "Because I will become one of the Elders in three days, I was given this honor—and believe me, it is truly an honor."

I smiled, glad to see Il'zaks. I had not been afforded much opportunity in which to speak with him for several weeks, and despite his proper nature, I had missed his company. In my mind, he would always be my mentor; I had learned much more about the Order and about being a summoner from Il'zaks than I had from Te'chok.

Il'zaks offered me his arm, and I took it in my own as he led me out of the library once more. Ke'tai followed quietly behind. As soon as we were out of earshot of Te'chok, I said, "I'm glad you're here to do this, Il'zaks."

He smiled, and nodded in a knowing sort of way. "So am I, Lady Ji'anne."

We headed in the opposite direction of the lobby from the library, taking a path I had not traversed previously. The corridor Il'zaks had taken us down was short, and ended at two very large, curved doors, both of which had been propped open. On each side of the door stood a summoner, neither of whom I recognized, and beyond them was a spacious room with a high ceiling and polished wood floors lined with rows of collapsible chairs. Every seat appeared to be filled, many with summoners, but many more with trackers, and everyone appeared to be dressed in their finest attire.

"We will wait here for a few moments," Il'zaks said softly, stopping several feet away from the doors. "Te'chok must enter first to announce you. I am certain he has already told you of this."

I nodded, beginning to sense butterflies forming in my stomach. Throughout the morning, I had been calm, but now I was starting to feel truly nervous. I sighed and dropped my gaze to the carpeted floor; a moment later Ke'tai had taken my free hand in his own in a gesture of reassurance. I raised my eyes to meet his, and he offered up a smile.

"You can do this," he whispered. "I know you can."

I managed a smile, but was unable to answer him because Te'chok strode up to us at that moment. "It's time," he said briskly, looking rather nervous himself. "I'll go inside and begin, just listen for the cue. You know when you're supposed to enter."

I nodded once, though I don't believe Te'chok actually saw the movement. As soon as he had finished speaking, he walked quickly toward the opened double doors, leaving me no further opportunity to ask him any final questions. I did the only thing that I could do—I watched Te'chok as he strode down the aisle to the front of the room.

As he neared the front of the room, a hush fell over the crowd of gathered summoners and trackers as they anticipated his next words. When Te'chok turned around to face the crowd, his face looked a bit paler than was usual, and his brow shone with a fine sheen of sweat that even I could make out from the corridor. Te'chok was clearly nervous, which did nothing to help settle my own anxiety.

"I want to welcome all of you here today," Te'chok began, his voice strong and steady despite his obvious trepidation. "As most of you know, this sort of ceremony has not been held for many, many years. A new summoner has been inducted into the Order, and she will serve as my replacement as head of the Order."

I glanced down, hoping that I would make a good first impression upon those gathered. I had chosen to wear a formal gown of midnight blue for the occasion, which had been one of the few purchases I had made on my shopping trip with Adele almost three months ago. There were only a small number of people whom I had met previously present in the crowd; the room was filled with strangers.

"Eight weeks ago, I began teaching this new summoner everything I could to prepare her for this day," Te'chok continued after a brief pause. "She is ready for this position, and it is my belief she will do well as our next leader." Te'chok shifted his gaze from the crowd to where I was standing just outside the opened doors. "I would like to introduce to you Lady Ji'anne."

Every pair of eyes in the room turned toward the door where we were standing. I swallowed hard and took Il'zaks' arm once again. Ke'tai squeezed my hand in reassurance, before he stepped back to allow us to pass through the door. I managed an uncertain smile as we entered the ballroom, and tried my best to ignore the whispers I heard as I passed row after row of people.

When we had reached the front of the room and Te'chok, Il'zaks released my arm and stepped to one side. Turning around to face the crowd, I noticed that the Elders, who occupied the first row of seats, had all risen from their chairs.

"May I present Lady Ji'anne, the new head of our Order," Te'chok stated, and then he too moved to one side, leaving me to stand alone in the center.

At that moment, Zy'driks broke away from the line of Elders to stand at my left side. "After I address them, turn to face me," he whispered. "I trust Te'chok went over this part with you earlier?"

When I nodded, he smiled somewhat mischievously. "He did not know that I had asked for this role in your ceremony. He doesn't look pleased." He chuckled under his breath for a moment, and then he turned to the crowd. "The Board of Elders has accepted Ji'anne's position as the new head of our Order. With that said, I will commence the induction ceremony."

Here we turned to face one another, and I could hear soft shuffling as the other Elders returned to their seats. Behind Zy'driks, I could see Te'chok standing with his thin arms crossed over his narrow chest, his face darkened like a storm cloud. It seemed that Zy'driks' decision to take over this part of the ceremony had thoroughly enraged him. I tore my gaze away from the angry countenance of Te'chok to focus on Zy'driks as he began to speak once again.

"Summoner Ji'anne, the Elders of the Order welcome you as our newest leader. From now on, you will no longer be merely a summoner, but the Lady Grand Summoner. As Te'chok's replacement, we will look to you for guidance on how the Order should be run. Do you accept these terms as part of the Order?"

I nodded, and then managed to say, "Yes, I do."

Zy'driks smiled in amusement. "Very well, this ceremony has now come to a close." He turned to face the crowd once more, and added, "There are refreshments ready in the cafeteria. After a brief meeting, the Elders and Lady Ji'anne will be there to greet you."

Suddenly the room erupted in a burst of noise and activity. Nearly everyone in attendance rose to their feet and began chatting as they filed out of the room. Now that the ceremony had concluded, I realized belatedly that there had been little for me to be nervous about, and that the whole affair had been anticlimactic. I breathed a sigh of relief, glad it was finished, nevertheless.

"Why didn't you warn me that you were going to play this part, Zy'driks?" Te'chok demanded in an angry whisper as he prepared to stride past us.

Zy'driks shrugged, flashing that mischievous grin of his. "Mostly to see how you would react, which, by the way, was just as I had predicted you would. We can discuss this later, if you'd like, Te'chok, but right now I have some obligations—as do you."

Te'chok's jaw clenched and his eyes flashed with anger. "You know damn well that I do *not* want to talk about it later. Go to hell, Zy'driks." He stormed away, catching up with the last of the crowd exiting the room.

Zy'driks chuckled, and did not seem offended. "I think he's been wanting to tell me that for quite some time now," he commented, his lips twisting into a smirk as his eyes followed Te'chok's progress out of the room. "We've never agreed upon how the Order should run, but I think you and I will, Ji'anne."

I nodded, unwilling to comment one way or the other. I understood intuitively that I must maintain an accord with Zy'driks—and the rest of the Elders. They were going to become a large part of my life within the Order, yet I did sympathize with Te'chok as well. Zy'driks had made a concentrated effort to anger the other man.

After a short and somewhat awkward silence, Zy'driks said, "We have a bit of business to discuss with you before we all head over to the cafeteria." He gestured toward the other Elders, who were now standing, and I walked forward toward them.

The meeting with the Elders took less than five minutes, and proved to be a mere formality in which they extended their official welcome to me. My first real duties as the head of the Order would begin tomorrow. Over the past few weeks, I had taken over more and more of Te'chok's tasks, and while I was confident that I could fill in for the daily aspects well enough, I was unsure of how I would handle situations that involved the more dangerous aspects of our work. Thoughts of Xandra often clouded my judgment.

As our brief meeting concluded, Ke'tai met me at the center of the room. "Ready for your party?" he asked with one of his endearing grins.

I nodded. "I'm as ready as I'll ever be," I replied without enthusiasm. I was still too nervous to truly relax.

His mouth twisted into a worried frown. "You are going to be great, Ji'anne—you have nothing to worry about. Take this party as an opportunity to have some fun and get to know some of the other summoners. I can introduce you to some of them, and if we manage to find Il'zaks again, he can introduce you to almost everyone here."

"Or I can," Zy'driks chimed in from behind me. I started, not having realized he was still in the room.

"Um, okay," I agreed, not wanting to start off on the wrong foot with the temperamental Zy'driks if I could avoid it.

Zy'driks grinned as he took the lead, motioning for us to follow him from the otherwise empty ballroom. I glanced uncertainly at Ke'tai, who simply took my right hand in his left and followed the Elder's lead. The corridors leading us between the ballroom and the cafeteria were empty, and our footsteps echoed hollowly. As we neared the cafeteria, however, a cacophony of sounds spilled into the empty hallway beyond, and I could see that every seat inside was taken and many other people were standing in clusters around the room.

"I'll make an announcement," Zy'driks stated just before we entered the crowded room. He strode into the crowd quickly, and was soon lost amidst the sea of people.

Ke'tai and I remained near the door, though it did not take long for some of the nearby summoners to take notice and begin to wander toward us.

"I wish there was less ceremony involved in all of this," I whispered to Ke'tai before the nearest unfamiliar face reached us to introduce himself. "I feel like Zy'driks is making a big deal about nothing."

Ke'tai smiled faintly, his expression one of sadness. "It *is* a big deal, though, love. This sort of thing happens only very rarely, and the rest of us are excited. You'll understand one day what this is like…when you've lived beyond your natural lifespan—" He was cut off at this point by Zy'driks, who had positioned himself atop a table near the center of the room.

"Excuse me, can I have your attention please?" Zy'driks shouted over the chatter. A hush quickly fell over the room, and he waited until it was nearly silent before continuing. "I came here to announce the arrival of the Lady Grand Summoner, Ji'anne. Please extend your warmest welcomes to her!" Zy'driks hopped down from the tabletop fluidly, grinning all the while.

I had little time for myself for the remainder of the afternoon, but I did manage to escape as it neared evening. Rather than taking the most direct route back to our apartment, I took a more convoluted path in an attempt to avoid unwanted attention. After the packed crowd inside the cafeteria, the air in the corridors outside was refreshingly cool and quiet. For the first time that day, I was able to relax. Ke'tai walked at my side; he had not strayed far from me throughout the long day. We took our time heading back to the apartment, savoring the time alone. In the weeks to come, I knew we would have very few opportunities for these moments, and I wanted to enjoy it while I could.

# 23

# UNDERGROUND

Over time, I came to be comfortable in my role as the leader of the Order, though I recall those first few months as being difficult and every week brought with it new trials. During the day, I attended to official business while Ke'tai often spent time at his lab when we were in the Boston area. Each evening, however, we were together and made the most of our limited time alone.

After a while, Xandra's position with the hunters became much less of a concern for me, though I never truly forgot about my sister and her new role. My worries surrounding her were pushed to the background while I dealt with more pressing issues. I strove to run the Order smoothly.

I recall that those first few years were busy, but they were also the most wonderful years of my life. I was happy, and Ke'tai and I were very much in love. I maintained a close friendship with Xen'din, Kai'lind, and Il'zaks, making an effort to visit them whenever my travels allowed it. As head of the Order, I was never in one place for very long; I was expected to travel to all areas of the globe to resolve specific issues unique to each region. Most of the time Ke'tai traveled with me, but during other times we were forced to move separately; he would act as my voice during those rare occasions.

It was during one such occurrence that my façade of happiness and the tenuous peace we had achieved with the hunters was ultimately shattered. I had been called away for business in San Diego, and as I was on my way there, I was also requested in Seattle. Ke'tai took it upon himself to deal with the issue in Seattle, and I made up my mind to travel there once I had finished my work to the south. I knew that the San Diego business would not take long; I was merely there to welcome a new summoner to the Order.

I made my visit to San Diego very brief; once my business was complete, I asked Marek to begin the drive north the very same day.

As Marek steered his black Camaro onto the interstate, my thoughts drifted back to the last time I had been in Seattle. It had been seven years since that fateful night when Ke'tai and Il'zaks had whisked me away from everything I had known, sparing me from what I now knew would have been a certain death at the hands of the gathering hunters. Since that time, the hunters had made a permanent home in Seattle, and our activities in the region had been severely limited.

Ke'tai had volunteered to meet with some trackers who were bearing a sizeable shipment of various materials from their summoner, El'lei, in China, and were to deliver this shipment to Ke'tai under the cover of darkness at the Port of Seattle. I worried for his safety, both because of the obvious threat from the hunters and because he had insisted on going alone with only Carlos to assist him. I knew from experience what the hunters were capable of, and the group from Seattle posed a more serious threat than most; they were led by a Stone-reader of great talent, a man by the name of Thaddeus Taylor.

The morning faded into afternoon, and as the afternoon grew closer to evening, we traveled north through California. The car ride was proving to be uneventful, and for that I was thankful. I fell into a light doze as true darkness fell, exhausted from the prolonged road trip. I do not know how long I had been asleep, but it seemed as though it had only been for a few minutes, at best. My cell phone was ringing.

I fumbled at the center console for a moment, trying to free the noisome thing from its charging cable. As the tiny screen came into focus, I felt my heart freeze—it was Carlos. He was not to call me directly unless something had gone wrong. Why wasn't Ke'tai calling himself?

Somehow, despite the whirlwind of panicked thoughts spinning through my head, I managed to answer the phone. "Hello?"

"Ji'anne, listen—I don't have much time." The voice on the other end of the line was not Carlos', but Ke'tai's, and he sounded frightened.

"What—?"

"Uh, I just got back from the Port, but the trackers never showed. Something is wrong, and I can't find Carlos. All of his stuff is here, but…Oh, god…"

"Ke'tai? What's going on?" My voice sounded shrill, and Marek glanced worriedly at me from the corners of his eyes. I felt the Camaro suddenly accelerate as Marek sensed the urgency of the situation.

"I think we were set up," Ke'tai replied in a choked whisper. "Carlos…He's dead."

I felt my heart sink, and I wanted desperately to break down and cry, but I knew I could not. I had to maintain my focus in order to help Ke'tai, and tears would only prove detrimental.

"Ke'tai, we're on our way, but I don't think we will be there for a few more hours yet…I'll call Zy'driks—he is in the Olympia area. But you need to get out of there *fast*!"

"I'm packing as we speak, love," he replied, his voice hoarse with grief. "I will go to the safe house north of Coeur d'Alene. I'll meet you there."

"Be safe, Ke'tai," I whispered into the phone. "I love you."

I forced myself into some semblance of composure as I ended the call. I must hold myself together long enough to speak to Zy'driks, to explain the situation coherently. I made that call brief, and Zy'driks agreed to contact Ke'tai and meet him for the journey to the safe house. He ended the call by stating he would notify me once he had met with Ke'tai and they were safely on their way.

As soon as I had ended the call with Zy'driks, I could hold back the wash of emotions no longer. I burst into tears, mourning the loss of Carlos, who had become a good friend during the past few years. His death would weigh heavily upon Ke'tai's spirit as well.

Marek remained silent as he guided the Camaro through the light late evening traffic; he knew from experience that I would tell him what had occurred in time. Marek was patient, which was part of the reason he had been selected to work with me.

Once I had managed to compose myself again, I told Marek the news. His face fell, and an unspoken anguish shone through his blue eyes as he focused even more intently on the road ahead. Marek and Carlos had worked together often during the past seven years, and the loss had hit him hard, though he did not vocalize his grief.

"Carlos was a good man," he said gruffly. "What are we gonna do now?"

I shrugged noncommittally; I had not planned that far ahead. "I don't know yet," I replied quietly. "Just keep driving, for now."

Several hours later, my cell phone rang again. By this time, we had crossed the Oregon border and were passing a city called Eugene.

On the other end of the line was Zy'driks. "Ji'anne, we have a bit of a situation here."

"What's happened?" I demanded.

"Ke'tai is on the run…From what I can gather, he was forced to leave the rental apartment very quickly, and it looks like he went underground."

I glanced at Marek, feeling my face drain of color. "Drive faster," I whispered urgently. "Underground? Do you mean the old city?"

"Yes," Zy'driks confirmed.

I sighed. Beneath part of Seattle's downtown district were a maze of underground corridors, some of which were maintained as part of the city's Underground Tour—a guided walking tour that featured the history of Seattle. Other sections of the underground warren were in disrepair and would be dangerous to travel through. The underground passages were the remains of the original buildings that had made up portions of downtown Seattle before the fire in 1889 had destroyed the entire business district. The industrious Seattleites had simply rebuilt right atop the devastation.

"Is Miranda with you?" I asked of Zy'driks. Miranda was one of his three trackers, and had the ability to seek out those with a summoner's power.

Zy'driks hesitated before speaking. "Yes, she is here, but she has the flu. I can see if she is up for seeking him out."

"Please do," I replied brusquely, attempting to keep the terrified, panicked feelings I was experiencing from coming through in my tone. Ke'tai had fled underground, and anything could happen there—for good or ill. I turned to face Marek, trying in vain to push those despairing thoughts aside. "How long will it take to reach Seattle?"

"If I follow the speed limit, about five hours, maybe six. If not, we could probably be there in about four."

"We'll be there in four hours," I told Zy'driks, feeling the black Camaro accelerate even further. I did not know how fast Marek was driving, and frankly, I didn't care as long as he didn't get stopped by the police for speeding. "Meet me in front of the Smith Tower, and bring Miranda."

The next few hours went by in a blur, a haze of worried thoughts obscuring most of the memory I had of the trip. It was nearing four a.m. when we reached Tacoma, Seattle's southern neighbor, and there was very little traffic on I-5, allowing Marek to cruise unhindered along the rain-dampened highway. It was early March; during that season, the Seattle area rarely saw the sun through the nearly constant drizzle.

We were only twenty minutes away from our destination when my cell phone rang. It was Zy'driks again.

"Ji'anne, we are at the rendezvous point—how far out are you?"

"Not long," I replied, "fifteen, twenty minutes, max. We're going through Tacoma right now."

Zy'driks' next words sounded relieved. "Good. I don't want to sit here too long—Jake senses there are hunters in the area. Several of them."

I swallowed hard, trying to push away my fears. "We'll be there soon," I promised.

As I ended the call, I let out a sigh. He had mentioned nothing about Miranda or Ke'tai, and I wondered why he had omitted that from the conversation. Was there something else wrong that he was afraid to disclose to me?

I stared out the passenger side window at the darkened storefronts while the fine mist beaded up on the glass, tiny drops forming quickly and running across the slick surface. It felt strange to be back in Seattle after so many years of exile, but everything still seemed so familiar. It was a bittersweet homecoming; I had so many wonderful memories from Seattle, but those had been overshadowed by my concern for Ke'tai's safety.

Within fifteen minutes, we were parked in the garage across the street from Smith Tower. I pulled my hair back into a ponytail and pulled my gray woolen coat on, drawing the hood up to cover my hair. I took a pair of dark sunglasses from the coat pocket where they had been stored and slid them on, knowing it might look strange to anyone we might encounter but that it was also necessary for my safety. Marek and I hurried through the parking garage, meeting up with Zy'driks and his three trackers in a matter of moments. Worried as I was, Marek had a difficult time keeping up with me; I was doing a poor job of keeping my faster movement speed in check.

"Glad you made it," Zy'driks said by way of greeting. He had a knit cap pulled on over his head and was also wearing dark sunglasses. "The good news is that Jake senses the threat from the hunters is gone—at least for now. I don't know what that ultimately means for us, but we should be able to search for Ke'tai unhindered for a time."

I nodded, motioning for the others to follow. "There's an entrance to the underground in the alley up ahead. Most of the passages are connected, so we should be able to go just about anywhere he might be."

Zy'driks nodded, indicating his trackers should follow my lead. I hurried past several darkened buildings, paying little attention to my surroundings. I had only one thing in mind—find Ke'tai and rescue him from the danger he might be in.

I found the alley, and part way along its length was a set of cement steps leading down to a metal door which had been painted a pale yellow. City tour guides led groups through periodically during the day as part of the historic Underground Tour of Seattle; I was pinning my hopes on the door being unlocked.

Marek placed a hand on my shoulder as I reached for the door handle, stopping me. "Let me go inside first," he said gently. "The hunters may be gone, but they may have left some of their subordinates behind to keep an eye on things."

I sighed, but acquiesced. Drawing his pistol, Marek opened the door quickly, pointing the weapon first one way, then the other. He nodded, motioning for the rest of us to follow.

Once inside I removed the sunglasses and shoved them into one of my coat pockets. In the darkness, Zy'driks and I would be needed to lead the group safely through the obstacles I knew we would encounter, and I would need to be able to see without the hindrance of the glasses.

As the door was closed behind us, I took note of our surroundings. We were standing on a slab of cracked concrete, and directly across from the door was a metal railing, painted a red-brown color. Beyond the railing was an expanse of crumbled chunks of concrete and uneven mounds of dirt and debris, followed by a pocked brick wall whose face was littered with the remnants of old cobwebs. To the right of the door, the concrete walkway continued, winding around a bend in the wall. To the left was another railing, constructed to block the way from tourists in the corridor; the path in that direction appeared to be somewhat less structurally sound.

Zy'driks mumbled something off to my left, and I realized belatedly that he was calling forth a demon. That was a wise course of action, I decided, since the threat of the hunters had diminished. I danced, calling my chimæra, knowing that it would be hard to visually detect, unless I willed it to take on a specific form.

Suddenly a light flared in the darkness. Blinking at the brightness, I realized Miranda had turned on a flashlight as she stood near the closed door. Miranda was very petite, standing perhaps five feet tall had she been wearing heels. Her dark hair hung limply over her eyes, weighted down from the drizzle outside, and her face was flushed and appeared feverish. I felt guilty for asking Zy'driks to drag her along on this venture, but at the same time, she was the only one nearby who could track a summoner.

In the light, I could make out foot prints leading away to the left of the door, preserved in the thick layer of dust that covered the cracked and uneven floor. There were several different sets of footprints, most from various types of shoes, but one set unmistakably belonged to the talon-clawed feet of a shadow demon.

Without looking at the footprints, Miranda pointed to her left. "Ke'tai is somewhere that direction. But…he seems far away."

Marek took the lead with Jake, and I sent the chimæra with them. Zy'driks and I went next, with Miranda and Aaron taking the rear along with Zy'driks' shadow demon. Aaron was tall and well-muscled; he was not in truth a tracker, but Zy'driks employed him as a body guard. What had transpired during the past day caused me to reconsider hiring someone of that sort as well—though Marek had served well doubling both as a tracker and body guard so far.

The passage ran straight for only a short distance, and then made a ninety-degree turn to the left. At the turn, the concrete ended and the rest of the passageway was covered in mounds of dirt littered with chunks of broken concrete, pieces of half-rotten wood, and sections of metal pipe. The footsteps led us through this maze of hazards and toward another slab of cracked cement some distance away, running parallel to the last.

As we reached the next paved pathway, Jake held up a hand for us to stop as he bent his lithe form to examine something on the ground. In appearance, Jake looked very much like Zy'driks, though he was slightly thinner; his face had a similar structure to it and the two were nearly the same height. Jake had the same hairstyle—short spikes held in place with gel—and he even dressed in much the same manner, wearing a long black trench coat, black pants, and a dark gray t-shirt with a laughing black skull emblazoned across the chest. Jake's hair was very dark, almost black, and his eyes were the color of chocolate, but had he been a summoner the two could have been mistaken for brothers.

He straightened slowly. "There's blood here…I think it's from a demon."

Without waiting for the others to react, I jogged to where he stood and knelt beside the dark splatters marring the concrete. The blood was dark, almost black in color, and at close range I could detect the distinct tang of vinegar.

Standing quickly, I nodded. "It is a demon's blood." My voice shook unintentionally; this revelation rocked me to my very core, threatening to dissolve my strength into a tidal wave of panic. The blood spatters were a clear indication that Ke'tai had traveled this way with the hunters in close pursuit, and his shadow demon had been injured during the conflict.

Zy'driks came to stand beside me, and placed a hand on my shoulder in an effort to comfort me. "We have to keep going, Ji'anne," he said softly. "We know he went this way, but to reach him and get him to safety, we must keep going."

I nodded, forcing my emotions to the background once more. We had to locate Ke'tai.

The trail of blood spatters led us along the concrete pathway for some distance, growing in number and size the farther we traveled. It was clear to me that the demon had been injured rather severely, and I began to push the others to go faster as my mind raced towards a blinding panic. The pathway turned sharply to the left after a time, and ended after only a few feet at a wooden door that was hanging crookedly upon its hinges. More blood was splattered across the surface of the door, and not all of it was the dark shade that belonged to the shadow demon.

# 24

# DEVASTATED

I stopped dead in my tracks as I realized what the surface of the door held. Dark, almost black demon's blood, and the redder blood of a human marred its partially rotted surface. The door was closed, but I did not know if I had the strength to see what lay on the other side. Perhaps it was a dead hunter, but perhaps it was something far worse.

The group fell silent as we came to the door, each studying it in their own way. Finally, Miranda spoke, her voice barely a whisper. "Ke'tai is inside, but…my senses tell me he is far away. It doesn't make sense to me. I don't know what this means."

My heart leapt at this news. Ke'tai was inside! If she could sense him, that meant he was alive. But what had happened? And whose blood was spilled across the door?

Marek took the initiative, and yanked the door open. He disappeared inside, along with Zy'driks' shadow demon and my chimæra. Using the chimæra, I could see what lay inside without entering the room myself. The interior was slick with blood, the small space rank with its metallic odor; the blood appeared fresh. Crumpled just out of sight to the right side of the door lay Ke'tai's shadow demon, its body riddled with bullet holes. The demon was still alive, though only just. It reached out toward my chimæra feebly, unable to summon the strength to move any further, its breath rattling in its massive chest. I allowed the chimæra to go to the shadow demon, to comfort it in its last moments.

With my demon otherwise preoccupied, I did not see what lay at the opposite wall of the room. After several long moments, Marek returned to the corridor, his face a mask of pain.

"Ji'anne, you need to go inside. Ke'tai…he's…"

I felt hot tears threatening to spill down my cheeks, but blinked them rapidly away. Ke'tai was inside, and he needed me. I shoved past Marek into the dark, blood-smeared room.

In the corner opposite the door, Ke'tai sat propped against the wall, blood running freely from a cut on his forehead. I ran to him, ignoring the treacherous footing inside, and knelt down beside him.

"Ke'tai," I whispered, "I'm here."

He managed a weak smile, and reached his left hand up to touch the side of my face. "Ji'anne," he said, his voice feeble, "I'm in bad shape..."

"Don't talk like that," I said, tears spilling from my eyes. "We'll get you out of here—"

He shook his head, and glanced down to his abdomen, where his right hand was firmly pressed. He moved his hand slightly, and blood welled up around his hand. "It's too late, love..."

I swallowed hard, trying to dislodge the hard lump that had formed in my throat. "You can't leave me, Ke'tai. I *need* you."

He shook his head again. "I don't want to go, love...But I'm fading fast. Listen..." He coughed, wincing in pain, while blood spurted from the wound in his abdomen. "The hunters found me out...It was a trap, just like I thought..."

"Who did this to you?" I asked in a choked whisper, unable to speak any louder due to the lump in my throat and the tightness of my chest.

"There were three hunters..." He gasped, coughing again. "I didn't recognize one of them, but...one was Dirk Musgrave, the summoner-tracker...and the other was...It was your sister."

I looked down, unable to conceal the pain and horror I was experiencing any longer. "No!" The word came out more like a wail than any actual vocalization, and I began to sob uncontrollably.

Ke'tai reached up with his left hand again, and touched my face once more. "Ji'anne...I love you...I love you..." His words were faint, barely discernable through another bout of coughing that left him with blood trickling from the corner of his mouth. His arm dropped back to his side, and his eyes closed slowly. "I love you..."

Through the tears that were streaming down my face, I managed to reply. "I love you, too. Please don't go...Please..."

My request fell on deaf ears. He was already dead, the blood no longer flowing from the wound in his abdomen, his chest no longer rising with each painful breath. I rose to my feet, my ears ringing with my own pained screams. I didn't want to live without him in my life.

I don't know how long I stood next to his lifeless form, crying, screaming, tortured to my very core. It might have been a few seconds, or a few hours later, before Marek and Zy'driks moved forward to guide me back toward the door. I tried to resist their efforts, refusing to leave Ke'tai's side, but in the end they persevered.

I was led through the maze of corridors toward the exit door that would lead out of the underground realm of Seattle. I was blind in my grief, stumbling over objects and paying no heed to where I placed my feet. Zy'driks and Marek spoke at intervals during our journey, but I was deaf to what was said. It didn't matter any more; Ke'tai was dead, and so was my reason for living, for having become what I was. I wanted to fall into the darkness that I felt encroaching upon me, leap toward it and never return.

Finally, we reached the door that would lead us outside. Zy'driks stopped and turned to me, placing one hand on each of my shoulders. "Ji'anne, you have to listen to me. I cannot imagine what you have just experienced, but you must listen."

I shook my head stubbornly. What was the point in going any further? Ke'tai was gone, stolen from me by my twin sister.

Zy'driks appeared frustrated, and he shook me roughly. "Ji'anne, you can't just give up. Not like this…"

Marek pulled the hood of my coat back over my head. "At least put your sunglasses on, Ji'anne," he said quietly. His blue eyes were filled with concern and sadness. "We'll go anywhere you want to. I'll take you away from here."

"I won't leave Ke'tai here," I mumbled.

Zy'driks sighed and dropped his hands. "Aaron and Jake are bringing him out. We were supposed to retrieve one of the vehicles. We'll hold a proper funeral for him—I'm not about to leave him here, Ji'anne."

I stared at him, uncomprehending. When had all of this been decided?

"You weren't in any condition to make a decision about this," Zy'driks went on as though reading my thoughts. "I'm so sorry, Ji'anne. Ke'tai was good for you…"

Tears spilled from my eyes once more, and Zy'driks sighed. "Marek, take her back to your vehicle. I'll get ours and bring it here, but I'd like you to follow. Once my trackers return with Ke'tai, I want to ride with you, to watch over her." He paused, and then said, "Ji'anne, release your demon. We cannot go outside with it following along behind you like that."

I did as he asked, but could do no more. Some distant part of me realized they were worried about what I might do to myself because of Ke'tai's death, but another part of me wanted to ignore everything they had said and simply give up. I didn't want to go anywhere, but I didn't want to stay there, either. The darkness was beginning to feel oppressive, and yet, I wanted to embrace it, to let it swallow me whole, so that I would never again see the light of day.

I felt Marek tug my sunglasses out of my coat pocket and place them on my face for me. He put one big arm around my shoulders and led me outside into the early Seattle morning. The rain had increased, slashing down at us in icy pelts. I imagined that even the sky was mourning for Ke'tai. Marek led me to the black Camaro, and guided me into the back seat, where I drew my knees up, hugging them to my chest. I began to sob once more.

I do not recall what happened immediately afterwards, but I came back to my senses sometime much later. I may have cried myself into an oblivious sleep, or my grief might have served to block out everything around me to the point that I was no longer aware of the world. In either case, there is a dark gap in my memories, and I resurfaced from the darkness almost a full day later.

I was laying in a bed, the weak light of dawn coming in through a window frosted with ice. The room was bare with exception to the bed, and my travel bag of clothing had been placed in one corner of the room. Outside, I could see evergreen trees dusted with snow, sparkling in the first light of day.

I sat up slowly, surprised to see that I still wore the same set of clothes I'd had on when we had fled Seattle's underground. My coat and shoes had been removed, but otherwise nothing else had been changed. My jeans were still dusty from the trek through the bowels of the city, and there were dried bloodstains discoloring both knees. I knew it was not my own blood, but that of my fallen beloved. Tears stung my eyes as the memory resurfaced, and a raw, searing pain tore through my chest.

I rose unsteadily, and did not bother to straighten the sheets of the bed. I needed to find Marek, or Zy'driks, someone who could tell me where I was and how I had come to be there. I made my way to the closed door of the room, and opened it slowly, peering into the corridor beyond. The corridor itself was empty, but I could hear hushed voices coming from the room at the end, which from where I was standing appeared to be a living room. I moved in the direction of the voices, hoping to learn what had occurred while I had been paralyzed with grief.

As I entered the room, the voices fell silent. I noted that Zy'driks was present, as well as Xen'din and their combined five trackers. Marek was also there, standing nearest to me. He was the first to act after my sudden appearance, moving toward me to take my arm and lead me to one of the sofas.

"Ji'anne, how are you feeling?" he asked gently, genuinely concerned.

As I sat down, I simply shrugged, unwilling to talk about it. "Where are we?"

"This is the safe house near Coeur d'Alene," Zy'driks replied from across the coffee table. "We came here after the events in Seattle. We've been waiting for you to wake."

I shrugged again. Why did it matter if I was awake or not? Nothing mattered any more.

"Ji'anne, we need to know what Ke'tai told you," Marek said, kneeling before me and looking up into my eyes earnestly. "We weren't in the room yet when you let out that scream. Something happened...You need to tell us."

I didn't want to return to those last, tortured moments with him; I knew I would be forever haunted by them if I recalled them now. I shook my head, but said nothing, feeling tears begin to threaten once more.

Marek closed his eyes briefly, his expression pained. He rose slowly to his feet, and took a seat at the other end of the couch. "She'll tell us in time, Zy'driks. I don't think any of us know quite what she's going through right now."

"You were always there for me in the tough times," Xen'din said quietly from across the room. He was standing near one of the windows, gazing outside. "I came here to help you through this, Ji'anne. As soon as I heard what had happened, I came."

"How long was I out?" I mumbled, trying to focus on something, *anything*, other than the events in Seattle.

"Almost a whole day," Marek replied. "You had me worried, Ji'anne."

I shrugged again in reply. I felt numb to everything around me, with the exception of the grief that I was so desperately trying to ignore. It was as if all the color had been drained from the world in one brutal instant, and the only way for me to regain some sense of normalcy was to embrace the pain that I wanted more than anything to avoid.

"We are going to hold a brief ceremony for Ke'tai later today," Xen'din stated, turning from the window to make eye contact with me. "You ought to clean yourself up and be present for that, Ji'anne."

I nodded, knowing somewhere inside that he was right. I should be there, no matter how painful it might be. I had to say goodbye to him one last time. "How much time do I have?"

"We'll have the ceremony whenever you are ready," Zy'driks replied, his voice somber. "We can talk about what happened when you are ready, as well."

Ke'tai's ceremony was a simple affair. A grave had been dug behind the safe house by Jake and Aaron during the afternoon I had been out, and it was Marek and Xen'din who lowered his body into the earth. Zy'driks spoke briefly, as did Xen'din. I don't remember what was said; my grief was so overwhelming that I was unable to concentrate upon their solemn words.

During the whole process, I stood nearby, my eyes frozen on the still features of the man I loved. He had been dressed in a clean suit—who it belonged to I did not know—and I could not see the bullet wound that had taken him so viciously from my life. The cut on his forehead was visible beneath his white hair, which someone had thoughtfully spiked for the occasion. Tears flowed in a torrent from my eyes, and I made no move to stop them or hinder their progress. I didn't care any more what anyone else thought; Ke'tai was dead, and with him, a large part of myself had died, too.

After everyone who wanted to had spoken, Xen'din led me away while Marek, Jake, and Aaron began to bury my beloved. I could hear the sound of the shovels as they slid into the pile of cold, partially frozen earth and dropped it down into the hole that was to be Ke'tai's final resting place.

"Ji'anne, if there's anything I can do..."

Hearing the shovels caused something inside me to break. The numbness I had been experiencing melted away, and was replaced by a sudden and violent anger. I turned to Xen'din, blinking away the last of my tears.

"You have to promise me something," I said to him.

He nodded. "I'll do anything."

"You have to help me with what I must do next."

"And what is that?" he asked, concern etching into his features.

I hesitated, and then said, "Have Zy'driks come inside. The three of us need to talk."

He nodded slowly. "Okay. Go inside, and we'll be there in a minute."

I returned to the safe house, and paced across the living room for a few moments, thinking over what I was about to propose to them. I knew they would object, but it had to be done. There was no other way to end my pain, to mend my grief-stricken heart. I stopped pacing when I heard the door open, and I turned around to face Zy'driks and Xen'din as they entered.

"I hear you want to talk," Zy'driks said slowly, his voice cautious.

I nodded. "I need to, but I don't think you're going to like what I'm about to say."

Both men frowned and appeared worried. "Ji'anne, I hope you're not planning on doing something stupid—" Xen'din began, but I cut him off.

"I need your help, both of you. I'm going to destroy the hunters responsible for this. Every last one of them."

# PART THREE

# VENGEANCE

# 25

# INTEL

"We need to come up with a plan," Zy'driks stated, pacing from one end of the living room to the other, his brow wrinkled in thought.

It was two days after the funeral, and plans were beginning to come together about what to do regarding the hunters in Seattle. Te'chok had arrived the day before and was steadfast in his resolve to oppose everything I intended to do. I didn't care; Zy'driks was on my side this time, although a part of me realized that it was likely out of spite for Te'chok. Xen'din had agreed to lend his assistance, albeit reluctantly—he still could not shake the attachment he had once shared with my sister. All residual feelings I might have had for her had disappeared with the death of Ke'tai, and I believed there was no hope that they would ever return. By pulling her trigger and ending his life, she had unwittingly destroyed a large part of me.

"I think we need to gather information first," I replied. I stood with my back to Zy'driks, gazing out the window at the frosted branches of the evergreens that surrounded the safe house. I could hear his footsteps as he paced on the opposite side of the small room.

"Information about what?" Xen'din asked. He was sitting on the couch behind me, next to Il'zaks, who had arrived only hours earlier.

"She means to learn about the hunters, I believe," Il'zaks replied quietly. He had said very little since coming to the safe house; the death of Ke'tai had hit him hard as well.

"Yes," I replied without turning to face them. "I want to learn everything we possibly can about them—where they meet, where they live, where they work, who they associate with outside of their little group...I need to know everything."

Zy'driks was the next to speak, and his voice was cautious. "Ji'anne, what exactly are your intentions? I know you mean to run them out of

Seattle, and I am completely in support of that. But we must know what you mean to do with them…or to them."

I stared out the window for some time, anger bubbling just below the surface. I wanted vengeance for Ke'tai, to make those hunters regret that they had ever agreed to join in the fight against us. I wanted to make them pay with everything they had, to make them suffer, but I knew I could not reveal these thoughts to the three men in the room.

"I…don't quite know yet," I replied evasively.

I heard Zy'driks sigh. "I know you're out for revenge, Ji'anne, I just hope you don't get in over your head."

I whirled around to face him. "I will promise you this, Zy'driks: Whatever I do regarding these hunters, I will take every precaution I can to keep myself and those helping me safe. I am not about to have another person ripped out of my life." My words had come out heatedly, my anger managing to break through.

Zy'driks nodded. "Good, then it's settled. We'll start gathering what information we can about these hunters."

"We should send out the trackers first," Il'zaks stated. "They will be safer than any of us when we go about on this scouting mission—most hunters are unable to seek out trackers."

I nodded. "Yes. Let's call them in here, then, and get this started."

"I would advise you to have Marek stay here with you until you find another tracker for yourself, Ji'anne," Zy'driks stated. "I can spare Aaron and Jake for this, but I'd like to have Miranda remain here, at least until she gets over the flu."

"I will send Carmine," Il'zaks said.

My eyes traveled to Xen'din, where he sat quietly upon the couch. "Vance can go," he said after a moment of silence. "He will be able to track the Stone-reader."

A twitch of a smile appeared on Zy'driks' face. "I hadn't realized he had that ability. Excellent."

I strode past the others to the door leading outside. We had asked Te'chok and the trackers to give us privacy while we discussed our next move; now that we had, I was prepared to allow them inside once more.

As I reached the door, Zy'driks said, "Ji'anne, wait."

I turned to face him. "Yes?"

"If Te'chok is still outside with them, he ought to be present for this, too."

Internally, I groaned. "Why?"

"In the event that all of this ends badly, he ought to know what we are planning. Just in case."

I shrugged and frowned in his direction before turning back to the door. I knew he was right, but I also knew that Te'chok was going to be a thorn in my side once he learned of what I intended to do. He was still clinging to the pretense of false peace and advocated that we abstain from any action against the hunters, but I no longer cared about his misgivings. He would have to deal with my choice to act, no matter what came to pass.

Outside, the air was frigid in spite of the bright sunlight that streamed from the sky. It still felt as though Idaho was in the depths of winter, even though it was March. Most of the trackers we employed were seated in a circle of tree stumps, chatting amicably and bundled up against the cold. Carmine stood off to one side, glaring about her while smoking a cigarette. Te'chok was sitting in the circle with the others, though he spoke little and looked less than pleased.

As I opened the door, all eyes turned to me. "We've finished our discussion," I said. "You can come back inside now, and I want to thank you again for giving us the privacy we asked for."

Marek was the first on his feet and the first in the door. As the others followed suit, he drew me aside. "Ji'anne, whatever you all are planning to do, I would like to make sure I am with you. Don't force me to go off and do something else—not after what happened to Carlos and Ke'tai."

I managed a faint smile. "You know, we were just talking about that. You'll stay wherever I am—that's already been decided."

The look of relief on the big man's face was unmistakable, and he nodded once before taking a seat. I smiled; I was lucky to have Marek working for me.

The meeting that followed was brief, and the trackers we had chosen to return to Seattle all readily agreed to our request. They had all been present in the underground, with the exception of Vance and Carmine. It appeared to me that they, too, wanted vengeance for their lost comrades. The only person in opposition was Te'chok. I ignored his protests, and plans were made—the trackers returning to Seattle would leave early the next morning.

A week went by before we received news from Seattle. I was restless and eager to move on, but knew we must wait while the trackers gathered information about the hunters. Knowledge was our greatest asset in this operation; I forced myself to remain patient while we waited out the days.

The day after the trackers had left, Te'chok made his departure as well. He was obviously frustrated and made it clear that he wanted no part of what I was planning to do. I did not care; our plans did not require his presence, nor did I need his approval. There was little warmth between us as we said our goodbyes.

Zy'driks kept himself busy by contacting the other Elders, and from what he had told me, most were in clear support of what we planned to do. He and Il'zaks spent long hours on the phone with the remainder of the Board. At the end of each day, the three of us would meet to discuss what had been said, though there was little variation between the conversations. It seemed the Elders had long been tired of Te'chok's complacency and felt that a confrontation with the hunters was overdue. Too many summoners had been lost during Te'chok's reign; the time to make amends for our sorrows was at hand.

It was late in the afternoon of the seventh day when Xen'din received a call from Vance. We had decided he would be the contact, since the remainder of our group would potentially be preoccupied with other workings of the Order. We wanted the information to come through immediately, and did not wish news to be forwarded to voice mail.

I was speaking with Marek in the kitchen when Xen'din appeared in the doorway. "Ji'anne, Vance is on the line," was all he said before disappearing into the living room.

"Come with me," I told Marek. "You will hear all of this eventually, so you might as well hear it now." With a nod, he followed me into the living room, where Xen'din had already gathered the two Elders.

As I strode into the room, Xen'din glanced at me briefly before pressing a button on his phone and setting it down in the center of the coffee table. "Okay, Vance, you're on speaker phone. Everyone's here."

"Yeah, okay," came the reply. "You're on speaker too...Carmine, Jake, and Aaron are here with me."

Zy'driks glanced toward me, questions blooming within his silver eyes. I nodded, indicating he should take the lead. He seemed to have something he wanted to say.

"Before we start into the real business of this call, I want to make sure you all are taking every precaution to keep yourselves safe out there," Zy'driks stated. "I do not want to have a repeat of last week."

There was a chuckle on the other end of the line, and it was Aaron's distinctly New York accent that replied. "We don't want that either, Z. We're being careful. I set up bugs—wire taps, I mean—and we're trying to keep everything at a distance. So far, so good."

Zy'driks nodded, a faint smile appearing on his face. "I'm glad to hear it." He paused a moment before continuing, collecting his thoughts. "Well, now I guess it's your turn. We need to know what you've learned."

Il'zaks stood suddenly and moved quickly to the small table near the door, taking a yellow notepad and a pen that had been left there. "We may want this written down," he commented as he returned to his seat.

"I want to start with their leader," came Jake's voice through the phone. "As you already told us, he's a Stone-reader, and by the looks of it, a pretty damned good one. His name is Thaddeus Taylor—he goes by Thad. He's mid-forties, single, spends most of his time studying up on the best ways to destroy demons...and you guys."

"That's fairly typical," Il'zaks replied matter-of-factly.

"Um, yeah, well, he lives in an apartment not too far from the college campus," Jake continued. "It's above one of those Vietnamese restaurants that are everywhere out here—the pho places. Carmine is working on an email with exact descriptions and addresses for all of these people."

"I'm also sending photos of these dumb asses," Carmine's strident voice called. It sounded as though she were sitting some distance away from the phone.

"Anyway," Jake continued, "he's the one that calls the meetings. They meet in this abandoned building—it looks like it used to be an office building, but now there's nothing in it. They meet in the basement, and sometimes Thad stays there overnight, too."

"Okay, so we have Thad," I replied. "Who's his second in command?"

There was a brief silence on the other end of the line, and then Vance spoke up. "It's…It's Xandra Grey."

I had been anticipating her name coming up during the course of our conversation, and I simply nodded, blocking out all emotion. "Fine, tell me what you've dug up on her."

"Uh, well, she's living in West Seattle," Vance said, his tone one of mild surprise. "She owns her own home, drives a black SUV—a Tahoe. She's the strongest they've got when it comes to hunting demons…it's almost unreal."

"Not surprising, given Ji'anne's abilities," Zy'driks replied. "Go on."

"Well, this part is going to be a little more difficult for you all to hear," Jake said. "We happened to observe them at one point when they were celebrating…It looks like she's the one that did it."

"Did what?" I demanded. I had a horrible feeling I knew what they would tell us next, and I was not sure if I was completely prepared to hear it. I braced myself as well as I could, and waited for their next words.

The other end was silent again for a time, and then Carmine spoke, closer to the phone this time. "Xandra was the one who killed Ke'tai."

I bit back the anguish and rage that threatened to take hold of me, and blinked back the stinging tears that had formed in my eyes. "I…thought she…may have," I replied in a wavering tone. "We'll take care of her, the same as the others."

"If you are able, Ji'anne, perhaps we should know a little more about her," Zy'driks said. His tone was surprisingly gentle. "If you aren't up for it now, there is always later."

I shifted my gaze to meet his, unable to conceal the anger rising within me. "I'm fine," I snapped. "So, what do you want to know about her?"

"Personality traits," Il'zaks replied smoothly. "Try to focus your energy, Ji'anne. Do not take out your anger and hurts on those who are undeserving. I know it has been difficult for you."

I nodded; I knew he was right. I was not truly angry with Zy'driks; I was simply frustrated because it was Xandra we had to contend with. Despite how much I wanted to hate her for what she had done, I still thought of her as family—and that served to stoke my rage even more.

"Well, Xan has always been impatient," I began slowly, trying to think carefully about what I was must say. "She has a very quick temper, and tends to become irrational when she gets angry. She was always athletic, always good at sports. I don't know how much of this still holds true—it's been over seven years since I left her."

"Were you close?" Zy'driks asked.

I shrugged. "We're twins. Fraternal twins, but still twins. We always did everything together growing up, but in high school we went separate ways for a while and didn't get along well. I mean, we fought sometimes. When we got a little older and went to college, things changed, and we became close again."

"What are her weaknesses?" Zy'driks pressed.

I stared at him, attempting to understand the meaning behind his words.

"I might be able to help," Xen'din replied. "Xan and I…before I started down this path, we used to date."

Zy'driks nodded, as though recalling something he had previously forgotten. "Go on."

"We were still together when Ji'anne had to flee Seattle. Xan believed her sister disappeared—she didn't know why or how. She was the one responsible for that whole police investigation, which, by the way, is still open as a cold case file. I think, if you really want to weaken her, it would be having Ji'anne meet with her face to face."

I turned to face Xen'din, outraged. "Are you out of your *mind?*" I practically shouted. "You know we can't do that!"

He shrugged. "He wanted to know."

"Actually, it may not be a completely ludicrous suggestion," Il'zaks cut in before I could say anything more. "If we were to deal with the others first, it may weaken Xandra's resolve enough to make a meeting between the two of you possible. If she were left with no other options, it could work."

"We would need something else, to use as leverage," Zy'driks pointed out. "Even if she were the only one left of the whole group, she would need something to motivate her, to force her hand, so that she must go through with a meeting."

"Can I add something here?" Vance asked from the phone.

"Of course," Il'zaks replied.

"From what it looks like on the outside, I'd say a couple of the hunters are interested in Xandra. I mean, romantically," he added. "She's single, and so are they. Not to mention they admire her abilities."

"And who are these two hunters?" I asked, tiring of his vague replies.

"The first one is a man named Kent Waterby. The other is Thad Taylor."

"Interesting," I replied. "I would imagine she'd be loyal to Thad, since he is the leader of their little group. What if we managed to take him hostage? I think that ought to be leverage enough, knowing her."

Zy'driks was nodding. "Yes! I think that could work. I think our true plan is starting to form."

"Okay, so tell me more about this Kent Waterby," I said.

"Kent is about thirty years old, and he works as an accountant during the day at Wachovia," Aaron replied. "Single, as Jake said. He lives in Bellevue, one of the suburbs. Has a nice house, makes decent money. He drives a brand-new red Mustang, which makes it easy to follow him."

"Who else do we have?" I asked.

"Dirk Musgrave is the one who can track summoners," Carmine replied. "If you're going to go about taking these bastards out, you'll have to deal with him first."

"Dirk is in his mid-twenties," Vance added. "He's a computer programmer, and does pretty well for himself, but he has an issue with authority. We've seen him and Thad butt heads a few times already, and we've only watched three of their meetings."

"Then we have Jack and Aria Swift," Carmine said. "They both started in the hunter training program about the same time, decided they liked each other and then they hooked up. Jack is sort of the strong, silent type, and he can definitely handle himself when it comes to hunting demons. He's the one that took out the shadow demon."

"And Aria?" Zy'driks pressed.

"She's an idiot," Carmine replied contemptuously. "She's been doing her line of work for eight years now, but she still asks rookie questions. And she has a weak stomach and scares easily, if the jokes we overheard have any merit to them."

"And I know what you're thinking, Z, but she's not blonde, either," Aaron chimed in, causing Zy'driks to chuckle.

"There's the priest, Father Thomas Moresby," Jake said after a pause. "He's in his late sixties, and is not as active in the church as he used to be. He helps out Thad's group as a kind of hobby, I think, but he's actually pretty knowledgeable about stuff."

"Catholic?" Zy'driks asked.

"Yeah, from what we can tell," Aaron replied. "We haven't been able to track down which church he is a part of yet, but we'll get that info for you."

"The last member of the group is Mina Jones," Jake stated. "She's just finished college, has an apartment right off the campus. She's the youngest of the group, and the least experienced. She and Aria seem to be friends, and they do have a lot of similarities. Mina's pretty emotional, and I doubt she would be very good in situations that require silence or stealth."

"Okay, well at least now we can prioritize what we want to do," I said after a moment. "We'll check for Carmine's email later tonight, when Miranda and Trey are able to drive into town and use the wireless internet at the café. For now, I think those of us in Idaho have some discussing to do."

Zy'driks nodded once. "Thank you for the information. Keep watching them, because anything we learn will be helpful."

"Thanks," I added. "Call us again when you learn anything else, or if something happens." I did not need to elaborate on the "something"; everyone understood my meaning without my having to say it. There would always be the chance our trackers would be discovered and the whole operation would have to be moved or placed on hold.

Once the phone call had ended, we laid Il'zaks' notes across the coffee table so that everyone present could see them. After almost three hours of discussion, we had a tentative plan as to what we were going to do. We had to take out Dirk first, since he could track summoners. Somehow, we had to devise a way to take Thaddeus hostage, and once those two had been taken care of, the rest of the group would be easier to handle. We would slowly whittle away at their group until only Xandra was left, and then we would arrange a meeting between her and I. Xen'din asked to be present as well, and I consented; not only would it be a blow to Xandra to see me, but seeing her former fiancée as a summoner would probably shatter her nerves beyond repair. I wanted to break her, but I did not want to kill her. After all, we were not the savages the hunters seemed to believe we were.

I wanted this plan to be executed perfectly, and I knew we could not afford any mistakes. We would have to continue to monitor the hunters for some time, to make absolutely certain of their habits and schedules, before we made the first move against them. It was going to take some time, but it would be worth the effort. The longer we waited to retaliate, the better; they would not be expecting our strike when it crashed down upon them.

# 26

# ZY'DRIKS' PLAN

Over the next few months, we were able to form a clear picture of each hunter's daily activities, their strengths, and their weaknesses. Ideas regarding how to proceed were discussed at length, and finally we came up with our master plan. We decided to wait for April of the following year before making our first move, and those of us who had remained in Coeur d'Alene's safe house went our separate ways for a while, agreeing to meet there again at the end of March. It would be a full year after Ke'tai and Carlos had been killed before the hunters began to experience the wrath of the Order.

During that time, I resumed my regular travel activities. I found two more trackers to work with Marek, a tall, thin man with an angular face and a hooked nose named Levi Jacobson, and a German man who was all muscle named Konrad Brauer. Konrad spoke English well enough to communicate, but his speech was accented heavily and at times he had difficulty translating what he wanted to convey, particularly when he became excited or agitated. Marek remained my primary tracker, though having the three of them in my employ gave me a greater sense of security.

Il'zaks, Zy'driks, Xen'din and I kept in close contact with one another and the trackers that we had instructed to remain in Seattle. When the time finally arrived to begin our operation, we had more information on that group of hunters than on any other group in the world. I was confident our plans would be carried out smoothly.

When March came around, we met once more at the safe house near Coeur d'Alene. I arrived on March twenty-fourth, and was the first of the summoners to do so. Konrad and Marek, who by this time had formed a strong friendship, insisted on entering first to secure the area and make certain there were no unexpected surprises awaiting us. I remained in the back seat of the car as we awaited the all-clear signal, while Levi sat in the driver's seat, ready to move at the first sign of trouble.

After a few minutes, Konrad appeared in the front door, waving for us to come inside. All was well.

I climbed out of the car, glad for the chance to stretch my legs. We had spent the better part of three days cramped inside as we made the long trip from Cleveland, Ohio. The air was frosty, and there was a thin layer of hard-packed snow on the ground that crunched under our feet as we made our way inside. The sun was shining, though it offered little warmth on that cold spring day.

The safe house appeared unchanged from the previous year. As far as I knew, no one had been to this remote place in the intervening months since we had departed. A fine layer of dust had settled over everything inside, and I knew we would be busy preparing the safe house for the others' arrival in the days to come.

Levi strode inside just after I had entered, carrying his luggage and part of mine. He glanced around the space uncertainly. "Where should I leave your stuff?"

I waved him to set it down where he was. "There's fine. I can get it myself in a bit, thank you."

Konrad had ventured into the small kitchen, and returned with a look of disappointment. "Wine in fridge, but no beer?"

I laughed. "One of you can go into town and get some stuff to stock the fridge," I replied. "Get whatever you like. I'm going clean up some of this dust before anyone else shows up."

Konrad nodded, flashing a grin. "I'll go, if Levi lets me use his car."

Levi shrugged. "I'm tired of driving," he said, tossing the big German his keys. "Just don't spend everything she gives you on beer. I'd like to be able to eat something, you know."

Konrad laughed loudly. "*Ja*, I'll get food."

Marek entered the room from the hallway leading back to the bedrooms. "I'll call Miranda and Trey, and let them know we're here and everything's all clear."

I nodded to him. “Call Kendrick, too,” I replied, referring to Xen’din’s second tracker. I knew Marek did not care much for Kendrick, considering the other immature and whiney, but the call needed to be made.

He sighed, but did not argue. “Will do,” he replied, disappearing down the hallway once more.

I turned back to Levi as Konrad made his exit. “I guess it’s just you and I, then,” I said. “Will you help me clean up?”

He nodded, and we started the process of dusting, sweeping and scrubbing away the grime and dust that had built up in our absence. Konrad returned before we had finished, and once he had the groceries put away, he pitched in.

“What all did you buy?” Levi asked him as he took up a broom.

“Beer,” Konrad replied with a mischievous grin.

Levi tried to feign annoyance, but ended up laughing. “What else?”

“Frozen pizza, noodles, milk, bread…You know, basic stuff.” He shrugged. “Go look for yourself, American. I not fail the lady, here.”

At that point, Marek reemerged from wherever he had been talking on the phone. “It sounds like Zy’driks will be here sometime tomorrow,” he said, picking up a clean rag from the pile I had left on the arm of one of the couches. “Il’zaks should be here in two days, based on what Trey told me. Xen’din is still in Florida, and won’t be able to leave for a couple days yet. He’ll probably be here next week some time. By the way, one of these guys gets to talk to Kendrick next time—I’m done with that little twit.”

“What happened?” I asked, mildly curious.

“Nothing new,” he replied with a shrug. “He was complaining about the timing of my call, even though they *knew* one of us would be contacting him soon.”

“You mean, ‘Hi, it’s Kendrick and I’m never happy with anything so let me whine to you about how much my life sucks’?” Levi asked, imitating Kendrick’s higher pitched, nasally voice.

Marek chuckled. “Yeah, that.”

Konrad finished up sweeping the wooden floors in the kitchen, and I could hear him rummaging in the fridge. A moment later he came back with three bottles of Beck’s, passing one each to Marek and Levi.

“I should have known you’d get some sort of German crap,” Levi said in a teasing tone as he popped the top off his bottle.

"*Ja*, but it can't be too bad if you drink it," Konrad replied with a grin. "I shop, I pick beer."

"Fair enough," Levi replied, taking a swig. His eyebrows rose after a moment. "Actually, this isn't bad."

Konrad nodded knowingly. "You should trust my judgment, American."

The rest of the afternoon was spent cleaning the bedrooms, and that evening Levi baked two of the frozen pizzas Konrad had picked up on his trip to the grocery store. We ate in the living room, talking and laughing. I knew that the next few days would be the last for some time in which we could experience some kind of normalcy, and I wanted to encourage the trackers to enjoy it while they could. The ensuing days would be difficult and dangerous.

It was nearing noon on the following day when Zy'driks arrived with Miranda. Jake and Aaron had remained in Seattle, continuing our surveillance of the hunters. As soon as Zy'driks was inside and somewhat settled, he made it a point to speak with me.

"Ji'anne, I have an idea," he said, his tone conveying barely concealed excitement. "I was doing some research a couple weeks ago, and this sounds like something we could use against the hunters. I wanted to wait, to tell you in person."

I nodded. "Okay, what's the idea?"

"Well, I was reading about something that Elder Nei'leil used a few hundred years ago to combat a Stone-reader," he began, practically bouncing up and down with anticipation. "I spoke to him on the way here, and he told me exactly what I needed to know to do this. I know our plan is to go after Dirk Musgrave first—since he can track *us*. Now, I don't really like this part of my plan, but I believe it's necessary. I need to lure him to me, and kill him, so that the last thing he sees before he dies is my face."

I stared at him, uncertain how I should respond. We had agreed to avoid killing the hunters if it was possible, and now he was telling me we had to kill the first one on our list? "Zy'driks, no. We agreed—"

"I know, Ji'anne, and I'm sorry. But I think this is the only way we can make it work. Will you hear me out?"

I sighed, nodding slowly. It couldn't hurt to hear his plan, even if I intended to shoot it down as soon as he had finished speaking.

"The important part of this is that Dirk sees me while he is dying—I have to be *the very last thing* he sees. From what we've learned about Thaddeus Taylor, he will use the ether stones to discover what happened to Dirk once they know he's dead." He paused, biting his lower lip in thought. "The next part is tricky...I have to be ready and waiting for him to use the stones. When he does, and he looks through to see for himself what Dirk's last moments were, he'll see me. When that happens, I have to be ready..."

"Ready for what?" I asked, curiosity replacing my previous annoyance.

"I have those few seconds, when he sees me through the stone, to make my move," Zy'driks replied. "Nei'leil told me what I have to do—it doesn't sound difficult, but I have to be prepared for it, and ready for a mental battle with Thad. See, what I'm planning to do is use the ether stones against him, and take control of the hunter's mind."

I stared at him in disbelief. "You can *do* that?"

Zy'driks nodded. "If we set this up right, it'll be no problem. If we can get into Thad's mind, we'll definitely have the upper hand. Not to mention that it will be a lot easier to take him prisoner if he can't make himself run away." He grinned wickedly.

I had been prepared to disagree with his proposal, but now I was reconsidering my stance. His plan would make our operation that much simpler, and if we were able remove both Dirk and Thad as threats, it would be a significant setback for the hunters.

"Let me think about this," I replied. "And I want Il'zaks' opinion about this, too, before we decide to go through with it. I don't like the idea of killing Dirk, but you have made a very persuasive argument."

Zy'driks nodded, smiling knowingly. "How about we call Il'zaks right now? He's probably stuck in a car at the moment anyway—what else does he have to do?"

"Sure, why not?" I asked wearily. Knowing Zy'driks as I did, he would not let the matter rest until he spoke to Il'zaks and received a final answer from me.

Grinning, Zy'driks pulled a cell phone out of his pocket and punched in the number that would connect him to Il'zaks. He set the phone on speaker so that I could hear both sides of the conversation, and we waited as the phone rang twice before Il'zaks picked up.

"Good afternoon, Zy'driks," Il'zaks stated pleasantly.

"We just arrived in Coeur d'Alene," Zy'driks said, grinning and unable to hide his excitement. "I told Ji'anne about a plan I have regarding the Stone-reader..."

I only half listened to the conversation as Zy'driks related his plan to Il'zaks. I had a feeling Il'zaks would agree with the other Elder on this matter, and I would be out-voted if I did try to fight this. Yet at the same time, I knew Zy'driks was right—if we followed this plan, it would save us a good deal of time and would make the fight with the hunters go more smoothly. I simply did not relish the idea of taking a life, of stooping to the hunters' level to even the score. I wanted to believe that we were better than they.

After Zy'driks had finished relaying his proposed idea, Il'zaks was quiet for a time. "It is an interesting notion, Zy'driks," he said slowly, thoughtfully. "I understand why you want to do it this way, and though I would like to argue with you, I think it is our wisest course of action."

Zy'driks gave me a meaningful look. "You could not have said it better."

I sighed. "Fine, we'll do it your way. I just don't like the fact you have to kill someone in order to get inside Thad's head."

"We cannot always operate as though the world is perfect, Ji'anne," Il'zaks replied. "Sometimes it becomes necessary to perform drastic acts in order to achieve the greater good."

But was this truly for the greater good? I wondered.

# 27

# DIRK

We had gathered in the living room of the safe house for a final meeting before Zy'driks left us for Seattle. Jake, Aaron, Carmine, and Vance had returned; Xen'din, along with his two trackers, had arrived the day before. The little room felt crowded. I had wanted everyone involved to be present, to make certain that we each understood our parts in this next act. The trackers did not yet know of Zy'driks' full plan, as we had only finalized it late the night before. It was now morning, and sunlight streamed into the room from the windows, making for a surreal scene, given what we were about to discuss.

I stood to one end of the couches, facing the rest of those gathered. As the leader, it was expected that I go over these instructions, loath though I was to actually carry through with them. I was glad Zy'driks was doing the dirty work here; I wanted no part of it.

"First, I'd like to tell you who all will be leaving with Zy'driks later today," I began. "He will need strong trackers, in the event that our plans do not go as we anticipate and you need to get him away safely. Because of this, Il'zaks and I both felt that Carmine and Vance should accompany him."

Carmine nodded, turning to produce a smug look over one of her narrow shoulders, directed toward Trey. It was clear from her reaction that they had been discussing who might be chosen to go on this mission, prior to our meeting.

"We chose Carmine because she is the strongest tracker here," Il'zaks added, "and Vance because he is able to track the Stone-reader."

I nodded. "This group has to be small. You must go in and get out as soon as Zy'driks has completed his task. Until Dirk Musgrave is removed from the picture, we cannot truly move into the Seattle area. This mission is only the first part of what we plan to do."

"What should we be expecting?" Vance asked casually. He had a cool demeanor and rarely allowed his emotions into the forefront.

"Zy'driks has chosen an abandoned warehouse building in the southeast corner of the city in which to carry out his part of the operation," I replied. "On your way there, I will send a message to Dirk Musgrave via nightwing. If the hunters happen to notice its presence—which I believe is unlikely—it will lead them out of the city. I doubt they will pursue it very far, based upon what we have observed from this group previously. The more likely scenario is that they will start hunting for a summoner within the city, near the location where the nightwing was encountered. Dirk lives on the northwest side, which is quite a distance from where Zy'driks plans to be."

I paused a moment, thinking over what I should say next. "My message to Dirk will state that he should go to the address of the warehouse at a specific time. Since Dirk is able to track summoners, he will be aware of Zy'driks' presence there. You two must be on your guard," I added with emphasis, looking first at Carmine and then at Vance. "Based upon what we know about Dirk, especially from the past few weeks, he will likely go alone. He wants to prove himself to Thad—and I want to use that desire to our advantage."

"Here's where Carmine will come into play," Zy'driks said. "When Dirk arrives, you'll know straightaway. I want to wait until he is outside of the building before I summon anything, so as to not attract the attention of any of the others. Also, Carmine—if he does not come alone, you'll be able to warn us in time to flee."

Carmine nodded once, and Vance gave him a thumbs up.

"If this goes as we are hoping it does," I continued, "Zy'driks will have his demon weaken Dirk, and—"

"—And then I go in for the kill," Zy'driks finished the statement.

Several heads turned to stare at the Elder in utter disbelief. The summoners gathered knew of his plan, but it was the trackers—those sworn to protect us—who were most concerned. Zy'driks had anticipated this reaction, and he was prepared with a response to their objections.

"I know what you all are thinking," he replied smoothly. "Don't worry; we have thought this through, discussed it until we were green in the face, and bickered over it enough to last a lifetime. This is the safest path forward—for all of us. In order for the next step in our plan to work, my face must be the last thing that Dirk Musgrave sees before he dies. There is no other way we can work this, without significant risk."

The trackers were collectively unhappy by this news, particularly the three employed by Zy'driks. Not only were they to remain at the safe house, but their summoner was going to attempt something unheard of. As I gazed around the room, I could see most of them wanted to argue, in the spirit of sparing Zy'driks from potential harm.

"You can't do this," Miranda said, a note of despair in her clear voice.

"She's right, Z," Aaron agreed. "You shouldn't do this."

Zy'driks shrugged. "I have to. It's the only way our plan will work, the only way we have to take the Stone-reader down safely."

Miranda narrowed her eyes, and then turned to face me. "What does the Stone-reader have to do with this? I thought we were going after Dirk Musgrave."

I nodded. "We are, at this point in time. Thad is next...And to get Thad out of the way, Zy'driks has to do what he is planning with Dirk. If Zy'driks is the last thing Dirk sees, he will also be the last thing Thad sees when he utilizes the ether stones after they learn of Dirk's death."

"So?" Miranda demanded.

"So, when he uses the stones, I will be able to control his mind," Zy'driks replied with a shrug. "It is similar to when we call demons and they bend to our will; I can do the same with Thad, so long as this little episode with Dirk goes as planned."

Miranda looked down, stunned. Murmurs rose about the room as the trackers thought over this news, whispering to one another.

"Are you really sure you want to be inside that man's head?" Jake asked after a moment.

Zy'driks shrugged again. "I'll deal with it. I'm sure I've encountered worse in my lifetime."

No one doubted his last claim; Zy'driks was the eldest of anyone present, and that included Il'zaks. He had more experience with people than the rest of us combined.

"Once you are in place inside the warehouse, I need one of you to call me here," I said. "We need to know if everything is okay. If anything seems off, get out of there as fast as you can."

Vance nodded once, his demeanor calm and collected. Zy'driks flashed a grin in my direction, while Carmine simply nodded and lit a cigarette.

"When are we leaving?" Carmine asked, taking a long drag.

"As soon as the rest of you are ready to go," Zy'driks replied. "I want to get this over with."

Forty minutes later, Zy'driks left the safe house with Carmine and Vance, prepared for their trip to Seattle. I worried for him—for all of them—because I knew how dangerous this game we were attempting to play might prove to be. As I watched the car pull away from the safe house, images flashed through my mind of Ke'tai, of the nightmare I had been a part of just over a year ago in the decrepit underground passages beneath Seattle. I did not want to lose more friends to Xandra and her cohorts. Even though I still felt sick at the thought of Zy'driks murdering Dirk Musgrave, a part of me wanted to believe the act was justified. It was an act of retribution, of vengeance for Ke'tai.

Tears stung my eyes as the car pulled away, and I did not hinder their fall. Thoughts of Ke'tai still pained me, even after a year's time had passed. Would the hurt I experienced never fully disappear? Would that empty place in my heart ever be filled again with love? I did not know the answer to those questions. Many years later, I still do not know.

I stood at the window, watching the car vanish amongst the pines. I remained there long after Zy'driks and the two trackers were out of sight, staring outside, my eyes focused upon nothing. I was startled when I felt a hand touch my shoulder.

"Ji'anne, are you okay?" It was Xen'din, his words whispered near my ear.

I turned from the window at last, facing him. Concern marred his good looks, and his brow was knitted by worry beneath the sweep of white hair that cascaded across his forehead. I recalled that before I had met Ke'tai, I had at one time been very much attracted to this man, who was then called Elliot Thompson. He was now merely a good friend, and would never be anything more.

"I'll be fine," I managed after a moment. "I was just…thinking."

He frowned slightly, and nodded. "I wish it had been me to take that job in Seattle," he said softly, "and not Ke'tai."

He turned away, striding quickly across the room toward the hallway leading to the bedrooms, and said nothing more. I stared after him, wondering what the meaning behind Xen'din's words must be. I sighed, pushing my melancholy feelings aside for the time being; I had work to do.

I went to the table in the kitchen, where I had left a stack of plain white paper earlier. Taking a sheet and a black ball point pen, I set to work, writing my letter to Dirk Musgrave.

*Mr. Musgrave,*

*I would like to arrange a meeting with you regarding an incident that happened approximately one year ago. It involved a summoner in the underground of Seattle—that is all I am willing to say at this time. Meet my associate at the following address at 7 pm on April 2.*

*Yours,*

*LGS*

Satisfied with the letter's contents, I folded the sheet of paper into thirds and slid it into an envelope. I danced to call a nightwing, and gave the parcel to the tiny demon as it perched atop my left shoulder. Walking with it to the door, I ushered it outside, willing it to sense out the man named Dirk Musgrave in Seattle. The nightwing hesitated only for the briefest of moments before it took flight, and I knew then that it had located its target and was homing in on him. Now, I simply must wait for word to come from Zy'driks.

Six hours after Zy'driks and the two trackers had departed, we received word that they had arrived in Seattle and had set up in the warehouse without incident. Carmine made it a point to let us know that no hunters were in the vicinity of the warehouse, which put all of our minds temporarily at ease.

Shortly after that, my nightwing reached Dirk Musgrave, who was alone in his home. I had the little demon place the letter beneath his door, and waited. It took him nearly an hour before he realized the letter was there; it was then that I released the nightwing, not wishing for any harm to come to the little creature, should Dirk open the door and become aware of its presence. The letter had been delivered; now we simply had to wait for the next evening to arrive.

Throughout the next day, we were on edge. There was no word from Seattle—we had agreed that they would call only once the deed had been finished, or in the event that something had gone awry and they were forced to flee. No news was good news in this case, yet I worried for them all the same. What Zy'driks was attempting to do was incredibly dangerous.

Il'zaks took it upon himself to inform the other Elders of what we were attempting. Nei'leil had already been informed by Zy'driks and was one of the few who were not overly concerned for his safety. Many felt his actions were rash and would result in his death—after overhearing a partial conversation on that topic, I stayed out of hearing range of Il'zaks for the remainder of the day.

As evening fell, those of us in the safe house gathered together for a dinner of chicken cacciatore that Miranda had prepared. Although no one spoke of Seattle, it was forefront in everyone's mind, and the atmosphere was thick with anxiety.

The clock on the wall ticked slowly by, passing seven, and then eight o'clock. By eight-thirty, Il'zaks was no longer able to maintain the pretense of calm, and began pacing to and fro across the room. Miranda had locked herself away in her bedroom, and when Jake had gone to check on her, he returned with the news that she was crying and unwilling to speak to anyone. I checked and re-checked my phone, terrified that I would miss a call from the trio in Seattle. There were few words spoken during that time, and as the clock neared nine, I began to fear the worst.

"Maybe we should try to call them?" Levi asked, voicing a question that had gone unspoken for quite some time.

"No," I replied adamantly, just as Il'zaks stated, "We cannot do that." Xen'din simply shook his head.

Levi looked down, a deep frown creasing his face, lines of worry etching his brow. Konrad stood up from his place on the opposite couch, and placed a hand on Levi's shoulder. Levi looked up at the big German with an expression of mild annoyance, but said nothing.

"They will call," Konrad stated with little emotion behind his accented tone.

Levi shrugged away from him and crossed his arms as he sat back against the couch. "The waiting sucks," he mumbled.

Several of the trackers nodded, but no one ventured to say anything more. The room fell into an uneasy silence as the wait continued.

Ten minutes past nine o'clock, my phone began to ring. Startled at the sudden noise, yet incredibly relieved, I nearly dropped the phone as I scrambled to answer it. I set it on speaker phone, and placed it in the center of the coffee table as everyone gathered around.

"Hello, Ji'anne," Zy'driks stated. His voice betrayed his exhaustion.

"Zy'driks!" I exclaimed, thrilled at hearing his voice once more.

"What is your status?" Il'zaks asked, leaning over my shoulder.

"We are on our way back to Coeur d'Alene," Zy'driks replied wearily. "It'll be early when we arrive—around two-thirty, I think. I'm exhausted right now…I'll explain everything to you when I get there."

"Is everyone okay?" I asked, voicing our primary concern.

"Yeah," he replied. "We're all fine. We'll be there in a few hours."

Most of the others were asleep within an hour of Zy'driks' phone call. I did not turn in; I wished to remain awake so that I could greet him when he and the two trackers returned. Marek and Il'zaks waited with me, and we passed the time playing card games. I was emotionally drained from the anxiety the long day had caused, and my repeated attempts to ease the trackers' minds. A few times during the round of card games, I found myself nodding off, only to be awakened after a few moments by Il'zaks.

When Zy'driks did finally arrive, it was a great relief. Without stopping to take off his long trench coat, he collapsed onto one of the couches unceremoniously; he immediately told the two trackers accompanying him to get some rest. Carmine appeared to be taking the lack of sleep in stride, and did not look at all tired, while Vance looked horrible. Dark circles colored the skin around his eyes, and his face appeared pale. Without argument, both left the room to find a bed.

I asked Marek to rouse Xen'din. He needed to hear what Zy'driks had to say just as much as Il'zaks and I did. It did not take Xen'din long to appear in the living room once Marek had gone to find him, and I wondered if he had managed any sleep at all.

"I'm certain the question you have been asking yourselves is, 'What exactly happened in Seattle?'" Zy'driks began as Xen'din seated himself on the couch opposite the Elder. "Our plan was executed flawlessly, if I do say so myself. Thanks to the reports we received from our trackers over the past year, there were no unwanted surprises and Dirk Musgrave played right into our trap, just as we suspected he would."

Zy'driks paused, allowing himself a moment to smile. "We arrived in Seattle without any trouble," he continued. "The warehouse was actually a very good place to set up—there were some vending machines that were still stocked with sodas and we brought enough food along to last us, so we didn't even have to leave. They even had a microwave," he added with a grin. "Anyway, we spent the first night there, and it was uneventful. Actually, it was uneventful until about six-thirty this evening…or I should say, yesterday evening." He sighed, and paused to rub his eyes, fighting his fatigue. "We didn't sleep during our time there, for fear of missing a hunter straying too near our hideout."

I nodded; I understood that concern well enough. "But everything was okay?" I pressed.

Zy'driks nodded. "Yes. No one came near where we were hiding, until Dirk himself showed up last night. He was there early—six-thirty, as I said—but we had expected that from him. Dirk Musgrave was a punctual sort."

Internally I shuddered at Zy'driks' casual use of the word "was". I knew Dirk was dead—that had been our plan—yet speaking of it made my stomach lurch. How could Zy'driks be so nonchalant about having just killed a man?

"He arrived at the warehouse alone, as we had anticipated he would," Zy'driks continued. "Carmine and Vance were just inside the doors, and it was Vance who let him inside. We ordered Dirk leave his weapons at the door, in order to facilitate the 'meeting' without causing an incident. He protested a bit, but in the end, Carmine made a very convincing argument." He chuckled. "She put a gun to his head and told him to do as we said, or he'd die on the spot."

Il'zaks nodded, an amused smile appearing on his face. "That does sound like something she would do."

"Once he finally decided to cooperate, they led him to where I was seated on the far side of the building. They had informed me when he arrived outside; I had summoned a shadow demon, and I kept it in the corner where the darkness of the room would make it difficult to detect. Since Dirk did not have the ability to track demons, he probably never realized it was present, until I willed it to show itself." Zy'driks shrugged, and let out a yawn. "Sorry, I'm tired. Anyway, once Dirk and I were face to face, he went on about this meeting we were supposed to be having, demanding to know what it was the Order wanted with him. I never spoke a word to him; I simply had the shadow demon come out from its hiding place and attack. Dirk never saw it coming."

Zy'driks sighed and shook his head regretfully. "It was a very cowardly thing to do, I'm afraid," he said. "I know there was no honor in what I did, but it had to be done..." He trailed off, dropping his gaze to the floor.

The room was silent for a few moments while each of us contemplated what to say or do next. It appeared to me that Zy'driks had disliked the task he had persuaded me to allow him to perform, but did not regret his decision to go forward with his plan. I was unsure how I felt about this; on the one hand, I felt that he had asked for that job and because of that he would have to suffer the consequences, but on the other, I pitied him. Had he truly understood what he was getting himself into?

"Zy'driks, were you able to complete the task as you had hoped?" Il'zaks asked after a time.

Zy'driks nodded tiredly. "After the shadow demon had him beaten down enough that he could not resist any further, I walked to where he was laying on the floor and looked down straight into his eyes. And then I had the demon tear him in two."

I looked away from him, unable to meet his unreadable silver gaze any longer. He had killed a man—willed his demon to take a life—and he expressed no more emotion than mild regret. I had believed that I knew Zy'driks well enough by now to be unsurprised by his actions, but this was something I was not certain I could handle. Here sat a murderer who showed little remorse for what he had done. And I had sanctioned his actions.

Il'zaks, who was sitting alongside me, placed one hand on my forearm, drawing my attention back to those gathered around the coffee table. "Ji'anne, do not hate him for this. We both know there was no other way."

I frowned, unwilling to accept this explanation. There might have been another way, but perhaps we did not look hard enough to find it. I made no attempt to respond. I expected Zy'driks would come up with some clever statement to justify his actions, but I did not wish hear it, repulsed as I was.

Surprisingly, it was Xen'din who spoke next. "Ji'anne, you *know* this was the simplest way to get to Thad. You said so yourself the other day. Besides, it's not the first hunter that he's killed, and I'm willing to bet it won't be the last. At least there was a purpose to his death. Think of it that way."

I glared across the table at him. "I honestly don't care if there was a purpose to Dirk Musgrave's death, or if Zy'driks has killed hunters before. That doesn't matter. What does matter is that I allowed this to happen, and I'm sick with myself because of it." I stopped, startled at my own words. I wasn't angry with Zy'driks—I was disgusted with myself.

Zy'driks' face softened, and he sighed. "What I did was not without its consequences, Ji'anne," he said softly. "I know you allowed me to do this, and I am sorry that it has made you upset. However, it is a reality that you must live with as the head of our Order. I don't mean to seem cruel, but I do not want you to end up like Te'chok—disliked and constantly subverted."

He paused a moment, and then said, "Because our operation was a success, I am forced to forgo sleep until Thaddeus Taylor decides to use his ether stones. I cannot risk missing the only opportunity we will have to bring him down, because I needed a nap. And then I am stuck with having that link between myself and Thad for the rest of his life…So punish me if you will, Ji'anne, but know that I am already suffering for what I have done this night."

I nodded, feeling suddenly drained as the anger and tension I had been holding onto melted away. I wanted nothing more than to sleep, but I knew I could not risk doing so yet. "Why don't the rest of you get some sleep?" I asked of Il'zaks and Xen'din. "I'll stay up with Zy'driks. We'll need to leave for Seattle in the morning, now that Dirk is dead."

# 28

# THE STONE-READER

Dawn found me crammed in the back seat of Levi's SUV, riding between Zy'driks and Marek. Levi was driving, and Aaron rode shotgun. We were on our way to Seattle; I had not ventured to return since Ke'tai had been killed over a year ago. I was dreading the trip now, afraid of what memories might resurface simply upon my return to the city.

Trey had found lodging for us in a rental home in Seattle's northeastern suburb of Everett. Our thinking was that it was far enough away from the warehouse Zy'driks had used that the hunters would not be watching Everett closely. Only time, and the arrival at our destination, would tell us if this had been a wise decision.

I managed to keep myself awake until almost nine o'clock, but by that time, my sleep deprivation began to take its toll. I had never intended to fall asleep and leave Zy'driks to his vigil alone, but that is ultimately what occurred. I awoke as it was nearing noon, having been startled awake by the sound of a car door slamming nearby. Blearily, I looked around, realizing we had stopped in front of a house. It had been Aaron's door that had slammed shut as he emerged from the SUV to secure the area with Konrad, Kendrick, and Jake.

As I stirred, Zy'driks chuckled. "I'm glad you finally allowed yourself some sleep, Ji'anne," he said. "There was no need to keep yourself up just to help me. I've gone without sleep for longer periods before."

I sighed, annoyed with myself. "I take it this is the place we're staying?" I asked, changing the subject.

Marek nodded. "They're checking it out, making sure it's safe before the rest of us go inside," he replied.

I nodded, and then turned to face Zy'driks again. "Has Thad done anything yet?"

He shook his head. "I'm still waiting."

I nodded, but found I had nothing else to say. We sat in relative silence for another few minutes while the three trackers scoured the insides of the house. Finally, Aaron appeared in the doorway, waving for us to follow him inside. I pulled on my coat and drew up the hood before exiting the vehicle, while Zy'driks pulled on a knit cap over his hair. We quickly made our way inside through the light drizzle that fell from the sky.

The interior of the house was nearly empty, and smelled of fresh paint. We had brought the extra food from the safe house along with us, so I knew the kitchen would be well stocked, but we would have few other comforts during our stay here. As the door closed behind us, I heard the heater kick on; at least we would not have to endure the cold.

Zy'driks strode into the center of the living room and looked as though he were about to say something when he stopped and stood motionless for several seconds. His eyes were unfocused and his breathing became rapid and shallow. I raced to his side, concerned that something was wrong.

"Are you alright?" I asked, coming to stand in front of him. His gaze seemed to go right through me, as though he could not see me at all. "Zy'driks?"

I glanced beyond his shoulder to where some of the trackers had gathered in the kitchen. Jake was the first to catch my eye, and I waved for him to come over. "Something's wrong!" I called to him. Without hesitation, he pushed past the others and jogged over to where I stood with Zy'driks.

"What's going on?" he asked, as he noted the distant focus of Zy'driks' eyes and the rigidity of the Elder's posture.

I shook my head. "I don't know. He just stopped all of the sudden…"

Jake put one hand on each of Zy'driks' shoulders and shook him gently. "Z? Are you there? Come on, man…we need you here."

Some of the other trackers wandered into the room, but kept their distance. Marek made his way over to me, his brow wrinkled with worry. I glanced up at the big man, unsure of what to do next.

"Call Il'zaks," I said to him. "See how far out they are, and tell him what's going on."

Marek nodded and headed away from the group so that he could make the call without the interference of our background noise. As he turned away, Zy'driks suddenly toppled to one side. Thankfully, Jake was quick to react and caught him before he hit the floor, laying him gently on the carpet. The Elder's eyes had closed, but his breathing was still rapid and shallow.

"I think he fainted," Jake said, his tone mystified. "Ji'anne, what just happened?"

I shook my head again, feeling helpless. "I don't know. I can only guess that something went on with the Stone-reader, but I don't know. We can't know until he snaps out of this."

Marek lumbered over then. "Il'zaks wants to speak with you," he said in a low voice. "I think he has an idea of what might have just occurred."

I nodded, taking his offered cell phone. "Il'zaks?"

"Ji'anne, Marek told me what has happened. I do not think we should worry overly much," he said, his tone soothing. "I spoke to Nei'leil earlier this morning in order to understand the details of Zy'driks' plan, in the event something went wrong. I felt it would be safer to have a backup plan—but Zy'driks did not agree. He does not know I made the call."

"Why should we not worry?" I asked slowly, questions spinning through my mind.

Il'zaks sighed. "Nei'leil told me that when he last performed this operation, he fainted. It is one thing to command a demon to do what we ask, but an entirely different matter to break a human being's will. Zy'driks must have undergone quite the mental battle. When he awakens, we shall know how he fares." Il'zaks paused, and I heard a car door in the background. "We have just arrived, Ji'anne. I will speak to you again in a moment."

I sighed and ended the call, handing the phone back to Marek. "Il'zaks just arrived," I said wearily. "It sounds as though the fainting is part of this process, and we should have been expecting it to happen."

"He never said a word about it," Aaron replied, crossing his muscled arms before his chest and leaning back against the wall.

I nodded. "I know. He's going to have to answer to me when he wakes up, and I don't think he's going to like what I have to say." I was angry at having been kept in the dark, and frustrated that Zy'driks expected me to keep everyone on task and updated when he could not find the decency to keep me apprised of his own schemes.

A moment later, the front door sprang open and both Il'zaks and Xen'din strode inside, followed by their entourage of trackers. The two summoners joined me where I was standing over Zy'driks' limp form on the far side of the room.

Il'zaks knelt beside the other Elder for a moment, checking his breathing and heart rate. He rose and shrugged his thin shoulders. "All we can do is wait, I suppose. Hopefully he will awaken again soon."

The next ten minutes were spent in a state of quiet apprehension. Little was said as we waited for Zy'driks to wake up from his faint, but everyone seemed to have the same questions. What had happened? If it was regarding Thad Taylor, had Zy'driks been successful? If he had failed, what had gone wrong? And what had the experience been like for him?

I stayed at Zy'driks' side during this time, as did Il'zaks. Xen'din paced the length of the room, while most of the trackers remained clustered together near the door leading into the kitchen. Jake and Miranda stood slightly apart from the others, whispering quietly, while Aaron continued to lean against the wall, glowering. He seemed as upset as I was with Zy'driks' failure to keep us informed.

Finally, Zy'driks opened his eyes and immediately sat up, rubbing his head as though he had cracked it against something during his fall. Il'zaks stopped him from an attempt at standing up by placing on thin hand on the larger man's shoulder.

"Not so fast," Il'zaks said quietly. "You have been unconscious for the last ten minutes. How are you feeling?"

Zy'driks squinted up at him with a look of annoyance. "I feel fine, besides the fact that my head feels like someone took a hammer to it."

"What happened?" I asked, voicing the question most of us wanted to ask.

Zy'driks bit his lower lip thoughtfully before responding. "Our Stone-reader did just what we had anticipated he would do. He decided to consult his ether stones after he found out Dirk was dead, and had determined it was the work of a demon."

"And...?" I pressed.

"I had the mental battle of my life," Zy'driks replied, wonder in his tone. "I had no idea it would be so difficult...But, I did come out on top. Thad's ours."

"Are you able to sense what he is doing, then?" Il'zaks asked.

Zy'driks broke into a grin. "That, and more, my friend. He's at their headquarters right now, sitting in a rolling chair but unable to move a muscle unless I allow it. I'm letting him explain his situation to the priest and your dear sister right now, Ji'anne. Apparently, he was unconscious, too."

I was unable to suppress the smile of relief that spread across my face. "So now what do we do?"

Zy'driks closed his eyes for a moment, then chuckled. "It seems Xandra wants to call a meeting, but they don't think it's safe for their leader to be present any more. She's going to move the chair to the elevator and then leave him on the first floor until they're finished. This is an opportunity we cannot pass up."

"What are you thinking of?" Il'zaks asked.

"We should take him prisoner," I replied before Zy'driks could say anything. "He'll have plenty of information for us, and you can extract it from him easily enough now. You're right—this is the perfect opportunity."

Zy'driks looked up at me and nodded slowly. "Yes, we'll kidnap him. I'm afraid I won't be able to summon and be any good at it until I'm able to release my hold on Thaddeus Taylor's mind. One of you will have to do this part."

"I'll do it," I replied without hesitation, my thoughts focused once more on what had happened to Ke'tai. They were going to pay; I would make them regret every ounce of pain they had inflicted upon him.

The two Elders glanced at one another, and then they both nodded. "Be careful, Ji'anne," Zy'driks replied, while Il'zaks said, "Caution will be your greatest ally."

I nodded once, forming a plan on the spot. Thaddeus Taylor was a career hunter, the leader of this band of murderers who had destroyed the life of the only man I had ever loved. As a hunter, he had been trained to hate demons, to kill them without question...What would be the worst possible fate for a man such as this one? To be captured by a demon, and made to be its plaything for a time. A succubus, I decided, would fit the role perfectly.

Dancing to call forth the sex-crazed she-demon, I allowed a bit of a laugh to escape my lips. This would be the perfect humiliation for the man who employed my conniving sister, and I couldn't deny the grim thrill I received from the thought.

The succubus appeared at my side a moment later, dressed in a short leather skirt barely long enough to conceal her buttocks and a matching tube top. Her olive-toned skin was smooth and unblemished, and her dark curly hair fell to her shoulders and over one eye in a playfully messy fashion. Her thoughts flitted quickly between each of the men in the room, fantasies about what she could do with them, given the opportunity, forefront in her mind. I had learned to be prepared for such thoughts with this demon, and had braced myself, prepared to ignore them as necessity required.

I pictured Thaddeus Taylor's face in my mind, recalling the photographs Carmine had provided to us, then I imagined the building he would be located inside. *Go to this building, and find this man,* I thought to the succubus. *Bring him back here—unharmed—and then you may have your way with him for a time. But you must not kill him.*

A thrill of excitement coursed through the she-demon, and a wicked smile spread across her darkly red lips. "I will do this," she replied, pausing to wink seductively at Xen'din who was standing a few steps behind me before striding to the door. Her gait reminded me of a supermodel striding down the length of a catwalk. She yanked the door open, spread her wings, and shot quickly up into the rain-filled sky.

"Why a succubus?" Il'zaks asked as I moved to close the door.

I smiled wryly. "She'll be the most humiliating for him. He will hate that more than any other demon I can summon, and I want him to suffer." I was surprised at the vehemence I heard in my own tone.

I could sense the succubus soaring through the clouds. The air felt cool upon her skin, but that did not seem to affect her. She enjoyed the freedom of flying, and the thrill of adventure at being in our world, on an important job for me, her mistress. Thoughts of what would come later with Thaddeus drove her purposefully toward her goal. As she reached the building the hunters were to meet in, I cautioned her to remain above the city, hidden within the cloud layer, until Zy'driks gave me the indication to proceed.

The clouds would shield her from the hunters' tracking abilities, and also protect her from the prying eyes of anyone below who might happen to glance skyward.

Zy'driks kept us apprised of the hunters' activities, using his new-found link to the Stone-reader to see what was happening through the other man's eyes. Xandra had left him alone on the opposite side of the empty room from the entrance door, but by turning his head only slightly, the summoner was able to watch as each and every one of the hunters entered the building and made their way to the elevator.

Once all of the hunters had gathered, Zy'driks said, "Now's our chance, Ji'anne."

I nodded once, and then closed my eyes to focus more fully on what the succubus must do. *Go to him now,* I sent to her. I felt the demon respond with a flash of excitement as she dove from the cloud layer toward a window on the second floor of the abandoned building the hunters used as a headquarters. The window was solid and could not be easily opened, but that did not deter the succubus. She kicked at the glass with her heel a few times and managed to break it open.

Once inside, she went to the stairwell and glided gracefully down to the first floor. The entrance to the stairwell was directly across from where Thaddeus had been abandoned by my sister. He was slumped in the rolling chair with his eyes closed, an expression of pain and anger marring his rugged features. I assessed him through the eyes of the she-demon, noting that in spite of being in his late forties, he still maintained a fit physique and was mildly attractive. The gray that had begun to invade his brown hair at the temples seemed to accentuate his looks, rather than detract from them.

"I see him," I said aloud, though I kept my eyes closed in order to maintain my focus.

In the building across town, Thad's eyes opened. I could see that he was still fighting for control of his mind. As he took in the succubus standing before him, I could see conflicting emotions flit through his eyes—he appeared at once relieved, but disgusted and angry as well. Zy'driks had taken control of his actions, but not his emotions.

The succubus sauntered toward the man in the rolling chair, one hand toying with the hem of her skirt. "The lady sends you her regards, Thaddeus

Taylor," she whispered, moving so that her lips were very near to his ear. "Let's say we leave this place, and go have a little fun. Hmm?"

Unable to move as he was, Thad's face darkened like a thundercloud. "Get out of my sight!" he bellowed.

The succubus backed up a step and batted her eyelashes at him, feigning a pout. "Oh, that's no way to talk to a lady, now is it? Let me rephrase what I just said, so maybe you'll understand it a bit better. You're coming with me. *Now.*" She smiled at him in a wicked sort of way, and then took to the air, grabbing him under the arms as she did so.

"We don't have time to flirt, now do we?" she asked him as she soared back up through the stairwell to the broken window. "The lady has need of you—once I'm finished." Her laughter cascaded through the stairwell as the helpless Thad was carried outside and up into the cloud layer.

*Bring him here quickly*, I sent to the she-demon before opening my eyes once more.

"He's on his way as we speak," I said to the others gathered in the room.

Zy'driks chuckled. "Yes, and he's quite unhappy about his situation now, too. Tell me, Ji'anne, are you really going to let the succubus have him first?"

I shrugged. "Why not? For all we know, it just might make him a little more cooperative."

Zy'driks sighed. "You do realize I'm going to have to stay inside his head until she's finished, don't you?"

I laughed aloud. I had not considered that. "Well, I guess you'll have to deal with that then, won't you? After all, you didn't tell us everything that might have happened when you pulled this stunt of yours with Thad."

Zy'driks' mouth popped open in disbelief. "You're punishing *me* now?"

There was scattered laughter around the room, and Il'zaks, who was standing near, said, "There could be worse things, you know."

"I'm afraid so," I said to Zy'driks, internally shuddering as I recalled Il'zaks' disturbing fetish with the succubus demons. "But let's call it even, once the demon's finished with him."

Zy'driks sighed, appearing resigned. "Fine," he said wearily, "we'll be even, then."

# 29

# INVESTIGATION

I stood outside of the closed bedroom door, hesitant to enter. Marek and Konrad had informed me that Thad was secured inside and that he "wouldn't be going anywhere," but I still waited. He had been inside our house for almost six hours by this time, but had only been in contact with three of the trackers—my three—and the succubus. I would be the first of the summoners to speak with him. I had confronted a hunter only once before during my time with the Order, but that had been brief, and the stakes had been much lower. I could not afford to make any mistakes.

As I stood in the hallway outside, I heard footsteps to my left. Turning, I saw Xen'din approaching from the living room at the end of the corridor.

"I've got some news for you," he said quietly. "Il'zaks and I have been spying on the hunters a bit…It seems they want to go take a look around Dirk's home for any clues as to why he took off to meet Zy'driks by himself. I think we ought to investigate his place ourselves, before they arrive, to see if there's anything useful to us. We have a plan."

I nodded, indicating he should continue.

"I'm going to send a demon their way, to distract them," he continued. "I know it's risky, but I think it's the best way. While they're distracted, Il'zaks is going to go to Dirk's house with Trey and Carmine. He'll take a look around, and then have anything pertinent that they might find destroyed."

"Fine," I replied. "Do it. I need to talk with Thad…"

Xen'din nodded before turning to go back the way he had come, leaving me alone in the hallway once more. I sighed, dreading the confrontation that I was certain would ensue. This would be unpleasant for the both of us.

Drawing a breath to steady my nerves, I opened the door and strode inside. The room, like all the others in the house, was empty of furnishings.

One of the trackers had covered the single window with a black trash bag and duct tape, blocking out any natural light. Thad was propped in one corner of the room with his back to the wall, naked except for his socks, his wrists secured to the wall with a length of thick chain that one of the trackers had bolted to the sheetrock.

I sighed, irritated that they had not returned his clothing. How were we to get any useful information from him if he felt he were being mistreated?

I turned back to the door and called down the hall for Marek. While I waited for him to arrive, I took a moment to face Thad. His brown hair was disheveled and there was a small trickle of blood drying upon his right temple. His gray eyes were stormy, his jaw set in an expression of angry defiance. He said nothing, merely studied me in the dim light that spilled into the room from hallway beyond.

When Marek appeared in the doorway, I turned my back on our prisoner. "Where are his clothes, Marek?" I asked, forcing disdain into my tone. "I told you to treat him kindly—and from what I see here, I am not being obeyed."

Marek knew from experience that this was part of the charade. He nodded once, and said, "I'll go get them," before turning away, the ghost of a smile surfacing upon his features.

I turned my attention Thad once more. "I apologize for the way they have treated you so far. It is unacceptable."

Anger had been replaced by wary uncertainty upon the Stone-reader's face. His eyes continued to study me, but they were unreadable. He maintained his silence while Marek returned with the clothing the succubus had taken from him.

"Help him dress," I instructed Marek. "I will return once you have finished."

I left the room, closing the door softly behind me, and waited in the darkened hallway beyond. A minute later, Marek exited the room, and flashed a grin in my direction. "He's presentable now," he assured me. "I like this tactic of making him somewhat comfortable…Maybe he'll open up to you now."

I nodded. "That's the plan, anyway. Would you mind staying out here, in case I need you for anything?"

Marek nodded. "You know I will."

"Thanks," I said before reentering the room. I closed the door again behind me, and strode toward our prisoner, keeping well out of kicking range should he choose to become violent. He was dressed in the same pair of faded blue jeans he had been wearing when I had abducted him from the hunters' headquarters, and a button-down cotton shirt with a blue-and-white plaid print on it.

"I hope you are a little more comfortable now, Mr. Taylor," I said. "Again, I am sorry for the way my subordinates have treated you. I will be speaking with them about it once we have finished here."

He nodded once, quickly, but said nothing.

"You must be wondering why I have chosen to bring you here."

He glanced down at the carpet, and then shook his head. "Not really, no."

"Then you know already?" I asked, genuinely curious.

He sighed, refusing to make eye contact. "I know more than I'd like to at the moment," he replied. "The other summoner—when he was in my head, I could sense what he was thinking. I know this has something to do with Xandra Grey, and that there are a whole lot of you trying to bring us down. The only question I have is: Why?"

I nodded, taking a moment to sit down cross-legged on the floor. "That is a valid question, Mr. Taylor. If I give you the answer, will you give me an answer as well?"

Again, his gray eyes became wary, as though he felt this were some sort of trap. After a moment, he closed his eyes and nodded, resigned.

"Very well. I would like you to recall an event that happened here a little over a year ago, Mr. Taylor. There was a summoner killed in the underground portion of the city, shot four times in the abdomen by none other than your friend, Xandra Grey."

"That's what all this is about?" he asked, incredulous. "You're bringing us down because of *one* incident?"

"He *died*," I shot back, venom in my tone. "He was my lover."

"Oh..." he said, as some sort of realization dawned on him. "Xan was so proud of herself, too. God *damn* it, why did it have to be someone important?" The question was not directed at me, but at himself. He was angry, frustrated, and something else... I could not quite put my finger on just what it was that I detected in his expression.

"I do not wish anyone else of your little organization to be hurt," I said after a moment of silence. "For that to happen, I will need you to cooperate with me. Can you do that, Mr. Taylor?"

Again, the quick nod. "Yeah, fine. Just don't kill Xan." His tone was almost pleading. Was he in love with her? I wondered.

"I have no intention of killing anyone," I replied. "What happened with your colleague Dirk was something I allowed only because it was the safest way to bring you here. No one else has to share his fate, as long as you cooperate fully."

"Anything you want," he replied, his gray eyes pained. It was not a decision he wanted to make, but he knew it was the right thing to do. He wanted to protect the others.

"Good. Now, tell me this: What made your group decide to go after Ke'tai? And why leave him bleeding and in so much pain—why not finish the job and end his misery then?"

This question had nagged at me for the past year. I had arrived in time to watch the one man I loved die of his injuries. While I was thankful that I had been able to speak to him one last time, the knowledge that they had let him slowly bleed to death in the underground of Seattle had hurt me more than I could comprehend. These hunters—my sister among them—were savages; ruthless and cold, killing and destroying without thought of consequence. Tears of rage stung at my eyes, but I blinked them back as I focused my heated gaze upon Thad once more.

"She told me he was dead when she left him," Thad muttered quietly with a slight shake of his head.

"He was *not* dead!" I shouted. "By the time I reached him, it was too late to save him. He was still *alive* when I got there—but only for a very short time. She let him suffer, and for that I cannot forgive her."

Thad sighed, his gaze dropping to the carpet once more. "Either she didn't realize he was still alive, or she lied to me," he replied. "Our rule is to ensure one of your kind are dead before we leave the scene—but not to prevent suffering, as you put it. It's to prevent their being healed and seeking revenge…" He shook his head, letting the words trail off. "Never had it occurred to me that you freaks could fall in love."

I stood, blind with rage, wishing that there was a chair in the room that I could hurl in his direction. Instead, I closed my eyes and clenched my fists, restraining myself.

"We all were human at one time," I said through clenched teeth, "no different than you or Xan. We have the same feelings, the same emotions. We'll continue this discussion later, when I don't have the urge to tear your head from your shoulders. I'm not going to go down the same path that she has—your blood will not be spilled by my hand."

Turning away from the chained man, I strode out of the room before my emotions escalated beyond my control. Marek was still in the hallway where I had left him, and concern was evident in his blue eyes.

"Are you alright?" he asked quietly as I closed the door. "I heard shouting..."

I nodded. "I'll be fine. I just need some time to cool off before I try talking to him again." I sighed. "Is Zy'driks still sleeping?"

Marek nodded.

"I'll just have to wait until he's awake again," I replied. "I think the next round of questions will go better if he's in the room. Get Thad something to eat, please...I don't want him complaining of hunger since I'm trying to be the gracious host here."

Marek chuckled at my dry tone. "Will do, Ji'anne."

Two hours later, I was half asleep and leaning against a wall in the living room when the front door opened and Il'zaks stepped inside, shaking moisture from his sleeves. Outside, the rain was coming down in a steady torrent, dripping from the eaves of the house and causing the street beyond to reflect the orange glow from the streetlights overhead.

"I found something at Dirk's home that may be of interest to us," Il'zaks said as he removed his coat and left it in a heap on the floor near the door.

I nodded. "Let me get Zy'driks and Xen'din," I said as I rose to my feet. "They'll need to hear it, too."

Zy'driks had been asleep since he had relinquished his hold on Thad's mind, having exhausted himself after going almost three full days without sleep. I decided to give him a few more minutes to rest. I went to the bedroom Xen'din had occupied after he began his mission to distract the hunters. I knocked on the door quietly, but heard no response from within. I waited several seconds, knocked again, but still heard nothing.

Frowning, I pushed open the door. "Xen'din?" I asked, searching the darkened room. Rain lashed at the windows, one of which had been left open, and cold water had begun to run down the wall and soak into the carpet beneath. In the center of the room, Xen'din lay on his side, knees drawn up to his chest, grimacing as though he were in terrible pain.

I raced to his side. "What's wrong? Xen'din, what happened?"

"I was careless," he gasped. "Ah, it hurts!"

Immediately, I recalled a discussion that I'd had with Te'chok during my training. I had asked him what would happen if a summoner's demon was killed, but the summoner remained alive. His response had been cryptic, but he had said, "I've been told it causes physical pain to the summoner, but beyond that I don't truly know. We are tied to the demons we call forth, so it would not surprise me if some part of us dies along with the demon."

I turned and closed the window, shivering as I did so. The air outside was cold.

"Xen'din, you've got to tell me what happened," I said quietly. "I know it hurts—but you have to focus enough to tell me."

"Well, my distraction worked," he managed, gritting his teeth against the pain coursing through his body. He slowly pushed himself upright. "Too well, I think."

As he sat up, I noticed a dark trickle of blood running from his ear lobe. "Xen'din, you're bleeding," I said, kneeling at his side.

He nodded. "I know...It isn't important." He shook his head slowly, as though to clear his mind. "I led the hunters away from their hideout, and into the opposite direction of Dirk's house...so Il'zaks would have more time," he explained. "It was going so well, I got cocky...and I made a mistake."

"What happened?" I asked again.

He glanced up at me with a wounded expression. "I let the demon stay too long in one place," he replied. "They caught up to it, and they killed it." He grimaced again as he tried to shift into a slightly more comfortable position. "I knew it was dead immediately...and then this pain started..."

I nodded, standing slowly. "I'll get Il'zaks; he just returned. Maybe he knows something that will help you."

Xen'din shrugged as though it were unimportant. I left him and ran headlong into Zy'driks as I exited the room. He and Il'zaks were in the hallway.

"Um, sorry," I managed.

"Ji'anne, what's wrong?" Il'zaks asked, having noticed my worried expression.

I motioned for the two to follow me back into the room. "Xen'din says they killed his demon," I said quietly. "He's in a lot of pain…"

Zy'driks sighed heavily. "Well, this will make things interesting, won't it?" he asked of no one in particular, his tone dry.

While Il'zaks knelt beside Xen'din, I turned to face Zy'driks. "What do you mean?"

"Te'chok was a lousy mentor, wasn't he?" he replied with a frown. "The only way to recover from a loss like this is to rest. The pain will make it almost impossible for him to function for a while, but only time can heal this type of wound. There's nothing we can do for him." He sighed, running a hand through his hair. "This means we are down one member of our squad for a while. It'll just be you, me, and Il'zaks now."

I closed my eyes, feeling suddenly weary. Te'chok had left me unprepared for many things; this was not the first such instance, and would probably not be the last. It was disappointing that Xen'din would be unable to help us for a time, but at least he would recover.

"How long will it take?" I asked Zy'driks.

He shrugged. "It's hard to say. It depends on which demon it was that he lost, but it still varies between summoners. Over time, the pain will lessen and finally disappear, just like a physical wound. Sometimes the healing process can be accelerated by the summoner calling another demon of the same type, but other times it doesn't help at all." He sighed. "It's best to just let him rest, for now."

I nodded. "Alright."

I allowed Zy'driks to lead me out of the room and down the darkened corridor toward the living room. Several of the trackers were asleep, bundled in sleeping bags or blankets along the near side of the room as we entered. Konrad was standing in the doorway leading into the kitchen, a bottle of Beck's in hand as he talked quietly with Levi, who was leaning against the wall to his right. Zy'driks headed for the empty wall opposite the hallway and sat down heavily. I sat down next to him, drawing my knees up.

"Did Il'zaks say anything to you yet?" he asked.

I shook my head. "Not really. Just that he had found something we needed to take a look at."

Zy'driks merely nodded and gazed toward the hallway, his face expressionless. I could tell he was still very tired and wanted this night to be over, but I understood him well enough to know that he would not rest again until our business had been concluded.

It was several minutes before Il'zaks emerged from the hallway and headed toward our location. His face was grave, but he said nothing until he had seated himself, cross-legged.

"Xen'din will recover," he said slowly, "but it will take some time. He lost his shadow demon."

Zy'driks nodded knowingly, as though he had expected this. "You found something at Dirk's house?"

Il'zaks nodded and reached a hand into one of his pockets, withdrawing a small, spiral-bound notebook with a faded red cardstock cover. "Yes, a journal. Take a look at the last entry."

I took the notebook, flipping through pages of scrawling script, searching for final entry. It was dated the day prior to Dirk's death.

"Read it aloud," Zy'driks encouraged. "I'm too tired right now to read it myself."

I nodded and began. "'I received an anonymous letter today not long after I returned home from a meeting with the H'—"

"I believe he means the hunters," Il'zaks commented. "It would fit the time line."

"Yes," Zy'driks replied impatiently, waving a hand absently in Il'zaks' direction. "Go on, Ji'anne."

"'The letter was signed LGS'," I continued. "That was my letter… 'I am to meet someone, an associate of this LGS, tomorrow evening. Thad will probably disapprove, but I intend to go alone. I have to prove to him that I am capable in this job, just as capable as he is. Once I put an end to this business with whoever "LGS" is, Thad will be forced to acknowledge me as one of his equals. It won't just be him and Xandra Grey any more.'" I paused, sensing there was more bitterness behind these words than we had suspected. I intended to ask Thad about his relationship with Dirk in the morning.

"'I have a feeling that this must have something to do with what happened last year,'" I went on. "'I told Thad, and I keep telling him, that the business with killing that summoner wouldn't bode well for us. He felt everything would be just fine, because it had to do with one of Xandra's accomplishments. He'd bend over backwards and kiss his own ass for her if she asked him to. Tomorrow night, I'll prove once and for all that I am more worthy of being his second than she is. I'm not going to tell Thad anything. I'll have Jack or Aria come and check on the dog, in case I'm gone for a while. I'll tell them I'm going to visit family or something. No one has to know until the deed is done.'"

"It is my belief that we should speak with Thad about this business between himself and Dirk, and where your sister fits in," Il'zaks said quietly after I had finished reading. "She must mean something more to Thad than he will readily admit."

I was unhappy when it came to talking about Xandra, and even less so if it meant I would have to confront Thad about his relationship to her. I knew I would have to speak to Thad about this in the morning, but I was beginning to feel it would be another heated conversation. Xandra had wounded me beyond repair, and I was determined to make certain she paid for it dearly.

"I'll speak to him in the morning," I replied briskly. "For now, let's all get some rest."

Zy'driks nodded and stood slowly, stifling a yawn. "Rest would be more than welcome right now, believe me."

He took three steps toward the hall when his phone rang. Muttering curses under his breath, he answered it with a surly, "What?" He listened for a time, sighed, and then said, "Okay, I'll let them know. Now let me get some sleep." He hung up, irritated with the interruption, and turned to face Il'zaks and I once more. "Aaron says Xandra and a couple of her friends have gone to Dirk's place to investigate. I hope you cleaned up after yourself, Il'zaks."

Il'zaks nodded, an amused smile appearing on his face. "You ought to know me well enough by now, Zy'driks. While I was searching for anything that might help us, I had a *Zombi Cadavre* busy devouring anything that might incriminate us. There is nothing to worry about. Now, go get some sleep; you deserve it."

# 30

# PREDICTABLE

It was just after dawn, though I could scarcely tell the position of the sun due to the thick layer of clouds overhead, when I strode into the room where Thaddeus Taylor was imprisoned.

During the previous day, Konrad and Marek had made a few modifications to the room—the door now only locked from the outside, the single window had been sealed with some sort of industrial glue, bars had been installed on both the interior and exterior, and the chains had been removed from the wall. Because of this, Marek had insisted on going into the room first, to "secure" our prisoner; in other words, he was handcuffing Thad for my safety. Once he had finished, I was allowed inside. I had chosen to confront him alone. Even without the handcuffs, Thad was of little threat to me.

Thad was sitting stiffly on an overturned five-gallon plastic bucket, the best we could provide as a seat in the otherwise unfurnished rental house. He had been given a change of clothing since I had last visited.

"Thad," I said as I entered the room, "how are you this morning?"

"How the hell should I know?" he replied with a sneer. "I don't even know if it really is morning. The window is taped up and all I ever see is darkness, until one of your kind shows up."

"Now, be honest with me," I said in as soothing a voice as I could manage, "we have treated you better than you would have treated any of us. Am I not correct?"

He did not answer, but his deepening frown and refusal to meet my gaze spoke volumes.

"Look, we found some information at Dirk Musgrave's home yesterday that concerns you," I stated, tired of mincing words with this uncooperative man. "It also concerns your friend Xandra Grey."

He looked up, meeting my gaze. "What does it have to do with Xan?"

Interesting. He was more concerned about her welfare than his own. I nodded thoughtfully; Il'zaks' assumptions had been correct.

"It seems as though Dirk didn't care much for Xandra," I said slowly. "Why is that? From everything we have seen, she does an exceptional job at exterminating people who only wish to be allowed to survive." The last sentence had come out rather acidly, more so than I had intended.

"Is that *really* what you are trying to do? Just survive?" Thad asked, his tone incredulous. "I have seen what you people can do, and it is nothing but a perversion of everything that is good in this world."

I had expected nothing less from Thaddeus Taylor. He was a fervent believer in the hunters' doctrine, and I knew nothing could sway him from his chosen path.

I shrugged. "It doesn't matter. You and I could argue all day about whose side is in the right and not get anywhere. But I did not come here today to argue—I came here to get answers. Why did Dirk dislike Xandra?"

His stormy gray eyes were defiant and cold, but I held his gaze unflinchingly. I was not about to leave without an answer.

Finally, he sighed. "Fine, I'll tell you. I know that if I don't, you'll do something to force me into it anyway."

I nodded, simply to provide him with confirmation, and waited for his next words.

"Dirk joined us a little over two years ago," Thad began, his gaze directed downward toward a patch of carpet. "He used to be a part of another hunting group, but his girlfriend at the time got a job transfer to our area, so he came to us." He sighed, and a scowl marred his features for a moment as though he were conflicted about divulging any further information. He fell silent, his jaw clenched.

I sighed. "If you don't tell me what I need to know, Xandra will die." It was a lie—I had no intention of taking her life—but his reaction was exactly as I had hoped it would be: one of fear and desperation. It was clear to me that he would do anything to keep her from coming to harm.

His eyes flicked up to meet mine only briefly, but his stony demeanor crumbled ever so slightly and he began to speak once again. "Dirk had talent," he mumbled with a shake of his head. "I had been on the lookout for someone who could track summoners for years, and his move to our area was perfect. He had been the second in his former group, but I already had a perfectly capable second—Xan."

"I take it Dirk didn't much like this."

Thad shook his head. "Not at all. He had issues with authority, and was always trying to subvert me one way or another. It was almost like he was out to prove to everyone that *he* should have been the one in charge. There were some…tense moments."

"Do you think this quirk of his personality had anything to do with his recent death?" I pressed.

His face hardened again and his mouth twisted into a frown of distrust. "Why are you doing this?" he demanded.

"I need to know what you're thinking," I replied, intentionally vague.

He sighed, a sound full of frustration. "I don't know why, but I'll be honest with you. Yes, I think it had something to do with his death. You people exploited his desire to prove himself, and he died because of it!"

"I appreciate your honesty," I replied. "I will also be honest with you, Mr. Taylor. I was against the taking of any lives in this process. I did not want to stoop to your level, and take a life without it being necessary."

A flicker of confusion passed through his gray eyes before they resumed their wary vigilance. "But in the end, you did find it necessary."

It was now my turn to sigh. "Unfortunately, yes. It was the only way to lure you into a trap in which you could not escape. To single out Xandra, we had to take you prisoner, and I am truly sorry for that."

"So, you had Dirk killed, so that…" he trailed off as realization dawned on him. His face became a mask of fury, his cheeks and forehead turning a deep crimson, almost purple hue. "He died so that that monster of an associate you have could take control of my *mind!*"

He rose to his feet more swiftly than I had anticipated he could, and aimed a kick in my direction. Thankful for my much quicker reflexes, I avoided the blow and moved to stand beside the door. He blinked in confusion, his eyes unable to follow the movement.

"How did you—?"

"It doesn't matter how I did it," I replied acidly. "I don't appreciate you trying to harm me. I did not agree with this plan to bring you here, but now I have to deal with the consequences of having done so in the end. Neither of us likes this situation, so bear with me and it will end up far more pleasant for you."

He appeared nonplussed, and returned to his seat on the bucket. I imagined that had his arms been free, he would have crossed them over his chest. "I seriously doubt anything that happens during my time with you people could be anywhere near pleasant."

"Certainly not, if you're going to have that kind of attitude," I replied. "Look, as long as you cooperate, Xandra won't be harmed, and I won't allow my colleague access to your head, either."

He frowned. "Fine, what do you want then?"

"For now, just the information I ask for."

"And you asked me why Dirk didn't like Xan," he said. "I guess I really only told you why he didn't like *me*."

When I nodded, he continued. "Jack told me once that he and Dirk had a long talk. Jack and Aria Swift were the only ones from our group that seemed to get along with him. They'd go to his place every so often, you know, have dinner, watch a movie with him, that sort of thing. Anyway, Jack told me that Dirk was upset with Xan getting all of the attention for what we did last year. It was Dirk who tracked him down, but Xan got all of the credit for taking him out. He was a little pissed off about that."

"I can't say I blame him," I replied, biting back other comments that I would have liked to say on the matter of Ke'tai's death. "Xandra always did like to take all the glory."

I dropped my gaze, and sighed. Damn, I had been careless.

"You know something more about Xandra than you're letting on," Thad said slowly. "You two must have some kind of history..."

I drew myself up and met his gaze. "We have far more of a history than you would ever guess, Mr. Taylor. I think I've said enough for the time being. Perhaps we can speak more about this later."

After my meeting with Thad, I found myself in Xen'din's room. He was curled up on himself in the midst of a swath of blankets, his eyes closed as though he were asleep, though I doubted he was. He looked to be in too much pain. I sat down heavily upon the floor, leaning my back against the wall, and merely watched him for a few minutes, waiting for some sign that he was aware of my presence. I did not have to wait long.

"Why are you here, Ji'anne?" His voice was hoarse, barely rising above a whisper. His eyes remained closed.

I shrugged, though I knew he could not see the gesture. "I don't know," I replied quietly. "I guess I just wanted to see how you were doing."

"If you believe what Il'zaks says, I'm doing as well as can be expected," he replied. "I feel like my guts are being ripped out."

I made a face; that had been a rather unpleasant visual. "I don't know what to do about Xan," I said after a moment's pause. "I think…I think Thad cares for her more than we initially realized. But, that doesn't really matter, I guess. I just don't know how to go on from here."

Xen'din managed to change his grimace into a frown briefly, showing his displeasure at my words. "Ji'anne, you said yourself that you didn't consider her family any more, that she had wounded you too badly for any kind of reconciliation. Why do you hesitate now?"

"It was something Thad said to me," I replied, thinking back to how he had reacted when we had spoken of Dirk. "She's lost someone already in this little game we're playing…I just want to know what the right choice is."

Xen'din sighed and sat up slowly, grimacing once more. He was shirtless as the blankets fell away, and again I was startled at just how perfect his form truly was. Had Ke'tai not come along when he had, I would have fallen completely in love with this man that now sat before me, but for all of the wrong reasons. Attraction alone was not enough to form the basis of a relationship; I knew that now.

"You can't think of this as just Xandra any more," Xen'din said. His arms shook as he held himself up, from weakness or pain, I was not certain. "She's a hunter, Ji'anne. She will not just come forward and talk; you'll have to persuade her with the only language she will fully understand—fear for her friends."

"Then we should continue." It was not a question, but a weary statement. I knew he was right—Xandra would not talk unless she felt there were no other way to adequately protect the other hunters. I sighed and looked down.

"I think this is just as hard for me as it is for you," Xen'din said quietly after a moment. "I hate myself for admitting this, but I still love her. After all these years, and everything that I've gone through, I still hold onto the hope that one day we can be together again. It's an irrational hope, and I know that, but…I still dream of it. I still dream about her."

"Even if you could be together, would you want that?" I asked of him, still focusing intently on the carpet. "She'll already look almost a decade older than you do…One day she will die of old age, but you never will. Would you really want that for her?"

He sighed. "I would want her to be able to choose which path to take, Ji'anne. Right now, she doesn't know that this path exists. I want her to know that it does, and to decide as she will."

I looked up at him, and his eyes were focused upon mine. "If she decides to choose a path that does not include me, I'm strong enough to handle it," he continued. "What I don't know is if you are."

I blinked, shocked that he would think this. After everything I had said over the past year, and everything that we had planned—all to bring Xandra down to the lowest depths of despair—he still questioned my resolve.

"Why?" It was all I could manage, but he understood the full import of that single word.

"So much of what you said was borne of anger," he replied, compassion in his eyes. "I can't fathom the pain you had to endure, watching him die, Ji'anne. But Xan is your sister, your family…I just don't believe that you are ready to abandon those ties completely. Or that you are truly willing to," he added.

"But you think we should continue?" I asked.

"In spite of everything you have said, I don't think you actually hate her, Ji'anne. You want to talk to her—I think that's been made pretty clear to everyone here—and that's what this game is all about. You want to make it so that you can do just that: talk to her."

I sighed, disappointed with myself for having made my desires so obvious to those around me. I *did* want to talk to Xandra, but I did not know where such a conversation would lead. I wanted the chance to explain myself to her, to tell her why I believed she was wrong in joining the hunters. But was I daydreaming? I knew Xandra was stubborn and quick to anger—she always had been—and once she had set her mind to something, only a shock of the greatest magnitude could hope to weaken her resolve. Would I be able to deliver that particular shock?

"I may not be strong enough right now to help out with your schemes, Ji'anne, but I want to be there when Xan finally comes to you on her own," Xen'din said quietly. "I know her nature as well as you do—alone one of us may not be able to get her to see reason, but together, I don't think she will have the willpower to resist. We both need to be there."

I knew he was right. I merely nodded, and stood up to leave. "Thank you, Xen'din."

He managed a weak smile and drew the blankets over his shoulders again. "You don't have to thank me, Ji'anne. I think I understand your intentions here better than the others do, even though I'm just a subordinate in this operation. I want the same thing you do, though…And I think that at times like this, I can be of a little more help than they can."

I nodded again. "Yeah, and that's why I thank you."

As I exited the room, closing the door softly behind me, I was nearly knocked over by a breathless and excited Zy'driks. He had been racing down the hall at top speed.

"Ji'anne! We have some news about the hunters," he explained, taking a moment to catch his breath. "I've been looking for you. You should come to the living room." He turned to hurry back the way he had come, pausing only to motion that I should follow him.

With a tired sigh, I followed his lead. Most of the trackers had gathered in the room, as well as Il'zaks and Zy'driks. Aaron stepped forward toward the center as I entered, making it obvious that he was the bearer of this news.

"What's this news about?" I asked him wearily.

"The hunters just had a meeting," he replied. "They're trying to figure out what to do now that their leader has disappeared. Apparently, they think he's dead." He allowed himself a brief chuckle before continuing. "It looks like a couple of them went to Dirk's home to look for clues, but it was after we had already been there. They didn't find anything, besides some indications that he resented Thad and was trying to prove himself—nothing new to them."

I glanced at Zy'driks. He had been excited about *this*? It wasn't news, just more of the same. I crossed my arms, somewhat annoyed.

"There's one more thing," Aaron said after a moment's silence. "Xandra refused to take the role of leader, so they decided it would be the priest."

The priest—Father Thomas Moresby—was like a father figure to the hunters. He was in his late sixties, a Catholic priest, religious almost to a fault, though we had found that none of his colleagues within the clergy knew of his dealings with the hunters. He would have been the reasonable choice.

I wondered how Thad would take the news that he had been replaced by the priest. Perhaps I should pay him a second visit today, but I was unsure if I was truly up for it.

"What are you thinking of, Ji'anne?" Il'zaks asked quietly after a moment.

I sighed. "I think I need to talk to our prisoner again. It will be difficult to single Xandra out if she is still following someone else's orders."

Il'zaks nodded, his face placid. "I shall join you this time," he replied. "Perhaps with two of us present, he will not be so unwilling to relate the information that we need."

I hesitated for less than a second, and then nodded my assent. "Fine, let's do this, then."

As had been the case earlier, Konrad insisted on securing our prisoner before we were allowed to enter, despite my protests. It was not necessary to handcuff the man when he was alone, especially not in a house full of people who were his sworn enemies.

After a few seconds, Konrad reemerged and gave us the okay to enter the room. He was grinning, obviously pleased with himself.

Ignoring him for the time being, I pushed into the room ahead of Il'zaks. Thad was sitting on the plastic bucket again, his hands cuffed securely behind him. He scowled at me, the expression darkening when he noticed I was not alone.

"What, I wasn't helpful enough to you earlier that you needed to bring reinforcements?" he asked, his gray eyes stormy.

I frowned and was about to say something, but Il'zaks replied first.

"I requested to come along this time around," he replied. "We have some news for you that you might find interesting, but in exchange, we require your cooperation."

Thad's fiery gaze shifted away from me to focus fully on Il'zaks. "What news?"

"They've chosen a new leader, Thad," I replied.

That wariness I had come to recognize came back into his eyes as he turned to face me once more. "They…being my people?"

I nodded once, watching as impassively as I could while his face fell. He looked down at the floor, disappointed; I could not blame him for feeling that way.

"That was very fast," he said stiffly. "Who did they choose?"

"They voted Xandra Grey as your successor, since she was your second in command," Il'zaks replied in a quiet tone. "She refused to take on that role. They voted a second time, and chose the priest."

Thad appeared thoughtful, though still hurt by the news. "The priest was probably a better choice for leader to begin with," he admitted. "Xan's temper tends to get in the way of her rationality sometimes."

He glanced at me as though seeking confirmation of his statement, but I merely crossed my arms and continued to gaze at him evenly. I was not about to let another shred about my past become known to this man.

"We know that this priest is rarely fazed by events, and has been working with organizations like yours since his career began," Il'zaks stated after a moment's silence. "Sending a demon or two his way will not bother him; he knows well how to dispatch them, and seems to keep his head well under stressful circumstances. What we need to know is how to unnerve him."

Thad frowned at Il'zaks, though there was a hint of something more than mere displeasure—uncertainty, perhaps—in his expression. "I'll be honest with you here—I don't actually know. I've never seen him become upset, never seen him angry, never seen him afraid of anything. Father Thomas has seen everything you people can throw at us, and has survived into old age, which is damned good."

"He hasn't seen everything," I replied hastily, thinking of the demon I had not called upon for eight years, Alastor. Perhaps now was the time to finally see what he could do for me.

Thad appeared unimpressed. "Yeah? Well, I'd like to see what you can conjure up that even *I* haven't seen yet."

I laughed mirthlessly, tempted to summon Alastor on the spot.

"Do not call it now," Il'zaks said evenly, placing one hand firmly on my shoulder. "The time is coming, but it is not yet."

The skeptical challenge had faded from Thad's eyes, replaced once again by that wary uncertainty I had come to be so familiar with. "So, there must be something…" he said to himself, though both Il'zaks and I could hear him clearly.

"We have always been forced to keep our secrets carefully guarded," Il'zaks replied. "If we do not, we are killed—no questions asked. It must be so much simpler to live life knowing that everything you do is right, and is justified by some higher power, or higher calling. We do not have that luxury. You ought to be grateful that you do, Thaddeus Taylor."

I was surprised by the undisguised bitterness I heard in Il'zaks' tone. He was always so proper, so careful with his words, and this was out of character.

Thad also seemed taken aback by the Elder's words. Confusion had settled across the planes of his rugged features, and he seemed unsure of how to respond. I allowed myself a bit of a smile; perhaps agreeing to have Il'zaks come here had been the best course of action I'd taken all day.

Silence settled over the room after Il'zaks' embittered statement. I kept my gaze fixed on the form of the unyielding man that sat before us, knowing that eventually there would be a crack in his stony resolve. I hoped that crack would develop sooner, rather than later.

Finally, Thad looked up with a weary sigh, his expression one of resentful submission. "Okay, there's one thing you might be able to do that would make the old priest begin to wonder just what you're really trying to accomplish." He fell silent and refused to make eye contact.

"And that is what, exactly?" Il'zaks asked after allowing the statement to hang in the air for some time.

"If you were able to get some sort of personal item—not necessarily from him, but from one of them—and send it to him, he just might be surprised enough to make some kind of mistake," Thad replied rather grudgingly. "I don't know what it was *exactly*—" he said the last word in a mockery of Il'zaks' previous statement, "—but something in his past really rocked him. It had to do with a summoner getting something of his mother's, but I don't know the situation there. And I don't even know if this will work; I'm only speculating."

A plan had begun to form in my mind as soon as he had mentioned the personal item. I had the necklace Ke'tai had given me, that Christmas so long ago, when everything had still been normal. I knew Xandra would recognize it immediately; I had never taken it off since that day. I reached up and tugged the chain from beneath my shirt, looking down to examine it in my palm. The gold, eight-pointed star with its incredible ruby set within its heart caught what little light filtered into the room, sparkling faintly in the gloom. Xandra had been present when I had opened Ke'tai's gift that Christmas, and I knew this was the item that I must send to Father Thomas. Not only would it possibly rattle *him*, but it would scare the hell out of Xandra, as well. This plan would have been perfect, if it hadn't been for the fact that I was forced to give up the necklace, one of the most treasured items I possessed from Ke'tai. I sighed; this was yet another sacrifice I had to endure in order to deal with my sister.

When I looked up again, both men had their eyes locked upon me. Thad's were curious and uncertain, whereas Il'zaks' were full of compassionate understanding.

Carefully, I removed the chain from my neck, taking it off for the first time in many years. "We will send him this," I said quietly, holding the necklace out for them to see it better. I felt tears threatening to spill from my eyes, but I no longer cared if Thad could sense weakness within me. "It won't bother the priest much, until he shows it to Xandra."

The hour following my latest visit with Thad passed by slowly as I prepared to send the necklace to Father Thomas. I felt as though I were moving mechanically; I knew that I had to do this, yet regretted the action all the same. I was surprised at how difficult it was to part with this trinket, as though I were giving up physical memories of my lost beloved.

I placed the necklace carefully in a small envelope, accompanied by a brief letter that had become a bit tear-stained by the time I managed to fold it and place it inside. I summoned a nightwing to take the envelope to the priest, instructing it to leave it on his doorstep before collapsing wearily against the wall in one of the empty bedrooms.

I was heartsick at the loss of my necklace, but if I wanted to see Xandra brought down, I knew it was the safest way to move forward. I wished that I could see her face when the priest revealed the envelope's contents; that would have provided me with some satisfaction. Unfortunately, I could not risk letting my demon be seen—let alone be present myself.

Time passed before Zy'driks took it upon himself to locate me. I don't know how long I sat hunched against the wall, alone in the darkened room; I remember only that I was miserable. Sometime before Zy'driks appeared, the nightwing dropped the envelope on the steps leading up to the priest's front door, and I dismissed the little creature as soon as it had. I felt Ke'tai's loss more keenly than ever, and it left me despondent and weary.

I rose slowly as Zy'driks moved inside the doorway, more a silhouette in the darkened room than a real figure. I did not want him to see me this way, upset and broken down as I was. I wiped hurriedly at my eyes; they were sore and puffy from the silent tears I had shed.

Zy'driks said nothing for several long moments. He merely stood at the opposite end of the room and studied me carefully.

Finally, I could take no more of the silence. "What do you want?" The words had come out more harshly than I had intended.

"I came to see how you were holding up," he replied, his voice subdued. "I know you don't have very many things to remind you of Ke'tai—"

"Stop," I said, holding one hand up. "I know you mean well, but I can't take it right now. I know I had to give up that necklace, but it wasn't easy. And now I have to live with that decision, on top of all the others I've already made during this endeavor of ours. I'll recover, eventually."

He sighed, as though he were dealing with a stubborn child. "Ji'anne, please let me speak."

I closed my eyes briefly. I didn't want to listen to anything he had to say, but I knew I ought to hear him out. I was Lady Grand Summoner; it was part of my job to listen to his concerns. When I opened my eyes again, Zy'driks had not moved an inch. "Fine," I said evenly. "I'll listen."

"Thank you, Ji'anne," he replied. "I know it hasn't been easy for you—and that necklace meant something more to you than I can imagine. But I wanted to tell you that I thought it was a very clever move. Il'zaks told me about when Ke'tai gave that to you...I'm sorry you had to part with it."

I shrugged, trying my best to ignore the whirlwind of emotions I was feeling. "It was the only way," I replied numbly.

He nodded, moving forward to stand before me. Here, closer to the windows, I could see his features more clearly in the feeble light seeping into the room from the edges of the dark shades. He was clearly concerned.

"I sent Aaron to conduct some surveillance on the priest and your sister for a while," he said carefully, never taking his silver eyes from my face. "I want to know how they react to the package you've sent them. I thought you should know."

I nodded again, feeling rather weary. I wasn't sure what I should say—if anything—but he seemed as though he were expecting something from me. I remained silent.

"I guess—" he began, but was interrupted by the untimely ringing coming from his cell phone. He sighed, and reached into the pocket of his jeans to produce the noisome thing. "Hello? Uh-huh…Hang on a second, Aaron." He pulled the phone away from his ear, and said, "Ji'anne, you need to hear this," as he punched the button for speaker phone.

"Am I good to go now, Z?" Aaron's voice came through the receiver. There was static in the background, as though it were windy at his present location.

"Yes, go ahead," Zy'driks replied.

"Okay, I'm outside of their headquarters right now," Aaron said. He sounded excited. "The priest found your package about a half hour ago, and called an emergency meeting of the hunters. I don't think he opened it yet, but I'm pretty sure he knew it was from one of you. Anyway, I had to take my time in getting to our surveillance spot across the street, so he wouldn't know I followed him back here. It looks like the others are just now starting to show up."

"Do you have the audio playing?" Zy'driks asked, and I wondered what he was referring to.

"Uh, I do now, yeah. Thanks for the reminder," came the reply.

"Il'zaks had Carmine and Kendrick go in, disguised as a cleaning crew overnight," Zy'driks explained to me quickly. "While they were inside, Carmine installed a device in the ceiling above their meeting place. As wary as these hunters are about their hideout, they certainly don't watch the floor above them very well." He chuckled briefly to himself. "The audio will play back to the handheld device Aaron has with him."

"So, we'll be able to hear them during their meeting." It wasn't a question, but Zy'driks nodded in affirmation anyway.

"Aha, here's our guest of honor now," Aaron said. "I mean—"

"It's Xan," I said flatly.

"Um, yeah..." He sounded a little deflated, and I silently cursed myself for allowing my personal disgust to invade our conversation. "They'll probably start their meeting soon," Aaron continued after a pause. "I think all of them are there now. I'm going to set the phone down next to the speakers."

There was a rustling sound and a soft thud as he set the phone down. I could hear faint static accompanied by muted voices, but none of the voices were clear enough to make out.

Zy'driks frowned. "Aaron, turn up the volume on the speakers. We aren't getting much coming through."

There was more rustling, and suddenly the conversational murmur blossomed into a dull roar. The voices were now clear, but it seemed the meeting had not yet begun; the topics of discussion currently featured someone's weekend barbecue and whispered questions regarding why they had all been gathered so unexpectedly. After a few minutes, there was the sound of a door opening and closing, a pause, and the room quickly quieted.

The voice that came through next was obviously that of an older gentleman's; I knew immediately that it must be the priest who was speaking. "Now that we are all here, we can begin. It seems our movements have been carefully watched, and that Dirk's death and Thad's disappearance are only the beginning."

The voice that spoke next was one I recognized all too well. "What have they done now, Father?" It was Xandra.

I imagined her sitting down, one leg crossed over the other and leaning back with her arms crossed, a position I had seen her take so many times over the years, one she assumed when she had something serious to think over, or a problem to solve. I could hear her cool demeanor come through in her casual tone, and I ground my teeth in frustration. I was so close to bringing her down, but I still had to lay in wait, spinning my web, ensuring that everything had been prepared perfectly. The only thing she'd had to do was pull a trigger.

"—given a present," the priest was saying as my focus returned to the conversation. I glanced up at Zy'driks briefly, but his eyes were glued to a solitary spot on the carpeted floor as he listened intently.

"Do you think it's safe to open it?" a female voice asked, her tone wavering toward shrillness. She was either inexperienced—a newcomer to their ranks—or one of those generally nervous types. My guess was that the voice belonged to Mina or Aria, based on the information we had gathered.

"It does not seem to have any sort of evil presence to it," the priest replied. "I do not know what the package contains, but I think it is best if we find out. It may give us some answers, or at least some clues as to what they are scheming."

There was a lengthy silence, and then Xandra's voice filtered through the speakers. "Fine, if nobody can make a decision, I will. Open it. Let's see what's inside."

I smirked. She had always been impatient.

There was a faint rustling sound as, I assumed, one of their number broke the seal on the envelope and opened the package I had left on the priest's doorstep.

"There is a note," the priest said slowly, "and a necklace. A rather expensive and unique necklace."

There was another bit of rustling, and then a gasp of recognition from Xandra. "That... That was my sister's." Her voice trembled, and I could hear the emotion behind her words. She was shocked, confused, perhaps upset. One thing I knew for certain, however: She had not expected this.

"Are you sure?" a male voice asked, incredulously. "I mean, how long has it been, Xan?"

"Just over eight years," she replied without hesitation, that note of confusion still hovering in her tone. "What does this mean?"

"Perhaps you should explain, Xandra," the priest said gently. "Not everyone knows the story of your sister's disappearance."

There was a pause, and I imagined Xandra's face crumpling into a frown as she composed her thoughts. She had never been good at expressing herself when it came to personal matters, particularly when in front of a crowd.

"I...I don't really know what to say," she mumbled, and the words were difficult to hear over the speakers. She sighed heavily. "I mean...That necklace, it was given to my sister as a Christmas gift by the man she was dating. That was...That was only a few weeks before she disappeared. No one knows what happened to her, and it's been so long..." The emotions had finally taken their toll on Xandra, and I could hear muffled sobs through the speakers.

"The police were never able to find any evidence of her sister's whereabouts," the priest said softly after a moment, continuing on for Xandra when she could not go on herself. "Thad and I met Xandra not long after the investigation began. We helped her get through that rough spot in her life."

I knew the priest meant more than just my disappearance when he spoke of Xandra's "rough spot"; he also implicated the events surrounding Xandra's boyfriend not long afterward—the apparent suicide of Elliot Thompson. I wondered how much her colleagues suspected regarding what had actually happened to him, and how much she had decided to tell them herself.

"You're certain that necklace belonged to your sister?" another male voice asked. This voice sounded concerned, and did not belong to the same man who had asked if she had been sure the first time.

There was another pause, and then, "Yes, I'm positive." Xandra seemed to have composed herself once more.

"What about the letter?" the nervous woman asked. "What does that say?"

"It says, 'To the priest friend of Xandra Grey, I have enclosed a certain trinket that has been very difficult to part with. Xandra will know its meaning, when you show it to her. If you want to see your leader returned in once piece, Xandra must meet me on Thursday evening alone. If she agrees to this, leave your reply in a sealed envelope where you last saw Thaddeus Taylor'." The priest sighed.

"Xan, you can't," the concerned male said as soon as the priest had finished. "It's probably some kind of trap they're trying to set for you. You can't go alone."

"I know," Xandra replied. This time she sounded weary. "We can still leave our reply, but it doesn't have to agree with their demands."

"Thursday is three days away," the priest said slowly. "We have time to figure this out, but I am in agreement with Kent. You cannot go alone, if you go at all."

"What will they do to Thad if we don't agree?" the nervous woman asked.

"That's the part we don't know," Xandra replied. "If not meeting them means he gets hurt—or worse—then I will go."

I smirked; she was still predictable.

"We should leave them a reply right now," Zy'driks said quietly, ignoring the hunters' conversation for a moment. "Let them know that if they do not meet your demands, more of them will end up missing, 'or worse' as your sister put it."

I nodded. "Yes, we should, but I don't have the energy for something like that right now. Why don't you do it? You can be very persuasive when you want to be, Zy'driks."

He chuckled. "Alright, I'll do it."

I returned my attention back to the conversation while Zy'driks summoned a nightwing and scribbled a brief note.

The hunters were in a heated debate over what action Xandra should take; all were opposed to her going alone, though she stated repeatedly she would if it meant Thad came to no harm. The debate was growing tiresome, but I continued to listen, hoping that something important would be said. In the meantime, Zy'driks had sent his demon flying toward their headquarters, intent upon the creature dropping the note at their door before they even realized it had been there. I hoped it would be fast enough to escape; having Xen'din out of commission was enough of a blow to our cause as it was. I could not afford to have Zy'driks incapacitated in the same manner.

After almost ten minutes of debate, the hunters grew suddenly quiet on the other end of the phone line. "There was something…" one said, and another stated, "I think I sensed something," almost at the same time.

I glanced at Zy'driks again, and he was grinning. "The mailman just finished his delivery," he replied. "I dismissed it as soon as it dropped the note. I did not want to take any chances."

I nodded, relieved that he had decided upon caution. Zy'driks had taken more risks than anyone else had during this mission, and he was the most important person to ensure the mission's success, after myself.

"Whatever it was is gone now," Xandra's voice said flatly. It seemed she was annoyed that they had missed this opportunity—however brief—to capture their winged visitor.

I heard the sound of the door opening again, and after a pause, it closed once more. "It seems that whoever is bothering us anticipated our decision," the priest's voice came over the line. His tone was no longer calm and self-assured; it now held a definitive note of uncertainty.

"How is that possible?" the skeptical male voice asked.

The priest sighed. "I don't know, Jack." There was a pause, and then the priest said, "This note is written by a different hand than the one that sent the necklace. We are dealing with more than one summoner here."

Murmurs arose, but quieted a moment later. "This second note says that if Xandra does not comply with the terms outlined in the first, there will be more casualties. They mean to take us out one by one, until they get their way." The priest sounded weary, and perhaps, even frightened. *Good.*

"Why do they want me?" Xandra asked of no one in particular.

"That's the mystery, isn't it?" the voice belonging to Kent asked quietly.

I looked up at Zy'driks, who was smiling grimly, pleased at what he had heard. "She won't do it, not yet, anyway," I stated. "We need to meet with everyone and decide our next move. Xan isn't going to come around easily, and she won't simply do as we ask until she is left with no other choice. You can stay here and listen to more of their pointless debate, but I have heard enough already."

As I turned to leave, Zy'driks put a hand on my shoulder. "Ji'anne, are you sure?"

I nodded. "It may have been a few years since I last saw her, but she is still my sister, after all. We're twins, Zy'driks. I know how she thinks."

"Let's see if we can make it *seem* like you go in alone," one of the hunters said over the phone, "but we'll all be right behind you. That way, they think you're doing as asked, but you aren't. It'll be an ambush."

"Yeah, okay," I heard Xandra agree. "Let's plan on something like that."

"See?" I asked Zy'driks. "She's predictable, to a fault."

# 31

# MISCALCULATION

We arranged a meeting with everyone the next day. With the hunters thrown into near-panic regarding our demands of Xandra, the trackers had been busier than ever with the task of maintaining our surveillance. Il'zaks had set the time for the meeting—four am—which was disagreeable to almost everyone involved, though his reasoning could not be held at fault; the hunters generally were asleep at that time, giving us a brief window of opportunity to speak as a group.

I was not particularly coherent at such an early hour, so I allowed Il'zaks and Zy'driks to take the reins for the meeting. I would give my input when it was needed, but no more.

Il'zaks began by stating that the meeting would not run long; he realized that several of the trackers had been busy throughout the night, tracing the hunters' movements.

"We don't have a plan, yet," Zy'driks admitted next, "but we do know that we must be prepared for Thursday, the scheduled meeting time with Xandra." He paused, and then added, "We called this meeting to get some ideas flowing. We need to throw them further into disarray."

"I'm in favor of trying to convince her—just one more time—to meet with me alone," I said, stifling a yawn at the end of my statement. "If she ignores the request a second time, it will be her own fault if something—" I paused, searching for the appropriate word—"*unpleasant* happens to one of the hunters."

"I think that would be an appropriate course of action," Il'zaks agreed.

"Perhaps if we have our prisoner ask her to come alone, she might listen?" Zy'driks mused. "Maybe I'll pay him a visit this morning." He smiled in grim anticipation.

"You are *not* to force him into doing *anything*, Zy'driks," I replied forcefully, causing his smile to falter. "I made a promise to him that I wouldn't allow you inside of his head again, and I mean to keep it. We are *not* going to stoop to their level, if we can help it."

Zy'driks nodded. "I understand. I can be very persuasive."

I sighed, uncertain of what he implied, but not thrilled with the images it conjured in my mind. I made a mental note to speak to him after the meeting had concluded.

"We can have Thad write her a note," Aaron suggested. "I know she'll recognize his handwriting."

"That's a good idea," I replied, shooting Zy'driks a meaningful glance, which he appeared to ignore.

"And what shall we do if she doesn't accept the offer a second time?" Carmine asked. "From what I have seen of this Xandra, I don't believe she will comply with our terms easily. It's a shame she's on their side."

I frowned in annoyance; I did not need a reminder of the damage Xandra had inflicted already. If only she weren't a hunter, things could have turned out much differently. Ke'tai might still be here. I sighed, fighting back the threatening tears. Would his loss ever become any easier to bear?

"I think if she does not agree to meet us, we should decide which of the hunters to go after next." It took me a moment to refocus and realize that it was Xen'din who had spoken. "We cannot go easy on her, not if we want her to do what *we* want. She's headstrong and stubborn."

Konrad stepped forward a pace from his post against the opposite wall. "I think the women should be next," he said brokenly in his German accent. "I see them…They protected by the men. We take them, and the men will go crazy."

"I think the German's on to something here," Aaron replied. "Aria's married to Jack, and he *is* very protective of her. If she suddenly disappears, it could very well play right into our schemes. I mean—"

"He means that Jack will go ballistic and get reckless," Carmine replied with a knowing smirk. "But Konrad said 'women', meaning both Aria and Mina, I believe."

Konrad nodded, but did not elaborate.

"Okay then," I said. "We will have Thad write another note to Xandra. If she agrees, we will meet her; if not, we'll take out Aria and Mina at the same time. We will need surveillance on Xandra, of course, but also on the other two women. Constant surveillance, if you all can manage it."

Most of the trackers nodded, and Marek said, "We'll get it done," speaking for the group.

"Good, now that all of this is settled, let's get to work," Zy'driks said eagerly, turning to head down the hallway to Thad's room. I had to move quickly to catch up to him.

"Zy'driks, wait," I said softly as I headed him off at the end of the hall.

As he turned to face me, I noticed he looked rather grim. "I will not delve into his head a second time, Ji'anne. I told you that."

"I know," I replied, not sure how to explain to him what I was thinking. "I trust you, it's just..."

"What is it?" he asked, his look becoming more concerned.

"Can I be there?"

He smiled wearily. "Of course, you can. You don't have to ask."

He sighed, running one hand through his hair, before he looked down at his feet. He appeared uncomfortable, which was so uncharacteristic that I couldn't help but ask what was bothering him.

Again, I received that weary smile. "I wish I could explain it to you, Ji'anne, but I don't think the timing is right. Perhaps when all of this is over..." He sighed again, leaving the statement unfinished. He did not speak again for several long moments. "Let's get this done, shall we?"

I frowned, confounded by his behavior. This was unlike him, and I knew he would have mentioned if something outside of our operation in Seattle were bothering him. Was it something here? Or someone? Surely, I would have picked up on that by now.

Zy'driks paused outside of Thad's room to unlock the door. Our prisoner lay curled in one corner of the room, his hands cuffed behind him, snoring softly. I flicked on the light switch as soon as the door had been closed again, while Zy'driks stood over the sleeping man, shaking him slightly in order to rouse him.

Thad opened his eyes slowly, blinking at the light as he tried to focus. "God *damn*, it doesn't feel like its morning yet," he mumbled. "What the hell do you want?" As his eyes came into focus and he realized who it was that was standing over him, he sat up suddenly and backed against the wall.

"Get the fuck away from me," he growled, his eyes darting about the room as though he were looking for some means of escape.

Zy'driks laughed humorlessly. "I'm not here to tamper with your mind again," he replied dryly, "although it would make our mission here so much simpler if I were allowed." He glanced over one shoulder at me, and winked once as though to reassure me he wasn't going to do anything that went against my wishes. "I'm just here to ask a favor of you, Thad."

"Fuck you," Thad practically spat, his legs working as though he were trying to back himself through the wall. "There is no way in hell that I'd do anything for you. Not after what you've done to me."

"You really ought to at least hear him out," I stated. "If you don't, there's a very good chance that Xandra will die." It was a lie, but one that I knew Thad would believe—one that would force him to comply with Zy'driks' request. I felt terrible, using his feelings for my sister to my own advantage, but I knew it was the only way to get this difficult man to cooperate.

His gaze flicked to me for the briefest of instants before returning to glare up at the elder summoner. "If I do what you want me to, will Xan be spared?"

Zy'driks nodded. "She will not come to any harm if you just do as I ask." He paused a moment, feigning thoughtfulness—I had to admit that Zy'driks could be quite the actor when he wanted to be—before stating, "You are actually very lucky that the lady is here to oversee this operation. If she weren't, I'd never have let go of the hold I had on your mind."

Thad's jaw clenched in anger, but he made no reply.

"What I ask of you is simple," Zy'driks continued. "I want you to write a message to your dear Xandra, asking her to comply with our wishes and to meet with the lady here alone. I promise that if she does this, she will not come to any harm, and neither will any of your other pitiful friends. But she *must* come *alone*."

Thad was unable to hide his skepticism. "Why do you want her alone?" he demanded, his gaze returning to meet mine. "Why is she so important to you?"

"I don't need to explain my motives to you," I replied as icily as I could. "Just do as he asks, or more of your friends will die." I whirled around and stalked from the room. Zy'driks should have no trouble getting our prisoner to write the message. Once he had, it would be a simple enough task to have it delivered directly to Xandra.

Word came to us from Vance shortly after noon that the hunters were gathering for another meeting. I realized that this was the perfect opportunity to leave Thad's message to Xandra. Not only would she be surrounded by the hunters when it arrived, but they would be in their headquarters, which were bugged. Everything that was said would be overheard.

Vance and Miranda were manning the surveillance station across the street from the hunters' hideout that afternoon. When word came to Xen'din from Vance that they were beginning to gather, Il'zaks, Zy'driks and I gathered around Xen'din's phone as he placed it on speaker.

Xen'din had been active for most of the day since our early morning meeting, and he was looking better than he had been for some time. I was glad that he was beginning to overcome the painful loss he had endured.

"Okay, I think the last of them just went inside," Miranda's voice came to us from the other end of the line. "We've got the mics on."

The hunters seemed to have gathered to discuss their options regarding a search for Thad. *How ironic*, I thought.

As they began their meeting, I summoned a nightwing, handed it the message from Thad, and sent it on its way. It would drop the note just outside of their door, and I would dismiss it once its task was complete. There was no reason to take unnecessary risks with this group—we had lost enough at their hands already.

The hunters' conversation was dull, and contained nothing of value to us. They went on for some time, but the conversation quickly died when my nightwing arrived with its note. They seemed to have sensed it outside their door, but it had vanished before they ventured to open it.

"Another message," I heard the man named Kent say after a long, breathless silence. "The envelope says it's for Xan."

I heard my sister grumble something in irritation before the sound of tearing paper could be heard over the speakers. This was followed by another lengthy silence.

"It's…it's from Thad." Xandra sounded stunned. "That means he really is alive. He's…a prisoner, it says. But…" She trailed off, sounding confused.

"What is it?" the priest asked.

"He says that they're giving me an option," she continued in a wavering tone. "Either I meet with their leader, alone, as they requested before, or someone else is going to die."

"Xan, you can't," Kent said immediately. "They're just trying to scare us."

"How do we know that for sure?" One of the other women asked, her tone sounding fearful. "What if they are serious, and someone else does end up dead?"

"Listen to yourself, Aria," one of the other men said in frustration. "We got into this business to rid the world of evil, and you want to send one of your own in alone! You're worried someone else will die, but what if that someone happens to be Xan?"

"Damn it, Jack, why are you always so insensitive?" Aria demanded.

"Guys, please, this isn't the time to fight," came the other woman's voice—Mina, I recalled. "We have to figure out something…"

"I believe the last time we met, we decided to make it *appear* like Xan goes to meet them alone," Kent reminded them. "Why don't we stick with that plan? She won't really be alone—at least one of us will also go with her. We'll just have to be…stealthy."

"Okay, who will be going then?" the priest asked. "Any volunteers?"

"I'll go," Kent replied, predictably, given his obvious affection toward Xandra.

"I will, too," Jack stated, though not without some protest from his wife, whom he apparently ignored.

"That's settled then." The priest sounded less than confident in their plan, but did not say anything more on the subject besides, "The three of you can figure out what exactly you want to do." There was a tired sigh, and then the priest said, "You all know it's Tuesday, and I have a Bible study group to lead this afternoon. I need be off."

I looked away from the phone at this point, lifting my gaze to meet that of Zy'driks. "I say if those two are going to go with Xan, then we go after the two women for sure."

Zy'driks merely nodded, but Il'zaks said, "Yes, I think that would be the best way to go about it. We can capture them—hopefully they are not together, because that will make our job harder—and then bring them back here, as prisoners."

"Well, I guess I'd best leave that response they wanted up where we left Thad," Xandra's voice said wearily on the other end of the line.

There was some rustling, and then the sound of the door opening and closing. Silence ensued.

"Konrad and Vance have been tracking Mina primarily," I said, trying to gather my thoughts into a coherent plan. "And Levi, Kendrick, and Trey have been monitoring Jack and Aria. We need to get them back here. I want to go over everything they know, to get an idea of where they'll be while Xan and the two men are preoccupied elsewhere."

"Ji'anne, wait a sec," Xen'din broke in. "Xan doesn't know what time to meet you yet—you said in that earlier message that you would give her a time once she agreed to meet with you."

I frowned. I had forgotten about that little detail.

"Perhaps we gather the trackers first, and determine then what would be the best time to schedule this meeting," Il'zaks suggested.

Zy'driks nodded thoughtfully. "We'll find a time when Aria and Mina are the most vulnerable. It'll be easier to deal with them then."

Forty minutes later, the five trackers in question had gathered at our hideout. It was decided that we would schedule the decoy meeting at nine o'clock in the evening; Mina was taking night courses at a community college, and had to walk across the campus during that time, while Aria was generally at home watching television. If Jack was away, Aria was vulnerable at any time of the day—she seemed almost completely dependent upon him, and had little confidence in her own skills as a hunter.

Il'zaks took a turn sending a nightwing to drop off our response; it would pick up the note Xandra had left for us in return. The hunters had vacated the premises after Xandra had departed.

Everything was finally coming together into a cohesive plan. I was pleased with the results so far, and was feeling confident. It was now a matter of waiting for Thursday to arrive. We would continue our vigilance in monitoring the hunters' movements, but for the next two days, we could take some time to rest and relax.

We were poised for our strike by the time Thursday morning dawned. Marek and Aaron, accompanied by Il'zaks and Xen'din, would stake out the residence of Jack and Aria Swift, and make their move upon Aria when the timing seemed appropriate.

Zy'driks and I would remain at the hideout; we planned to send demons to pick up Mina as she made her way across the poorly-lit college campus that evening. If anything should go wrong with our plans, Konrad, Jake, and Trey would be monitoring Mina's progress across the campus after she had finished her class. If she somehow managed to take out both demons, the three trackers would be nearby to complete the job.

Vance, Kendrick, and Carmine were tasked to follow Xandra—and likely Kent and Jack as well, since they had refused to allow her to go to our meeting alone. As she moved toward the nonexistent pre-arranged meeting place, Carmine intended to approach her with a handwritten message from me. This left Levi to watch the hunters' headquarters alone, while Miranda would remain at our hideout to prepare another of the rooms for the two women we intended to capture that evening.

At just after six o'clock that evening, the trackers, Il'zaks, and Xen'din departed our hiding place to travel to their respective destinations. Aaron had come up with the idea of acting as a lost pizza delivery man in order to confuse Aria; his plan was to knock on her front door and act as though he were attempting a delivery. Earlier that day, he and Konrad had left and come back with the necessary outfit, apparently from a nearby second-hand clothing store. I had given him my approval—if we could apprehend Aria without attracting any notice from her neighbors, all the better.

The plan with Mina would not be so simple. Zy'driks and I had decided to abduct her using a pair of shadow demons. Being the newest member of the hunters' team, and one of their weakest when it came to her sensing ability, we felt we could snatch her from the air before she realized she was in any danger. Konrad had objected mightily to this plan. As a compromise, we opted to have him and the two other men nearby in case something went wrong with our initial scheme. I was confident that it would go through smoothly, however.

As the trackers left and the house fell into relative silence, I was unable to sit still knowing what I was required to do next. It was exciting to be upon the precipice of action, but it was also a bit terrifying. If anything were to go wrong, I risked finding myself in a state of near-constant pain similar to that which Xen'din had endured, or worse. I attempted to block out those thoughts by focusing on our goals. The nervous energy coursing through me would not abate, and eventually, Zy'driks lost his patience.

"Ji'anne, sit the hell down before you drive me crazy!" he snapped.

I stopped in mid-stride and glanced down at my watch. It wasn't even seven o'clock. With a sigh, I sat down where I was; he was right. Pacing would not make the time go by any faster.

He chuckled briefly, and then strode toward me to join me in the middle of the floor. As he made eye contact, I could see there was some level of amusement twinkling in his eyes.

"Ji'anne, I know how you are feeling," he said slowly, never taking his gaze from mine. "I was there once—we all were there once. This is the first major operation you have been involved in, and it's exciting—but I sense you are perhaps a tad bit worried about the outcome as well."

I bit my lower lip before nodding.

He smiled in a knowing sort of way. "That's typical, and that is why I wanted to be with you tonight. Il'zaks has a lot of experience, but he's still got quite a few years to catch up with me. I wanted to be here to help you—to get you through this without any major hiccups. What I need you to do now is to try and relax. If you don't, you'll have a harder time concentrating when the time comes for our strike—and you will probably need every ounce of concentration you can muster." He paused a moment before continuing. "I know how strong you are as a summoner, but even the most powerful summoners sometimes make critical mistakes when under pressure."

"Like what?" I asked without thinking.

A wry smile surfaced on the Elder's face. "I'll give you one example. Perhaps it will open your eyes a bit as to why I dislike certain people."

I raised an eyebrow. "Do you mean Te'chok?" I asked.

Again, he chuckled. "Yes, Te'chok. I was trying to be subtle, there, but you always see right through that." He smiled genuinely this time. "I was working with Te'chok quite a few years ago on a project—and by quite a few years, I mean that it was not all that long after he became a summoner. We were in Germany at the time; that is where the headquarters used to be, just outside Hamburg. Anyway, there were a pair of hunters that kept crossing into our perimeter. They knew about us, just as most of the hunters here in the States know that Boston is our city right now, and they know to stay away. But this pair didn't care if they crossed into our territory, and they started to cause us some trouble there. We lost several apprentices to them, but Te'chok was afraid to confront them. Finally, the Elders convened and told him that something must be done, that he couldn't hide from them any longer."

"What did he do?" I asked, fascinated by his story.

"Well, you know how Te'chok is," Zy'driks replied with a shrug. "He tried to dodge the fight and find a way around it. He issued orders for the headquarters to be moved—that is when we established our foothold in Boston. The Elders decided that I would stay in Hamburg with Te'chok to make sure he did not leave before his appointed time, because we felt there was a very good chance that he would bolt at the first opportunity. That is how I came into this story.

"Two nights before we were supposed to leave, that pair of hunters again crossed our borders. I told Te'chok that we had to act. As I'm sure you can imagine, he was very reluctant, but confronted with the orders issued from the Board of Elders, he was forced to make his move. He was a nervous wreck while we were trying to plan—or rather, while *I* was trying to plan—and he would not settle down.

"We decided to send a shadow demon and a dragon—I told him we ought to use two shadow demons because they would attract less notice than a dragon, but he has always been stubborn and chose to send his dragon anyway. The hunters sensed the dragon well before they could see it, and they were ready for a fight. Te'chok, however, was not prepared at all, and he lost his dragon that night."

My eyes widened in shock. "I can't imagine what that would be like," I said, my voice barely a whisper in the quiet room.

Zy'driks shrugged, as though the young Te'chok ought to have known better. "He was unbearable to be around, to be honest. Screaming constantly, weeping, unable to function for almost a month. Your friend Xen'din handled his loss much more gracefully, if such a thing can be called graceful." He chuckled briefly before continuing. "I told Te'chok that night that it was his own damned fault that he'd lost his dragon. He should have listened to me—I did not make it to Elder status by being reckless. Of course, he doesn't take criticism well either, as I'm sure you have noticed."

I nodded, recalling several instances when Te'chok had become angry and defensive when the least of his actions were called into question.

"That night was the beginning of our long dislike for one another," Zy'driks commented. "He is weak, and I never felt that he did the Order justice as its leader. I continued to hope for the day when his replacement would arrive—it just took quite a bit longer than I would have wished." He smiled amiably at me. "So far, I think you have done very well, Ji'anne. And I am grateful that you would sit through the long ramblings of an old man, and choose to learn from his advice."

I laughed; it was difficult to think of Zy'driks as being old. He typically dressed as though he were about to go on stage at a rock concert, and he acted so very much like he was a member of my own generation, rather than one that had long been forgotten, that I tended to forget his true age. He seemed much more modern than Il'zaks, but I knew that Zy'driks was far older.

"Why do you laugh?" he asked, mischief sparkling in his silver eyes.

I shrugged. "I just never thought of you as being old," I replied. "I mean, you don't *act* like you're old."

He grinned. "And that is how I keep my sanity, Ji'anne. I wear the body of a young person, but I am very, very old. One could even say that I am ancient. By attempting to fit in with the trends of each generation, I feel like I am better able to cope with the changes in society that happen as time marches on. Maybe you don't understand that yet, but I believe that one day you will."

I was uncertain of what to say. His words implied that he believed I would live to see the passage of as many years as he had. I wasn't sure that I wanted to. Perhaps if Ke'tai were still alive, my view would be different, but without him, the world had become a very dreary place. Did I truly want to spend so many years in a state of such profound gloom? Or would I simply become accustomed to the loss eventually, and move on? I had no answers to those questions.

Something in my expression must have alerted Zy'driks to my change in mood, because he said, "Ji'anne, times like these are always difficult, but you have to focus on the good times to keep yourself moving forward. Don't allow this to weigh you down forever."

I sighed, trying to hold myself together. I could not let thoughts of Ke'tai overwhelm me tonight; I had to focus in order to complete our job correctly the first time. I nodded once, swallowing the lump that was beginning to form in my throat, and glanced at my watch again. It was just after eight o'clock—we had been speaking for over an hour.

I glanced at Zy'driks, who nodded knowingly. "Yes, it is nearly time, but don't get overly excited on me and do something stupid. You handled Thad's kidnapping well enough, but that was easy compared to this. Thad was incapacitated. Mina will have some fight in her, and she will be able to sense something of the shadow demons as they approach. Tonight, we will see what you are truly made of, Ji'anne."

Zy'driks had an aura about him that spurred my determination to go on, one that kept me looking forward. I realized belatedly what an asset he had been to me during the past year. He had always been there when I needed someone to talk to—no matter what time of day or night it happened to be—and he had always provided guidance for me in difficult situations. I had been taking his help—and his friendship—for granted, I realized guiltily.

I looked up from the worn carpet to meet his gaze once more. "I think this is long overdue," I said, "but I want to thank you—for everything. I should have said something sooner..."

"Now is not the time to beat yourself up about a little detail like this," he replied briskly, "although your being grateful has not gone on deaf ears." He flashed a grin. "Let's get started—it's about that time."

Zy'driks rose to his feet and offered a hand to me, which I accepted with a smile. Once I was on my feet, he pulled his cell phone from one of his jeans pockets.

"I'm going to call Jake and get this thing started," he said to me as he pressed a button and held the phone between us as it began to ring on Jake's end of the line.

"Hey, Z," came Jake's amiable voice a moment later. "I thought you were going to call at eight."

"So, it's what? Eight-eighteen now?" Zy'driks asked with a laugh. "We were discussing some last-minute details, and I wanted that covered before we started. By the way, you're on speaker so Ji'anne can hear you."

"Are you in position?" I asked before Jake could say anything else. I wanted to focus on our business, and not become distracted by idle chat.

"Yeah, we've been here for just over an hour," he replied. "Mina went to class as usual. Trey and I are watching the doors she usually leaves from, and Konrad is at the other exit with the van, in case she goes that way."

"Good," Zy'driks replied, glancing down at his watch. "She is usually done with class at eight-fifty, correct?"

"Yeah," Jake affirmed.

"Alright, I want our demons to be there before then—maybe five minutes or so. It's going to take them about ten minutes to travel from where we are to where you are. They'll remain in the air until we have visual confirmation of Mina's location, and then we will strike. Got that?" Zy'driks asked, all business now.

"Roger," Jake replied. "I'll radio Konrad and let him know the details."

"Good. Stay on the line, so we can keep in the loop of what's happening on the ground," Zy'driks stated. "We have to time this perfectly."

"Got it, Z," Jake replied, and then there was some muffled talking on the other end of the line as Jake relayed the conversation to Trey.

"We have ten minutes then," I said as Zy'driks carefully placed the phone on the floor between us.

He nodded once. "We will need to summon the demons a few minutes before we send them out. I don't want to sound preachy, Ji'anne, but we have to let them know what our plans are, just as the trackers need to know. This really is the first time you have been in this sort of situation, and I want to make sure you're prepared for it."

I nodded impatiently, ready to be moving.

"Alright, good," he said after a moment's pause. "Go ahead and summon your shadow demon, and I'll summon mine."

I closed my eyes in order to concentrate, and began to dance. It had been quite some time since I had last called the shadow demon to me. In truth, I had not had the heart to do so since seeing Ke'tai's broken and battered, as it lay dying in Seattle's underground. I had always been afraid the memories would be too overwhelming, too painful to bear.

When the shadow demon came through to our plane, things were not what I had feared they would be. I could sense the creature's power, its desire to hunt, its somewhat savage nature barely restrained by the desire to please its summoner. I opened my eyes slowly to look upon it for the first time in well over a year. The pattern of pale scars on the gray-black flesh of its chest were just as I remembered them, though it seemed to have acquired a sturdier pair of armor-plated leggings than it had worn on its last summoning. Its crimson eyes were focused on mine, and I could sense it was eager for my commands.

Zy'driks' shadow demon was much shorter than my own, but what it lacked in height it made up for in bulk. It appeared much more muscular, and its crimson eyes glared with a defiance that could only have been born upon another world.

I drew my gaze back to my own demon, and began to feed it the information it would need to know about our plans for the evening. It seemed pleased to have been chosen for this task, and its untamed spirit lusted at the prospect of the upcoming hunt. Once I was certain that it understood Mina was not to be hurt or killed, and that it knew its role, I turned to face Zy'driks.

"Is he ready, Ji'anne?"

I nodded. "Yeah. So am I."

"Good. It's time to get this thing started." He picked up his phone, then strode to the sliding glass door at the back of the room. "Let's go."

I closed my eyes in order to focus more fully on my connection to the shadow demon as it made its way through the door and launched itself forcefully up into the night sky, trailing Zy'driks' demon by only a few feet. I could sense the cool, damp air as it rushed over and around the demon's head and shoulders, and I could see the city as it rushed by beneath the near-silent beat of its wings. A thin fog had settled over the city, making streetlights and headlights alike blur and cast halos as they failed to penetrate into the surrounding gloom.

As the demons neared the college campus, Jake's voice sounded once again over the phone. "I hope you aren't too far away, because it looks like class was let out a bit early this evening. No sign of our target yet, though."

"I can see you and Trey," I replied as the shadow demon halted overhead, its wings beating methodically to keep it airborne. The two trackers were seated on a plastic bench that served as a bus stop, in an attempt to appear inconspicuous.

"Is Z ready, too?"

"I am," Zy'driks replied.

I could see his shadow demon through my demon's eyes; it was keeping its place above the building's roof, about midway between the two doors. Mine was directly above the bench where Trey and Jake were sitting. A few students at a time were trickling out of the building, singly or in pairs for the most part, chatting and blissfully oblivious to the two creatures that hovered overhead waiting for one of their comrades to appear.

I heard the radio Trey carried crackle, both through the demon's ears and over the phone. "She came out this way!" Konrad's German-accented voice called out in excitement. "She is looking around—I think she knows we are here!"

I focused my energies upon the shadow demon's actions, guiding it quickly to the other end of the building just behind Zy'driks' demon. As it glided almost noiselessly over the edge of the building, Mina came into view, her face upturned as she scanned the sky. It appeared as though she were trying to perceive shapes through the fog. She was alone, and it seemed the rest of her classmates had exited through the other door. The sidewalk and the street beyond her were empty.

"Hold up a moment, Ji'anne," Zy'driks' voice came to me, as though from far away. My senses were almost completely joined to the demon's as I continued to concentrate on the task at hand.

I nodded, acknowledging his statement, and withdrawing my focus only slightly from the shadow demon. I needed to hear what he had to say.

"We must execute this perfectly," he said quietly. "I will count to three; on three, we will both strike. Ready?"

Again, I nodded.

"One…"

I returned my focus fully to the demon, anticipating the count.

"Two…"

Zy'driks' voice sounded much farther away now, and had taken on an almost dream-like quality while I was in this other state. The shadow demon was poised to strike, every muscle tensed with excitement and anticipation. Its gaze focused upon Mina, alone on the damp sidewalk below, as she moved slowly away from the building, glancing over her shoulder and up into the foggy night sky.

"Three!"

The demon flew faster than I had realized it was capable of, its wings folded back to streamline its descent. Less than an arms' length away, Zy'driks' demon did the same, the pair rocketing out of the fog toward our target. Mina turned around, her dark eyes wide with surprise and terror as the demons suddenly broke through the gloom and became visible. She was only a few yards away, and began to sprint along the sidewalk, the backpack she wore bouncing from side to side with each step, threatening to throw her off balance. She ran in a straight line, and chose not to glance behind her. She was quick, but the shadow demons were quicker.

My shadow demon was upon her first, snatching her up from the sidewalk and wrapping its muscular arms about her torso, pinning her arms. She flailed her legs in a futile attempt to break free, screaming and sobbing as the demon soared higher into the night sky with its quarry. Zy'driks' demon kept pace with mine as they flew back toward our hideout.

I relinquished some of my hold on the demon, withdrawing into the reality of the rental house. Zy'driks had picked up the phone and was rapidly talking to Jake on the other end of the line. It seemed as though the trackers had made their way to Konrad and the van, and were leaving the college campus. Zy'driks was beaming, pleased at how smoothly our operation had gone.

The two demons arrived some time before the trackers returned; they entered through the sliding glass patio door they had taken off from. Mina had long since given up trying to fight the much stronger demon that held her, and had gone limp in its arms while sobs wracked her thin frame. I told the demon to keep a firm grip until our other trackers arrived, while Zy'driks dismissed his own shadow demon. Miranda appeared from the hallway at about the same time, standing alert with her right palm resting on the butt of her gun, her unwavering gaze leveled at the hunter in our midst.

It was several minutes before Mina mustered enough courage to look upon her new surroundings. When her eyes fell upon Zy'driks and I, she began to sob anew. "What do you want with me?" she moaned. "I didn't do anything…"

Zy'driks chuckled mirthlessly. "None of you ever say anything different," he replied dismissively, turning to face Miranda. "Is the room ready?"

She nodded, but did not take her eyes from Mina. "It has been for a while, now. I moved the gear we had stored inside to the room at the end of the hall."

I watched our new prisoner carefully as she hung limply in the shadow demon's grip. She appeared young—nineteen, maybe—and there was no mistaking that she was terrified. This was probably her first real experience with a demon or a summoner; I recalled she had been recruited by Thad's group not long before the events leading up to Ke'tai's death had occurred, and that she had not been a part of them. I sensed that Mina was convinced her first experience with us would be her last.

"As long as you cooperate, we aren't going to hurt you," I said quietly, moving closer to where my demon held the girl. "We aren't monsters, you know."

Mina's gaze rose to meet mine, and for one brief instant, I could see the desperate hope that she clung to, reflected in her eyes; hope that what I said might be true. That instant was shattered by the front door banging open as Konrad, followed by Trey and Jake, filed inside.

"Excellent," Zy'driks said, beaming at the trio of trackers. "Let's get our newest acquisition to her living arrangements, shall we?"

Konrad and Jake relieved the demon of Mina, Konrad holding her arms while Jake locked cuffs around her thin wrists. Her eyes rolled toward me, filled with fear and uncertainty; I merely nodded, hoping it would encourage her to cooperate. She hung her head, but allowed the two men to escort her down the hallway and out of sight. With a relieved sigh, I dismissed the shadow demon.

Zy'driks turned toward me, beaming. "That went perfectly," he said. "There were so many things that could have gone differently, but they did not. I think you have definitively proven yourself to the Order tonight, Ji'anne."

I smiled; it was nice to hear praise for a job well done. "I think—"

I was cut off by the sound of my phone ringing where it rested on the kitchen counter. I jogged into the other room, and as I picked it up, I saw that it was Xen'din calling. I hoped their hunt had gone as well as ours had.

"Ji'anne, hi," Xen'din said rapidly, and a touch breathlessly. "We have a bit of a problem, I think."

Just as with our own mission, theirs could have had a thousand things go amiss. I hoped for all our sakes that it was something that could easily be remedied. "What happened?"

"Aria suspected Aaron's pizza man ploy from the start," he explained. "Thankfully, Marek thought to go around the back side of their house just in case. As soon as she opened the door and saw Aaron, she bolted. Marek caught her, but she managed to get away—" He paused, and there was some conversation in the background. I could hear Marek's voice, and that of Il'zaks as well.

"What happened?" I asked again, more firmly this time.

"Um, sorry," he replied quickly. "When she escaped, she climbed to the top of their backyard fence, but she fell going down the other side. There's a steep slope behind the fence that borders a pretty major street. She was laying on the side of the road the last he was able to see."

"And you left her there?" I demanded.

"We had to," he explained. "Jack came home about then and we had to abort in a hurry."

I sighed, disappointed and frustrated. "Okay, just hurry back. If he follows you here, it's not going to be pretty." I punched the button to disconnect the call before he could say anything more.

Zy'driks approached slowly, concern marring his handsome features. "Ji'anne, tell me what happened," he said slowly. "Whatever it was, we can overcome it."

I felt my annoyance and frustration melt away with his words. He was right; he was always right. We *could* overcome this. As calmly as I could manage, I explained to him what had transpired with Aria.

He frowned in thought, and ran one hand through his hair. "Well, this could definitely go either way. Depending on the level of her injuries, and how long it takes Jack—or someone else—to find her, she could either recover or she could die. If Jack suspects we have anything to do with this…" He trailed off with a shake of his head.

"He's hot-headed, just like Xan is," I replied. "He'd probably do something pretty reckless."

Zy'driks shrugged. "We can't count on the probably's, Ji'anne. All we can do is wait, see what happens, and then we act accordingly."

I nodded. "Once everyone is back here, we ought to send a couple of the trackers to monitor Jack."

"I'll go right now," Miranda offered from the other end of the empty living room. I had forgotten she was there.

I nodded. "Go ahead, then. Just be careful—he'll be watching everything a little more closely from now on. We'll send someone else to join you in a little while."

She nodded once, and disappeared through the front door into the foggy night. I turned back to face Zy'driks, whose eyes had never left my face during the whole exchange with Miranda.

"You are coming into your role as leader very nicely," he said softly after a long moment of silence. "We have needed someone like you for a long time, Ji'anne."

I shrugged, suddenly uncomfortable, and looked away. "I'm just doing what needs to be done," I mumbled.

The phone rang again—Zy'driks' this time—breaking the heavy curtain of silence that had fallen once again between us. Digging the phone from his pocket once more, he glanced at the screen and said, "It's Carmine. I'll put her on speaker."

"Hello, Zy'driks," she said, sounding casual. "Is our fearless leader there also?"

"I'm here, Carmine," I replied, doing my best to ignore the jab in her words.

"Okay, then, I can get to business. Everything went just like we had planned. You should have seen the look on that bitch's face though! Disappointment is an understatement. She was hoping to take you out and down tonight, and was not happy to only get a letter." Carmine broke into one of her harsh, dry laughs. "How did things go otherwise?"

"We brought Mina in without any trouble," Zy'driks replied quickly, glancing at me warily. I could see he feared I would take offense to Carmine's attitude and begin an unnecessary argument, as had happened more than a few times in the past. "Aria was injured, and the group had to bail...We'll discuss this some more once everyone is back at the hideout."

"So, our fearless leader is more than just talk," Carmine said, this time with a little more respect in her tone. "Glad to hear it. I should be there in about ten." There was a click as the call was disconnected.

Zy'driks shook his head, seemingly amused by something. "I do not know how Il'zaks puts up with her most of the time," he said to himself.

"Ugh, I don't either," I replied. "She grates on my nerves something awful."

Zy'driks chuckled, and nodded knowingly. "I've noticed. At least our plans regarding Xandra were carried out as expected, and we brought in Mina without any trouble. This evening was a success, if you overlook our little miscalculation with Aria. We should know how serious that will prove to be within a few hours."

# 32

# JACK

After a relatively brief rundown of the successes and failures of the night's proceedings, I was finally able to get some much-needed sleep, if only for a few hours. It was still very dark outside the thinly curtained windows when Zy'driks had gently roused me from my slumber. He said not a word until we had moved some distance down the hall.

"Levi just arrived," he said in a hushed whisper. "He followed the other hunters from their hideout to a hospital after the priest got a phone call—we are pretty sure it was from Jack."

I nodded, rubbing the residual sleep from my eyes. "Have you talked to Levi yet about anything besides that?"

Zy'driks shook his head. "I thought you ought to be there to hear what he has to say first."

I nodded groggily, and followed him out of the hallway toward the kitchen, where I could see Levi leaning against the counter near the fridge. There was an unopened can of German beer Konrad had picked up on the countertop beside him. Konrad was also in the kitchen, standing opposite Levi, a can of his own in hand. As usual, Konrad appeared to be in good spirits, grinning and chatting in spite of the early hour. Levi was much more subdued than his counterpart.

I ran my hands through my hair quickly, in an attempt to make myself look somewhat presentable after having just been awakened. Zy'driks chuckled in amusement beside me.

"It looks fine, Ji'anne," he whispered as we neared the kitchen. "You have nothing to worry about when it comes to your looks, believe me."

I turned towards him, at once surprised at his statement, but also uncertain of what he was trying to imply. Was he just being nice, or was he flirting with me? I hoped it was the former, because I was not willing to tolerate the latter. His comment reminded me of Ke'tai, of how much I missed him. I focused my gaze upon Levi then, doing my best to ignore Zy'driks and whatever his intentions might have been.

"I hear you have some news about the hunters," I said as I stepped into the kitchen.

Levi nodded. "Most of them went to Swedish Medical Center all of the sudden," he replied. "They got a phone call—we think it must have been from Jack."

"And?" I pressed. This was nothing new; Zy'driks had already given me as many details in a shorter span of time; I was not feeling very patient, having been awakened at such an early hour.

"I did some checking around after they got there," Levi continued. "Aria's there, and it sounds like she is in pretty bad shape. When she took that tumble over the fence, I guess one of the cars on the freeway must have hit her, but the driver took off."

Behind me, Zy'driks swore under his breath. "Perfect. Now they'll think we were responsible for that, too."

Levi nodded in affirmation. "Yeah. And Jack is super pissed off. I think he's planning something, because the priest kept trying to talk to him, like he was trying to change his mind. I don't know for sure—I was just spying on them through the window of the hospital. I didn't want to get too close."

"We need to keep an eye on Jack at all times," I said after pausing for a moment to think the situation over. I met Konrad's gaze. "I know you were busy with Mina's capture earlier tonight, but would you mind checking on Jack for a while?"

Konrad grinned, and downed the remaining contents of his beer can. "I thought you would never ask," he replied. "I got sleep in the afternoon; I can go for a while longer."

"Thank you," I said to him as he brushed past Zy'driks and I on his way to the front door.

"I'll wake one of the others also," Zy'driks said quietly. "We ought to have one at the hospital, and one at Jack's house, just to be safe. We know he has a history of trying to take matters into his own hands, so we need to be very careful."

I nodded without turning to face him, and waited until I heard his footsteps retreating to turn away from Levi. Things were becoming complicated, and it was poor timing. We were in the midst of a very major operation, and I wanted to devote all of my attention to it. I did not want to become distracted by the potential attraction Zy'driks seemed to suddenly have for me. He was a good friend, and had become a sort of mentor for me since I had become the head of the Order, but I was no longer certain about my own feelings toward him. I wanted to believe his earlier comment had been nothing more than a harmless remark as he attempted to bolster my self-confidence, but I could not be certain.

I leaned against the wall with my eyes closed, taking the brief period of silence provided me to simply think. My thoughts focused upon Ke'tai, and how much I missed him. I wondered—not for the first time—if I would ever meet someone who could even partially fill the void that had been left within me after his death. I had been lonely, but I was determined to ignore it as I pursued Xandra. As I thought over Zy'driks' comment, I began to realize that it was not the first time he had said or done something that could be interpreted as suggestive. I could not be certain what his intentions truly were.

Footsteps from the hallway jarred me away from my thoughts, and as I opened my eyes, I saw Zy'driks striding into the living room. His eyes were focused upon me, and he smiled faintly. Behind him were Xen'din and Miranda, both struggling to awaken.

"Miranda will be leaving to monitor Jack," Zy'driks said as he moved toward me. "I told her to call Konrad and take whichever position he does not. She will call me once there."

I merely nodded, glancing behind the Elder as Miranda exited the house. Xen'din walked over, stifling a yawn, and stood next to Zy'driks.

"What time is it anyway?" Xen'din asked, shaking his head and blinking in an attempt to clear the residual sleep from his brain.

I shrugged. "I don't know, but it's early."

"I was thinking about this whole thing with Xan," Xen'din said slowly. "We ought to try and get her to meet you again, alone this time. After what happened to Aria, she might actually listen."

"We will have to plan this very carefully," Zy'driks replied with a slight frown. "Jack is unstable—and we must keep an eye on him."

"I understand that," Xen'din said, "but what I'm trying to say is that it might just be the perfect time to do it. Xan will be shaken up, and she's always more vulnerable than she'll let on when she's scared. She'll be easier to convince right now, than she will be in a couple days, after she's had some time to process the situation. I'm not saying we need to schedule the meeting for today or anything, but I think we ought to try and convince her to meet."

Zy'driks appeared thoughtful, although I sensed he still wanted to disagree. I took the opportunity to give them my opinion.

"Xen'din is right. She will be more vulnerable right now, and much easier to convince. Once we are able to get her to commit to meeting alone, she'll follow through with it—she's incredibly stubborn, and won't let any of the others try to sway her. We just have to convince her to make the decision."

Zy'driks sighed, and then nodded slowly. "Alright, we'll do that then. You both know her better than anyone else does. Perhaps we convince Mina to write her a note this time? It may work better if they know she's okay—and if they know that both she and Thad are our prisoners. It'll give us a bit more leverage."

I nodded. "That sounds like a good plan to me. We can go in and speak with her in a little while, when it's not so damned early."

It was nearing seven o'clock when Miranda called to inform us of Jack's movements. He had spent the night at the hospital, never once leaving Aria's side, until her monitors began to go off and the doctors were forced to whisk her away for an emergency surgery. She had not yet regained consciousness, according to what Konrad had told Miranda, and Jack was in a foul mood.

While his wife was in surgery, Jack had taken a brief hiatus from the hospital to return home, where he began investigating what had happened. It quickly became clear that he felt we had been involved, but based upon Il'zaks' and Xen'din's account, he would find nothing at the scene that would point to us. Jack had not stayed at his home long before returning to the hospital. He was seen pacing through the surgical waiting room for much of the morning.

While Miranda was filling us in, Konrad returned to our hideout to get some rest, and Jake volunteered to take over for him. Vance had gone to spy on the hunters' hideout earlier in the day, and we had sent Carmine and

Marek to follow Xandra. None of the other trackers had called in to report anything. Miranda ended her call not long after, promising to report to us again if anything changed for Jack.

I motioned for Zy'driks to follow me, and led him to the door across the hallway from Thad's room. "We need to talk with Mina," I said. "Now is as good a time as any."

He nodded. "Call one of your demons first, if you insist on going in there unannounced by one of the trackers. I'm not about to allow you to get reckless at this stage of the game, Ji'anne."

I knew he was right, and once again I was glad to have him around. He was always there to remind me of the little things that I had a tendency to overlook. I closed my eyes and danced, calling forth the shadow demon once more.

"Good, I'll call a *djinn*," Zy'driks said. "Perhaps we can filter a bit more information out of her that way."

I sent the shadow demon into the room first, in order to restrain Mina should she decide to become violent or attempt to run. She did not fight the creature, but simply allowed it to grasp her wrists behind her in an act of tired submission. Once she was restrained, Zy'driks and I entered the room, his *djinn* floating in orb-form above his left shoulder.

"Mina, I need to ask something of you," I said as I closed the door behind me.

Her dark eyes were fearful and wary, like those of a wounded animal. She made no reply, but simply nodded in acknowledgement.

"I would like you to write a note to Xandra," I continued. "Ask her to meet me alone this time. We knew what you all were planning last night, and I am no fool. I will not meet with her when she has trigger-happy friends tagging along."

Mina bit her lower lip, her expression one of uncertainty. "If she meets with you, are you going to kill her?"

I frowned, but it was Zy'driks who answered. "Of course not. We are not savages, and we do not take someone's life unless our own is in danger."

"So Dirk—?" Mina began, cutting herself off by biting down on her lower lip once more.

Zy'driks sighed. "Dirk's death was unfortunate, and I would not wish to see another die by my hands. All we want is to talk with Xandra, nothing more."

Mina looked down, swallowing hard, and then nodded. "Okay, I'll do it."

"She must come alone," I repeated. "We will know if she decides to bring someone else along."

Zy'driks produced a small notepad and a pencil from one of his pockets, and offered it to Mina as I had the shadow demon release her right wrist. The demon kept her left in its iron grip; I wanted to take no chances with her. Zy'driks held the notepad while Mina scribbled down her note hurriedly. When she had finished, she handed the pencil back to Zy'driks, biting her lip again.

"Thank you, Mina," I said, taking the notepad from Zy'driks. "I will have one of the trackers bring you breakfast soon. If Xan agrees to our conditions, we will allow you to go free after the meeting."

Mina's eyes widened with surprise and a wild hope. "You mean, I'm not going to be kept here forever?"

Zy'driks chuckled as he made his way to the door. "Of course not. What would we do with someone like you?"

I had most of the morning to myself, which was unusual, but I was grateful; it gave me time to think. We were now very close to our goal, and although this realization excited me, I was also filled with a profound wave of dread. When we met with Xandra, any number of things might happen, very few of them good.

We had not received any additional news regarding Jack's movements—or his mental state—nor had we heard from the trackers that had been assigned to monitor the hunters' meeting place and Xandra. Zy'driks had sent a nightwing bearing Mina's note to Xandra shortly after we had finished speaking to her, but either Xandra had yet to look at the note, or she was preoccupied with other things and was putting off telling the other hunters about it. Carmine had reported in briefly around noon to say that Xandra was still at home, though they had no indication she had received Mina's letter.

To top it off, there was the matter of Zy'driks. I was still uncertain of his intentions; on the one hand, I felt he might be acting as he was simply out of friendship, but on the other hand, I had a hard time believing that friendship was all he had in mind. His behavior had not changed since my first encounter with him, just over eight years ago; in fact, he was very much the same. It was because of this that I remained uncertain. If he *did* have feelings for me that were more than mere friendship, they had been present all along and I had simply never realized it.

I thought again of Ke'tai. I had loved him with a passion I did not believe I would ever experience again, and I missed his presence terribly. I was lonely, and it had become exhausting being my own support structure, yet I was also afraid to make a commitment to someone else again. To risk experiencing such a painful loss a second time was something I was unwilling to pursue. As a summoner, the risk of such loss would be ever-present.

I found myself leaning against the trunk of one of the trees in the back yard, protected somewhat from the cold drizzle coming down by its thick branches, when my thoughts were interrupted. Il'zaks exited the house, moving quickly toward me in a business-like fashion. I knew immediately that something must have occurred. I pushed myself away from the tree as he approached, feeling weary.

"Xandra has convened a meeting at the hunters' headquarters," Il'zaks stated. "Carmine has just called to inform us of her movements. Xen'din is calling Vance so we can listen in on their conversation again." He paused, a brief frown crossing his usually placid features. "You have me worried, Ji'anne."

I shrugged, unwilling to talk about my feelings at present. "I'll be fine. Let's go inside."

Il'zaks did not argue, although he did not appear entirely convinced that I was "fine". We entered the living room together, and he slid the glass door closed behind us, brushing tiny droplets of water from his narrow shoulders as he did so. It had been raining harder than I had realized, and I wondered just how bedraggled I must appear.

Zy'driks had been facing away from the door as we entered, but he turned around quickly. He offered up a smile that was quickly replaced by a look of concern. He left Xen'din standing in the center of the room with several of the trackers and hurried toward us. I sighed; I did not wish to speak of my current state of mind.

"Ji'anne, how long were you out there?" he asked in a low voice. "You're completely soaked."

I shrugged. "I don't know, a while." I kept my gaze focused on the floor, afraid that my eyes might betray some of my own misgivings.

He sighed. "Why don't you go change into some dry clothes," he suggested. "I think we can handle things for a few minutes without you."

I raised my eyes to meet his, and was startled at the expression I saw there. It was one of concern, but also something more; his look reminded me so much of Ke'tai in that single moment that I felt my knees buckle and I was forced to look away in order to keep my composure. Ke'tai had given me that look countless times during my training as a summoner, and many times afterwards when I had done something reckless. Zy'driks' concern for me was genuine, and that was something I could no longer deny.

I nodded briskly and brushed past him, making my way toward the hallway and the duffel bag of clothing I had stashed in the single remaining bedroom.

"Ji'anne?" Zy'driks asked uncertainly from behind me.

I chose to ignore him and continued on down the hall. I heard rapid footsteps behind me, and I knew without having to turn around that he had followed me. I closed the door to the bedroom after noting it was empty, to allow myself a bit of privacy while I changed into dry clothing. When I had finished, I took a moment to run a brush through my hair—it provided me with a few more seconds in which to brace myself for what lay on the other side of the door.

He was leaning against the wall a few paces away, his arms crossed, that same concerned expression upon his face. I was torn; I wanted to be left alone with my misery, yet at the same time, I knew I needed someone that I could speak with openly. We were so close to completing our business with Xandra, but I felt as though each step I took closer to the goal became ever more painful. I was forced to rethink and relive that awful day when I had watched Ke'tai's life fade away, time and again. I knew in that moment that I could not do this alone; I needed Zy'driks' help, if I were to succeed. He had been a good friend to me, through my months of grief, but I continued to ponder his motives.

"Ji'anne, are you feeling alright?" he asked softly.

I shook my head. "I don't know. We should go—"

"Il'zaks and Xen'din can handle listening in on the hunters without us there," he replied gently, cutting me off. "I need to know if you are okay. This mission depends so much on you, Ji'anne."

I sighed. "I know. I'm okay. The thing that's been bothering me the last couple of days has nothing to do with the hunters…It's something else."

His gaze was unreadable, and he was silent for several long moments. His eyes never left mine. "You miss him, don't you?" he asked finally.

I managed a weary smile. "Yeah, I do. I feel very alone, Zy'driks. I know you and Il'zaks and Xen'din have all been here for me, but…it's just not the same." I sighed and looked away, unable to meet his gaze any longer.

He was silent for another lengthy period of time, and then he said, "I'll always be here for you, Ji'anne. Remember that."

Startled, I looked up to meet his gaze, but he had already turned around and was heading back toward the living room and the others. I sighed, following his lead, but lost in my own tangled web of thoughts.

As we entered the living room, it seemed that things had already wrapped up with the hunters. Xen'din extracted himself from the group of trackers and Il'zaks to fill us in on what had happened.

"Xan got Mina's letter," he said as he approached. He eyed me critically, and a frown manifested itself on his handsome face. "Ji'anne, is everything alright?"

I sighed in frustration and nodded impatiently for him to go on.

"Okay, we can talk later," he replied, still frowning. "Anyway, she's agreed to meet alone this time, and was going to leave a note for us in that same location as the last time. I think Kent is planning on tailing her, even though she was pretty emphatic about him staying behind." He looked down, sorrow filling his features now. "Kent cares for her…It's hard for me to sit here and listen to him talking to her." He sighed, running one hand through his hair.

I reached out to him, touching him lightly near his right elbow. "Xen'din, don't…Xan doesn't know you're still alive. Anything could happen when we meet…" I sighed, trying to put order to my thoughts. "Look, I'm going to need you for this meeting, and I need you to be strong.

Things might change for you…We have to meet her, and see what happens."

He looked up to meet my gaze, a tired expression on his face. "That's all I can do, I guess. I just wish I could force my heart to move on. I know nothing good is going to come of Xan and me."

"You don't know that," Zy'driks replied from beside me. "You won't know until you try. Don't give up now, when we need you the most."

Xen'din nodded, though he appeared doubtful. His gaze met mine again, and he said, "Would you care to talk now, Ji'anne? We can go somewhere a little more private…"

I sighed; he would not let up until he knew the reason for my melancholy. I shrugged in response, hoping that he would leave the matter be. Instead, he took me by the elbow and steered me toward the hallway, to the empty room at its end. Once there, he closed the door and sat down against the wall.

I remained standing several feet away from him. I crossed my arms; I did not want to have this conversation. I already knew what he would say to me in the end, and I did not want to hear it.

"Tell me what's been bothering you lately," he said, genuine concern in his tone. "I have a feeling it's not about your sister. I promise I won't tell anyone."

He had always been sincere, and it made it difficult for me to maintain my frustrated silence. I frowned, struggling with the decision to speak or to walk away. Finally, I decided it couldn't hurt me to finally say something; I knew he would keep his promise to me. Some part of me believed that talking might lessen my worry and improve my mood.

I walked toward him and sat down rather ungracefully upon the floor. "It's Zy'driks," I said softly. "I don't know what to do."

His eyes narrowed in thought. "What do you mean?" he asked. "The two of you seem to work very well together…"

I let out a bitter laugh. "Yeah, but that's not the problem."

"Then what is?"

I sighed, finding it hard to voice my concerns even after finally giving in to Xen'din's request to talk. "Well…I think he wants more from me than just friendship. I don't think I can do it."

Xen'din laughed softly. "Xan always did say you were oblivious to things like that, Ji'anne. He's had those feelings since the day he met you."

"What?!"

Xen'din laughed again, louder this time. "You heard me, Ji'anne. He and I talked for a while on the day you became Lady Grand Summoner. He said he was happy for Ke'tai, but he wished it had been him in that position instead. He agreed to help you with this deal here in Seattle when most of the other Elders felt it was unwise that he become involved, because he loves you. He always has." Xen'din shook his head. "It's been hard for him, Ji'anne, seeing you in so much pain. I just didn't think he'd actually come out and say something to you. He's not like that."

I frowned, once again thrown off balance by the thought of Zy'driks. I had known him for over eight years, and seven of those I had been with Ke'tai. If what Xen'din was telling me were true—and I had no reason to believe he would lie to me—that meant Zy'driks had not acted as a mentor because he felt it was the right thing to do. He had been acting as he had because he cared for me, but he had never admitted his feelings to me. I didn't know what to do, and I was at a loss for words.

"Did he say something?" Xen'din pressed.

I shook my head. "Not really. I've just noticed some things lately..."

Xen'din chuckled, appearing amused. "If you want my honest opinion, Ji'anne, I think he would be good for you. You've sort of isolated yourself from everyone here, and he is the only one who can talk sense into you when you get over-emotional."

I gave him a warning look, but he simply laughed again.

"You *do* get over-emotional, Ji'anne," he repeated. "I don't know how he does it, but he always manages to find a way to make you see reason. And the way the two of you work together...it's like you're a perfect team, you know? I suppose you don't want to hear this, though."

I nodded and looked away. I couldn't allow myself to have that type of relationship with Zy'driks—I felt it would be a betrayal to Ke'tai's memory. I wasn't ready to move on. Zy'driks was level-headed and kept his cool in situations where I was unable to do the same; Xen'din was right in his assessment that we worked well together. Ke'tai had never been able to do that—if anything, his temper was often amplified by my own. Ke'tai and I had been two of a kind, and perhaps that is why I struggled so much with the very *idea* of becoming involved with Zy'driks, who was, in many ways, quite my opposite.

"I can talk to him and tell him to back off, if that's what you want," Xen'din offered. "I can't imagine how hard it's been for you—"

I surprised myself by cutting him off. "No, Xen'din, I don't want you to talk to him."

"Then you'll do it?"

I bit my lip, much in the same way, I imagined, that Mina had earlier in the day. What did I intend to do? I didn't know yet myself. I *did* know, however, that if I were to allow Xen'din to talk to him, I would risk losing a very good friend. That was a risk I was unwilling to take.

I lifted my gaze to meet his again, and shook my head. "I think you're right...about some things. I'll talk to him later."

His eyebrows rose in an expression of surprise. He was about to say something more when there was a loud knock on the door. "We have a problem," I heard Aaron's voice call from beyond the door. "Z wants you guys to come back out so you hear this."

I rose swiftly to my feet, following Xen'din out of the room. We had only taken perhaps three steps when he paused to take my hand in his. "Follow your heart, Ji'anne. Do what you feel is best." He squeezed it once, and then hurried ahead to catch up with Aaron's retreating form.

I sighed, uncertain of what to do, but no longer afraid to act. I followed Xen'din into the living room, noting that Il'zaks was on the phone, a strained expression upon his face. Zy'driks was speaking rapidly to the trackers that had remained in the house, delivering rapid instructions. I wondered what had happened while we had been shut away from the others, and made my way toward Zy'driks.

He acknowledged my presence with a brief nod, but did not stop speaking. "...need to be on your guard from this point forward. Anything could happen, especially if he is able to locate us here." He paused a moment, and then said, "Go get ready—do whatever you need to do."

As the trackers dispersed, Zy'driks moved to stand next to me. "We just got word from Carmine that Aria has died," he said quietly. "Jack was angry before, but now he is borderline psychotic. He was ranting to the priest, who was at the hospital with him, that he was going to take matters into his own hands now. Hopefully the priest will be able to calm him down, but this may be an opportunity for us to lure him out."

"What are you suggesting?" Xen'din asked from behind me. I startled; I had forgotten he was there.

"Jack's temperament being as it is, it would be child's play," Zy'driks said, a mischievous glint in his eyes. "All we'd have to do is send a single demon to a location *near* where he is, and once he's alone—"

"He would follow it without thinking," I said cutting him off. "He would go after it solo, thinking it would lead him to us, and we could take him prisoner like the others."

Zy'driks nodded his approval, flashing a grin in my direction. "Exactly." He glanced up to locate Il'zaks, who was still on the phone at the other end of the room. "Give me just a moment."

While Zy'driks spoke quickly to Il'zaks, and then took the phone himself, Xen'din nudged me with his elbow. "Things like that prove my earlier point, Ji'anne. You know, about being the perfect team."

I made a face at him, which provoked him into laughter. The brief moment of light-heartedness was broken however, as Zy'driks handed the phone back to Il'zaks and made his way toward us once more.

"I told Carmine of our plan," he said. "She will notify us as soon as Jack is alone. We have to be ready when she calls." He paused a moment, studying my face carefully. "You seem to be in better spirits, Ji'anne. I'm glad to see that."

"Sometimes I don't want to admit it, but talking to someone usually helps me figure things out," I replied, never taking my eyes from his. "I think I'm going to be okay."

Nearly four hours passed before Carmine called again. Jack was on the move—he had stormed out of the hospital and appeared to be returning home. He was alone, and this could very well be the only chance we had to strike. Zy'driks had decided to take it upon himself to send a demon in Jack's direction, leaving the rest of us waiting in anticipation.

The plan was to have a demon waiting nearby when he arrived home. Given Jack's current state of mind, we had no doubts about what his course of action would be. The demon would lead him to a place Aaron and Konrad had chosen, and the two of them, along with Miranda and Kendrick, would subdue him there and bring him to our location. Trey and Jake had remained in the house with us, and together had quickly moved our meager belongings out of the last remaining bedroom in order to transform it into yet another holding cell.

While Zy'driks was busy with his demon, Carmine and Marek kept the rest of us apprised of Jack's movements as he made the journey from the hospital toward his house. Marek was driving, and it sounded as though he were trying to keep three cars between his own and Jack's, to remain unnoticed by the distraught hunter.

"We are about six blocks away from his house," Carmine was saying. "Aha! He's turning away—I think he must have noticed our lure."

I glanced at Zy'driks, who was standing apart from the group with his eyes closed. He nodded once, a very slight up and down movement of his head, but it was enough to serve as a confirmation.

"Zy'driks knows he is being followed," Il'zaks stated.

"I'm leading him toward the trackers," Zy'driks said quietly, his voice seemingly distant.

"What was that?" Carmine asked.

Il'zaks repeated the statement for her, and she let out one of her harsh, cackling laughs. "Perfect! We'll keep tailing him until he gets there."

Ten minutes later, my phone began ringing. I answered it to the sound of Konrad's excited voice. "We are bringing him in, lady," he said. "He's a fighter...Kendrick is hurt bad, and I think Miranda broke her arm."

Somewhere in the background, Miranda said, "*I* didn't break it, that stupid bastard did." Her voice was strained, and it was obvious she was in pain.

"We'll have someone take her and Kendrick in to a clinic once you're back," I replied, knowing they could not afford a detour with Jack in tow. "We'll be ready for him when you get here."

"Good, *ja*," Konrad replied. "We will be there in ten minutes, I think."

I disconnected the call to inform Trey and Jake to be ready for the newcomer. Zy'driks was talking with Il'zaks and Xen'din, but abruptly ended his conversation when he saw I was no longer on the phone. He made his way toward me.

"I think that went well," he said. "Jack put up a fight—I think Miranda might be hurt, and Kendrick definitely was—"

"Yeah," I replied. "Konrad said her arm is broken. Kendrick is not in good shape."

He frowned. "Well, they will heal. It could have been worse." He sighed. "He had a gun stashed in his pickup. He took it with him when he followed my nightwing. He almost hit it."

"Oh no…"

He offered a tired smile, and shrugged as though it did not matter. "Almost doesn't count," he replied dismissively. "I'm okay, and with the exception of Miranda and Kendrick, so are the trackers. Konrad is really an asset to you, Ji'anne; he was ready for the fight and had the gun out of Jack's hand almost as soon as he had fired that shot."

"I'm glad you're alright," I said without thinking. "I…" I cut myself off, surprised at myself for what I had almost said—that I needed him.

Was it true, that I needed this man in my life? Or was I simply just reacting to the near-miss, the thought of having him incapacitated as Xen'din had been? It was true that *we* needed him for the confrontation with Xandra, but I was not sure if what I had nearly said had been so simple. I bit my lower lip, lowering my gaze to the ground as I tried to sort out the complicated mix of emotions swirling through me.

"We need to be wary when Jack arrivers here," Zy'driks said quietly, choosing to overlook the awkward silence that had suddenly grown between us. "He is out of his mind with grief and rage—which, given his misguided ideas, is understandable. But he will be a danger for everyone here, and we especially must be very careful."

I looked up to meet his eyes, nodding in agreement. "I'll be careful, Zy'driks. I promise."

The smile that broke across his features was one of amusement. "I know, Ji'anne. I just worry. Humor an old man, will you?"

I couldn't help but laugh. "I've never thought of you as being old," I reminded him, "and your age shouldn't matter anyway."

He raised an eyebrow but was unable to make any sort of reply. My phone began ringing again, abruptly putting an end to our conversation. I glanced at the screen before answering; it was Konrad.

"We are at the house," Konrad said. "I wanted to warn you before we brought him inside."

“Thank you,” I replied. “We’re ready.” I disconnected before he could say anything more.

“They’re here,” I called to the others in the room.

Instantly the anticipatory atmosphere changed to one of tense silence. A moment later, the front door opened to reveal Miranda, gingerly cradling her left arm to her torso. She held the door open with her foot, while Aaron and Konrad maneuvered a blindfolded and handcuffed Jack through the threshold. Trey beckoned the two men restraining Jack to follow him, while Jake moved across the room to examine Miranda’s arm. A moment later, she gestured outside, indicating that he ought to see to Kendrick’s injuries first.

As Jack was moved through the room, he turned his face directly toward where Zy’driks and I were standing. Zy’driks shifted slightly so that he stood between me and the others, and I was forced to lean to one side to see around his broad shoulders.

“I know you’re here!” Jack shouted angrily, his voice raw with emotion. “I’ll be damned if I don’t fucking kill you all!” He twisted in an attempt to break free of the two men holding him, but both trackers kept hold of his arms, pushing him roughly toward the hall. “You will pay for what you did to her. I won’t stand by and let you get away with this! Fuck you all!”

“Well if Thad didn’t know what was going on with Jack, he does now,” Zy’driks said in a low voice. He shook his head in disappointment.

Jack’s shouts and screams of frustrated rage could be heard even after he had been locked in the room at the end of the hall. I doubted I would get much sleep that night, even if I was given the opportunity. I knew all too well the sort of pain and anguish the hunter must be feeling, and I knew that even with time, the wounds would never fully heal.

# 33

# RETURN

Surprisingly enough, sleep came to me that night, albeit at a very late hour. Some time before that, Jack had quieted down, apparently having worn himself out with his useless curses and shouts of rage. My sleep was light and dreamless, and when I was awakened by quiet conversation on the other side of the room, I knew I would not be able to return to my slumber.

I opened my eyes slowly, noting that gray daylight was spilling into the room from the glass patio door. Il'zaks was talking quietly to Trey and Carmine near the front door. I rose as quietly as I could manage, not wishing to awaken any of the trackers that were still asleep. As I moved carefully across the room, I noted that Xen'din was in the kitchen speaking with Zy'driks. I made my way toward them, stepping around the sleeping form of Konrad as I did so.

"Morning, Ji'anne," Xen'din whispered rather cheerfully, smiling.

I frowned. I had not been awake long enough to determine if the morning would prove to be good or not.

Zy'driks chuckled softly. "Give her a few minutes to wake up, and then we can get to business."

"What business?" I asked.

"I have a plan as to what exactly we should do with Xan," Xen'din replied. "I was just running it by Zy'driks to see what he thought before I told you…But he thinks it'll work."

A few minutes later, during which time I had made a pot of coffee and downed half a cup, Il'zaks wandered over to join us. He and Zy'driks also took some coffee before we began to discuss Xen'din's plan.

The first part of the plan would be simple—he wanted to have Thad write a message to Xandra, detailing a time and place for the meeting. Included in this letter would be the fact that all of our prisoners would be released unharmed if she came alone as requested. The time was still up for debate, but the location was decided by the two Elders—they wanted her to meet us in the underground, in the same area in which I had lost Ke'tai. I objected; I did not wish to relive those painful memories. Il'zaks gave me a gentle reminder that I would never be able to move on with my life if I could not manage to face my past. I knew he was right, but the thought of returning to the underground soured my stomach. I left the remainder of my coffee unfinished on the countertop behind me.

We decided to make the prisoners visible to Xandra—perhaps kept under guard outside the very room where Ke'tai had been murdered. Xandra would encounter them before she was to meet with any of us. Xen'din suggested that I speak with her first, revealing myself in front of the prisoners so that they would witness her reaction. It was universally agreed upon that she would recognize me, even after the changes I had undergone to become a summoner. Xen'din said he would reveal himself when he felt the timing was right, and again, the prisoners would be there to gauge her reaction. He felt she would recognize him as well.

It was at this point in the conversation that Zy'driks intervened with a proposition. "Ji'anne, perhaps that will be the perfect time to see what your Alastor is capable of. Summon him there, so he is ready for your sister's arrival."

"We will ensure that she is disarmed well before she reaches us," Il'zaks added. "I do not want to take any risks."

Xen'din nodded. "Yeah, I was thinking about maybe having a couple of the trackers meet her near the entrance, and you know, take away her weapons and whatnot. They can escort her in."

Now that we had a plan, it was time to begin setting it in motion. This meant I must meet with Thad—and answer the inevitable questions he would have about Jack. It had been impossible to keep the raging hunter quiet after he had been brought in. It was unlikely that Thad had failed to recognize the other man's voice.

I took a moment to steel myself while Trey went into the room to restrain Thad. I had to convince this stubborn man to write another note to Xandra, and I must not lose my temper. Growing angry with him would only serve to make matters worse.

Trey nodded to me as he reemerged from Thad's room, confirming that it was safe for me to venture inside. I drew a deep breath and entered to find Thad standing up and facing the window, peering through the bars into the small back yard. The window covering had been removed since my last encounter with him. His expression was resigned and thoughtful, but he said nothing as the door was closed behind me. I remained near the door, exercising my patience as I waited for him to acknowledge my presence.

After a long silence, the Stone-reader turned around, his gray eyes sad. The wary look I had grown so accustomed to seeing was no longer there. What had occurred to elicit such a change?

"I suppose you are here to ask something else of me," he said after studying me for a moment.

I nodded, and waited for him to continue.

"I heard Jack last night," he said quietly. "You are taking us out one by one, until you get what you want. Has she still not agreed to meet with you, then?"

I sighed. "She has agreed to a meeting, finally. We have Mina held here too, you know."

Thad nodded. "That wouldn't explain Jack's anger," he said, mostly to himself. "What happened there?"

I closed my eyes and drew a breath, uncertain of how he would react to the news of Aria's death. "We tried to take Aria and Mina on the same night. We managed to get Mina here without any trouble, but Aria tried to run...From what I have been told, she tried to climb over the fence behind her house, but fell instead. She was hit by a car..."

Thad looked away, his jaw clenched in sudden frustration.

"We were not trying to harm her," I stated firmly, wishing with all my being that he would believe me.

He nodded, raising his eyes to meet mine once more. "I've been here long enough to realize that," he replied. "At least now, it explains why Jack was so pissed off last night. He lost her, didn't he?"

I nodded, looking down at the floor. "We never meant for that to happen."

"Maybe one day I will be able to convince Jack that you were not entirely to blame," Thad mused. "If we are ever allowed to leave here, that is," he added sourly.

"I had Mina write Xandra a note yesterday, asking her again to meet with us alone," I said, ignoring his last comment. "Part of the conditions of her meeting with us is that you, Jack, and Mina will be released after it takes place. She has agreed to the meeting."

"So, what exactly do you want from me?" Thad asked.

"I'd like you to write another note to her, telling her to meet us in the underground, at the same location where…the incident took place last year." I had managed to keep my voice steady, even though the thought of returning to the scene of Ke'tai's murder was painfully difficult. I drew a shaky breath before continuing. "We want to meet with her tomorrow, at ten pm. She must come alone—if that overprotective Kent follows her again, it will be the last thing he does."

Thad's gaze was unreadable as he nodded. "I will write the note," he said.

I turned and exited the room before he could say anything more. I instructed Trey to bring paper and a pencil to Thad, and to bring me his message once he had finished writing. Trey nodded and went about his task without any questions, while I headed back toward the living room to seek out one of the other summoners. I needed someone to talk to, and I was hoping Xen'din would be available.

Unfortunately, he and Il'zaks had disappeared on some errand or another, and the only other summoner present was Zy'driks. I sighed, pausing at the end of the hallway to debate whether I truly wanted to speak with him. I knew he would listen to me, no matter what I had to say, but I did not want to waste my energy attempting to decipher his motives. After Xen'din's revelation the previous day regarding Zy'driks' feelings for me, I found I had a difficult time trying to keep my mind on the business at hand. Zy'driks had become a distraction, a puzzle that I still had not solved.

I was spared from my internal struggle by Trey, who returned bearing Thad's message to Xandra. I thanked him as he turned away, while he shrugged and said, "Just doing my job." I scanned the letter quickly, noting with some amusement—and worry—that Thad had not mentioned anything regarding Kent keeping his distance. He had underlined the statement indicating that Xandra should come alone, but I wondered if Kent would follow the Stone-reader's implied commands. I folded the letter carefully and summoned a nightwing to carry it to the hunters' headquarters, hoping for the best when the meeting finally took place.

The day had been filled with preparations for the confrontation with Xandra. Marek and Miranda had been sent to the underground area where the awful events surrounding Ke'tai's murder had unfolded, to ensure that the area we intended to use remained blocked from the public's access.

Miranda's arm was now in a cast, but she did not complain; Kendrick, however, had been admitted to the hospital, and would remain there for some time while he recovered from his injuries. Their altercation with Jack the previous evening had taken its toll upon us, and Xen'din was down one tracker.

Levi and Jake had taken on the task of monitoring the hunters, and had relayed that Xandra fully intended to comply with our demands to meet us alone. Kent continued to object, but if he followed her, the trackers would be in place to capture and restrain him. The two Elders, Xen'din, and I had finalized our plans in the early evening. I believed that I was ready for this final showdown with my sister. I did not know what the outcome would be of this meeting, but whatever transpired, I believed that I was prepared for it.

As we concluded our preparations, Zy'driks remained with me while the other two summoners left to conduct business of their own. With the trackers busy outside of the house, or monitoring our prisoners within, we were left entirely alone. I was uncertain if I liked the scenario.

I moved to walk away from Zy'driks, but he reached out and took hold of my elbow gently. "Ji'anne, can I talk to you for a while?" he asked. Something in his tone caught my attention—was it fear, or something else?

I turned around to face him, and nodded uncertainly. He glanced toward the glass patio door, and then turned once again to me. "Let's go outside," he said. "It's not raining tonight—for once—and it will give us a little more privacy. I…need to talk to you without any interruptions."

I frowned, unable to discern what he was planning, but nodded in acquiescence. I followed him out the door, which he slid closed behind us, and was surprised to see faint stars twinkling high in the sky. Not only had the rain stopped, but the nearly perpetual overcast gloom that was typical of Seattle had lifted, revealing the clear night sky. The air was cool, being early spring, but it was not cold.

"I'm concerned about what tomorrow may bring," Zy'driks said quietly, breaking the brief moment of silence. He was standing near the center of the small yard, his back toward me as he gazed toward the night sky.

"I think we'll be fine," I said slowly. "We've been planning for this since the beginning. Everyone knows their part."

He was silent for a long moment, and then he turned to face me, a sad smile playing at the corners of his lips. "We cannot know what will happen until it does," he replied. "What we are going to attempt tomorrow is dangerous for everyone involved. I want to believe that Xandra will keep her promise and come alone, and I want to believe that she will come to this meeting without it erupting into a battle, but belief isn't enough. The reality is that anything is possible—and some of those possibilities are not very appealing."

I looked down at the grass between my shoes; I knew what he said was true. We could plan for a million different scenarios, but there would always be something we had overlooked, something unexpected that might occur. If anything happened to go wrong, the outcome could prove devastating. I sighed.

"I'm sorry, Ji'anne," he said softly. "I did not bring you out here to be so negative..." He sighed, allowing his words to hang in the air between us. I raised my gaze to meet his, but he was looking down at the ground. A myriad of expressions flickered across his features, betraying his internal struggle.

Without realizing it, I had taken several steps, closing the gap between us. "Zy'driks, tell me what's wrong."

He met my gaze and managed a weak smile. "I need to tell you something," he said, his voice little more than a whisper. "I've been meaning to tell you this for many years, but it's much harder to say this than I had expected it to be." He shook his head, appearing slightly amused at his own perceived inadequacy.

"Tell me," I pressed. I understood what he planned to say, thinking back to my earlier conversation with Xen'din. I needed to hear it from him.

"As I said before, anything can happen tomorrow. And I need you to know this, in the event that something goes wrong…"

He closed his eyes, clenching his jaw as though he were bracing for something unpleasant. When he finally opened them again, he met my gaze and held it for several seconds before he spoke again.

"Ji'anne, I love you. I have since the day I met you, all those years ago. You were so happy with Ke'tai, and I would never have done anything to get between the two of you. And when you lost him, it hurt me to see you in such agony…I want you to be happy again, but I don't know if I could ever take his place. I'm not asking for that, I just…need you to know what I feel."

There it was, finally out in the open, and I was left with one of two choices. I could step back from the precipice, turn my back on Zy'driks, and always wonder what might have been, or I could take the plunge and hope he would be there at the bottom of the cliff face to arrest my fall. I hesitated, uncertain of my own feelings for him, and bit my lower lip in worried thought.

After a moment of silence, he sighed and his expression became pained. "I should never have said anything. I'm sorry, Ji'anne; I've been a fool."

He moved as though to walk past me, toward the patio door. I knew if I was going to take the plunge, I must do it then.

"Zy'driks," I said impulsively, reaching my hand toward his arm, "wait."

He swung his miserable gaze in my direction, and the haunted, pained look I saw there caused my heart to ache, my resolve to crumble. I was the source of his grief, and I needed to make this right. I found that I wanted to make it right, that some part of me longed for him—a part that until now I had kept buried deep inside, ignoring its very existence. I wanted to reject those feelings, but I was particularly vulnerable and unsure of myself; I wanted to experience happiness again—however briefly.

I rose up onto my toes, my lips meeting his. He resisted at first, seemingly surprised at my sudden action, and then he relaxed and returned the kiss, his arms slowly encircling my waist as he bent his head toward me. I felt my heart racing, caught up in the moment, and I realized belatedly what the extent of my loneliness truly had been. I did not want this moment to end, and it seemed, neither did he. He had been there to catch me after all, reckless though I had been.

After an interminable amount of time, Zy'driks suddenly straightened and turned to look toward the door. I followed his gaze to see Aaron just outside of the door, his mouth gaping in shock. I was unable to suppress the nervous laugh that bubbled up from my throat, and only then did Aaron manage to recover some measure of his composure.

Aaron cleared his throat loudly, his face turning crimson with embarrassment. "Uh, Il'zaks sent me to look for you, Z..."

"Tell him we'll be there in a minute," Zy'driks replied, amused, before turning back to face me. He reached one hand up, touching the side of my face gently. "Ji'anne, I have dreamed of this a thousand times, but my dreams did not compare to this. I have been alone much longer than you can imagine...And I was afraid..."

I smiled up at him, uncertain. "You don't have to be afraid of me," I replied, although I was beginning to have some misgivings. I silently cursed myself for being so impulsive; I knew this thing between us—whatever it was—could never last. I had committed the most colossal of blunders, by giving in to my vulnerability as I had.

The smile the lit up his face then outshined even the most brilliant of smiles Ke'tai had ever managed, and rather than making me happy, it made me feel guilty. "Yes," he agreed, "but for now, we have work to take care of first. If we make it through tomorrow, we can take some time to be together, just you and I."

I nodded, offering him a wavering smile, though I felt horrible about what I had done. What had I been thinking? I did not want to hurt him—he had become a very good friend—but what had just transpired was the result of my own impulsivity, my own selfishness. I knew I must tell him, but found that my guilt weighed so heavily upon me that I was unable to speak.

I hung my head as I followed Zy'driks into the house. I wondered how long we would have before Aaron spread the word to everyone else. I knew that Aaron was not prone to gossiping, but it had been such an obvious shock to him to find us kissing, I felt he was bound to say something.

It appeared that most of the trackers were still away on various errands; only Aaron and Trey were within the room as we entered. Il'zaks and Xen'din were standing together near the kitchen's entrance, and when Xen'din saw us he waved us over excitedly. I frowned; I had the distinct feeling that Aaron may have already said something to the pair.

"The hunters just had a very brief meeting," Il'zaks said as we approached. "Since there are only three of them left, there was not much argument taking place."

"Xan's ready to meet with you tomorrow," Xen'din said, practically bouncing in place with nervous excitement. "I think Kent is still going to try to follow her, even though she made it very clear to him she did not want him anywhere near her. We'll have to watch out for him."

Il'zaks nodded, and then turned his gaze fully upon Zy'driks. "I do hope you knew what you were doing outside," he said, his tone even and business-like. "The timing, in my opinion, was not ideal."

I turned toward Zy'driks, the color draining from my face. They knew what had happened. Furious, I spun around to face Aaron, and he flinched as though I had physically slapped him; he shrugged uncomfortably before turning his gaze toward the floor.

"You *told* them?!" I shouted at Aaron, who looked as though he wished for all the world that he could simply make himself disappear.

Zy'driks' reaction was somewhat less explosive than my own; he shrugged, and then placed a hand on my arm in an effort to defuse some of my sudden outrage. "We cannot know what tomorrow will bring, Il'zaks," he replied quietly. "If I had not said what I felt tonight, I may have never been given the chance to do so again. And to be honest with you, what Aaron happened to walk into was not something I had counted on. In fact, I had prepared myself for quite the opposite."

He had expected me to resist—why hadn't I done so? Things would be so much less complicated right now had I held my selfish impulses in check.

Il'zaks did not appear pleased with the answer; he frowned and crossed his thin arms over his chest. "Yes, and the opposite reaction—which you had been anticipating—could have been much, much worse for our entire operation." Il'zaks rarely showed any signs of true anger, but he was unable to conceal the fact that inwardly, he was seething. "Sometimes you are a real fool, Zy'driks."

Zy'driks rolled his eyes in exasperation and sighed heavily. "I never expected you to understand," he replied, managing to keep his tone even. "I have never allowed myself certain pleasures that others of our kind happen to indulge themselves in. My time to for happiness is long overdue."

"Happiness has nothing to do with it!" Il'zaks shot back. "You have jeopardized our entire mission in a matter of ten minutes. We need her to be thinking clearly tomorrow, and you could not keep your damned mouth shut until we had finished." He shook his head, his mouth a tight line of barely suppressed anger.

I sighed, quickly becoming frustrated. I shoved my emotions aside, and said as evenly as I could, "We can't change what just happened. So, let's deal with it constructively instead of becoming angry and wasting time. The two of you arguing is not helping our mission, either."

Il'zaks clenched his jaw, and then with a sigh seemed to deflate. "You are right," he acknowledged after a moment, though he refused to make eye contact with Zy'driks. "This anger of mine is counterproductive, and I need to set it aside until after we deal with your sister."

"Thank you," I replied, "and as for the matter of me thinking clearly, I feel like I'm doing better right now than I have in months. I know what needs to be done tomorrow, and I will do it. We'll stick to our original plans, and things should work out just fine."

Il'zaks nodded once. "I am glad you are feeling better, Ji'anne. I apologize for my outburst." He looked up to meet Zy'driks' gaze, a slight frown reappearing to one side of his mouth. "I still think you can be a damned fool, Zy'driks, and I hope you did not just cost us everything we have been working towards." With that said, he turned away and walked toward the glass patio door, preparing to spend some time alone.

"If you want my opinion," Xen'din said once Il'zaks had gone, "I think it's about time you finally said something, Z. I hope it works out for both of you."

I wanted nothing more than to turn away and burst into tears, but I managed to hold my composure. *What had I been thinking?*

I was awake well before the sun had risen on the next day, full of nervous energy. This was the day we had been preparing for; all of our actions for the past thirteen months would come to their inevitable conclusion, and only when I finally met with Xandra face to face, would we know for certain what the outcome would truly be. I knew I had taken a risk in pursuing her as I had, but today could only have one of two outcomes—either it would go very well for me and the other summoners, or it would go very badly, and we would be lucky to escape unharmed. I was prepared, but I was also terrified to the very core of my being. We could find ourselves in a life or death struggle.

Throughout the day, the trackers monitored Xandra's movements, reporting in at set intervals. We decided to move the three prisoners to the underground after sundown; our goal was to do so between seven and eight o'clock, after the tour guides would be finished for the day. Our preparations in place, the remainder of our time was spent in waiting.

I spent a lengthy span of time speaking with Zy'driks. It had quickly become obvious that word of the previous evening's kiss had spread; we received numerous furtive glances, overheard myriad whispered comments. Il'zaks maintained an air of disapproval, but refrained from any further argument with Zy'driks. I was grateful for his silence, although it served to heighten my resolve to inform Zy'driks I believed it had been a mistake. Now that the time for my long-overdue confrontation with Xandra was upon us, I needed his support more than ever. I forced myself into silence, and said not a word regarding my guilt or misgivings. After our encounter with the hunters had concluded, I would tell him what I must in order to set things aright once more.

Finally, as the clock neared seven-thirty, we began moving toward the underground. Thad was taken from his room first, handcuffed and blindfolded as he was led to one of the trackers' vehicles; he would be transported in the same car as Mina. Thad maintained his silence as he was led into the garage, as did Mina when she was escorted out minutes later. Konrad, Carmine, and Jake were assigned to the same vehicle. The prisoners were to remain cuffed and blindfolded until we reached our destination.

Jack was taken from his room next, escorted by Trey and Aaron, who, along with Miranda, would follow the vehicle bearing Thad and Mina. Jack had grown silent, but his very presence emanated hostility as he was marched through the house. Of the three, Jack would need to be watched most carefully.

Levi and Vance called Xen'din at eight-fifteen to report that Xandra had returned to her home; they suspected it was to prepare for our meeting. They were asked to meet us at the underground, and would survey the area carefully until Xandra arrived. I wanted to ensure that if Kent followed her, they would be ready to subdue him.

This left Marek alone with we four summoners. As we exited the house, I pulled up the hood of my woolen coat; I did this in an effort to hide my hair, but it had also begun to drizzle once more. I sat in the back seat of Marek's SUV between Zy'driks and Xen'din, while Il'zaks rode shotgun. I had the distinct feeling that Il'zaks had taken that position due to his continued anger with Zy'driks.

Zy'driks and Xen'din spoke quietly on the car ride to the underground, but I paid little attention to their conversation, even though I was sitting between the two. I held my gaze fixed upon the scenery gliding by through the rain-streaked window as Marek guided the vehicle expertly through the Seattle traffic. Even at this time of the night, the traffic was dense.

My thoughts were upon Xandra, and what I wanted to say to her when we did finally meet. There had been a time when I knew the precise words I would speak, those words fueled by anger and the pain of loss. As our operation had progressed, my feelings had become numb and I no longer understood how I would react to her presence. I still harbored a dark anger, smoldering deep inside, but it was no longer as poignant as it had once been.

Marek brought the car to a stop in an alleyway just beyond a door that would lead us into the underground. I recognized the two vehicles parked ahead of Marek's as belonging to Jake and Trey, and noted that Levi was lounging against the wall of the building alongside the door. Everyone was in position; all we had to do was wait for Xandra's arrival.

I tugged the hood of my jacket over my head once more before exiting the vehicle behind Zy'driks. Levi opened the door for us, nodding once to me in acknowledgement as I passed, though he said nothing. As I entered the darkened passage beyond, I had expected to feel anguish as a wash of unpleasant memories came unbidden to my mind. Instead, I felt a cold determination, fueled by my long-suppressed anger, course through me. I would make Xandra regret what she had done.

I turned as we entered, pulling my hood away from my face as I did so. I found myself leading the way to the metal safety railing meant to block people from going off the specified path designed for the walking tours. I ducked below the railing and stepped onto the uneven ground. The trackers and their prisoners had left a tangle of footprints behind in the hard-packed dirt. I did not wait for the others as I forged ahead—I had waited long enough. The endgame was upon us, long overdue.

Zy'driks caught up to me after a few moments. He did not speak, and did not need to; it was his way of letting me know he was there for me, that I was not alone. I glanced over my shoulder once, just before I rounded the first bend in the tunnel, noting that Il'zaks and Xen'din were not far behind. They were speaking quietly with one another. Marek had remained behind with Levi to monitor the door.

Together, Zy'driks and I made our way through the chunks of broken concrete and the mounds of dirt that filled the tunnel, finally coming to a short span of cracked pavement. This path would lead us to the door of the room where Ke'tai had been so cruelly ripped from life forever. Once more, I had braced myself for the overwhelming cascade of emotions that being in this place once more should have brought forth. I found I felt nothing more than burning rage. My determination to see this through was stronger than it had ever been. As I set my gaze upon our final destination, I resolved that Xandra would not walk away the same person she had been upon her arrival.

Our three prisoners had been placed at intervals along the wall adjacent to the door, still handcuffed, though their blindfolds had been removed. I noted with some surprise that ankle shackles had been added to Jack's restraints; I was uncertain of where they had procured the shackles, but it had been a wise choice to further subdue him. He was the most likely of the three to cause trouble, given the altercation that had taken place when we had captured him. The trackers kept wary eyes locked upon the three captives, and—I noted with some amusement—Konrad and Aaron were flaunting the fact that they were armed and unafraid to shoot at the first sign of misbehavior. I knew they would not, unless one of the summoners were in danger; they were simply putting up a show of force to ensure our meeting went smoothly. Battery-powered lanterns ringed the space, providing pale, yellow light.

I stopped before the door; it was closed. I paused for a moment to take a deep breath and assess my current state of mind. Zy'driks placed one hand on my arm, and I looked up to meet his gaze.

"We must follow the plan, Ji'anne," he whispered. "I cannot imagine how difficult this must be for you..."

I nodded once, steeling myself for what lay beyond the door. With a quick movement, I pushed it open. The room was dark, and very little of the light from the battery-powered lanterns made its way through the doorway to penetrate the gloom. It seemed that the room had been cleaned at some point—perhaps by city workers, or perhaps by one of the trackers out of concern for me—but the blood that had once stained the floor was gone. I found this strangely unsettling, yet it was a relief all the same. I stared at the place where Ke'tai had struggled for his last breath, reliving those nightmarish moments, my heart breaking anew at the memory of my loss.

I drew another breath, forcing my emotions aside, and turned to face Zy'driks. His eyes were full of concern and uncertainty. I knew he was trying to assess how I was holding up, and I was not about to disappoint him by breaking down. I could not afford to lose myself in another bout of despair when so much relied upon my actions tonight.

"I'm okay," I told him. "Stop worrying about me."

He managed a weary smile. "I can't, and I won't, Ji'anne. That's part of the price we have to pay if we want to make this work, you know." He paused briefly, looking down, and then said, "I wasn't sure how you'd react to being here again."

I shrugged, trying my best to ignore the guilt that gnawed at me. "To be honest, I wasn't sure, myself. Right now, I want to bring her to her knees more than ever before...I want her to feel my pain." I was surprised at the vehemence I heard in my own voice, and Zy'driks raised his eyebrows.

"I just hope you are able to keep your temper in check," he said quietly.

I nodded once, and turned to look through the doorway. Il'zaks and Xen'din had arrived, and Il'zaks was speaking quietly with Carmine. I glanced at my watch; it was almost nine-thirty. Xandra would be arriving at any moment.

I left the room, intending to speak to Xen'din, when the radio clipped to Aaron's belt crackled. Vance's voice suddenly cut through the room like a knife.

"I have a visual confirmation—she is on her way to the doors, Levi. I'll keep an eye out for any followers."

A moment later, Levi replied. "Roger, that. I see her. We'll bring her in."

# 34

# ALASTOR

The room had fallen silent with the revelation that the trackers had Xandra within their sights. Even Jack, who had been mumbling and cursing in a near-constant stream since we had arrived, had become quiet as we waited to hear what the outcome of her arrival would be. Time seemed to stretch, the seconds taking hours to tick by. Finally, Levi's voice cut through the breathless silence once more.

"We are on our way. Target has been disarmed and seems to be cooperating."

Aaron pulled the radio from his belt to make his reply. "Roger. We're ready for your arrival."

Il'zaks turned away from Carmine, leaving his conversation with her unfinished, and nodded once to me. "It is time," he said quietly. "We must go inside."

I turned around; Zy'driks had not moved from his position in the doorway. Vance spoke again through the radio. "I have visual on Kent Waterby."

"Damn him!" I was surprised to hear Thad's voice, but it also gave me an idea.

"Aaron, tell Vance to grab him—and to be careful. Then have Mr. Taylor explain to Kent why following Xandra is not in his best interests."

Aaron's eyebrows rose in disbelief at the notion, and he glanced helplessly at Zy'driks, who merely nodded. With a sigh, Aaron lifted the radio to his lips and relayed the message to Vance. While we filed into the room, Vance confirmed that he had cornered Kent near the entrance to the underground. I could hear Thad begin to speak rapidly, urging Kent to return to his car until our business had been settled. A few more seconds of silence passed before Vance relayed that Kent had departed. Vance intended to stay near the entrance to make certain Kent would not return.

"I think you ought to summon Alastor now, Ji'anne," Il'zaks said quietly from the rear of the room. His voice was hollow, as though he were struggling with some internal turmoil and it was slowly draining his energy. I wondered how much being in this place was affecting him.

I closed my eyes, clearing my mind of misgivings, and began to dance. As I felt Alastor's arrival, I heard Jack shout something outside, having sensed the demon's presence. He was quickly silenced by a sharp remark from Carmine, but it was clear to me that the hunters were uncomfortable with this turn of events.

I had not called upon Alastor since the day I had become a summoner. I could sense his thoughts—he was starkly aware of the anger I bore Xandra, and this knowledge seemed to strengthen him. I allowed him to venture near the doorway, just beyond the illumination from the lanterns, while we awaited her arrival.

Alastor was eager for the confrontation, was craving it. Some remote part of my consciousness quailed at this realization, but another, stronger part ignored the warning signs and urged Alastor on. If the demon could sense my inner turmoil, he did not acknowledge it. He merely waited in an anticipatory stance, much like a cat sitting outside of a mouse's hole, eager for a glimpse of its prey. Alastor was a predator by nature; I did not know what his world must have been like, but I knew that his very essence reeked of malevolence. He lived for moments much like this one.

I waited in the darkness, using Alastor's keen eyes to see what lay beyond the doorway, my own eyes closed in concentration. My surroundings began to feel distant, as though I were merely observing the goings-on of people on a television screen, and I were no longer a physical part of the scene that was about to play out around me. I could sense each individual nearby through Alastor, could even intuit their emotions; Jack was terrified to his very core, his senses screaming to him of Alastor's threat, Mina was scared, but was more deeply concerned about Xandra's well-being than her own, and Thad was merely worried based upon Jack's sudden outburst. Thad, being a Stone-reader, could not sense the presence of a demon, I recalled. Most of the trackers were neutral to Alastor, though Carmine gave off a distinct aura of annoyance; I imagined she was standing in front of Jack with her arms crossed and that characteristic smirk playing at the right side of her mouth. To my surprise, however, Alastor could not feel the emotions of the other summoners in the room, though he could sense their presence more strongly than any of the others nearby.

It seemed that hours passed before Xandra appeared around the bend in the corridor, flanked on either side by Marek and Levi. Her arms were restrained behind her, probably hand-cuffed, and her dark eyes were cast down as she concentrated on maintaining her footing. She took only a few steps further, before she stopped suddenly, staring directly at the place where Alastor crouched in waiting. What little color had been in her cheeks quickly drained away, and I could sense her emotions shift quickly from uncertainty to wary fear, bolstered by a fierce determination. She would see this through, if only to see the other hunters freed.

Through Alastor's eyes, I watched as she was prodded, urged to continue moving forward. Her face had changed little during the past eight years. When last I had seen her, she had been sitting on the couch in our apartment beside the man who had once been Elliot Thompson. She was still pretty, although fine lines had begun to appear at the corners of her eyes, a subtle sign of aging as she approached her thirty-first birthday. Her dark eyes were serious, her jaw set in defiance as she took her final few steps forward. She stopped several feet away from the doorway. I could tell she knew that Alastor was present, and his presence seemed to frighten her more than the mere notion of the meeting had.

I watched Marek and Levi back away from Xandra, leaving her to stand completely alone before the doorway. She glanced once to the side, perhaps taking note of her friends—our prisoners—as they stood in a line against the cracked concrete wall. She feared for them, but she did not show any outward sign of it; she had always been good at hiding her emotions, especially those that left her feeling vulnerable.

I felt a gentle pressure on my arm, just above the elbow, and a voice whispered, "Ji'anne, you must act now." I was so absorbed in Alastor's presence that I could not identify which of the three men nearby had spoken, though I suspected it must have been Zy'driks. I did not acknowledge the words, but simply encouraged Alastor to move forward toward the light.

I watched Xandra's jaw clench as she took note of the movement in the darkness beyond the doorway, felt her tense in preparation for the unknown. "I know you're in there," she called, her voice steady in spite of the cold fear that flowed from her in unseen waves. "I don't know what you want. I came here because you asked me to, in exchange for my friends' freedom."

The sound of her voice triggered my ire. I had been trying my best to keep it buried, but it burst forth like a beast that had been caged too long. Remotely, I realized that I was quivering with rage. I felt a hand fall onto my shoulder, sensed words spoken that were meant to reassure and soothe, but which I could no longer hear. Alastor had grasped at my anger and held onto it as if it were his own, pulling my very consciousness with him as he absorbed my emotions like a sponge.

The part of my mind that had been terrified by the thought of Alastor's obvious desire to confront Xandra began to panic blindly. I had ventured too far into Alastor's being, and I was no longer in control; I felt helpless and frightened, unable to break the connection that had been established between us. I was now merely an observer, looking through his eyes, sensing the environment only as he interpreted it. I wanted to scream, to break free of my mental prison, but I was unable to do anything except watch as the events unfolded before me.

Alastor took a few slow steps, stopping when he stood upon the threshold. His form was obscured by the loose black garment he wore, its hood pulled up to shroud his face. I heard Jack shouting profanities, but Alastor ignored him. He kept his focus solely upon Xandra, the object of my anger and his own dark hunger. Xandra's eyes widened as he stepped into the light, the stench of her fear becoming more pungent. I felt Alastor's unseen face break into a wicked smile. He relished her terror.

"You have wronged my mistress," Alastor said as Jack's unheeded words died away.

The sound of his voice reminded me of the wind as it blew through tree branches in late autumn, after the trees had dropped their leaves and were left barren. Until that moment, I had never heard him speak aloud, and the sound chilled me to the core. I battered at his mind in an attempt to regain control, but it was a futile endeavor. His grin stretched wider.

"Your…mistress…?" Xandra managed after a moment. I could detect a distinct tremor in her words. Her stoic façade was beginning to crumble.

"Yes," Alastor replied, moving another step forward. "She is very powerful. She has called upon me to seek revenge for your terrible deeds."

Xandra's eyes darted to the side, as though she sought reassurance from the hunters lining the wall. She was facing an adversary that, even had she still been armed, would have been a challenge for her. As it was, she knew she could not defeat Alastor alone if he decided to act upon her.

I knew he intended to do something, and again, I tried in vain to reassert my dominance over him. It had been a mistake to summon him here, but none of us had known just what this demon was truly capable of. I hoped I would be able to stop him in time; the snatches of thought I could discern from his mind were filled with malice. She had killed Ke'tai, and had caused more anguish than she could have ever realized, but she was still my sister. I didn't want to see her tortured—or worse, dead—at the hands of Alastor. My renewed mental assault caused the demon to pause, if only briefly, but I believed I could regain control if I concentrated my effort.

Alastor took another step forward, stopping at arm's length from Xandra. "Do you have anything to say?" the cold, hollow voice asked, the tone clearly anticipating what was to come next.

I battled against him again, but only managed to give him another moment's pause while Xandra managed to find her voice, unsteady though it was. "I suspect this has something to do with that summoner I killed a year ago," she said slowly, "and had I known that my actions would lead to this, I would have spared him a thousand times over. I swear that to you." Her tone had become desperate; she knew something unspeakable was about to occur.

Alastor chuckled, a sound that would have raised goose bumps on my arms had I been aware of my physical body. Trapped inside Alastor's head, the sound served to make me recoil.

"Your apology comes too late," Alastor replied, stretching one skeletal hand toward Xandra's face. "You must feel the pain he felt...Experience it for yourself."

Xandra doubled over, but with her hands cuffed behind her, she could not brace her fall. She crashed onto her side on the dusty concrete. She drew her knees up toward her chest, as though the pain that Alastor was inflicting upon her were localized in her abdomen. The bullet that had taken Ke'tai's life had been in the same area. I must stop Alastor before he caused any further damage.

He bent over Xandra, maintaining his cold touch upon the side of her face. I could hear her cry out as her body convulsed beneath his repulsive caress, and I could sense the horror of the spectators surrounding Alastor. He gained a perverse sense of pleasure with his role as the instrument of Xandra's torture. Distantly, I could hear shouts of alarm from somewhere behind the demon, where my physical body stood rooted in place. I renewed my assault upon him, finding renewed strength as I realized Alastor's true intent. I would not allow him to kill my sister, no matter what she may have done.

Furious with Alastor for taking advantage of me, I threw all of my mental prowess against the barriers he had erected to defend himself from me. Abruptly, I found myself staring directly into Zy'driks' face. His hands were on my shoulders and he was shaking me as though he had been trying to wake me from a deep sleep, his eyes wild with fear. I was shocked to see unshed tears in his silver eyes.

For a moment I stood as though frozen in place, stunned that I had broken free of Alastor's hold. I shook my head, as though to clear it, and focused again on what the demon was preparing to do. He was bent over Xandra, and I could hear her moaning in pain. I clenched my jaw, and quickly put a stop to his actions by releasing him to the perverse realm he had come from. Immediately, Xandra fell silent. Xen'din pushed past me, making his way into the light.

"Ji'anne?" Zy'driks asked uncertainly. "Are you with us again?"

I nodded; in that instant, the strength fled from my body, and I nearly collapsed. I would have fallen onto the floor had Zy'driks not been standing in front of me and had caught me in his arms. He pulled me into a rough embrace that I was too weak to resist, and he held me to him for some time.

"Alastor seems to be a very dangerous demon," Il'zaks said from his post to my right. "I have never seen a demon take control like that, and he did it so swiftly..." His words trailed away in ponderous wonder, and I merely nodded again.

"I never want to call that monster here again," I said, my voice little more than a whisper against Zy'driks' shoulder. "He was going to kill her."

"It's going to be okay," he said in an attempt to reassure me. "You were able to stop him. That's what matters."

I shook my head. "I don't know if I was able to stop him in time." I shuddered involuntarily as I thought again of how difficult it had been to regain control of myself after the demon had taken hold. "I couldn't do anything..."

"I didn't realize he would react that way," Zy'driks replied quietly, his tone apologetic. "I'm sorry I made the suggestion to call him here. What matters is that you're okay—that everyone is okay. You came back to us, which is probably something most other summoners would never have been able to manage, given the situation." His arms tightened around me for a moment, and then he said, "I was afraid I had lost you, Ji'anne."

I sighed. I knew it was not the time to bring up the fact that the brief moment of intimacy we had shared had been nothing but a mistake on my part, and it was unfair to him.

"Ji'anne, what's wrong?" he asked, one hand reaching up toward my face.

I turned away before the contact could be made, and I shook my head. "We need to talk after this is over."

I felt him withdraw, heard him sigh, a sound of utter defeat. I could not bring myself to meet his gaze. I had come here to confront Xandra, and I needed to finish the job. I sincerely hoped I had not come too late in dismissing Alastor.

I made my way toward the doorway, stopping just outside of the light's radius. Xandra lay curled on the floor where Alastor had left her, and Xen'din was bent over her, silent tears spilling down his cheeks. Her chest was rising and falling rhythmically, but her eyes were closed; she appeared to be unconscious.

Xen'din must have noticed my approach, because he looked up, his face a mask of fury. "What the hell were you thinking? You nearly killed her!"

I looked down, unable to answer him, clenching my jaw in an effort to stave off the tears that threatened to overcome me. Xen'din would not understand what had happened between myself and Alastor, and I knew trying to explain it to him would be a waste of my breath. He was still in love with Xandra, after all this time; his feelings had blinded him to what had truly occurred, just as mine had blinded me to Alastor's true intentions.

"I'm sorry," I managed feebly, unable to meet his gaze.

He made a sound of disgust. I knew at that moment, in spite of the history we had shared, our friendship was forfeit and there would be little chance to salvage it. Not only had Alastor nearly ruined everything I had been working towards, but now this had been destroyed, too. I wanted nothing more than to find a dark corner in which I could curl up and wait for the inevitable darkness to take me. I had failed.

After several moments of tense silence, I heard a shuffle of movement outside. Looking up, I saw that Xandra's eyes had opened and she had backed a short distance away from Xen'din. Her eyes were wide with surprise and fear—and recognition.

Her tone was uncharacteristically shrill when she finally found her voice once more. "*Elliot?*"

# 35

# NEW BEGINNING

Xen'din tilted his head to one side, considering Xandra's exclamation as though she had posed a complicated mathematical equation to him. Finally, he said, "What did you call me?"

Xandra's eyes narrowed in confusion. "Elliot. That's your name...I'd know you anywhere."

He shook his head, a mystified expression upon his face. "No, it's not."

I sighed. This argument could continue all night if nobody stepped in to put a stop to it. Xen'din could not remember going by the name of Elliot Thompson, and Xandra would never have understood his apparent amnesia.

"He cannot remember that name," I cut in just as Xandra was about to make another argument.

Xandra's eyes narrowed further as she turned her face toward the door. She could not see me yet, but I knew she had recognized something in my voice. "Come out into the light, where I can see you," she implored, rising stiffly to her feet. I noticed that she winced a little as she straightened, and her left cheek bore a scrape from her unimpeded impact with the concrete.

"I will come out in a minute," I replied. "First, I'll let you two enjoy your reunion."

Xandra frowned, but turned back to Xen'din. "So it *is* you," she said. "I knew it had to be...But I thought you were dead!"

Xen'din shot a glare in my direction before he replied to Xandra. It was obvious he no longer wanted to be any part of this ordeal, but he had little choice but to go on. He sighed and ran one hand through his hair.

"Xan, I had no other choice," he said in an attempt to explain. "You were found out by Thad, and you were so excited about the 'new job' you tried to be so vague about. But I had already started my training...If I hadn't done what I did, they would have killed me."

Xandra's jaw clenched in that familiar way it did when she was angry. "How do you know that?" she demanded. "You don't know anything about us."

"I know from experience that you've been trained to shoot first and ask why you did it later," I replied dryly, unable to keep silent on that account. "Thad and the priest would have had him killed, if they had known what he really was."

"If you're going to be a part of this conversation, you'd better stop hiding from me!" Xandra shouted angrily toward the doorway.

"Xan," Thad said from behind her, his tone soothing, "they are telling you the truth, and you know it. Our mission has always been to exterminate their kind, regardless of how they may be connected to one of our own."

"Shut up, Thad, you aren't helping," she growled before turning to face Xen'din. "I was in love with you, and then you go and…fake a suicide? You claimed you couldn't live without my sister in your life—you used my greatest weakness against me! You can't actually expect me to up and forgive you for that."

Xen'din closed his eyes briefly, and drew a breath before he said, "I am not trying to ask for your forgiveness, Xan. I only wanted you to know that I still do love you—I've never stopped. I don't expect you to understand." He sounded weary, as though the conversation had sapped all of his remaining energy.

She frowned, though some of her anger seemed to have dissipated. "I'm sure you only did what you thought you had to," she replied guardedly. "It doesn't make it any easier for me to see you suddenly appear after eight years, especially when it's obvious you're a damned summoner. I've sworn to fight against your kind, and that isn't going to change just because you decide to show up and attempt an apology. Which, by the way, was a pretty pathetic one at that."

Xen'din's face fell. I knew he had been hoping that she would understand his position, but Xandra tended to be stubborn. Unless something else occurred to shock her sense of reality, she would not allow herself to even consider his side of the story. It was time for me to make my final move.

"You have always been so quick to judge everyone, without bothering to hear them out first," I replied, finally stepping into the light where she could see me. I crossed my arms in front of me, and leaned against one side of the dusty door jamb.

Xandra turned to face me, and her jaw dropped open in shock. She shook her head in disbelief, and took a couple steps backwards toward the line of hunters restrained against the wall.

"This can't be happening," she said, her voice coming out in a strained whisper. "This isn't possible."

Behind her, I saw Thad's eyes narrow in suspicion, and recalled the morning I had nearly spilled my secret to him. I knew he had to suspect some previous connection between us, but what I was about to reveal was something none of them could have prepared for. If we had been identical twins, my appearance in the doorway would have been enough, but since we were not, I would have to spell it out for them.

"Hello, sister."

I noticed Thad frown slightly and nod to himself, as though he had been suspecting this outcome. Mina and Jack both appeared stunned, though Jack appeared to be suspicious of Xandra as well as the trackers and summoners around him. As Jack tensed, Carmine swatted at his shoulder as though he were nothing more than a pesky insect. She whispered something in his ear that elicited a glare, but he kept his mouth shut.

Xandra closed her eyes, and sank to the floor on her knees. "Everything that I've worked towards…This will destroy everything…"

"Only if you let it," I replied.

"What choice do I have?" she demanded. "I can't go on with this…Not knowing you're on the other side. Not after I fought so hard to find out what happened to you, why you disappeared." She sighed and shook her head. "I guess I know what happened now, don't I?"

"You only know a small part of the story," I replied, my words coming out a little more harshly than I had intended. My thoughts had returned to Ke'tai, the reason that I had desperately wanted to have this conversation in the first place. I needed her to understand what she had done, and why I had spent so much time slowly dismantling her whole operation in Seattle.

"I know why you left," Xandra replied sullenly, "and I know what that 'night job' you had really was. You were in training."

"Do you remember Kevin?" I demanded. "You spoke to him once on the phone."

She nodded. "Yeah. He gave you that necklace…I have it with me, but it's in my pocket. I can't get to it with these handcuffs on." She hung her head and sighed.

"You can release her," I said to Marek, who appeared skeptical, but went about unlocking the handcuffs on Xandra's wrists anyway.

She rubbed first at one wrist, then the other, as though reassuring herself she was no longer bound. She reached into one pocket of her jeans, and withdrew the necklace in question, the necklace I had been so loath to part with. Cautiously, she stepped forward, and held it out to me.

"You ought to have it back," she said quietly. "But what does he have to do with all of this?"

I sighed as I accepted the necklace from her, the painful memories I had been trying to keep locked away pushing to the forefront once more. I looked down, unable to speak the words that she needed to hear.

"You killed him," Xen'din said from somewhere beside me. "That's what started all of this mess. You killed the man that she left everything behind for, and I've had to sit by and try to help her through it. And you don't even want a damn thing to do with me," he added bitterly.

I heard a shuffle of footsteps, and looked up through a blur of tears to see Xandra only a hand span away from me. Konrad and Marek had abandoned their post with the three prisoners to intervene, concerned for my safety, and now held her at bay.

"I'm so sorry," Xandra whispered, tears in her own eyes. "I never knew…"

"You wouldn't have believed him even if he had told you, I'm sure," I replied. "Just like you didn't believe the man that against all reason still loves you. He does, Xan, and he's been beating himself up for the past eight years because of how he was forced to leave. You ought to at least try to give him a chance to explain. Give him the chance you never gave to Ke'tai."

"Ke'tai?" she asked, confused.

"That was his name. Ke'tai," I replied. "It wasn't Kevin. I made that name up, so you wouldn't get suspicious."

She sighed, and turned to face Xen'din once more. "Elliot, I'm sorry…You know how I can be."

Xen'din glanced at me, though his gaze was unreadable, before he spoke to Xandra once more. "I told you the truth, Xan. I still love you, even though I know I shouldn't, and I wish most of the time that I didn't. But I know we can never be together—even if you decided to quit being a hunter. Maybe once upon a time, it would have worked out, but things are too complicated now..."

Her expression was pained, but she nodded. "I understand. And you're right, you know."

He sighed, and ran a hand through his hair once again. "This is really hard for me to say, Xan, but I have to say it. There are two men that you've worked with that care for you as much as I do, but I don't think you've taken the time to realize it. One of them would be a bad fit for you, but the other one...He would take care of you. He's worthy of being with you, and he has sacrificed a lot to protect you. Just open your eyes, Xan...You don't need to be hung up on a dead boyfriend any more." He swallowed hard, and focused his eyes on the floor. "I hope you are able to take care of her as she deserves, Thad." The words came out in a strangled whisper, and he turned to disappear into the darkened room.

Xen'din had done something I had never expected him to do; he had given up on his doomed love of Xandra. I had assumed he would attempt to persuade her to join him, but something had occurred during the course of the conversation—or during his time spent in the house with Thad—that had changed his mind.

I hoped that once he had a chance to compose himself once more, he would be open to hearing the story of what had actually happened between myself and Alastor. I valued his friendship, and I did not want it to end because I had lost control of the demon. He was going to need the few friends he had more than ever, now that he had finally let go of Xandra. I had discovered a newfound respect for Xen'din, and I wanted to be there for him as he had always been there for me.

Xandra glanced over her shoulder toward Thad as Xen'din disappeared; Thad merely shrugged, but did not deny any of what had just been said.

"I wanted to speak to you, Xan," I said after a moment's silence. "That's what all of this was about. I couldn't just walk up to your front door and expect you to hear me out—your friends would have killed me before I had the chance to say a word. I was forced to eliminate them one at a time, just so that we could have this meeting."

Jack growled something angrily under his breath, and I sighed. "I did not want anyone to be hurt," I said firmly, looking directly at him. "We intended to pick up Aria just as we had with Mina, but she surprised us a bit and took off running. She fell going over the fence. We did not intend for her to die…And for what it's worth, you have my condolences."

Jack glowered at me, but said nothing.

Xandra was quiet for a time, contemplating my words. Finally, she said, "You wanted me to know what had happened…What I had done was wrong. This was the only way…I understand."

I looked beyond her to where Carmine was standing. "You can take Jack and Mina back to the entrance. Let them go home."

Xandra's eyes were filled with uncertainty, and she said, "What about Thad?"

I managed a tired smile. "Once they're gone, I'll let him go, too. I think the two of you probably have things you'll want to talk about away from the others."

She glanced at Thad again, and he offered her a weary smile as Jack and Mina were marched back the way they had come by several of the trackers. "I can't go back to being a Stone-reader for the hunters any more, Xan," he said quietly. "They'll never trust me again."

I watched Xandra carefully as she walked across the concrete to kneel down beside him. She glanced toward me, as though asking for permission to speak with him, and I merely nodded, exhausted from the ordeal.

"What do you mean?" she asked him. "We need you, Thad."

"The hunters don't need me," he replied. "I've been…compromised. But you know that, Xan. You were there."

She nodded. "I had forgotten," she admitted. "With everything else that happened…"

He managed a tired chuckle. "At first, I didn't want to listen to them, Xan, but they aren't bad people—not really. I've realized that maybe we've been wrong." He lifted his gaze to meet mine. "Your friend in there, the tall one—he offered me a job the other day, and I didn't think he was serious. But he was, wasn't he?"

I made a face, uncertain of what he was referring to. "I don't know—"

As if on cue, Zy'driks emerged from the room behind me. I suspected he had been listening in on the conversation from the very beginning, just out of sight, but ready and waiting should something have gone wrong.

"It was a serious offer," he affirmed. "The Order could use your abilities, and given all that has transpired during the past few weeks, I believed you might consider it."

Thad nodded, and looked up at Xandra. "It means I have to move away, Xan."

Zy'driks flashed a grin in my direction, but I had no energy to return his sudden good cheer. I still had to talk to him about my mistake from the previous night, and I was dreading that conversation.

"I'll go with you," Xandra replied. "I don't care about the hunters any more. I can't do it. I can't fight my sister...We did enough of that as kids."

I nodded to Konrad, who went about the task of unlocking Thad's handcuffs. "We'll be leaving in the morning," I told Xandra. "You might want to think about going home so you have a little time to pack. Konrad can give you the address of where we will be tomorrow. We're leaving at ten, so don't be late."

Xandra managed a smile, and said, "I hope you can forgive me one day, Chandra...If that's even your name any more."

I laughed, and it felt good. "It isn't, but I can tell you about that later."

It was nearing two in the morning when we finally returned to our hideout. Xen'din had said not a word to anyone since Xandra and Thad had left the underground together. He had shown a measure of selflessness that I knew I would never possess myself, and I admired that in him. I couldn't imagine how difficult it must have been to act as he had.

I stopped Zy'driks as he headed toward one of the bedrooms, and asked if he wouldn't mind talking just a bit longer. He gave me a knowing look, and nodded, following me to the empty kitchen where we would have some semblance of privacy in the crowded house.

"I think I know what you are going to say," he said, initiating the conversation himself. "And you're probably right, Ji'anne, but you ought to tell me yourself so I'm not guessing any longer."

I frowned; telling him that I did not want a relationship was much harder than trying to ignore the guilty feelings I had been experiencing since the previous evening. He deserved to know, but I had left him uncertain and waiting for this conversation for several hours now.

"I think…I think that last night was a mistake," I managed, unable to meet his gaze. "I was vulnerable. What you said made me feel better about things, but as soon as I had kissed you, it felt wrong. I should have said something sooner, but I was afraid—"

Zy'driks' chuckle caused me to snap my head up and look at him directly. "You didn't need to be afraid of me, Ji'anne," he said, smiling in spite of my words. "It would not have mattered if you had reacted in the opposite manner last night, or exactly as you did. I would have still gone through with this business today, and it isn't going to change what I feel about you. I wanted you to know; it is simple as that."

"So…you aren't upset?"

He chuckled again, obviously amused. "I did not live to my age without realizing that it isn't worth getting upset about the little things, Ji'anne. I'm not saying I'm going to give up in my pursuit of you—but I will give you the space you need until you're ready to move on from the bad memories this dreary city has held for you."

I wasn't certain of how I felt regarding his blatant admission that he wanted more than mere friendship, but I was glad that he was willing to give me space, to allow me to come to terms with everything that had occurred.

Still smiling, he said, "Good night, Ji'anne. Just remember, tomorrow is a new beginning for all of us."

# EPILOGUE

# MELODY

It had been three weeks since we had left Seattle behind, but I had only just returned to our headquarters in Boston. I had taken a short detour to Las Vegas on the way to talk things over with Kai'lind. He had always been a good friend to Ke'tai, and I had promised that when things were concluded in Seattle, I would pay him a visit. It had taken a few days—and many lengthy conversations—but in the end he was satisfied with the outcome. I was still uncertain about the prospect of working with Thad and my sister, but I did not relate my misgivings to him.

Upon my arrival in Boston, Te'chok had been in the lobby awaiting me. He had two things to say to me; first, that Thad was proving to be a valuable resource in finding information on the hunters nearby, and second, that Zy'driks wanted to speak to me privately once I had settled in. I must have appeared uncomfortable at the mention of Zy'driks, because Te'chok had smirked and commented that he already knew about our adventures in Seattle. I was told Zy'driks could be found in his apartment.

As I approached his door, I could hear music playing; the melody was complicated and somewhat haunting, but it was beautiful, nevertheless. The door was propped open, and as I peered inside, I saw Zy'driks seated on the bench in front of a piano. He had his eyes closed, but his long fingers deftly found the keys he sought, and the music played on flawlessly. I stood in the open doorway for an interminable amount of time, content to merely listen. I had known that Zy'driks was a musician, but until this moment, I had never been afforded the opportunity to hear him play. He seemed to be quite skilled, at least to my untrained ear.

After a time, the melody began to fade, and as the last of the haunting chords died away into nothingness, Zy'driks turned away from the piano to gaze toward the door. "How long have you been standing there, Ji'anne?"

I shrugged. "I don't know, a while. That was really beautiful."

He smiled knowingly. "It should be; I wrote it while I was thinking of you." He chuckled as I began to protest, and held up one hand. "It's the truth, Ji'anne—the melody is complicated, yet at times discordant, though it still maintains its beautiful quality. It is a musical expression of your personality."

I frowned, unsure of how to respond, and crossed my arms instead. "I was told you wanted to talk to me."

"I did," he replied, and beckoned for me to enter.

He led me to a pair of chairs placed on either side of a small, round dining table on the far side of the room. He had a silver pitcher of water ready, and two glasses set out. I hoped that he was not attempting to turn this into a date.

"I wanted to talk to you, Ji'anne," he explained, pouring us each a glass of water. "About where things go from here."

"Okay..."

He laughed. "Not regarding the two of us, but the Order as a whole. Il'zaks and Ai'zhanna made the decision as to who should speak with you about this business, and Ai'zhanna felt it would be best if I did, since we have worked so extensively together." He flashed a grin. "Il'zaks said he would allow me the honor, since he knew I would pester him about it anyway."

I rolled my eyes. "You really were serious about pursuing me, weren't you?"

He chuckled. "Of course, I was, Ji'anne, but let's get down to business. First off, the Elders want to know what you plan to do with Xandra, since she really isn't much use to us. We all know that whatever you decide will also mean something for Thad, since they are engaged now."

I stared at him in surprise. Nobody had told me of this new development. "She's engaged? When was someone going to tell me?"

"Uh, I guess right now," Zy'driks replied. "Sorry, I thought you knew."

"Well, okay then," I managed, trying to focus on the business at hand. "I guess she could work as someone's tracker. Who that is we could leave up to her. I personally don't think I could work with her...I'm still trying to recover from what she did, you know?"

Zy'driks nodded. "Actually, Il'zaks suggested the same thing, but we wanted to run things by you before we made a final decision. You know, typical stuff between the Elders and our leader." He shrugged. "I think Il'zaks was actually thinking about employing her himself. Trey has asked for his retirement."

I nodded in understanding. Trey had been working for Il'zaks for many years, and was nearing fifty. He probably wanted the opportunity to settle down and live a somewhat normal life before he became too much older. I had no problem with Xandra working for Il'zaks, although I could not imagine that she would get along with Carmine. I hoped Il'zaks was a good mediator.

"The second thing is about finding someone to train a new would-be summoner," Zy'driks said after a moment. "Nei'leil found a man up in Siberia with the talent. As an Elder, he cannot train a newcomer, so he must defer the training to you."

I sighed. "You know I can't teach anyone," I replied. "Not with the way I summon."

Zy'driks smiled knowingly. "Let me rephrase what I said...The Elders cannot train newcomers, so the choice as to who does the training is left up to you, as head of the Order."

I nodded. "Okay, who is close to that area right now, besides Nei'leil?"

"Tho'vaer is in Moscow," Zy'driks offered. "He is probably the closest one, geographically."

"Alright, then let's have him do it," I said, growing weary of this business conversation already. "How is Xen'din?"

Zy'driks sighed. "He seems to be holding up alright. He decided to go to Europe, for a change of scenery, but I suspect he'll be back sooner than he was initially planning. He will miss his friends, after a while. Speaking of which, he left a letter for you, Ji'anne. Let me go and get it."

Zy'driks strode quickly away and disappeared through a door, which led to the bedroom, I presumed. He reemerged after a few seconds, holding a sealed envelope. He set it down on the table in front of me as he took up his seat once more.

I carefully tore the envelope open, so as to not destroy its contents before reading them. Inside was a single sheet of lined paper, folded in half.

I recognized Xen'din's handwriting as I opened the letter, and immediately began to read.

> *Ji'anne,*
> *I wanted to write this before I left for Europe, and I left it with Zy'driks (I hope that was okay, given what happened between the two of you. He assured me that it would be, but I'm not so certain). I was upset with you back in Seattle, and I wanted to apologize. Il'zaks explained to me on the way here what had happened when you summoned that Alastor demon. I didn't know what had happened, and I thought you had decided to break our agreement and kill Xan. After hearing what you said to her after I left, I know I was wrong to think you would do something like that. I hope that my actions haven't destroyed our friendship. I don't know how long I will be in Europe, but I will try to call you or Zy'driks at least once a month to see how things are going, and to check in. I will be coming back eventually, and I hope things between us can go back to what they were before Seattle. Tell Thad to take care of Xan for me.*
> *XD*

"I think things are going to work out just fine," I said to Zy'driks as I finished reading and refolded the letter. "Xen'din said he'd call one of us once a month, and it doesn't sound like he's mad at me any more."

Zy'driks nodded. "Il'zaks and I explained to him what happened with Alastor. We waited until after he had settled down a bit, emotionally, so that he could fully understand what we were trying to say. When he did finally realize, I think it scared the hell out of him."

"Well, I'm glad he's doing okay now," I said. "I was worried…"

"I know," Zy'driks replied. "That's one of the things that makes you so complicated, one of the things I was thinking about when I wrote that song."

"Would you play it again for me? I missed the beginning last time, and it really is a beautiful song."

Zy'driks smiled. "Of course, it is; as I said, I wrote it for you."

# ACKNOWLEDGMENTS

Thank you for taking the time to read Hunted! If you enjoyed the read, please consider leaving a review.

Hunted was a book borne of my own inner darkness and demons during a time in my life that was filled with emotional turmoil. I hope you enjoyed my book.

Foremost, I want to thank my husband and my brother for their feedback during the writing process, for their patience with me during that time, and especially for understanding my need to be "ready" to publish. Hunted took me 2 1/2 years to write, but I didn't pursue anything further for another decade. It was a long time in coming, and without their encouragement, this book would not be in your hands today.

I would like to thank the talented Sheena Sampsel for her editing skills, and for helping this book become publication-ready.

If you enjoyed Hunted, please consider signing up to my newsletter at https://www.ajcalvin.net, and clicking on the newsletter tab. I release additional content via that outlet, and it will be the first place for you to discover my upcoming books.

# ABOUT THE AUTHOR

A.J. Calvin is a science fiction/fantasy novelist hailing from Loveland, Colorado. By day, she works as a microbiologist, but in her free time she writes. She lives with her husband, their cat, and salt water aquarium.

When she is not working or writing, she enjoys scuba diving, hiking, and playing video games.

For more information on the author and news about her writing, please visit her website at www.ajcalvin.net.

# OTHER TITLES BY A.J. CALVIN

THE RELICS OF WAR:
- The Moon's Eye
- The Talisman of Delucha
- The War of the Nameless

The Ballad of Alchemy and Steel

Serpentus

THE CAEIN LEGACY
- Exile
- Guardian
- Harbinger
- Legend

HUNTED

WRAITH AND THE REVOLUTION

www.ingramcontent.com/pod-product-compliance
Lightning Source LLC
Chambersburg PA
CBHW020604310726
48979CB00008B/1334/J